Mori

Kiensei, Volume 1

Justin Hobbs

Published by Justin Hobbs, 2024.

This is a work of fiction. Similarities to real people, places, or events are entirely coincidental. Similarities to other works is coincidental.

MORI

First edition. January 30, 2024.

Copyright © 2024 Justin Hobbs.

Written by Justin Hobbs.

For my daughters, who I will forever encourage to follow their dreams... no matter how long it takes.

Prelude

IN THE HEART OF AN evergreen forest, where time itself wavered like boughs in the wind, an evanescent spirit existed at a nexus within the Essence of the Ki. The fading screams, the searing pains, the darkness, all dissolved within a warm embrace and soft light of organic and cosmic energies. Ancient trees, standing tall as sentinels between realms, whispered secrets of distant worlds, their breath heaving from boughs and becoming the essence of time. One realm was between existences – a place where past, present, and future coalesced into a tapestry of possibilities. The grasslands that stretched beyond appeared to undulate like waves of oceans of time, carrying the spirit toward an uncertain waypoint.

The spirit existed suddenly at a crossroads of this reality. As energies ebbed and flowed with it, around it, and through it like song and wind coalescing, the boundaries between the material and the metaphysical began to blur. The dappled sunlight was like a kaleidoscope, painting its features with the hues of forgotten memories and untold futures. The fragrances of the forest were no longer confined to physical essences; they flowed effortlessly as angelic harmonies of song.

Amidst the flora, a tranquil lake beckoned to the spirit, it's still waters mirroring not only the infinite sky above, but also the paths around it. The spirit extended itself, its—fingers— like growing tendrils, breaking the surface tension like ripples in time's pond; the ripples echoing vague moments in time. The reflection that stared back was not just its own, but that of the choices it had made and those yet to be forged.

Time seemed to move around it, and suddenly, a surge of surreal energy, a penetrating light, an otherworldly echoing voice sounded from the darkness that mingled with the light. A soothing female voice whispered upon the winds and called to the spirit. The forest gave way to a river of stars, a cosmic tributary flowing through the very fabric of reality. Nebulae, quasars, and galaxies suddenly appeared, like apparitions of destiny. Their gravitational pulls guided the spirit through the corridors of possibility. The serene lakeside morphed into a portal, a place that bridged—her—ethereal existence with the tapestry of eternity.

A voice within the portal called to her. In she dove, without cause nor care nor even reason.

In this celestial plane, stars wheeled underfoot, maelstroms churned in the trees, and emotions took on hues of color unseen in the living realms. A day became a life age in the threads of time here. Her—heart— began to beat with the ebb and flow of this world beyond worlds, a symphony of choices and destinies. Past, present, and future all comingling in balance.

She searched for the source of the voice. Tears from the firmaments began to flow, shimmering like stardust. The forest, the grasslands, the lakes, and rivers merged seamlessly with the cosmic web. She—stood— on the boundaries between terrestrial and the transcendent, once blurred, and indistinguishable. Her—eyes— began slowly coming into focus. She saw the intersections of a journey laid out like constellations, each one a reflection of pivotal moments where fates had intertwined, though she could not divine a meaning.

And then, with the gentlest of embraces, the river of stars and the voice ushered her. Coaxing her back towards whence she came. Her steps rippling with reverberating sounds never heard before. A winged creature materialized and called out as it wheeled overhead. The forest's secrets melded with the revelations, a bond between dimensions. The evergreen whispers and the cosmic harmonies intertwined, guiding her back with newfound... purpose. She carried with her the enigma of these experiences, forever marked. The winged creature soared overhead, dove downward, and with a quiescent gentleness, rested on no visible *support in front of her. It stared at her, unmoved. A light blazed forth from a singularity at the feet of the creature. The source of the voice revealed itself and became an event horizon that she walked toward and willingly crossed. The increasingly blinding light surrounded her and drew her towards itself. She surrendered, completely, and fell into infinity with the screech of the creature, an owl, echoing around her.*

Then, silence. And the black of nothingness.

Luminance, like hands, clasped her—face— though she could not see its source as her eyes searched. A feeling of warmth caressed her. The female voice spoke weakly, yet clearly as if directly in front of her.

"The Ki flows within me, and the Ki flows for me."

"The Ki flows within me, and the Ki flows for me."

An urgency was felt, and she was compelled to speak. The two repeated the mantra in unison. Her own voice materializing as a gentle, silky alto.

"The Ki flows within me, and the Ki flows for me."

"The Ki flows within me, and the Ki flows for me."

The voice was silent as she repeated the mantra again.

"The Ki flows within me, and the Ki flows for me."

Her eyes focused quickly and viewed the swirling of many worlds far, far away. Distant stars instantly stretched into untold thousands of lines of brilliant lights, flashing like lightning in multitudes of color.

The voice, barely a whisper, trailed off into oblivion in her—mind— as a grain of time falling in the hourglass of eternity. "I am... Amamikoto ... and now you are... the light."

All at once, fresh air rushed into her lungs as she coughed to expel the stagnation of death. Her mortal body aching for the breath of life to return. Her senses fired; her mind awoke as from a dream. Her eyes blinked as a familial embrace wrapped around her.

"Hey ka'ze." Kina said quietly with deep relief. Ka'ze was his affectionate pet name for her. She absolutely hated it at first, but it had grown to be a sign of friendship between them.

"What's... going on?" Ashira replied wearily.

"Uh. Not much" he said. "It's good to see you."

The Kage had selfishly forced his will upon Ashira and had launched her towards the precipice of oblivion. The Amamikoto had unselfishly sacrificed her last glowing embers of life to return her. For what reason and towards what end the Ki had willed this to occur remained to be discovered. Though she couldn't explain what had happened or what she had seen, Ashira knew a destiny awaited her. A destiny and calling from the Ki itself.

Ashira's experience of the Ki had always been rooted in nature. She heard its winds whisper, felt its rivers flow across her skin and sensed its trees dancing when she called upon it, or when it called upon her. Now, the Ki had changed for her. Her perceptions had fused to include elements of the celestial world, a world beyond her understanding for now, and a being she had barely met. She was both intrigued and perhaps anxious at what had transpired, but her trust in and hope of the Ki was unwavering. And when the Ki called to her, she would answer it.

Chapter 1

Standing in the Hikarino-Kiensei Grand Council Chamber, a beacon of hope, peace, and justice that stood for thousands of years, streams of amber light from a Korosento sunset poured in through the large, arched windows. Snowcapped mountain peaks rose to the north while expansive city skyline sprawled to the south. The Grand Chamber, situated atop the singular pillar of the Kiensei Monastery, towered high above the city skyline as a guardian, watching over the realm as it had done for so long a time. Kina Wykera, a tall, human male, stood in line with six Demio of the Grand Council. His apprentice, or Nisi, Ashira Mori was in front of them, standing at her full height, her arms crossed in gentle expectation but cautious defiance. Her fearless attitude was present but laced with a tinge of bitterness and sadness given the recent events.

Ashira Mori. The young girl that had been assigned to a Runan of the Kiensei, as a student, at fourteen standard years of age. Assignments were unconventional but not *too* unusual in the history of the Kiensei Establishment. Especially now that the need for Kiensei on the battlefield became more of a focus than the passing of institutional knowledge. The millennium of tradition had long been that nisi were selected by Runans, or warriors, and Sesnei, or masters, at the annual tournament on Korosento or at the behest of the Grand Council to undertake the Seishin; the tests of skill and spirit.

For some, to be assigned meant improvement. That a specific personality trait, or some other personal weakness had been identified in one or both candidates and that the Kiensei Grand Council, in all their understanding, sought to strengthen the pair in many ways. For others, it was a sign of advancement. Just another layer of training woven into an already complex fabric of monastic life.

And for another group, it was a sign of honor. Not to be confused with hubris, but that out of the thousands of Kiensei in the realm, the council had identified a specific pair of people, their light within the Ki ebbing and pulsating in a way that complemented each other. A destiny within the Ki, as it were.

The overarching goal, of course, was to make the two Kiensei stronger than they otherwise would be and to pass on the experiential knowledge of what was learned from one to another.

Once long ago, battlefield promotions were normal, but had been suspended until recently, the need for added Kiensei personnel supporting the realm's civil war efforts was requested by the High Minister who effectively ruled the realm under the Emperor. For many aspiring Muhashki, the initial title given to younglings, this was a welcomed opportunity. Ashira was one of them.

Her assignment as Kina's nisi by Harichi, the oldest, wisest, and most senior of the establishment, was a definite reversal of the old wartime policy. An exception to the rules, as it were. A *'slippage'* as she put it, of the usually rigid norms of the Kiensei. Or maybe it was because of her skill level at such a young age?

Ashira Mori. Accomplished war veteran who fought alongside the Roosan Battalion for the better part of three years, earning the admiration and trust of the organo-robotic Tsugint soldiers that served under hers and Kina's command. A challenging task. Not to mention her many solo missions and other less-than-spectacular moments... but who was counting, right? It was exciting, she remembered, the first time she rode in that *Haru-class* gunship. Her spirits high, her heart pounding nervously, her adrenaline surging.

She had boarded the craft as a Muhashki of the Kiensei and emerged as a Nisi Commander in the Imperial Army of Korosento, searching for her new sesni in the war-torn city of Phisis.

Ashira Mori. Wrongly accused of burning the archives of the Kiensei Monastery... her home. Wrongly accused of murder and sedition of a conspirator. Both of which were capital crimes that carried capital punishment. Framed by someone who she thought was her friend. Reikuno... the woman and fellow Kiensei from the city of Artepyx who openly despised war, had openly attacked her own. Because of this betrayal, Ashira had been hunted down like an animal, arrested, and imprisoned. She had been expelled from the very monastery she so vehemently defended and supported for the majority of her young life. Her nisi ribbons were ripped from her head and then she was tried as a criminal by the Imperial government she equally loved and served. Now... here she was, standing in the Grand Council chamber far above Korosento, cleared of all wrongdoings that she never committed to begin with.

Here she stood... as if at a junction point on a lonesome, hard packed, dirt country road. And she already knew what to do; what *must* be done.

As soon as the military tribunal at the Center for Military Operations had ended, she was set free. She recalled the expanse of the cold and imposing tribunal chamber had hummed and echoed anticlimactically with the low conversations of attendees as they milled about amongst each other or shuffled drily out of the concluded proceedings. The prosecutor, Heim Takashi, "slime ball..." she thought, scowled at her as she equally shot him a look of contempt.

She had hugged her legal counselor, Prefect Damae Miada, and thanked her for everything. Her sesni, Kina, had approached her with a warm and sincere smile, putting his hand on her shoulder in comfort. He had informed her that the Demio Council asked to see her as soon as she arrived back at the monastery.

Asked... not summoned... as was the norm.

The aura within the hallowed council chamber hung thick with remorse. With shame. With *embarrassment*. The venerable Demio of the Kiensei Council... wise and respected, stood like muhashki who were about to be scolded after being caught sneaking out of their childcare suite in the middle of the night. Demio who, just a brief time ago, stood towering over Ashira in the Well of Judgement, with yellowish lights shining upward transforming the revered masters into glowering and imposing figures like predators staring at their next meal. Those same Demio who capitulated to public outcry, judged her guilty, and passed a sentence of expulsion from the monastic order now stood in front of her.

Humbled now, with softer eyes and hopeful smiles.

All except Demio Mako Rinji, of course. His rigid stoicism and constant grimace were unmatched amongst any other Kiensei that Ashira had ever, *ever* encountered.

"Ashira," Kina began with a sigh of true and deep remorse dripping from every word, "I'm *so* sorry... about everything."

Ashira knew her sesni was sincere. He never apologized for *anything*, let alone with that much emphasis. The problem was, Kina didn't do anything wrong, yet here he was trying to mend a wound between her and the Establishment... her and the council. The same council that he, himself, would defy – *has* defied when his own understandings and impulses clashed with their directives. Ashira was sure that if there was one person who could feel the gravity of the situation, it was Kina.

It was her sesni that stood by her against the onslaught from both the government and the Establishment surrounding the sabotaging of the Kiensei Monastery. It was her sesni who raised his fists and voice against the Kiensei Grand Council's judgement and was threatened by the monastery security guards. It was her sesni that brought a lauded prefect to be her legal representative at the military tribunal. It was her sesni who scoured the depths of Korosento's slums, outside the purview of the Kiensei Council, seeking out long-time rival and former Kageatsu apprentice, Jessa Tressnu, hiding within the slums of Korosento to gain facts and clarity of the situation. The Kageatsu being the longtime enemy of the Hikarino-Kiensei.

It was her sesni who confronted Reikuno... who Ashira *thought* was her friend... and literally battered her into submission in a duel to gain her confession of the truth, as witnessed by a cadre of muhashki and Sesni Busen. She had felt some of this through the Ki.

It was her sesni... fighting for *her*... ever since she first joined his side at Phisis.

Ashira, with relaxed arms by her sides, looked at his gentle yet gleaming blue eyes and saw the simmering emotions just behind them. He was holding back, she could tell. She could feel it. She returned his pure gesture with a gentle nod – her mouth curling up slightly at its corners in a slight smile of acknowledgement and of respect.

"He's struggling." she thought. "And it's only going to get worse." It was all she could do to *not* say 'I'm sorry Kina' right then and there.

"You have our deepest and most sincere apologies little 'Shira." Demio Kai Asato said in his deep, steady voice.

His long-fingered hands were clasped together at his chest. A sign of both inquisitiveness and respect from his native Rodlek tribe. 'Little 'Shira' was a parting gift from her father, Demio Asato once told her in confidence. Though it was generally frowned upon to discuss a muhashki's biological family, Demio Asato offered this precious morsel a few years after her arrival at the monastery as both an offering of friendship and trust in repayment of her own towards himself.

"*Our* apology? Or just *yours*?" Ashira puzzled cautiously to herself.

She couldn't tell whether he was speaking on behalf of the council or himself under the guise of unity. It had been a punch to the gut to see her founder and mentor, from her early years at the monastery, stand over her and play a part in her condemnation in the Well of Judgement. Demio Asato had been one of the few Kiensei in the order that Ashira maintained a close friendship with, which made the sting of his distrust in her that much more painful. Now, it was equally difficult to hear his apology. Demio Asato is her friend... was her friend... she didn't really know at this moment. Harichi did mention that the Council was not in total agreement, and she held on to a shred of hope that the Rodlek Demio was one of the dissenters.

"The Kiensei Council was remiss to accuse you," Asato concluded. Ashira quietly understood that he was, indeed, speaking on behalf of the council. This made her wonder briefly what he would say outside of his official duties.

The usually quiet and reserved Demio Haruka Shiro at once joined in the verbal parade. His voice was smooth and articulate, more human than his horned Kimori features would suggest. This surprising address surprised Ashira as she turned to face the near-human male. Demio Shiro wasn't known to speak much unless he had carefully considered the conversation and the will of the Ki. Come to think of it, she couldn't remember the last time she actually heard him speak.

"You have demonstrated a great deal of strength and incredible resilience in your efforts to *prove* your innocence" Demio Shiro said.

The look that Shiro shot over to both Haruka Sawaku and Mako Rinji revealed his feelings and intent to now support Ashira. His steely eyes conveying a sense of both honor and humility. Ashira took this as a genuine compliment. Something she wasn't overly used to especially from a council member.

Her innocence *was* proved... by her own *sesni*. The problem was, she shouldn't have had to *prove* it in the first place. If only they would have considered all of her accomplishments and characteristics into account, her commitment to the Kiensei Establishment, and her loyalty to the government before they hastily imposed a guilty verdict upon her at the behest of Takashi, the opposing legal counsel. If only the Grand Council would have trusted her as they had for years instead of capitulating to politics. Maybe, just maybe things would be different.

Demio Haruka Sawaku at once followed Demio Shiro. His light, even toned, and logical Erecan voice saying, "this is the *real* heart of a Kiensei Runan." Erecans, with their large and bulbous heads, were known to be deep thinkers with their expanded brain capacities.

"*Runan*?!" Ashira thought with surprise. "First they condemn me, now they want to *bribe* me?!"

She noticed the subtle one-sided grin coming from Mako as he turned his head to look at his fellow council member. That, she could do without. Both Sawaku and Mako Rinji were known to be loyal to one another. Ashira was not placated by the subtle offer nor the attempt at reparations for what they ripped away from her.... her honor and dignity.

"As punishment, you are expelled from the Hikarino-Kiensei." Sawaku's words from her time in the Well of Judgement echoed in her mind. Of course, she had wanted to be a Runan. What nisi didn't? Why else would she endure countless hours of training, hundreds of missions with the Tsugints, studying endlessly in the library, and of course... the meditation time. Can't forget that. Why else was she *here* if not to learn, serve others, and advance?

"Why else indeed?" she thought seriously to herself.

Sawaku had always considered her and Kina's adventurous nature to be unusual, maybe even unbecoming of the Kiensei establishment. At least that's what Kina told her. Ashira thought, given the different brain structure of the Erecan peoples, Demio Sawaku would be able to see her side of the situation in addition to his own.

"Maybe he did? Maybe he deduced that promoting her to runan would appeal to her ambition?" she mused to herself, mentally. He obviously didn't know her very well. Or maybe he realized that a person can never please everyone at once and that there are stark consequences for mistakes of this magnitude. She let the thought pass quickly.

"It has been revealed to us that this was your Great Seishin." Demio Mako Rinji spoke at once following Sawaku with a hint of smugness behind his rigid posture. Mako was a light-skinned human male with eyes that appeared to kiss in the corners. His long, dark hair was neatly pulled up into a bun that sat neatly on the back of his round head.

Sawaku returned the grin to his fellow Demio as he spoke.

"Now we understand that" Mako continued. "We understand that the Ki presents itself in strange manners..." he paused.

Ashira was uninterested in hearing a half-hearted retraction mixed with redirection. Her face hardening slightly while crossing her arms once again. Her eyes narrowing a bit with disinterest at what the famed Kiensei Champion had to say. Rinji had a reputation for being cold, dismissive, and rigid amongst many in the establishment, but he was a fierce and gifted warrior when needed, no doubt.

"... and because of this struggle, you *have* blossomed as a greater Kiensei than you would have otherwise," Rinji concluded.

Ashira had mixed feelings at that statement. His tone and demeanor had softened a bit, and he did make a small point. An exceedingly small point. She had grown as a Kiensei in certain areas, though not the ones he was likely alluding to. The word 'jaded' just didn't seem to encompass the entirety of her feelings and emotions at this point.

The way she understood it, her ordeal on the remote island of Wahaska was her Great Seishin. Surviving the cannabilistic hunters that had kidnapped her from the battle of Phelima all while rescuing not one, but two lost muhashki was one of the most challenging things she had experienced thus far. Ungosh Harichi, the highest-ranking member of the Kiensei, had spoken to her about her ordeal after her Ji'enpuku ceremony under the Sacred Emblem of the Order. The rank of Ungosh was only given to the most senior, most experienced, wisest, and most revered member. She recalled that intimate ceremony vividly where she received her last ribbon extension as a sign of her growing maturity.

"Now *that* was a 'Great Seishin' experience if ever there was one," she recounted to herself. She had nothing and nobody, not even her swords. And yet, she survived using only her training. "Thanks to Kina," she thought.

Ashira expected Demio Teka Suromasa, who was standing next to Mako, to speak next. She expected some eloquent apology and political reasoning to flow from the usually quick-witted human male Demio. She expected to hear some sort of logical diatribe about her place in the monastery and how the Ki had a plan and purpose for her. Blah blah blah. She expected Teka Suromasa, the great negotiator, to barter with her in hopes of staunching the discontinuous blood-letting that flowed in this moment between her and the Council. But he didn't. He unexpectedly remained silent with only a dejected expression painting his mustachioed face. Come to think of it, he didn't speak at her tribunal either. A rare thing to relegate the usually loquacious Demio to silence. She counted that as a win.

Instead, Harichi, the ancient Ungosh of the Hikaro-Kiensei spoke up in his gritty voice. Ashira turned her blank expression upon the diminutive, elderly man. The last things she remembered about Harichi had been his eyes, golden, blazing, and baring down upon her as if to burn a bolt hole from an energy weapon through her with his usually soft voice booming throughout the Well of Judgement. His gentle demeanor replaced with resounding seriousness and scorn.

Now, the Harichi she had known since her time as a muhashki had returned. His large, round eyes returning to their gentle and cheerful gaze. A smile appearing from his wrinkled little mouth. His fading hairline seemed to mimic the snowcapped mountains behind the monastery. It flowed neatly and framed his wizened face, ending in small inward curls under his knobby chin.

"You may return to us, Ashira," he said plainly. His voice, light and pleasant.

Ashira's expression deteriorated. Her eyes looked at the floor, away from any other's glances. Her mouth morphing into a saddened frown. Her own emotions now starting to rise up inside her.

"Back? ... back to *what* exactly?" she questioned to herself.

The Grand Council had effectively discredited her and embarrassed her. The government had publicly shamed her, disseminating her image across the entirety of Korosento and possibly the world. In the name of what? Justice for the Imperial Government? An attempt to polish an already tarnished Kiensei image in the eyes of the people? Placating the prefects of the Assembly? Vilifying her to bring closure to the multitudes of protesters of the raging civil war? She couldn't place a finger on the exact reason, but she knew things would never be the same if she returned regardless of the situation. And what if she *did* come back? What would be there waiting for her? Would the Council issue a bulletin statement throughout the Kiensei Establishment formally acknowledging their error? Would the infallible Demios of the Grand Council embrace their own teachings of humbleness and subject themselves to ridicule to restore her good name?

Doubtful.

"They're wanting you to return, Ashira." Kina said with a hint of military bravado.

She was used to hearing this tone of voice, having served by her sesni's side on countless missions. Her gaze returned to his face once again and changed to one of respectful remorse. She watched as he approached her with a yielding yet solemn purpose in his eyes. He stopped in front of her as if to, yet again, intervene between her and the council itself. Reaching for his hip pouch on his utility belt, Kina palmed an object. Extending his cybernetic hand towards her, he spoke with his most sincere, heartfelt voice. As a mentor, a friend... a brother. That hand, she remembered, was the first thing she remembered about him. He had lost it in a duel with the opposing side's Field Marshal some years ago. He didn't speak about it much, but she would catch him fiddling with its mechanics from time to time as if fine tuning it to his combat style.

"*I'm* asking you back," he said gently. His gloved cybernetic palm opened up to reveal a string of ribbons.

Her ribbons.

The same ribbons that were aggressively ripped from her head by the Guardians. Her cherished rank and mark of being a nisi learner. One of the only material possessions she had other than the clothes she wore, a few trinkets and her... well... she was going to think about her swords, but they had been taken when she was arrested.

Ashira looked at them briefly, then raised her eyes to meet Kina's. Her eyes conveying the hurt, the shame and discomfort of what she was feeling at the core of her being, but also conveying the resolute spirit of what was to come. Her eyes returned to the ribbons once again. Her life's work thus far summarized into an unassuming and humble piece of jewelry. Everything she had worked for, strived for, fought, and suffered for laid innocently within her sesni's hand, drooping, and swinging slightly on both sides. A hand of friendship, of apology, of hopeful wishing. Kina nudged his open palm a little further toward her as if to convey that it was her turn to act.

Ashira looked up into her sesni's face once more. Her eyes conveying hesitation and a stubbornness to react. His brow creased slightly, urging her to reach out and take her life back, to join him once again. Kina's expression softened, his open hand extended slightly further, begging almost, as if to say "please."

Another statement he rarely made.

She stared once more at her sesni's hand, then at her beads, remembering the entirety of her life as it had been in this single moment. And how it was no longer who she really was or wanted to be.

One. Last. Time.

The air was completely still within the chamber. The sound of silence was inundating. No one moved, no one made a sound. She reached out hesitantly, but with intention. A hopeful smile began to return to Kina's face seeing the gesture from his friend. She clasped her right hand underneath her sesni's and with her left hand, she gingerly closed his fingers around the symbol of her Kiensei identity. She lifted her face to meet his. Every ounce of emotional suffering and wounded sorrow poured out of her into this moment between them.

A demoralized look of surprise and slight fear painted Kina's face as her hidden intention was finally revealed.

"I'm sorry sesni. But I won't return," Ashira said with a somber yet tender resolve.

She took a step backwards. Her first step of many, away from this life. Turning her back to the Demios of the Grand Council without speaking a word to them, an act of silent, peaceful defiance...

MORI

Ashira, with sorrow weighing heavily on her shoulders, walked out through the doors of the Grand Council Chamber and away from the Hikarino-Kiensei.

17

Chapter 2

It was done. Though it wasn't pleasant by any means, the thought of leaving the Kiensei had weighed on Ashira's mind for some time. It started small, like a fleeting curiosity of 'what if.' But eventually growing into a gangrenous spot in her mind after reaping her reward of spent loyalty from the Kiensei to whom she had given it... except Kina. That was different. *He...* was different. She was certain he would come after her, wanting some reason or explanation for her decision. She just didn't have the willingness to give it, not right now at least.

A tempest of emotion was washing over Ashira as she rode the lift down the spire. She had to leave. She had to get out. And she had to do it as soon as possible. She just couldn't stay here any longer.

There was nothing left for her here anymore except the overarching feeling of distrust in her from everyone.

She had no possessions to gather. She had her trusty utility belt and that was enough. She had no credits secreted away. The few trinkets she owned held no tangible value and weren't worth bothering with. Not even her few spare outfits were worth the effort so there was no need to stop by her quaint little abode on the way out. She knew this, but Kina did not.

She could feel her sesni's presence in the Ki, reaching out to her, calling for her. He was coming after her, ethereally pleading with her to stop. She just couldn't bring herself to answer. She tried pushing it away, out of her mind but her focus wasn't where it needed to be. It was, however, on her small room... what it looked like, what it smelled like... in hopes of swaying his limited ability to track her. It wasn't as if she didn't want to see or speak to him ever again. She just needed some time, some space. She needed to figure this out... this... whatever it was.

Ashira had gotten to the lift descending from the central tower before Kina could stop her, so it gave her a bit of a head start. She knew she had to be quick because Kina would be on her heels in no time. She knew him, and he knew her, so she had to be deliberate in her exit path. After all, Kina *did* hunt her down in the maze of the city's sewers once. The monastery would be easier than that.

The lift chimed its arrival at the requested destination and the doors opened to the spacious plaza at the base of the spire. Turning right out of the lift towards the offices and support areas of the Scientific Exploration Sector instead of left towards the centralized Sacred Obelisk, Ashira ran with nimble grace.

Determination fueled her every step as she looked to escape the Monastery's confines. She ignored the surprised looks from the other Kiensei meandering about their daily business as she sped past some and dodged by others. One elderly woman in particular scowled at Ashira as she accidentally brushed by, nearly knocking the poor lady over. "Sorry!" she called back hastily for her brief unfocused clumsiness.

"I need to be more careful. Creating too much disturbance will give me away," she thought. Navigating a monastery full of Ki-sensitives without creating ephemeral waves was not an easy task. Everyone knew who Kina was and, by association, they knew she was his nisi.

Ashira skillfully maneuvered through the many corridors and open areas. She ran down voluminous arched passages. She weaved through throngs of Kiensei and service personnel alike ... her lithe figure a blur amidst the sea of robes, cloaks, hoods, and the occasional metallic glint. She scurried down several expansive and ornate hallways, with natural light pouring in from elaborate arched windows as if the Monastery, itself, was guiding her way out. All the while with her sesni searching earnestly for her. She would have to be crafty because Kina, she felt, was on his way.

Kina Wykera was distraught. His heart weighed heavy within his chest as he hurried through the doors of the Grand Council Chamber. His partner, his friend, his nisi, his *responsibility*... just... left? "She quit!? She can't do that!" He ruminated. The lift was already on its way down with Ashira onboard. Had he been a moment sooner, he would have been able to join her in the lift and speak to her on the way down. Though, he sensed that was not her plan when she walked out.

At the moment, that's all he *needed* to do. He just wanted to talk to her. He had to know. He couldn't just let her go without a fight, figuratively speaking. All he wanted was to hear her answer to the splintery question "why?"

He *could* take the emergency stairs down the spire but quickly reasoned that it would take longer than the express lift itself. Pacing back and forth in front of the lift door, he waited, and disliked every second of it. His former sesni, Teka, had emphasized too many times on how patience often leads to success. Well, his patience was running a bit thin at the moment. Kina grumbled aloud, his emotions beginning to boil over. He watched anxiously as the lift indicator stopped, then continued to display its return to his location, seemingly to mock him with its calm and happy chime.

In his frustration of the lift's clear tardiness, he continuously pressed the call button hoping it would lessen the travel time. Out of sheer irritation, he bashed the call button so hard with his cybernetic hand that the ornate, backlit cover shattered. Small sparks flew out signaling the consequence of the lift not moving fast enough for his liking.

The chime sounded the return of the lift. "About time" he growled through clenched teeth and steely eyes as the doors slid opened.

As the lift started its descent, Kina was silently counting the seconds in his head and trying to calculate where and how far Ka'ze might be within the monastery given her advantage of the poorly opinionated slower-than-embernectar lift he was currently on.

"Ugh. Can't this thing go ANY faster?" he bit out with choleric frustration. Patience was not something that would work in this situation. He needed to find Ashira fast before she got too far ahead. He considered bashing a hole in the floor of the cab with his fist and just vaulting down. He had already obliterated a simple little button, "what's so bad about a hole in the lift cab floor?" he cynically reasoned to himself. He knew in the back of his mind that this would not go over well with the Grand Council, and he already had enough problems with them at the moment.

His emotions eddied in a tempest of sadness, desperation, and a lingering sense of loss on the ride down the spire. Ashira's rejection of the Grand Council's offer—*his* offer—to return to the Kiensei establishment had shattered his hopes, leaving him with an emptiness that he already knew too well.

Closing his eyes and reaching into the Ki, Kina sought to connect with his nisi, but it was chaotic, noisy even. He took a deep breath and focused. Closing his eyes, he saw brief, fleeting visions skitter across his vision. A small space? Window. Bedroll.

"Her room," he whispered aloud with assumed clarity.

The lift chime sounded the arrival to the lobby floor. Kina snapped back into focus and burst out of the lift. Turning left towards the Sacred Spire, he ran with both reckless purpose and measured disregard like a beast charging through a homewares shop.

Pushing past startled civilians, autonomous robotic valets, and fellow Kiensei, Kina navigated the monastery's latticework of paths on the way to the Okami section of the monastery with a mixture of urgency and anxiety. His eyes darted left and right, scanning every face, searching for the distinctive silhouette of his nisi as he charged down corridors, passageways, stairs, and various open areas. With his heart yearning for a chance to speak to her, to understand the reasons behind her decision was the singular focus of his entire being right now.

Turning the corner to an all-too familiar hallway, Kina hastily arrived at her unassuming door. Normally he would press the chime button or knock gently to announce his presence before entering. Instead, he opened the door with rash abandon ready to accept whatever consequence... only to find it empty. She wasn't here. She never was here.

His eyes narrowed slightly in annoyance. "Where are you Ka'ze?" he said, focusing his efforts. Stepping back and allowing the door to close, he turned around and closed his eyes. Reaching out again to the Ki, he pressed harder, breathed deeper, and concentrated further.

Repulsor lights. Mosaic flooring. Cavernous. White ceiling. Tables? *Long* tables.

"The Formal Dining room!? What are you up to Ashira?" he questioned aloud. The looks from passersby did not faze him. They, on the other hand, tried not to look as though they were curious as to what the famed Kina Wykera would do next. He did have a reputation in the monastic establishment, as it were, and whether it be good or bad, they knew who he was.

This illogical location dumbfounded Kina slightly. If she wanted to leave, to get out of the monastery, then the fastest route was through the central connector of the Sacred Obelisk. Why would she go there?

"She must have cut through the Scientific Exploration Sector. But that's out of the way? And the Formal Dining room, that's...." he broke off from his soliloquy. His eyes widened as he discerned what he believed Ashira's plan was.

Looking swiftly left and right to regain his bearings, Kina dashed off towards the Grand Entrance. If she was going to be crafty, he could do the same. She might have decided to leave, but she wasn't getting out that easy. He would have his say. He had to try. He had to do something, anything, before she was gone. Nothing or no one would deny him that.

Ashira turned a corner and stopped briefly after appearing from the well-hidden staircase originating from the Formal Dining room's narthex. The staircase, she remembered from her time as a muhashki, was a shortcut she used to bypass the roving Security Guards after lights-out when she felt the need to explore or just get away from everyone. Its real purpose, she had learned after getting caught once and having to write a report on the history of the Hikarino-Kensei as punishment, was used for dignitaries and other persons of importance should they visit the monastery for a formal event; to usher them quickly to and from specific points without parading them through the monastery. Most outsiders of status preferred a slight tour and longer walk just to see some of the inner areas of the monastery. What was commonplace for Kiensei was a rare experience for outsiders.

She stopped to examine the immaculate foyer of the Grand Entrance before her. She couldn't remember the last time she wasn't rushing somewhere enough to marvel at the millennia-old architecture. Having grown up here, it's beauty gradually becoming mundane in many of its inhabitants' eyes.

The towering archways and windows of the entrance hall loomed ahead, bathing her exit path in a warm, golden light. The sunlit glint off of the bronzium statues created what looked like star patterns on the walls and ceiling. The massive pylons dedicated to the establishment's original founders standing as distant sentinels through the main archway.

Her way out.

The serenity of the Ki resonated within those hallowed halls, reminding Ashira of her deep-rooted connection to its ethereal energy. The sea of beings ebbing and flowing before her in a symphony of peace. Reminding her of how things *should* be, not as they are. A quick scan of the expansive space showed no sign of pursuit from Kina.

Maybe... with the tiniest bit of disappointment, Kina wasn't coming after her after all? It wasn't as though she didn't want to speak to him. Just not right now. She just needed some time to process and the space in which to do it.

Taking a deep breath, her resolve solidified; she embraced the moment and stepped out of the shadows and into the meandering crowd of Kiensei, valets, visitors, and workers alike.

"Almost there," she sighed slightly to herself.

Not wanting to draw attention to herself, even though quite a few beings knew who she was, all thanks to the council and the tribunal, and the fact that Kina was her sesni, Ashira walked toward the exit at an even pace. She purposefully avoided direct eye contact with anyone, unwilling to engage in the countless looks and subsequent questions she knew would arise. Word tended to travel quickly in the monastery, especially when the word was bad or controversial.

She was a quarter of the way through the foyer when all of a sudden, a familiar presence surged forth—a whirlwind of passion, determination, and unrestrained concern. Her sesni had arrived.

Ashira could feel his presence in the Ki billowing as he leapt down gracefully to the polished floor. Ignoring the surprised and puzzled onlookers passing by her, she could single out his echoing strides resounding with a mix of urgency and desperation as they clapped against the detailed mosaics. There were a few benefits to being a hybrid. Especially when it came to sensing moving objects around you. Her mother was human, her father a Teekan. She had retained the beauty of the human form and features and had gained the ability to hear more clearly and sense things around her like the Teekan's possessed. Her skin, however, possessed the lightest of blue markings, like stripes. Another gift from her Teekan heritage.

Sensing his approach, her pace quickened. She bit her lip slightly, her somber expression dissolving temporarily. Her eyes quickly scanned her surroundings looking for an avenue of escape. She darted towards a nearby loop-thru alcove, its hidden shadows beckoning like a sanctuary. She thought it would offer an avenue to sneak away should Kina close in on her. Slipping into its concealment, she pressed her back against the cool, ancient stone wall, trying to blend into the surrounding dusk. Her senses at full awareness. Her breath, still. Footsteps coming closer.

Kina had appeared from the winding service corridor onto an elaborately ornate and cleverly concealed overhead gantry. He had the high ground. The grandeur of the monastery's main entrance hall stretched before him, its vastness a testament to the ancient architecture. The soft glow of sunset filtering through glass windows bathed the vast cathedral-like entrance in glowing hues of yellow and orange, casting long shadows that melted across the floor and the beings flowing across it. His intense blue eyes scanned the crowd and then fixated on a fleeting glance of Ashira. Kina's eyes widened; he was getting close.

He leapt down into an open space in the crowd, landing smartly on both feet with one hand on the ground, his face forward. The crowd around him parted swiftly having been startled by this unusual and somewhat aggressive arrival amongst them. Many of them voicing their displeasure at the brashness they had been witness to. Some just brushed it off as if they weren't surprised that he had done something like that.

He didn't care one bit and ignored everyone.

He sensed Ashira's presence nearby. It fueled his determination to catch up with her. His footsteps quickened, echoing through the hallowed halls, rising above the audible din, as he chased after her elusive figure.

Suddenly, he caught a glimpse of her, a flash of blue markings amidst the currents of occupants. She seemed to glide effortlessly through the throng. No small feat seeing that she tended to stand out amongst crowds. Her lack of a cloak was his advantage.

Kina moved linearly with a single-minded purpose, but as he closed in on her, Ashira's form vanished in the shadows of an alcove. A *looped* alcove. Stopping briefly, he looked across his left shoulder to see the alternate entrance to the loop. An old double-back escape tactic resurfaced in his mind. He would cut her off. He hoped so at least.

Kina's footsteps stopped abruptly, then resumed quicker than before. Ashira could hear him coming, echoing through the other side of the loop.

"Good." She thought. Her plan had worked.

She appeared quickly from the alcove and headed immediately towards the entrance archway resuming her swift stride, her mind firmly set on the path ahead. If he was going to catch her, it would have to be outside, away from everyone. She had no desire to create a spectacle though she knew he wouldn't care. She had had her time in the spotlight, and she certainly was over it.

Passing by the statuesque guards stationed on either side of the arched doorway without fanfare, Ashira had finally made her exit onto the Processional Path outside of the monastery.

Chapter 3

Descending the first flight of stairs, Ashira slowed a bit from her brisk walk. Her forlorn face numbly pointed at the ground, not skyward as she once did to marvel at the large stone pillars that created a modular stonecrete forest just outside the monastery. She would run no more. She didn't have to. She had made it outside with her sesni eagerly chasing her once again. That's all she wanted right now, to just get out of there.

Behind her, the familiar echoes of running boots permeated through her ears. Kina was coming and fast. There was nothing she could do about it now and there was certainly no stopping or evading him any longer.

"Ashira! Wait!" Kina shouted while quickly closing the distance between them.

Ashira kept walking without a single acknowledgement. She really didn't want to speak to him, she didn't think she could. But this was unavoidable. If she was going to have to face her sesni... *former* sesni now, then outside with a bit of privacy would be best. She owed him that much at least, she reasoned. She carried on walking a steady pace until the last possible moment.

"Ashira, please talk to me!" he exclaimed with a shade of desperation in his voice.

"No point in delaying the inevitable." Ashira sighed to herself. Her pace slowing and stopping, her head lifting to the horizon.

The distant Korosento sunset cast long shadows off of the two figures on the plaza, the sky was dappled grey with hues of cream and orange. The sun was setting on Korosento and setting on a once powerful partnership between two remarkable Kiensei.

Ashira turned slowly to face her former sesni, her face and eyes rising to meet his as Kina came to a bedraggled halt just a single pace in front of her. He exhaled a coarse breath to clear his lungs so that fresh air could take its place and to give himself a moment to think. His palms turned upward in friendly surrender as he spoke.

"Why..." he inhaled sharply, trying to catch his breath "... are you *leaving us*? Leaving *me*?"

Without even thinking before speaking, Ashira's face turned to a light scowl as she slightly leaned forward at the waist towards Kina.

"The Grand Council didn't trust me..." she spoke.

Her gaze softened as she began to reveal her inner thoughts and feelings to her former sesni. She turned to look away as she divulged what Kina had so desperately chased her down for.

"... so how can I trust the decisions I make for myself?"

It was painful for her to admit her own faults. But doing so gave her a moment of clarity as to how Kina must have felt in the Chamber. Ashira turned completely sideways and crossed her arms in mock protection. Her emotions were beginning to pour out.

"What about *me*?" Kina replied softly, leaning towards her while gesturing towards himself with his cybernetic hand. It was fine, he thought, if she didn't trust the council or want anything to do with them anymore. He didn't either but he was still there.

"*I* believed in you and stood by your side!" his voice elevating as his own emotions began spilling out, matching hers. Ashira turned back to face Kina. Her eyes rising to meet his.

"I *know* you believe and trust in me Kina, I'm so very *grateful* for that," she said, her face emanating every ounce of respect she could muster.

He *had* believed in her. Stood by her. Fought for her. Fought *with* her at times. And for the last several years he was one of the few she could truly count on. She had been a large part of his life, just as much he had been of hers. They had become something that both of them had empirically sacrificed for the illustrious Kiensei establishment... a family. Brother and sister.

Ashira owed so much of what she had learned and experienced over the past few years to the man that stood before her. She even owed him her life. Had he not intervened in the secluded monastery of Rigort, she'd be dead... she *had* been dead. Through the grace and will of the Ki it was Kina, the Singularity of the Divination as he was known, who with the help of the Kamimoto, drew the last bit of ethereal life essence from the luminescent spectral figure known as the Amamikoto. He channeled it and poured it into her, bringing her back to life.

"But this isn't about you" she said with mild defiance. "I can't stay here any longer." A sudden wave of sadness rushed over her as she looked away. "Not now at the very least."

With a longing stare and arms crossed, Kina accepted her declaration about himself. He believed her. What he couldn't understand was why she would give up everything she had known, everything she had become a part of. In his quick wit, he decided to probe deeper to gain a better understanding. A fleeting memory of his own former sesni's goading of 'patience' was taking a toll on him in this moment.

"The Kiensei is your *life,* your *reason,* your entire *being,* your *purpose,*" he declared.

This simple mantra had been imposed upon every single member of the monastic group since their arrival at the monastery. From admittance to fiery burial, this was a foundation the Kiensei stood upon.

He pleaded, revealing his innermost thoughts on the matter at hand. "You can't just... discard it as if it doesn't hold meaning! Ashira, you are making a *mistake.*"

Ashira looked away from him, arms crossed with a thoroughly downtrodden look across her face. Her entirety of tutelage under Sesni Wykera had been freckled with her mistakes. A result of her own brashness and recklessness that mimicked his own. Such was the Kiensei ways under the Sesni-Nisi structure that had stood for millennia. One to make the mistake, one to correct it, both to learn from it. She didn't resent it. She had embraced it and had gained much from its long heritage. But she could no longer stand by it.

Kina had been there for her in every mistake she had made. Kina had been there constantly to guide her through those mistakes no matter how harsh it seemed. She even saved him a few times as well. In this however, Kina had failed to allow her the pain of growing on her own. It was her turn to save herself. It was her turn to be the person she had long been groomed to be. It was time to let go.

She snipped in retort. "I might be. But I have to figure this out on my own. Without the Kiensei..." Her piercing blue eyes matching his own momentarily. Her voice becoming steady with a sagacious essence. "...and without you." She turned away from him, her face returning to a despondent stare under the crushing weight of the moment.

Sadness gripped Kina's chest. He, too, turned away slightly from Ashira. His face an equal projection of hers. Sadness at the fact that they had come to this moment. Sadness at the fact that the establishment in which both of their trust was placed had failed them. Sadness at the fact that irreparable damage had been dealt by forces beyond their control and yet... they were the ones made to bear its consequences. Another casualty of a conflict they did not start but were bound to play a part in.

The bond between sesni and nisi shouldered this sentiment equally.

Sensing the resolute rebelliousness that he had cultivated and nurtured in the young hybrid Tesska, Kina did something he had never done before... well, not willingly anyway.

He admitted defeat and surrendered.

Taking up the pseudo-mantle his own former sesni had constantly bore in their long history of bickering, he allowed Ashira to win. His own teachings had bested him.

He succumbed to the fact that his friend was leaving, and there was nothing he could do about it. Kina had always been guarded. He had always kept his innermost thoughts and feelings carefully locked away inside. Allowing none, save one person, a glimpse of the scars he bore in his heart.

As an act of true friendship, he offered her a parting gift. An honest feeling from deep within. Something beyond the usual banter they had shared or the formal conversations whilst in front of others. Something he had wanted to do for some time now but couldn't find the courage. It was these types of feelings that led to affection, something strictly forbidden by the Kiensei, but constantly subverted by himself. Something else that the council mandated that Kina had selectively chosen to ignore. It was this special part of him, the forbidden love he shared with Damae, that he wanted to share with his friend. A gift of personal vulnerability that displayed the fullness of trust.

"I understand," he sighed. "More than *you* know or think you know, I understand... wanting to leave too."

With that, he had opened the proverbial cage that held a boontari, a native simian-like animal, and then set its tail on fire. It was painstakingly difficult yet soothingly satisfying at the same time. There was also something else to his statement—a hint of jealousy.

Ashira recognized the passion emanating from him and she knew exactly what he meant. He cared. Genuinely cared. That was one thing she would deeply miss and what made her decision to leave a distinctly painful one. The fact that he deeply and genuinely cared for others was what made him one of the greatest Kiensei she had ever known. She turned her head slightly to look over her shoulder and with her last statement, she returned his gesture of open vulnerability with one of empathy, a verbal hug as it were.

"I know." She said gently. Her words carrying the force of a thousand truths.

Kina's face melted into sheer surprise. "She knew!?" he thought. "How could she…? Wait. What?" His mind was in a flurry. "All this time and she *knew*, and yet, never said a word?" His mind began to spin in measured shock. It was like the loosed boontari had wrecked the shop and set it ablaze. "Of course! She *had to have* known," he at once reasoned with himself. Ashira had a natural gift through the Ki to sense feelings and intentions of others. Yeah, he knew that. Demio Asato had mentioned as much once. She could always tell when he was silently frustrated with some ridiculous assignment or secretly overjoyed to be coming home to Korosento for some regenerative leave. Right?

But there was that one time…

He had always tried to be incredibly careful when he and his wife were together in official capacities or around prying eyes and ears. I mean, sure, there were occasional slip-ups where he would allow his emotions to well up and he would accidentally put the wrong inflection to his words when speaking about her or to her in front of others. Teka was certainly suspicious, nothing new about that. He always was—and— he liked to meddle in Kina's business too. But there *was* that one mission to the city of Ra'andal. That had to be it.

Kina had done some pretty uncomfortable things to earn certain assignments before, but that one was definitely worth it. He suspected that Teka took pleasure in seeing him squirm at the thought of aiding Lady Aidial in the library or having to spend extra time answering questions for the various clans of muhashki…

he especially disliked that. Muhashki asked the most obtuse and ridiculous things and they had absolutely no patience whatsoever. Worst of all was giving lame tours of some of the communal areas in the monastery to some of Korosento's many primary schools. More kids. No thanks to the Conclave of Reconciliation, another layer of bureaucracy within the establishment, for that. With the war, there were many anti-Kiensei dissenters, and, in their infinite wisdom, the council thought it would be a great idea to show the citizens of the world that the Kiensei weren't warmongering bigots with a penchant for killing by offering watered down tours to school children. Great.

But... it had all been worth it. Just to garner a private security detail with his prefect wife. And in beautiful Ra'andal for that matter. He had planned it out to be like a second honeymoon, and it was going to be amazing.

He remembered stepping off the boxy and lightly armed *Lakhshmi-class* shuttle and seeing his wife Damae advancing toward him in all her beautiful splendor with her attaché of shonyin, or handmaidens, behind her. Like a bride at a wedding, he thought. For a moment he imagined that it was what it would have looked like if things were different. Their eyes met with hidden joy and after a brief exchange of formal pleasantries, he had ushered her to board the vessel. Just when he thought all was going splendidly... "Sesni!" he heard, immediately recognizing the voice of his nisi. And there she was... Ashira... eagerly running toward them with a smile on her face with a waving hand—exactly where he didn't want her to be.

A shared moment of exasperation between him and his wife was followed by the patient acceptance of her presence ... by Damae first. They *were* friends after all. Ashira had let it be known that Teka was the culprit behind her assignment to the mission after he had queried her. He remembered distinctly assigning her to youngling duty to fulfill some of her teaching requirements for promotion. But, since Teka sort of outranked him, Ashira was bound to oblige the higher order. Kina made a mental note to repay the favor to Teka. His old sesni would need saving at some point in the future, he was sure of it.

Soon, however, after liftoff it became clear that it was actually good fortune to have Ashira with him... like that time at the ancient Chitnade stronghold where she actually saved him for once. An unexpected brush with a guerilla cell, through no fault of his own he claimed, caused them to take evasive action and return fire. He had sensed imminent danger to his wife as her starboard side gun pod was about to be raked with plasma energy shots. He remembered taking immediate action by leaping from the pilot's seat to grab his wife, pulling her from the gunner's seat and shielding her with his own body. He held her tenderly and she shared the embrace as only lovers would. A protective instinct that had taken over in the heat of the moment.

All witnessed by Ashira.

"That had to be it... that's how she knew." Kina thought. There was some solace that she had kept his innermost secret intact since then.

Had she not been there to quickly take the helm and expertly navigate them out of the area, they likely wouldn't have survived, that much was true.

The trip overall ended up on a positive note. He and Damae got to spend some much-needed time together and Ashira had unusually kept her distance, except when official duties required otherwise. Now he understood why. "Wonder why Damae never mentioned it?" He thought in passing, his focus returning to the present.

Turning slightly towards his now former nisi, Kina watched longingly as she began to walk away. His face vaguely able to express what his heart and spirit were aching to pour out. He watched her slender outline as it passed between the towering sentinel statues and began to descend from the monastery amidst the setting sun; a few rays piercing through the wispy grey cloud veil over the distant skyscape of the expansive cityscape cast a long, dark shadow of her that appeared to reach back at him.

In a matter of moments, she sank beneath his line of sight and was gone from that life.

35

Chapter 4

The echo of her own footsteps reverberated around her, resonating not only off of the stone steps but also in the depths of her shell-shocked mind. Passing the towering Founder's Statues, Ashira felt the lingering grip of the bond between sesni and apprentice, a connection that clung to her relentlessly through the Ki. It pleaded with her not to leave, while a faint whisper, a gentle urging in the recesses of her thoughts, assured her that this was the path she had to tread, the path she must follow. The wounds on her heart were still fresh. Only moments ago, she had stood her ground, bared her soul, and turned her back on everything she had known—"them," she murmured under her breath—the Grand Council, the establishment, her entire life as she had once embraced it. Kina had been right about one thing; the establishment was her life. The only life she had ever known. And now it was over.

She sensed his presence, all too familiar, reaching out to her through the Ki. She could feel Kina's pained gaze boring into her as she descended the long, majestic stairway, leading her towards the plaza and the surface streets beyond. "I'm not coming back," she whispered to herself, a quiet affirmation that resonated within her, echoing the moment in the Grand Council Chamber. The moment that had changed everything.

Each step on the processional staircase, trod upon by countless others before her, felt like a painful reminder—a reminder of the grandeur of the Kiensei Monastery, once a sanctuary that had nurtured her mind, body, and spirit, now standing as a stark testament to the fractures and flaws within an establishment she had once held dear. With her acquittal from false charges, she had been presented with an opportunity—an open door beckoning her back into the embrace of the monastic establishment, the promise of promotion to full Runan, a chance to mend the strained bonds that had brought her to the brink of breaking. But Ashira, her heart tempered by the trials and tribulations of a massive planet consumed by war, knew that her place was no longer among their ranks.

Yet, there was something else; a persistent phrase that had anchored itself into her mind. Not a thorn of thought, but rather a constant, gentle voice reminding her soothingly. *"Are you happy, child? Are you treated well?"* She heard it again like a fragrant wisp of smoke meandering through her mind. She shook her head slightly as if to dispel the thought. Like déjà vu, it reminded her of a strange occurrence years ago.

Pausing briefly, Ashira glanced to the side, her gaze capturing the vibrant hues of a waning Korosento sunset cascading over the majestic architecture of the Kiensei Monastery. The long shadows crept upon the towering walls, and Ashira, her spirit weary but resolute, continued her measured descent. Each footfall carried the weight of her decision, an unyielding choice that would forever alter the course of her life.

As Ashira looked ahead at the vast expanse of the Grand Causeway, the Imperial District, and the surface thoroughfares woven about it, she saw a multitude of avenues, each leading to a new path, a new possibility. The bustling crowds of pedestrians flowed like rivers across the surface, going about their daily lives. Lives vastly different from the rigors of monastery life. Her cerulean accented features became slightly alarmed. "What do I do now?" she pondered briefly. What would she do? Where would she go? She admitted to herself that a lack of thought, and planning didn't help her situation much.

Her mind raced momentarily, consumed by the brash urgency of her decision to leave, causing her to overlook the practicalities of living once she stepped beyond the boundaries of the monastic complex. Taking a deep breath, she calmed herself, drawing upon her battlefield training from Kina and the Ki techniques she had learned in her training. She needed to assess her surroundings, to familiarize herself with the world beyond on a different level beyond what her eyes had once beheld. She reminded herself that she had patrolled these surface streets, navigated the alleyways and main thoroughfares before. She had a general understanding of the area. That was a start at least. In the distance, the *100 Ecumina* stood as a pinnacle of affluence and power within the vast metropolis. It was the tallest building in the vast metropolis. Its angled visage was discernable from any angle for hundreds of miles around. She had never stepped foot inside, but she wondered about the regal figures who resided within its walls, aside from the Emperor and High Minister, of course.

The Kiensei beliefs stated that its followers were supposed to forego material possessions and embrace an air of honored poverty, so the concept of overt opulence was one she had seen many times but had not lived herself.

At its base, in perspective, the omnipresent angled roofline of the Planetary Assembly Building loomed—a place she had visited countless times and knew quite well.

A fond memory washed over her upon seeing that enormous building, a welcome respite from her current emotions. She remembered a time when politics had been a distant pulsating star, far removed from her realm of knowledge. It was a memory of empathy, of a secret journey to Maxiss alongside her friend Damae, where she had come face to face with Mariss Butark and her son Lusec—both enemies of the government and supporters of the opposing side of the civil war, yet the former a friend and mentor to

Damae. It had been an encounter akin to gazing into a mirror. Their shared purpose: the pursuit of peace.

She savored the memory of that journey. She had discovered that the Divisionist Movement, as their enemy in the war, held hopes, dreams, and ideals similar to those of the Imperial government. She had seen that the taste of war was equally bitter on the opposite side of the civil conflict. Things weren't so black and white, she thought, as she had come to understand that the term "loss" was universal. Above all, she had discovered that problems could still be solved without the wielding of a Ki-infused sword in war; that the promise of peace had not met its demise.

As a Kiensei, she had been ingrained with the understanding that lethal force was the last resort, that the artful use of emphatic thought and words exemplified true strength, goodwill, and peace. The Kiensei were peacekeepers. Yet, she had wielded her weapons more often than she had employed her consular words. *Far* more often. Moreover, she had seen a different kind of warrior in Damae. Her friend possessed the most tactful mind and fierce heart of any battle-hardened warrior, yet it was *how* she wielded her weapons and the battles she chose that opened Ashira's eyes to the true meaning of service. Kiensei were meant to serve the people of the planet. All of them. But were they truly living up to that creed? Had *she*?

Teka Suromasa stood alone before a towering arch of a transparisteel window, nestled high within the ancient walls of the Kiensei Monastery. His presence commanded the space, casting a long shadow that stretched longingly into the dimly lit anteroom. Like a stoic statue, he remained motionless, surrounded by centuries-old artwork whose warm hues now appeared muted, their beauty dulled in the face of his somber contemplation. With arms crossed protectively over his chest, his left-hand fingers grazed his mustachioed lip in a gesture of deep introspection.

Below, two tiny figures moved in a slow, divergent path as if pulled apart by unseen forces. One towards the light of sunset, the other towards the shadow of the columned entrance.

Kina's bond with his former nisi persisted, just as Teka's with his own. Remaining unbroken. It had taken time for Teka to adjust to the fact that Kina was no longer his sole responsibility, that they now stood as equals in their service to the Ki. Yet, his concern and genuine care for his friend never wavered. Yes, it was true that Kina had saved his life on many occasions, Teka would never forget that and would forever remain as humbly grateful as possible. But no, that blackmailing incident on Harte Minosa still does not count. He had everything under control then but alas, Kina still managed to show up as he was inclined to do and together, they were able to assuage the local government from killing them both and joining the dissention movement. Teka fleetingly smiled to himself at the recollection of the memory.

"My dear Kina, how painful this must be," he said to himself, knowing full-well how he felt. He had trained the young man ever since he was a child, so he knew almost everything there was to know about the famed 'Singularity.' Even then Teka knew that Kina carried a heavy burden of lonesomeness within. Losing someone so close had happened to the elder sesni too many times already. His own sesni and... Raxshi.

As one of the more astute members of the Grand Council who had opposed Ashira's expulsion, Teka had chosen to voice his opposition openly during the closed-door deliberation amongst his fellow Demio, yet silently during the trials. Duty bound him to uphold the Kiensei Code, presenting a united front, even if it meant sacrificing his personal convictions. Slowly turning on his heel and resting his arms behind his back, he embarked on a purposeful journey down the corridor, seeking solace and guidance from someone far wiser than himself.

In time, the door to Ungosh Harichi's chamber slid open, granting Teka entrance into the sacred space. There, Harichi sat upon a small, cylindrical, padded stool, positioned near one of the chamber's mostly veiled exterior windows, offering only a glimpse into the outside world. His favorite waterfall burbling to the side. The aged ungosh's room was unassuming as were most of the occupants' accommodations in the monastery. No outlandish decorations, no paintings on the walls. Though it was slightly larger than most, it was mostly plain, save for the two rectangular tables with candles that the wizened man burned constantly during meditation. It was quiet and serene. The only major differences were that this room was curved into a hemisphere on one side with large columns set between four windows. A pattern in the intricately laid stone flooring mimicked a sunrise or sunset mirrored the rooms layout. A central, darker circle with alternating rays reaching out to the external columns. The only major piece of technology present was a small virtuaprojector nestled atop a spindly base that trumpeted at the top for when the ungosh communicated privately. No, Harichi was not one for opulence.

Stirred from his customary meditation, the ungosh opened his aged eyes and welcomed Teka with a subtle nod of his time-worn head. The wrinkles in his face smoothing slightly in some areas, deepening in others as he sent a smile; his gnarled ears perking upward slightly. The waning rays of daylight filtered through slatted shades, casting fragmented patterns that played upon the chamber's age-old walls and floor. Upon his entrance, the weight of seriousness that Teka carried with him transferred itself to the air within the room, usurping its usually warm tranquility.

"I apologize for disturbing your meditation, master," Teka spoke softly, aware of the reverence that enveloped the room.

"No apology necessary Teka," Harichi's gentle yet gravelly voice stirred, carrying the authority of countless years. "I understand why you are here. Your heart is troubled for your former nisi is it not? I noticed your reaction in the Grand Chamber."

"Yes, master," Teka acknowledged, grateful for Harichi's perceptive wisdom affording him mercy from having to admit his own feelings. Approaching Harichi's position slowly, Teka settled cross-legged onto an adjacent stool, joining the venerable Ungosh in a moment of shared connection. Their gazes met, mirroring the depth of their collective burden—the consequences of a plan gone awry. In the ensuing silence, an unspoken understanding passed between the two, each grappling with the weight of recent events and the uncertain future that lay ahead. Finally, with a heavy sigh laced with remorse, Teka broke the stillness.

"Ungosh Harichi, I fear our decision years ago to assign Ashira as Kina's nisi has had unintended consequences. I believe we underestimated the depth of their bond, the strength of their connection, and perhaps the extent of Kina's attachment. I worry that this imbalance will have far-reaching effects on him. He is not taking this situation well and likely blaming himself."

Harichi remained serene, closing his large eyes briefly as he took in a deep breath. Exhaling slowly, his expression softened, infused with empathy as he responded to Teka's concerns.

"I equally see and share your concern, Teka," he said pointing a finger. "The bond between sesni and nisi is deep and sacred. It is natural to feel loss when the nisi is gone. Usually, it is a joyous occasion, like the promotion to Runan. Though it can be sad when a nisi is killed or becomes a tendril within the Ki. This was not such an occasion. It was a severance. It has left a void, and such a void can fester with anger and pain. It is a treacherous path for one so young as Kina. A path to the Kage, the darkness it opens up. For the Kiensei, affection is a constant struggle. Your former nisi needs guidance, and guidance you must provide, Teka, just as I have for you. We set out to lessen his need for affection, and we may yet still achieve it."

Silence once again settled over them, and Teka allowed the weight of Harichi's words to sink in. It was uncommon for the aged Ungosh to speak at length, so he wanted to make sure to assimilate all that was said. His gaze wandered, fixating on a dusty, unused corner of the dimly lit chamber. Lost in profound thought, his mind digested the wisdom it had just heard. Slowly, his hand resumed its gentle stroking of his chin, a gesture that mirrored the journey his mind embarked upon.

"Sesni," Teka spoke again, his voice filled with respect and vulnerability as he turned his attention back to Harichi. "Kina's emotions run deep, like an endless wellspring. Throughout the years, I have strived to guide him in channeling those emotions, to prevent them from overwhelming him. We would spar, we would train together, I assigned him tasks—all to give him purpose, to keep his mind busy, and to help keep his emotions in check. I even allowed him to store and keep junk in his room to tinker with. I trained him the best that I could. He needs time to process the recent events, but he also needs an outlet. I don't believe another apprentice is the solution; he would resist it, even if it were mandated. Imposing mandates upon him is the last thing he needs right now."

Harichi's eyes met with Teka's, his voice both soft and sincere. The aged man grunted in deep thought. "We were so certain that young Wykera was ready for a nisi, weren't we? Yes. The Ki revealed it to us. You saw it too, correct? Muhashki Beithial was a good match for young Wykera. Though she chose another path. Yes."

"But my idea of Ashira was a better one," Teka quickly interjected.

In some of his downtime, Teka could be found wandering about the various youngling training areas, watching from afar or making a brief appearance at a group training session. He was in fact, considering ever so slightly the idea of taking on another nisi since Kina had been elevated to the rank of Runan. He just hadn't committed to it yet.

It was in his millings about the monastery years ago that he happened to spot Ashira in mock combat with a fellow muhashki; a female from Tholo who appeared to be a few years her elder and who, by his initial observation, was more skilled than her. In one of Battlemaster Areeno Sive's sessions, he watched as the young Tesska hybrid employ a variation of the Ryod style to a very competent degree. Yet her technique seemed mismatched to her strength. She definitely wanted to prove something. It was then that the young one had surprised him. The spindly Tesska evoked a smile from him by spouting off a colloquial barb to distract and disrupt the Tholo's concentration. Not overly unlike himself of course. As the mock contest progressed, he noticed the Tholo became increasingly sloppy in form execution as the verbal quips continued to flow between the two. Out of nowhere the young Tesska quickly switched to a reverse grip... something he hadn't seen in quite some time and certainly not used much anymore. It was then that his internal criticism of her strength versus technique became misappropriated.

In combination with the change of grip, she began fluidly combining elements of Rutara and Ashimak forms of swordsmanship to her attack and quickly became a whirling dervish of knobby little knees and elbows. The spritely little young one employed flips, cartwheels, and other Ki-augmented movements landing three marks of contact with her training sword in quick succession thus bringing the contest to an end. It was not unusual to hear verbal barbs or to see elements from various combat forms appear from the young ones as their training progressed, but the young Tesska had shown exceptional skill in utilizing multiple, different skill sets and tactics for one of her age. What surprised him the most however, was the gentle kindness the little one showed to her opponent as they walked away from the mat. Sesni Sive had spotted him observing the session from afar. Catching one another's eyes, Sesni Sive raised an eyebrow and extended a slight nod towards him as if to show his own impression. Returning the nod with an impressed grin, Teka knew at that moment she was one to watch.

"Hmm," Harichi murmured in contested agreement, a hint of a grunt punctuating his voice. It was at *his* suggestion and *his* authority that the young Tesska be assigned to Wykera. Teka considered taking her on as his own at first but was undecided whether he even wanted another nisi. His wrinkled visage smiled slightly as he sensed the younger sesni's playful curtness towards him, but his features quickly turned more consular. His wise gaze met Teka's, filled with compassion and insight. "For any Kiensei, it is a great challenge to master one's emotions. Yet, a challenge all must face. Constant vigilance and training are needed. A formidable opponent young Wykera faces. We know this, you, and me. I agree—he needs an outlet. I have concerns about the dangers that lie ahead. Down a sinister path it may lead. You must, *must* be careful."

Teka considered the words of the wise master as he spoke, allowing the longstanding friendship they shared to permeate and soothe the uncomfortable nature of the conversation. His eyes slowly wandered about the space, noticing slight imperfections on the ancient walls as he thought intently on a course of action.

"Unfortunately, master, I won't be able to keep an eye on Kina for the time being," said Teka. "Our efforts in the Outer Havens have me grossly occupied for the near future." He paused briefly to contemplate further. He spat out questions and comments as if no one was listening. "Kina cannot stay here. That certainly would not be received well by him. It would drive him mad. Perhaps some recreation time? What if he could be reassigned to aid me? Or just reassign me? At least then I could keep an eye on him. I could keep him occupied."

"This isn't possible," Harichi abruptly replied with a frown. "Our efforts along the Purchant Trade Route need our gravest of attentions. Your strengths, Teka, are needed there. We will send Wykera to the station at Verdict Ridge. There he will aid the Kiensei twin sisters Pleeti and Plarti. As a group, they can support one another as Plarti also recently lost a nisi herself. Help him, she can. His strengths would be a benefit to their effort. Yes. They can help one another."

"I doubt Kina would entertain a spiritual handholding session. Even so and also pressing," Teka redirected, "are we to immediately just throw him back into the fray, master? Force him back into battle without guidance, acknowledgement of his situation or to offer some solace first? I do not believe that to be wise, regardless of whomever does," Teka said, a tinge of passion flaring up with a thread of his deceased sesni's defiance woven in.

Immediately he caught his own emotions in his throat. Their eyes met across the space. The galvanizing stare from Harichi quickly centering him once again.

Harichi considered Teka's words, his ancient face etched with a lifetime of wisdom and understanding. Many a time in his hundreds of years of training Kiensei he had seen this type of situation play out. Some instances he could not rightly remember very well, others were quite clear. Time seemed to stand still as he deliberated, weighing the possibilities.

"Perhaps we should allow the will of the Ki to present itself," he said lightheartedly. "Kina Wykera must be empty first to be filled once again. He must learn how to manage himself. In this, he will grow into a fine Runan. A stronger Kiensei, he will be." He pointed a weathered finger at Teka. "Your nisi? You have to let him go, Teka. Or it will dominate *your* mind. To teach the lesson, one must first learn the lesson. You shall guide Kina, but he must be allowed to follow his own path."

It had taken some time for Teka to stop calling Kina his *apprentice* or *nisi* and to begin addressing him in many ways as his peer, but he had certainly gotten better as time went on. Detachment was a foundational component of the Kiensei way, but so was compassion. He had learned from many missions with him that *caring* is also a way forward, though technically outside of the mandates. *That* was something Kina excelled at.

He settled the matter within himself. Sifting the advice from the wise master Harichi in his mind, he decided that he would counsel his nisi—his *friend*—but allow him the freedom to grow. All the while observing from a distance with a ready ear should he be needed. He would be Kina's brother in this situation, part of a family his friend never had. This was the way to help him.

Rising slowly and regaining his footing, Teka proffered a respectful bow to the Ungosh. "Thank you, sesni. Apologies for my brashness," he said as he turned to exit the chamber to search for Kina.

Unbeknownst to Teka, a slight smile crossed the ancient master's mouth as he watched the door to his chamber close. Truly a complementary lineage that line of trained Kiensei had produced. From himself, to the fallen Orlozin, to Misharka the obstinate, to Teka, to Kina, and now Ashira... the undercurrent of pushing boundaries and challenging authority in measured ways had not been lost, though Olorzin was a different sort. Harichi recalled that he had been about 160 years old when he finally learned not to be so obstinate. Many believed the diminutive human Kiensei to be completely rigid in many facets of the Establishment. There were a great many things that the various people of the world believed about him that simply were not entirely correct. This did not bother him at all, and he was not about to change his outward persona based on the opinions of others. Much of his own past mischievousness had been forgotten or lost to time and he had no desire to dredge up things from the past, unless of course, there was a lesson attached to it that could be passed on. Worrying about any of these things had never added a single second to his strangely long life and it never would. He simply lived his life in service as the years passed by, learning from both success and failure, constantly in search of the Ki, but always continuing on regardless.

He believed that gentle nudging, not brazen enforcement of boundaries was necessary to grow as times and beings changed. Quick, large, sweeping alterations were reckless, like the Civil War of this age. Small, calculated, precise changes were more prudent. In his time, Harichi had seen such changes occur throughout the world. He divined this as the will of the Ki at work; its continuous reaction to balance the actions of those living in symbiosis with it and vice versa. To the Ki, time had no meaning, he surmised. In his younger years, he had derived this philosophy on a mere whim. Once, in his first century (or was it his second?), on the newly discovered continent of Mastillion, he was a part of an early exploration group. They were aboard an antiquated ship that sailed the waters within the continent amongst the scattered islands documenting flora and fauna alike. Their rudder had broken after striking something in the undocumented shallows, leaving a small, nearly useless stump. While many were concerned the trip was doomed, the captain remained steadfast and unfazed. Harichi remembered that this captain was still able to guide the large ship with such a small stubby rudder as long as he planned far enough ahead and made many small, calculated changes in their course. A lesson from the Ki he believed. Many lessons indeed, from the Ki.

Ashira was more than halfway down the expansive Grand Causeway, still searching for a direction, any direction to head toward. She couldn't very well wander about the entirety of

Korosento's massive sprawl aimlessly, that much she surmised. Any direction was better than no direction, except of course the direction back to the monastery. Off in the distance she spotted a valley of sorts in the shadowy skyline of towering structures. A rarity for the metropolis.

"Momento Pliaza" she said to herself with slightly narrowed eyes. It was as good a destination as any at this point. At the very least it would offer a place to collect her thoughts and decide what to do next. She could lose herself in the crowds that gathered there constantly, tune out the chaos for a bit, plan, and do what she needed to do...whatever that was.

The sun was setting and certain areas of Korosento weren't overly safe after night fall, even in the secured Imperial District with its constant patrols of artificially intelligent police robots and the Korosento Tsugint Guards. Come to think of it, Korosento wasn't overly safe even in broad pseudo-daylight a mere ten levels down. Ashira didn't feel discouraged by this, however. She was confident she could handle herself well in just about any physical confrontation. Even without her swords, she still had her unarmed combat skills and the Ki. Still, it was better to remove as much risk as possible. Especially now that she was on her own with no one to supply backup support.

Her measured and steadily cadenced steps continued forward into the quickly approaching darkness of night. The air becoming cooler against her skin as the sunrays climbed ever higher on the sprawling multitudes of towering buildings. The sound of hundreds of hovercrafts, levitators, and other flying transports overhead, droning against the many angular surfaces surrounding her. The Ki, she felt, becoming less and less turbulent. It was odd, she thought, that her intuition through the Ki hadn't revealed itself more than it did all throughout her ordeal. A Kiensei was supposed to feel it ebbing through them at all times. But as events had unfolded through the sabotaging controversy, the Ki had felt distant, slightly coarse. Unsettled. Heavy. Like trying to peer through a thick haze across a lake. For now, it seemed to normalize slightly.

She didn't fully understand what was happening or had happened to her connection to the Ki. Something like this had happened before, but in a unique way. Was it because she was technically *not* a Kiensei anymore? Would the Ki just stop interacting with her now that she was no longer affiliated with the establishment?

"No," she chided herself while rolling her eyes. She knew better than that. She had learned through her many academic lessons that sensitivity to the Ki doesn't just turn off like a toggle switch on a virtuadeck console. Though it *was* documented that some Kiensei practitioners could close themselves off, likely due to a traumatic incident... not unlike her own actually. She also knew that physical injury could diminish one's ability to wield the Ki as well. She often wondered whether Kina's missing limb had weakened him or not and if it had, then what would his power capacity be with it back? It was in these types of instances that the famed Dr. Niomea or one of the other Kiensei Consular doctors could step in and help the ailing person. Dr. Niomea was, however, more adept at diagnosing mental or spiritual ailments as the traumatic stresses of the Civil War itself took its toll on the minds of many Kiensei.

At last, she had reached the edge of the monastic monastery complex parapet. Behind her, the life of a Kiensei. One of conflict, war, sacrifice, and belonging, or so she thought. Below and in front of her, many pathways, many possibilities and... well... Ashira didn't really know what was out there for her. All she knew is that this is the direction her feet had taken her, and she would continue forward with the next opportunity, and the next opportunity until she found what she was looking for or all the opportunities were spent. One thing was clear though, there was no way she would subject herself again to the political placation and misplaced trust in the Kiensei establishment again. At least not right now.

Ashira looked down at the linear sprawl of the thoroughfares below. The beeps and hoots, the thrum of the crowds, the discord of city life teeming below. Her place in this world was out there. Where exactly remained to be found, but she had to start somewhere.

She stepped onto the lift to the streets below and turned around. The imposing figure of the castle-like monastery stood towering in front of her. Serene. Elegant. The snowcapped peaks of the Manilate Range behind it providing such a beautiful and peaceful backdrop. A flock of birds appearing as mere pinpoint specks against the ashen hues of the stone monastery walls in the sunset light. Closing her eyes, she took a deep breath in. She held it just slightly longer than usual before opening her eyes again and exhaling slowly. She repeated this three times over. It was a simple breathing technique that Sesni Asato taught her to help calm herself long ago. There it was again. She snorted lightly at the notion of her mind constantly returning to the Kiensei. She'd have to work on that. Ashira turned again, her back now to the monastery, her gaze lowering towards what lied beneath her. Reaching out to the side, she gently pressed the actuator.

The old lift shuddered momentarily, then with a metallic clank and slight jolt, it began its descent below.

Chapter 5 – Then

The swirl of the gravitunnel collapsed into lines, then into objects. A transport emerged from portalspace further away from the normal emergence zone than usual, but purposefully so. A single, gloved hand moved across a control panel in the cockpit, flipping switches and pressing buttons to stabilize the quasardrive and to cool the empedimental heatsinks. The control panels bordering the cockpit were of brushed metal and soft-glowing interfaces, each surface etched with the unique patina of countless journeys across the massive planet. A panoramic transparmor viewport stretched across the forward-facing wall, offering an uninterrupted vista of the world beyond. Through it, the vibrant green and blue glow of the continent of Karinar shone in the distance. A short-range scan of the immediate surroundings of the flat, saucer-like contours of the EZR-1210 light freighter yielded that the ship was alone and well outside of the atmospheric scanning capabilities of the continent.

Seats of supple, brown, well-worn leather hugged the contours of the pilot with the wrinkles telling tales of years spent in the embrace of travel. Amidst the array of instruments, a virtuaprojector sat just off center of the heads-up display. A few more clicks and beeps and the *Pyrixis* settled completely back into normal airspace.

The swiveling of the captain's chair and a clicking sound of the comms controls being activated signaled the opening of an encrypted communications channel.

"Baron Vohlm, its Sereeah. I've arrived at the Karinar continent. There wasn't much info from trade dispatch other than I had been specifically requested by you. So, what's with all the hush-hush?" the silky, female voice said.

The compact virtuaprojector blinked to life as the flickering light blue shape of a Hallen nobleman rose into view. His muscular repto-mammalian figure was imposing even at such a smaller scale. The long, dark robe heavily accented by scale-like embroidery. The triangular shoulder pauldrons rising to points framing his sharply featured head. His chiseled facial features consisting of high cheekbones and sharply arched eyebrows reflected a strong and stern countenance. His squared cranial structure that resembled a mohawk traversing the middle of his skull met with a long black tail of hair at the back. His eyes locked onto hers as he spoke in a deep and commanding voice.

"Good. You were hired specifically for this task Sereeah. I trust your earlier successes—and failures—will see to it that this task be completed. One would shudder to think what would happen should it not," he said sardonically.

"Now, now Baron. Let's not begin this little arrangement by being ugly... well, easier for you than me of course," Sereeah replied with a sly grin.

Vohlm was not amused by the aloofness of the vermillion skinned Rishka woman and so, cut her perceived insolence short.

"Let me remind you" he growled, "that the Mercenaries' trade cannot shield you from us. You have a debt to pay, and you *will* pay it or you and those who you hold dearest will suffer the consequences."

"Promises, promises" she said coyly with a slight smile and her most fake 'come hither' look. It wasn't the first time someone had threatened her or those supposed others with some dire set of consequences should she not do something of value. The fool. She was alone on this deity forsaken planet. There was no one that he or anyone could hold in ransom over her, but he didn't know that, and she wasn't about to let on otherwise. But that debt she owed;

it was true. At one point in her checkered past, she had fallen in with a cadre of slavers. Not something she was particularly proud of, but it was a means to an end. And that end came when their cadre was arrested during a sting operation. She sang like a songbird at the threat of a life sentence in exchange for a plea bargain. She had been young and naïve, she had done her little bit of time, and she had moved on... but not the Dark Fire. They certainly did not forget about her transgression and made certain she didn't either.

She shrugged the comment off nonchalantly. "Let's get on with it then Baron. What's the job here?"

"Our sources have picked up on a rumor of an undocumented Ki-sensitive child on the continent. Your task is to find it and bring it to a rendezvous point on the island of Cho'ckto in the Phustama Protectorate," Vohlm said.

The air within the cockpit became immediately solemn.

"That's a difficult task and also highly illegal" she shot back at once. "Kidnapping a child is a capital crime, you know, and is not afforded exemptions or protections under the law that trade members are typically extended via licensure. Plus, Karinar is a decently sized continent and with no other information to digest, it would be pretty challenging to find one child amongst the entire population. But that's not the crux of it all; the child is Ki-capable? You planning on raising some mystically powered merc, or something?"

"That is where you come in," Vohlm said wryly, "and the reasons are not yours to be concerned with trade-wench. Our benefactor has asked for this, and we shall deliver. And if *you* deliver, consider your debt to us expunged."

Sereeah cocked an eyebrow at the wavering blue hologram. The thought of not having to owe those green-faced hooligans was very tempting as was not having to live a life with the constant thought that she would be at their disposal, much like right now. "So, you want me to just fly my pretty little culo over there, say 'give me the wizard kid' to the locals and then just walk away," she snorted. "Why haven't the Kiensei come to claim the kid already? Don't they usually do the kidnapping? Albeit in a more legal manner?"

Vohlm smiled a deep fanged grin. "Precisely. On all points."

Sereeah was confused and her face reflected it. It wasn't usual for her assignments to come wrapped in a puzzle. She didn't like starting out from a place of mystery. She also didn't enjoy it when people spoke in circles or riddles. She liked to get to the point of things and take control of otherwise irrational situations. She enjoyed the ability to choose her own assignments and plan them accordingly instead of a direct request. Such was the way of the Trade and that's just the way she liked it. Straight forward with no nonsense and under control.

Having left her home on the continent of Prima Rishkais at an early age, Sereeah Trakkiss was forced to learn things the hard way. The best teacher in her opinion. She never was one for academics, though she did very well in all of her primary school studies and rarely had to study to pass exams. She discovered a love for material things early, no thanks to her deadbeat parents, and thus pursued the abundance of money and the freedoms it provided her. She wasn't afraid of arduous work by any means but prided herself on working with her mind more than her muscle. She had spent some of her earlier young adulthood working as an exotic performer, which is how she came up with the money to buy her ship. Her ticket to freedom. It was also there where she refined her abilities to engage with and subtly manipulate people. As such, most of her mercenary work consisted of information retrieval, surveillance, infiltration, and subterfuge.

She was considered beautiful by many, though, she was not a vain person. At least that's what she told herself. This exotic beauty, coupled with her natural ability to experience the feelings of others around her, allowed her to gain insights which made her suitable for her chosen trade. Whether it was consulting, befriending, or seducing, oh yes, there was money to be made in ways other than just hunting people. It could be made by simply manipulating them to divulge what otherwise might remain hidden. But now, this. Called to action like some hound to its master and for what... a child?

"Look Vohlm, I'm not in the mood to play 'guess the gauntlet' with you. Just spit it out already so I can get to work and get it done."

The Hallen's small virtuagraphic figured seemed to grow larger as his demeanor became more imposing.

"The fact that the child *hasn't* been acquired by the Hikarino-Kiensei is one of the more intriguing aspects. Especially since Karinar is part of the Expansionary Region and relatively close to the capitol. Which means the Kiensei don't know about it... *yet*" Vohlm said.

Sereeah's brow furrowed slightly. "How can they not know? Every child in the realm is blood-tested at birth, right? Wasn't that mandated by some rule or law or something long ago?" she questioned. Something was amiss here but she couldn't put her finger on it yet. It really didn't help that she couldn't tell what the brute was feeling.

"Ah. But Karinar isn't fully a part of the realm now, is it?" Vohlm said knowingly with a fanged grin. "It, like a few others, is associated with the realms monarchy only through treaties penned well over a standard century ago. They're technically neutral, but the details of which are mostly lost to time. So, unless one wants to go immerse themselves in ancient laws, no one alive today really knows the intricacies of the politics. Representation without responsibility, as it were. A... *beneficial*... result of a bygone conflict."

Her gaze softened as she began to unravel the implications of this little nugget of information. She, like many others assumed that all kingdoms, regencies, and fiefdoms from the capitol through the

Middle Region were inherent subjects of the realm. "So, what you're saying is that Karinar isn't required to blood-test then. Interesting. Ok Vohlm. Now you've got my attention. What else you got?"

"According to our asset, the child lives in one of the remote tribes away from the capital city of Kanónsoni'ta. Which one, we do not know. That is part of your task," he said with a slight nod.

Sereeah sat silently for a moment to consider her options and to ponder further questions. Partly to give herself the benefit of thought and partly to annoy the Baron. She did enjoy her petty torments from time to time. She wondered in the back of her mind how he knew such intricacies and details. It unnerved her slightly as to what else he may be hiding.

Vohlm scowled. "Are we done here Sereeah?"

"Not just yet. I'm thinking"

"Be quick. I have other pressing matters to attend to."

"So. What about the Kiensei? How do they play a part in all this? They serve the Emperor and the Prefects, but Karinar isn't really a part of the realm. Why would they be there and how would they know to go there?"

The baron bit out in frustration, "I am not here to enlighten you on the history of the planet you little red glush nor am I here to do the job for you."

"Alright, alright" she said in mock retreat. "I'm just concerned that I might run into one of those sword-wielding cultists. I wouldn't stand a chance against them in a fight, and I certainly don't want to spend time in jail by meddling in their affairs."

Vohlm glared at her. "*Why* would the Kiensei come if they're already *there*? Hm?"

Now the truth started to come out. The baron wanted her to impersonate a Kiensei, which was another capital offense. If she understood it correctly, she would arrive under the guise of a Ki-wielder, and the Tesska that live on Karinar would lead her to the child. She would take the child, and no one would be the wiser. The parents would assume her to be legitimate, the government wouldn't question it, and if something were said to the contrary she'd be long gone before anyone could do anything about it. "Hmm... not bad" she thought. Kidnapping wasn't really something she wanted to do. Information brokering might still hurt others, sure, but simply gathering it or bartering it didn't do so in such a direct way. However, this was a tangible person; a living, breathing being that she would have to coerce from its parents. "Man, it would really stink to be a Kiensei coming to collect a kid. How do they live with themselves?" she considered privately.

Sereeah twirled a piece of her thick, dark purple hair between her fingers. "Ok Vohlm. What say I don't feel like illegal kidnapping? Unless you've got a Tradesman medallion to hand me..." she was cut off.

"Then *you* will be the next target, Sereeah" he seethed. "Like I said, *you* owe us, and *you will* pay up one way or another. We have other resources within the Trade as well. Your dispatch was well within the regulations of the Trade though your task was not specified. How you handle it from there is entirely up to you."

Sereeah knew she couldn't talk her way out of this one and didn't want to poke the empyrlizard any further. Looks like she was stuck between getting arrested by the Kiensei or getting killed by the Dark Firc Organization. But if she succeeded, maybe she'd be free once again. "All right" she said cooly. "You got a contact for me at least?"

The baron crossed his arms across his large chest. "Your contact's name is Kel-so. I'll send you his private comm key. Don't land directly in Kanónsoni'ta. That piece of junk you call a ship isn't one the Kiensei are known to use. You don't want to cause suspicion."

Sereeah let out a small sigh. "All right. I'll get right on it... boss" she said sarcastically while rolling her golden eyes. "Call you when I've got the kid." Before she could say another word, the baron closed the channel down. "Well goodbye to you too. Mmm... a Kiensei huh," she tapped her cheek, "lemme check my reference store to see what I need to do about that."

She rose from her seat and walked back through the ship to her quarters. She snickered to herself as she recounted the 'junk' comment from the baron. She had sunk many a hard-earned credit into upgrading and modifying her ship to be a little more robust than the base model. She had bought it fairly cheap in the industrial city of Kormoran from an overstock yard and her chosen outfit that day certainly had *nothing* to do with that little extra dealer incentive she received during the purchase. They were practically giving the blasted things away due to their unpopularity. While it didn't have all the teeth she wanted, it could still bite. She wasn't a weapons specialist so most of her mods were in upgraded thrusters, armor plating, and shields so it could take a beating and get her hide out of town if and when things got too sporty. But along with the usual mods, she had also added a Grothian GB-MIN3 comms jammer to the starboard hardpoint and was planning to talk to her mechanic in the Trade about a signature scrambler from the black market.

She called up reference material on the Kiensei, specifically their attire. Checking her vast wardrobe in her cabin, she selected a tan colored homespun tunic that could be easily changed to look like the double-breasted robes in the diagram. She happened upon a plain cream-colored frock that could have its sleeves removed and neckline modified to give her some distinctive flair, as if she were one of the sesnis. No, that would be too forward. She needed to be a regular runan to keep skepticism down. Ah, a surcoat of similar color. That would do just fine with some work. A belt, no problem. Boots, why yes, she had plenty and quickly found a lovely pair of leather knee-highs with just enough scuff to appear like she'd seen some action. A hooded cloak, hmm... it wasn't the deep blue but nothing she read or saw made her believe that it couldn't be dark brown. That just left "... the sword. How in the planet am I supposed to come up with that?" she asked herself. One slip up with that critical piece and the ruse would be spoiled.

She spent the next half hour searching spare parts canisters, cluttered cargo holds and harvesting unnecessary metal embellishments from the ship and yet another hour cobbling together something that looked like a sword of the venerable Kiensei. It literally was just an amalgamation of common metals and carboplast, but it would fit the bill as long as no one wanted to hold it or see it in action. In total, she spent about three standard hours assembling, building, cutting, sewing, and modifying the various components into a complete and very passable disguise. She proudly stood before a full-length mirror marveling at her handiwork. She brushed her smooth, shoulder length hair then pulled it back into a simple bun. No embellishments allowed on this mission. With a smirk, she pulled the hood of the cloak over her head and giggled to herself "I am a Kiensei."

Baron Roulte Vohlm closed down the communications channel from the well-hidden comm station positioned on the perimeter of the conference room and turned to face the rest of the Dark Fire Council.

"Lord Grunnery, our asset is in route to collect the child on Karinar," he said.

"Very well Baron Vohlm. Our benefactor will be pleased to hear of this" the Hallen chairman said. "While you continue to monitor that dispatch, I will see to it that our cover is intact should things digress." Rising from his chair, the burly Hallen proffered a slight bow of his head to each of the council members as they also rose and bowed deeper in respect to their leader. "Gentlemen, I bid you good day."

Lord Grunnery left the council chamber that doubled as the Toomas Ferrying Systems executive boardroom and headed to his private office overlooking the southern lava pits of the volcanic continent of Phustama. The ornate steel door slid open with a silent hiss. The auto illuminators glowed to life revealing a large, windowed space. The floors were of a stone polished like obsidian glass with natural textured portions left for effect. The walls were burnished duralumium plates with vertical strips of polished titanium that touched a ceiling of black glass that, itself, was embellished with flowing gold accents depicting flora and fauna in an ancient art form. From his elegant perch above the volcanic chaos, he could survey the various natives, mechs and fellow Hallen going about the daily events of his namesake company. Just a simple shipping company, nothing more, he smiled. The ghostly hue of the shields protecting the workers, platforms, ships, repulsors and the building itself could barely be seen, adding to the frightening magnificence of the construction. He stepped over to the black polished stone desk that had inlays of gold akin to the ceiling and took a seat. He fingered a small control pad and with a whirring sound, a life-sized virtualgram appeared in front of his desk.

"Greetings Chairman." The flickering blue virtuagram said in a brooding voice. "To what do I owe the occasion?"

"My Lord, our asset is in route to acquire that which you requested" the Hallen said in a low, even tone whilst bowing his head. The hooded figure in the virtuagram made no motion at all. His face was completely covered by the shadow of its dark cowl and his body concealed by a long, dark robe.

"Excellent" the figure said with authority. "It is a challenge to acquire living subjects of this type outside of prying eyes let alone outside of the knowledge of the Kiensei. I have had several attempts fail because of them. Spare no expense in your efforts. You will be handsomely compensated above and beyond for your troubles. Be cautious and discreet, however. Leave no trace," the figure said.

The stern face of the Hallen relaxed a bit as he waved his hand in a formal fashion towards the holographic figure. "Thank you for your patronage, my Lord. I will contact you again once I have news that is worthy of your time." The dark figure's hologram motioned in what would have appeared to be a nod and was gone.

Sereeah seated herself back into the captain's chair in the cockpit. Looking at her comm station she saw that she was in range of the nearest relay beacon to send a message. She typed in the key, clicked the comm on and waited. A few seconds later, a voice crackled to life on the speaker like leaves rustling.

"Yes? Who is it?" a male voice said.

"Is this Kel-so?"

"And if it is?"

"My name is Sereeah. I've been sent here to pick up a... *package.* Yours I'm told." Sereeah said while adding a bit of playful sass in her voice. "I need a place to land outside of the capital. Think you can manage that for me? I'd hate to just land in your lap." Sereeah thought she'd gauge the response of the unknown contact to see if there was anything to glean about his personality. Never know when and how a person could be used unless you know what makes them tick.

"Good. I'll send you coordinates. Don't be late." Kel-so said.

Evidently this one was more of the thick-headed type she thought. Oh well, if she was playing the part of a Kiensei, she might as well act the part.

"Oh, I'll need your ship ID too so I can clear it through security when you get in airspace" he said.

"Roger that. See you shortly" she said in a more professional tone, ignoring the latter question. She wished she had that scrambler right about now. Firing the thrusters, she steered her ship towards the distant continent.

63

Chapter 6

Kina stopped and stood sideways on the staircase landing amongst the pillars of the monastery founders. Unable to process fully, he stood there looking toward the grand staircase. Waiting. Waiting to see if his friend experiences a change of heart and comes walking back up. Secretly he was willing it to happen, speaking his desire in his mind and into the Ki that flowed within. He knew the chances were slim to none, but he just couldn't let it go. He said nothing at all, his lips unable to convey what his mind produced. He had lost himself to thought amongst the ecumenopolis' familiar sounds surrounding him as they echoed by and between the squared and exquisitely carved pillars.

Hoping. Watching. Waiting.

He had lost track of time when he finally noticed the sun had completely set and the distant stars had begun to dimly shine through the atmosphere; the cooler evening air caressing his face. He needed to eat but wasn't hungry. His belly was filled already with other things less appetizing, so the thought of food wasn't overly pressing. Eventually he resigned himself to reenter the monastery.

She was really gone.

Time seemingly stood still as he robotically placed one foot in front of the other. He didn't rightly remember walking the halls and corridors. He spoke to no one even if they spoke to him. Kina found himself in one of the many mezzanines near the Sacred Obelisk when he realized how far he had walked. He felt angry, frustrated, and decided to head to one of several dojos reserved for runans and above in rank. He needed to do something, anything really, and some exercise might be what the doctor ordered to ease his troubled mind.

Opening the double sliding doors, he quickly checked to see if any scheduled sessions were on the data screen just outside. It was later than when most regularly scheduled training sessions took place, but there were always some private sessions or special events happening in the after hours.

None this evening.

Stepping inside and feeling the smoothly thatched floor underfoot, the doors closed behind him with a muffled sigh from the actuators. Kneeling down to the right side, he opened an access hatch near the ground. His years of tinkering on his own and repairing other's tech afforded him the knowledge and ability to override or disable doors, especially ones here. It wasn't necessary to hard-lock many doors in the expansive monastery and the dojos were no exemption, so this task was an easy one. He didn't feel like being disturbed anyway. Disconnecting the exterior motion sensor and disabling the automatic panel outside was all that was necessary to ensure his privacy for a time.

Since he reasoned no one else would be there, Kina shed his utility belt and leather tabard, leaving his dark colored robe. Tossing his outward implements to the side, with the exception of his sword, he took a quick glance around the large dojo. Darkness from outside permeated the high windows. The gray homespun cloth on the ceiling to disperse noise and prevent cacophonous echo hung like storm clouds, mirroring his mood. On the paneled, cream-colored walls hung various assortments of primitive hand-held weaponry, black and white tapestries, and vertical hanging racks of training weapons. The wooden implements, made from Larkwood, framed the square thatched panels of the floor and walls. They served as structural and decorative components and brought a visual warmth to the space. A few heavy bags hung on opposite corners to be used for unarmed strikes and other associated training.

Kina reached out his left hand slightly behind him. Slowly, with two extended fingers, he manipulated the lighting controls with the Ki. Darkness flooded the room.

He closed his eyes and took a deep breath. He palmed the hilt of his sword with his cybernetic hand feeling the muted metallic taps as the miniature servos slowly closed the individual metal fingers around it. Clasping his left hand around the other, he placed the silvery hilt at his waist and pointed it upward. The blade shimmered to life with a slight hum as he focused the Ki, imbuing the blade with that cerulean and ethereal power. The blade, merely centimeters from his nose, hummed smoothly as it bisected his face. He slowly opened his eyes with his features morphing into a blue-hued menacing look. His brow crumpled deeply; his lips curled into a snarl like a prowling Manxcat glowering at its prey.

Taking the ready position, he began slowly by harkening back to his own muhashki days and that of the Prolan regimen and the Efficacies. Step by step, Kina recounted with his hands and feet the various movements, strikes, blocks, parries, and reposts associated with the earliest of lessons learned. Only a few moments passed before he had completed the entire series with ease. He snickered at the rudimentary nature of the sequences. He hadn't even broken a sweat with the simplicity of movements associated.

But he was only getting started.

Teka sauntered down the expansive corridor towards the Sunburner section of the monastery that housed Kina's domicile, searching his mind for the words to say to his ailing friend. He knew that losing one so close to oneself was difficult, only too well. But this was different. Teka had lost his own sesni honorably in battle against the recently emerging Kageatsu. Kina had lost a nisi to politics, in which there was little to no honor to be found. Politics, he thought, were a necessary evil and one in which the Kiensei should never be involved, though now the monastery found itself interwoven more often than it should be. He paused briefly in quiescent reflection, turning to look out of one of the high arched windows overlooking the Imperial District. Millions of twinkling lights shone in the distance mirroring the stars themselves, as if the expanse of space had invaded the massive city. He had to be tactful in how he approached his former student. Kina was quick to shut out and shut down. Perhaps he would lightly prod him into a light-hearted banter? Or maybe a more straightforward approach? He turned and continued walking towards his destination, hand stroking his mustache in deep thought.

Arriving a few moments later, he pressed the button for the annunciator. No answer. He knocked gently on the door. Again, no answer. He reached his hand over, tapped the button and opened the door. To his mild surprise, the room was dark. Kina's trusty mech ID-241 was over by the bed in a customary low-power mode. Teka stepped into the room and the automatic system faded the illuminators into a mild glow. The usual things were there, crates of various bits of technology that had been scavenged from nondescript places and spare parts unaccustomedly lifted from the detritus bins from around the city, and a workbench with something Kina had been tinkering with. From what he had deduced in the years before, surrounding himself this way with all manner of bric-a-brac was similar to his former home back on Toonakeen, and it was a slight comfort for him. It kept his hands busy, kept his mind occupied. Across the room on the desk, he saw Kina's communicator. "No chance of reaching him that way," he thought. He'd have to remind Kina later that his communicator should be on his person at all times while on duty, but not right now. In that instance, the little mech came to life. After a quick boot sequence, the little mech turned his conical head and chittered a string of its robotic language to Teka.

"Hello there Four-One, I'm looking for Kina. Have you seen him?" The mech replied in the negative.

"Did he say anything to you about his possible whereabouts, maybe?" Again, a negative response.

"Hmm... odd. Don't you think?" The brief series of beeps, chirps, and squawks from Four-One conveyed agreement, but nothing out of the ordinary and to also suggest that Teka try to use his communicator.

"Yes Four-One, I thought of that at the onset, but he's not wearing it. See? Its over there on his desk," Teka pointed. A brief pause hung in the air as the little mech processed the information. Turning his head left and right, ID-241 posed a solution with a chirrup that sounded more like a question.

"Good idea my little friend. We'll keep that amongst ourselves, OK? Let's go plug in somewhere and see if you can locate him." The little mech had posited that he could access the video surveillance system to see if he could track Kina's whereabouts. Though not one to blatantly break the rules, Teka knew it wasn't completely in line with security policies to hack the monastery's networks. But this was important, and he knew Four-One was capable of not getting caught. ID-241 ambled over to a spot near the desk, he turned his head and beeped a request for Teka to move a crate so that he could access the terminal link. The Kiensei sesni's face morphed into a mix of shock and surprise as he hadn't realized there was one already present in Kina's room. His idea was to find an empty training room or somewhere they wouldn't be noticed. His mind briefly soared over the implications of such a revelation as he moved the crate. Soon enough, Four-One had the internal socket quickly blinking wildly as he parsed the network.

Activating his virtuaprojector, ID-241 played various angles of communal areas, searching for Kina. After a few moments, Four-One chirped and highlighted the outline of Kina as he had been spotted passing through the entrance foyer, accessing a lift, walking a hallway and... there... entering a dojo. "Which room is that Four-One?" Teka asked. The little mech beeped a response. "Thank you, my friend. Care to join me?" Another set of affirmative chirps and the two set out to intercept Kina.

Arriving at the dojo, Teka at once noticed the door's auto-open sensor wasn't working. He waved his hand at it just to be sure he had created enough motion to activate it.

Nothing.

He reached over to the door control panel and tapped the manual actuator button. Still nothing. He quickly realized that both the sensor and panel was non-operational, which was suspiciously odd.

In an instant he barely heard what seemed to be a howling roar on the other side of the door. "Somethings happening in there. Four-One, I need you to open this door as quick as you can," he said authoritatively. The mech squawked acknowledgement, ambled quickly to the access panel and set to work.

Kina's emotions were stirring as his memories caustically regurgitated themselves. From his reasoning with a fatuous council all the way to a riotous outburst in the Well of Judgement, the fires within were burning in his chest and the flames were steadily growing.

He grumbled and launched himself into his own modified version of Quieku. He had noticed over time that Ashira would meld elements of the form with her more dominant Sooien, giving her better mobility.

While aggressively interrogating Jessa Tressnu in the bowels of the Korosento slums, she had verbally assaulted him and the establishment in an effort to save herself from Kina... and she wasn't wrong. Come to think of it, the usually vindictive witch was actually defending Ashira.

"I realized that your fallen nisi and I had shared commonalities." He remembered her verbal gut-punch whilst nursing a neck sore from the crushing strength of his hand while trying to catch her breath. There was *no* way the two were anything alike.

He belted out a yell at no one as he swung his sword at thin air. Switching to his trademark Dai Kin form, heated emotions continued to rise within the Kiensei runan as he furiously slashed, feinted, attacked and otherwise became a veritable hurricane of assault and passion. He felt the Ki begin to dance strangely around him, within him, as he progressed through the form. It began to surge within his chest with an icy malevolence.

The light from his rapidly moving blue-hued sword strobed upon the walls of the dojo, and along with his percussive footwork became like the violent symphony of a thunderstorm as he physically recited the intricacies of each movement. With occasional grunts and other non-verbal vocalizations, he steadily yet violently performed the entirety of the form. Upon conclusion, he stopped briefly, his breathing much more pronounced. Sweat had begun to form on his brow and pronounced patches of moisture began to appear on his robes. He stood near the far end of the dojo with is arms hanging slackly by his sides with his head slightly inclined backward. There was silence in the room save for the sound of his breath. He silenced the Ki from his sword, returning it to the black scabbard on his hip causing the darkness to envelop him.

Kina stopped for a moment to focus, but the murkiness of Ashira's departure ate at him. Before her kiradrik-like dive into the dank air rising in the massive underworld portal that spanned the sublevels of the massive city, she had pleaded—no—criticized him for not even trying to come and help her when she was imprisoned, as she put it. Instead of responding harshly, he had tried his best to stay calm and convince her to stop running and return to the monastery with him. He tried to placate her with calm logic, he tried to show her he cared. He tried to explain to her that he, in fact *had* tried, and that the situation was more delicate than she knew.

"But I could have done more. I *should* have tried harder," he chided himself. The word 'failure' just couldn't describe what he had done.

His hands began to shake slightly as the tension in his mind began to build yet again. The story of the fire-beast his mother used to tell him when he was a boy welled up inside. His own simple truth, his own creed, alongside it. He was Kina Wykera, the Singularity who was supposed to simply *find a way*. Remembering his own self-reflection after the Harte Minosa incident caused another wave of anger to swell within. Gripping his sheathed sword tightly he cocked his right arm back and flung his precious implement against the wall with a primal shout. It clanged loudly as it struck the wall and fell to the floor having not been imbued with Ki.

Two of the three moons of the planet began shining through the windows from behind the overcast sky, casting a vague, eerie glow about the spacious room. A lone heavy bag was lightly illuminated near the corner. Kina spotted it and decided the unassuming thing was to be the victim of his next salvo. Bringing his arms to bear and balling his fists, he launched himself at the bag. He felt a surge of energy, as the Ki began moving darker around him. Darkness pulsed through his arms and legs like lightning as he pummeled the unassuming object.

His mind wandered back to his interrogation of Tressnu as he launched wave after wave of punches and kicks. The spectraxite fibers holding tight together as the punishment was doled. Normally used for mooring lines, towing lines, and other high strength applications where the use of anchor beam technology was moot, spectraxite was specifically used in some commercial textiles for its inherent strength and flexibility. This instance, in particular to the heavy bag, to counteract the Ki-augmented strikes that were common in Kiensei.

"My sesni left me, abandoned me, and that's exactly what you did to her... you and your precious Kiensei establishment," Tressnu had said with venom dripping from every word. Kina believed she was right, much to his chagrin.

With thoughts and emotions laid bare to himself, Kina stood three steps away from the unassuming bag. He had failed Ashira. Just like he had failed his mother. He judged himself guilty with a self-imposed sentence of pain. The fire-beast of his mother's beloved story bellowed within him. His emotions roiled into a volcanic geyser. Summoning his anger to the surface, he roared loudly, filling the dojo with his voice. The Ki surged within him with a power he hadn't felt before, and it felt.... *good*? No. *Easy, maybe*? He unleashed that power and his fury into one final punch with his cybernetic hand. The myriad items on the dojo walls shuddered ever so slightly as the pent-up energy was released in one, singular, quaking moment.

Throughout the monastery, those Kiensei who were most attuned to the Ki stopped momentarily in confusion or concern as a strange, evanescent ripple in the Ki propagated around them. Because of how quickly it came and went, most dismissed it almost instantaneously. Some looked around in confusion, Others just blinked in a moment of curiosity.

The doors to the dojo slid open as he struck.

Teka Suromasa stood in the double-doorway. Light from the corridor streaming past him and spilling into the darkened dojo. He stepped into the dimly lit space and stopped short only a few steps inside as he saw his former nisi at the far end. He noticed Kina was breathing heavily, his robes wet with sweat. The unfortunate heavy bag next to him with a gaping hole, spilling its contents onto the floor. A pang of worry crossed his mind as his face wilted slightly.

"Kina?" he questioned softly.

"Not now Teka," Kina said with annoyance whilst glancing over his heaving shoulders.

"Kina are you alright?"

"I'm fine."

"Better than that bag, I'm sure," Teka quipped gently.

Kina hunched over, placing his hands on his knees. "I'm not in the mood right now Teka. I just want to be alone for a while," he said taking a deep breath.

"I understand," Teka feigned in retreat, "but I could hear you from outside the door and I thought I heard shouting. Looks like you had quite the workout in here." He looked around the space with his gaze settling on Kina's crumpled effects on the floor. "Kina, I'm not here to judge. I only want to help," the experienced sesni said cooly.

Teka could sense something was amiss. Though he thought it best to try and keep the mood somewhat light, he could not help but feel the smallest presence of something strangely dark, and it was quickly retreating... like ashen tendrils of shadow creeping slowly back to their source.

ID-241 lumbered slowly into the dojo and took a position next to Teka. Turning his conical head to focus his photoreceptor on Kina, he chirruped quizzically.

"I'm alright buddy," Kina said between breaths. "Just needed a little stress relief, that's all."

Four-One's head slowly panned left and right. The little mech cheeped a doubtful response, having had to undo his sesni's handiwork on the door controls and the state of his surroundings in the dojo. The little mech ambled across the sectioned mats and past his sesni to the side wall. A noticeable dent was present in the cream-colored panel, like something had struck it. Extending a grasper arm, ID-241 picked up the sword that had landed nearby. He turned and trundled up to his sesni, extending the arm.

"Thanks buddy," Kina said calmly, gazing down softly at the orange and white mech while placing his human hand gently on its head. Teka approached his friend with his tabard and belt in-hand. His face soft and welcoming having sensed Kina's need for a friend rather than a sesni.

"You know," he said coyly, "there are much better ways of handling your emotions than allowing them to explode like this. Much healthier and safer ways. I understand your feelings surrounding Ashira. I, too, feel responsible. I can't say that I condone your actions, but I also can't say that I condemn them either, given the situation." He extended his arm holding Kina's implements. It wasn't often that the two spoke openly about topics of this magnitude. Sesni Misharka had been much better at delivering harsh realities and life lessons, Teka thought.

"I don't want to talk about it," Kina said flatly, brushing off the notion. He grabbed his effects and slowly walked past his former sesni. Restoring himself to his complete Kiensei attire and look, he casually strapped his sword back into his belt. He ran his fingers through his disheveled brown hair and started for the doors.

"Kina," Teka said gently.

He stopped and looked over his shoulder but said nothing. A moment of silence passed between the two Kiensei before he spoke.

"Don't worry master, I'll make an apology and take my punishment for damaging the dojo," Kina said with exasperation, turning back to face the double doors. Probably more scut work around the monastery, he scoffed to himself.

Tasseling a few whiskers from his mustache, Teka extended an appeal. "I wasn't going to mention anything, to be honest. I can simply state the accidental nature of the damage to the maintenance staff and leave it at that. As a return favor though, I wanted to know if you would accompany me to the dining hall or perhaps to one of the gardens? I can understand you not wanting to talk about Ashira right now. I won't press the issue, my friend. I just want you to know that I'm still here for you and will be ready to listen if and when you are ready. I do, however, want to discuss your emotional outburst here." He gestured to the now deflated heavy bag.

"Here it comes," thought Kina. He had hoped to be long gone before anyone knew he had been in the dojo. But as usual, Teka was there to hamper his intentions. Kina stood silently without acknowledging his sesni's comments. He didn't have the energy to deal with it at this point.

Walking up to face Kina and placing a hand on his shoulder, the senior Kiensei looked his former nisi in the eyes, a gaze of peace meeting a look of war.

"You know this isn't healthy Kina. Anger is a natural emotion that we all struggle with as Kiensei. You don't have to give in to it, especially so haphazardly or alone. There are other ways, my friend."

"I really don't feel up to one of your lectures right now Teka," Kina said with a slump of his shoulders. His natural tendency was to retreat within himself when emotional strife appeared. It was his conditioned reaction based on years of slavery. In this moment, he missed his mother. She had always found a way to calm and comfort him when things got tough. She was his safe place for many years. He could always hug her with his head on her chest, the sound of her loving heart beating in his ear, her gentle hands wrapping around him like a warm blanket. But those days were gone and yet, replaced by his wife. He needed her right now. He needed to talk to her and be with her. Hearing the memory of her voice in his head was enough to douse the flames. If he could just be with her for a while, that would help.

"I'm not trying to lecture you, Kina. I only say this because I *do* care," Teka said. He thought something he had learned from his nisi was worth a try. His reputation as being cold and uncaring preceded him constantly. "In the future, if you feel the need to vent, please come to me. We can spar, we can talk, we can do whatever is within our means, just don't bottle it up and allow it to explode like this. Please?"

"Yes master," Kina sighed. His face an expression of exhaustion. The will to argue was gone. "I'm going to eat. I haven't had much food in the past while... haven't really felt like it."

Teka proffered a half-smile and patted his friend on the shoulder. "Very well my friend. I understand. Food it is then." The pair began slowly walking toward the lighted corridor with ID-241 rolling along just behind them.

Teka thought some distraction would help in the moment. "On our way, we can discuss your next assignment if that's alright?" Kina gave a silent nod. "But before that, how in the jook-milker's joy did you wind up with a data link in your room?" he said with a wry smile. Kina's eyebrows rose in nervous surprise as he turned his head to look at Teka, his mouth opening to speak; the doors closing behind them.

Chapter 7

The sights and sounds of the Neethola lower market district were different this time. Considered as Level 116 by Korosento Standards, it was situated just below the topmost level of structures of the expansive Imperial District. Its myriad of walkways and passageways were open to the sky above and bordered by storefronts, restaurants, night clubs, and the occasional trendy mobile food stand. Its many patrons enjoyed the same conditioned environment and filtered air as those who were considered 'topsiders' and as a result, the affluency of the district was more than clear to the general populace with all the latest in goods and fashions for sale from all across the massive planet. In the past, Ashira had been here on general patrol or to run some kind of errand in an official capacity, but this time it was different. Now, instead of having to be on the lookout for suspicious activity or to scan faces looking for a fugitive or narrowly focusing on a task at hand, she just... walked. No pressing duties, no mission, no nothing. For the first time in quite a while she could just listen to the sounds of the various shop owners hawking their wares, the background conversations of patrons and bystanders, the pulsating club music filtering out of an entrance or just the hum of the hive-like city's utility infrastructure in the background. She could stop without worry of delaying her mission and just waste time watching some comical virtualnet advertisement of some obscure product or service.

She had nowhere to be and no one to expect her.

She walked amongst the citizens of the realm in pleasant obscurity as one of them and indulged herself in the knowledge that she was, well, free. Free to do as she pleased, go where she pleased and be... *whatever* she pleased. But what did that look like exactly? She didn't know.

As she continued along, the various scents of fine soaps, perfumes, and incense filled her nose. It reminded her of the many continents and diverse civilizations she had visited with the military and how, at times, they would have the simple joy of passing by a native flowering species. Secretly she enjoyed taking in the experiences of the natural world, wherever she may be. She loved nature, always had. It made her feel connected to the planet and the Ki more than any other experience. On a few missions to the lusher continents and islands, Ashira found it more peaceful and serene to camp outside the usual bivouac and sleep under the stars. Instead of a basic cot or the confines of a portable shelter, she enjoyed the feeling of a cool evening breeze on her skin, listening to the symphony of creatures in the night and smelling the sweet, alluring scents of the native flora as they closed themselves up for the evening.

Her daydreaming was interrupted briefly at the sight of an approaching platoon of Korosento Tsugint Guards. Their crimson and gold accented armor was unmistakable. Her mind quickly switched to military mode and her senses became laser sharp. She continued walking at a steady pace as not to draw undue attention to herself. With all of the fast-moving confusion surrounding her trial, she wasn't sure if the message of her acquittal and self-imposed exit from the Kiensei had made its way through the ranks just yet. As the platoon approached, she slid over to the side of the walkway while keeping a wary eye on them. Her breathing steady, she continued along her chosen path and watched with a wary eye as they continued on their route past her without even so much as a quick glance. Ashira had been around Tsugint soldiers for the past several years and this is the first time a formal greeting, salute, or some other form of militant exchange hadn't occurred. It felt... "*weird*" she said aloud for lack of better terms.

"Excuse me!? What did you say girl?" The Natook male bouncer guarding the entrance to a club shouted at her. He looked down at her crossly as if to demand an explanation for her alleged insolence.

Ashira stopped quickly and turned to face him. "I'm sorry! I didn't see you there," she said apologetically, holding up both hands in a mock surrender. "I wasn't talking about you. I promise. I was talking about the guards that just walked past."

The guard snorted through his flat black canine-like nose while folding his bulging brown arms across his chest.

"Hmph. Yeah. Been seeing more and more of them lately. You watch yourself kid."

"Kid!?" Ashira thought. It was insulting to her to be considered a simple kid. If he only knew who and what she was... but she wasn't that anymore she corrected herself in her mind. She waved a friendly hand at the bouncer and turned to continue on her way. She wasn't the tallest or bulkiest creature on the planet, but she was most certainly NOT a kid. Good thing he didn't see her eyes roll as she turned around and continued on her way. She'd hate to have to hurt the guy.

Emerging from a large sweeping corner, she saw a distinctly long and straight section of the market district. She still had a few clicks left to walk before coming to the Pliaza. This stretch was long. Long enough that the market seemed to collapse into a point of singularity in the distance. "Where's a scootster when you need one?" she said aloud to herself.

After walking a few kilometers, she stopped briefly to rest. The sound of breezechimes swaying and the gentle tinkling of a stringed instrument suddenly caught her attention. She stared at the lighted sign of a spa situated above its own windowed storefront. The name was crafted using a sweeping violet gradient color and a slanted and flowing version of the written and universal Uvadish language to give it a more luxurious look. The semitransparent windows were softly backlit and revealed a calm and inviting interior. Ashira became lost in thought for a moment, the entrancing light of the sign reflecting in her eyes.

There were times in the past when she wondered what it would be like to just be a young woman instead of a peacekeeping soldier; to do the things she had seen other women do like getting a manicure or something. Even though a hairstyle was seemingly out of the question, seeing as she didn't have experience with hair due to the strict rules of the Kiensei, she had always held a curiosity at the assorted styles Damae had worn. It was Damae who had once caught her staring in curiosity as the prefect's handmaidens were brushing her hair and dobbing makeup on her face in preparation for a semi-formal meeting. The prefect had once offered a similar experience to her, to which she politely declined as it was prohibited by the establishment. She remembered that Damae had told her with a gentle truthfulness that Ashira *"was always wearing hers anyway"* as a compliment, referring to the subtle but distinct markings on her hybrid species' face.

There were also instances where she had been slightly curious to experience the relaxation of a massage, though the thought of being touched made her anxious. There was one thing though. "Oooo... a long soak in a tub," she dreamed with a slight grin. Now *that* was something she could be *incredibly happy* with right now. The only other times she had anything remotely similar was a soak in a rejuva cylinder to heal battle-sustained injuries, which wasn't at all too bad. The liquid was warm and slightly more viscous than water and tended to leave a slimy feel after coming out of the tank. As for a regular bath in water... it would be nice just to have a relaxing steep untethered to a breathing machine and harness.

All these things were generally frowned upon by the Kiensei, unless used as part of a ruse on assignment... but now... she was *no* Kiensei. And... well... she had *no* money either, so this little curiosity of hers would have to wait a bit longer. Still, the prospect of chasing some of her dreams was encouraging and right now and she needed a little bit of that.

It was well into the night when Ashira finally made it to Momento Pliaza, a large and expansive area that served as the most popular tourist attraction of the metropolis. The stars of the night shined brightly over the large square complex with the moons Xatan-2 and Isperdium in full view with the former waning away into the night. The perimeter of the expanse was lined with evenly spaced ironocrete spires approximately ten meters high with blue flames dancing atop them. Virtuagram banners reaching to the sky at the four corners undulated and shifted in both color and text signifying cardinal direction and time. Even at this hour, the night life of the massive city teemed in and around the four large, cone shaped structures that appeared to be guarding the centralized monument of Matume, the most ancient and mysterious artifact on the planet. When in fact, they housed shops, food stalls, observation decks and cocktail lounges just like the rest of the perimeter structures that formed the external borders. The entirety of the area was divided into four individual quadrants. Each housing its own variation of fountains, lighted walkways, seating areas, public artworks and virtuanet projectors. It was a tourist's spot for sure.

Korosento never slept.

She stood on one side of the squared plaza and took stock of her situation. Her stomach groaned a warning. Placing a hand on her midriff just inside her crossed tunic, she secretly grimaced. The thought of hunger was one that had constantly been in the back of her mind since she left. In her survival training, she remembered it was shelter first, then water, then fire and food. It was advantageous being in Korosento as even the most rudimentary forms of shelter could be obtained easily, and the climate was mild enough with well-forecasted rain showers. Water could be obtained from a public refresher station fountain though the quality of it might be questionable. Fire was certainly not necessary and would likely land her in jail again. Food was going to be a problem though. She usually had several ration bars in her belt pouch just in case she needed something nutritious while away from a supply base or her assigned battleship, but not anymore. She also made sure to eat before a mission just in case the opportunity didn't present itself. At least she had had the opportunity to fill her belly during her first stint in a holding cell. Food was one of the only boons she had received while awaiting her fate for allegedly suffocating Latissa Chormarind using the way of the Ki. Commander Xima, a decorated Tsugint, had seen to it that she was well fed at the very least. Ashira knew she could last a little longer even though she had walked over ten kilometers by her reckoning, but she would need to find something to eat sooner rather than later.

Scanning the area, she saw a large VirtuaNet News projection in the center of the nearby southeast quadrant displaying a slowly rotating visage of Melia Ad'nya, a well-known Throlick newscaster from the Korosento News Desk. She decided to head that way to see what was happening around the area and to just sit down for a bit.

There were small, grey, independent seating pods set around a central rounded projector. The interesting concavity of the architecture allowed those seated to instantly hear the sounds associated with whatever was displayed without disturbing those outside. Ashira quietly slipped into one of the unoccupied pods furthest away from the central projector. It appeared that a repeat of an earlier broadcast was playing.

"...*citizens can expect the following atmospheric conditions across the following districts. In the Imperial District, clear skies and moderate temperatures will prevail. Amscray District will experience scattered rain showers, while the Cormorand District is set for a partly cloudy day. As for Luxoria Heights, a fog advisory has been issued due to ongoing maintenance of the atmospheric moisture condensators in that sector, which could make visibility low and navigation challenging. Commuters are recommended to exercise caution while traveling in these conditions while repairs continue.*

And speaking of Luxoria Heights, onto our next story.

The tranquil walkways of Luxoria Heights have been plagued by an increase in reported pickpocket thefts. Residents of this peaceful district have been reporting missing valuables and personal belongings in numbers not seen before. Authorities have not made any arrests at this time and residents are advised to remain vigilant and take necessary precautions to safeguard their belongings. Security measures within Luxoria Heights have been intensified to counter this unexpected wave of criminal activity. As a result, one can expect to see more than just the usual police presence.

And in our newsroom this evening, some late breaking news.

In our ongoing coverage of the Kiensei Monastery sabotaging, new details have emerged into the suspected culprit.

In a courtroom drama that has captivated the world, former Kiensei Nisi Ashira Mori has been acquitted of all charges."

The newscaster's image was replaced by Ashira's. It rotated slowly so that all who watched would eventually get a good look. In seeing this, her heart raced briefly as she quickly looked around to see if anyone recognized her. Seeing no one in particular looking over at her, Ashira sank ever deeper into the pod in an attempt to hide herself.

"*Mori stood trial for her alleged involvement in the sabotaging of the Kiensei Monastery that occurred just days ago. However, in a stunning turn of events, key evidence was presented that pointed towards the true perpetrator: A Artepyxian female named Reikuno Nortee. Nortee, now a former Kiensei herself, confessed to the court to orchestrating the burning, revealing a deep-seated resentment towards the Kiensei establishment's perceived hypocrisy and detachment from the planet's suffering. The following video of her confession may be disturbing for some viewers, so discretion is advised."*

Ashira's image was replaced by the face of her former friend. With her hands bound behind her back and flanked by Monastery Guards, the video of her confession in the courtroom was played for the masses.

"I did it," Reikuno had said. *"Because I've come to realize what many people in the realm have come to realize. That the Kiensei are the ones responsible for this civil war. They have so lost their honor that they have become the true perpetrators. They are the ones that should be put in shackles. All of them! And my burning of the Monastery was one of protest to what the Kiensei have become. An army fighting for greed and dissidence and moral decay. Fallen from the honor that they once held so dearly. This dynasty is failing! It's only a matter of time."*

The image of Melia Ad'nya returned to continue the story.

"This revelation has sent shockwaves through the whole of the realm, exposing internal issues and questions about the Kiensei establishment's role in the ongoing civil war. Many are left wondering how such a rift could have gone unnoticed and how the establishment's leadership failed to address these grievances. Mori's acquittal has raised concerns about the establishment's ability to recognize and rectify its own mistakes, leading to speculation about the future of the once highly revered institution.

As of right now, VirtuaNet News has not heard any sentencing information for Nortee and all attempts at contacting the Judicial Offices and the Kiensei Monastery have not been returned."

Ashira had heard enough. Rising swiftly out of the pod, she quickly looked around and began heading towards the nearest souvenir shop in the perimeter mall. The pale blue flames of the spires casting a pall upon the area as opposed to a warm glow.

Seeing her own face displayed virtuagraphically at 5 meters high and attached to a very shameful, very public newscast didn't do much to elevate her spirits. Even though the audio was only available to those in the pods, she knew the entirety of the planet and possibly the whole realm had seen and heard the broadcast.

On her way to the shop, she anxiously yet discreetly looked around as it felt like a thousand eyes were staring at her when all of a sudden something caught her eye. She stopped in her tracks to ensure she could focus on what she was seeing. A mischievous looking little green face was peering out of the shadows of some leafy potted plants just behind a couple of Scarbeck lovers sitting on a nearby bench. The couple was so smitten with each other's company that they didn't notice the little arms and hands reaching for their parcels located on the ground just beside them. In a flash, the items disappeared into the foliage with the lovers completely unaware of the crime. Not wanting to draw attention to herself, Ashira did not call out to the little thief or alert the Scarbecks, but instead walked briskly to the backside of the potted plants preparing to catch the perpetrator by surprise. When she peered around the edge of the largest plant, there was no one there. Standing to her full height, Ashira quickly scanned the crowd to see if she could spot the little being.

"There!" she murmured to herself. Through the throngs of tourists and natives alike, she spotted... "a child?" she said in surprise to no one in particular.

Scampering about in hurried fashion was a little green Multorn girl with two parcels. One under each arm. She was headed towards a public refresher station on the edge of the pliaza next to a side alleyway, bobbing and weaving with her little head tails swaying playfully on the top of her head as she trundled along. Ashira at once matched the little one's pace in pursuit. A myriad of questions rolled through her head as she gave measured chase. They ranged from wondering what a child was doing out and about at this hour to where the parents were. She watched as the little girl slipped into the refresher at about 20 steps in front of her. Stopping just outside, she quickly scanned to see if anyone was following and tapped the red button to open the door.

The scent of many a use of the facility and lack of proper cleaning caused Ashira to blink profusely and recoil slightly as she tried to adjust to the assault on her nose. About half of the lights were working. A line of blue partitioned stalls was at her left, stained ivory washing stations to her right. The obvious lack of maintenance showed itself clearly as she moved further inside.

"Hello?" Ashira called out. "Don't be afraid, I won't hurt you," she entreated. Her amplified senses through her ears noticed some sounds of crinkling plastoid in the rear partition. She began walking very slowly towards the back. As she inched closer the sound became somewhat louder until the little one burst suddenly out of the partition and bolted for the janitorial closet in the back. At a quick glance, Ashira noticed the little one had no shoes of any kind and what appeared to be the dirty remnants of an otherwise once decent outfit. The usually locked door slid open with a creak as the little Multorn palmed the operator console, glanced at Ashira quickly with fearful eyes, and disappeared inside with one parcel still underarm.

As the door shut behind the little girl, Ashira quickly ran to the closet. Opening it she saw... nothing... but some empty cleaner bottles and a derelict janitorial mech that was covered in grime and looked as though it had quit working some time ago.

The little one was gone.

A quick survey of the small closet revealed a tiny, square metal access hatch that had obviously been used many times due to the numerous dirty handprints along its edge. A large enough opening for the little girl, but too small for Ashira. At closer inspection, the hatch was merely a place to access a utility chase that appeared to service the pliaza. Leaving the closet, she went to investigate the partition. She pushed open the creaky and heavy metal door. Besides the expected disgust of what she saw... there was a wrapper laying on the floor with a bit of what appeared to be some form of sweetbread with a few distinguishable bites missing.

Ashira's heart sank.

As if she couldn't feel any worse than she already did, Ashira came to a stark realization. That little Multorn was hungry... and homeless... and she had just interrupted a meal that the little one may have desperately needed. "Way to go Ka'ze," she spoke aloud mimicking the usual condescending tone of her former sesni. As if the burden wasn't heavy enough, now the deprivation of a child weighed on her shoulders. With disappointment at the situation, Ashira left the refresher and returned to the pliaza.

Chapter 8 – Then

Sereeah put her ship down on a crude but functional landing pad near the small town of Tsit'awih about fifteen kilometers east of the continental capital of Kanónsoni'ta. Upon her entry into the outer security zone, she had been made aware of the expectation to abide by all laws, rules, and customs of the Tesska by a databurst, so as not to insult the people or the ancestral spirits they still held with esteem. One thing she was most pleased about was the ability to keep her shoes on. Her contact, turned host, had apprised her of the progress the indigenous peoples had made on certain customs: shoes or foot coverings being one. In times long past, everyone, including visitors, were required to remove their foot coverings when in public as the Tesska's spirituality mandated the utmost respect for the ground beneath them. For now, that custom was no longer in effect, though the spiritual inclination remained. One could still choose to follow it at their whim. But that would not be her as she was quite fond of footwear and despised dirty feet.

One final check of her disguise as she stood at the threshold of the loading ramp inside the *Pyrixis*... all good. She smacked the operating button with an open palm to lower the ramp. A loud clack, some low whirring noises of the jack screws rotating, a hiss, and the ramp touched down. Sereeah raised her blue hood over her head and began the short descent into the sunlit landing zone. Before she made it halfway down a deep voice crooned to her from beyond her vision.

"Ka'kwha, hello!" the voice said using both the native Tesska language and Planetary Common. "Neyo muypaa tikwa (*Do you speak this language*)?" the voice said. Sereeah wasn't familiar with the Tesska language, so she made no response as she continued down the ramp. "Do you speak this language?" the voice said in Common as the knee-high leather boots of the approaching person began to appear in the grass outside the ship.

"Greetings!" Sereeah said aloud. "Yes, I speak Common." She regarded the leather tasseling along the sides of the boots and how she simply must have some for herself. Maybe she would get the opportunity to pick up a pair before she left. Sereeah watched as the tall and muscular male Tesska came into full view as she descended the ramp. To her surprise, his tan face immediately morphed into one of fearful wonder; the white markings surrounding his eyes and mouth accentuating the movement of his features.

"Mi rawatah! *(By the Creator!)*" he exclaimed in surprise. Blinking in astonishment, the word "*Kiensei*" slipped from his dark lips. He balled his right hand into a fist and placed it near his chest. He bowed his head deeply and closed his eyes. As he did so, he uttered a phrase that Sereeah didn't understand but it seemed to be a formal greeting of sorts.

"Troa meckine voro namoro nirick," the man said softly with an inviting sense of respect.

Sereeah decided to return the gesture as a sign of mutual respect. She wasn't overly versed in Tesska culture or its nuances, so she decided to employe the "simian see, simian do" mentality. That generally worked in other arenas *so why not here* she thought. She made her bow as similar to what she had seen as possible, and her counterpart responded with acknowledgement.

"Are you Kel-so?" she asked.

"No no no master Kiensei." the man said with supplication. "I am Mata-ru and I was sent here by Kel-so to greet you and to bring you to him."

'Master Kiensei' she thought in amusement. She liked the sound of that. It had a distinct ring of authority and power behind it that tickled her fancy just right. She would play that little Polyp card as often as she could... well... so long as no one wanted to see any Kiensei-related magic or trickery anyway. She could already tell that this lackey was a pushover. She felt he had a subservient countenance to him, and her little ruse had worked perfectly.

"Very well good sir, let us be on our way then," she said in her most regal voice.

The pair walked casually through the relatively small town without stopping at all to take in the sights or local flavors. Mata-ru didn't speak and neither did she. She could sense a slight bit of apprehension, possibly at her, or what she appeared to be was more like it. As they walked, she remarked at the beautifully sculpted architecture. Its colors and designs were as beautifully diverse and intricately unique as the facial patterns of the native inhabitants, though the forms varied from angular to smooth. Some structures reminded her of buildings from other worlds while others mimicked the shapes of the head growths of the Tesska themselves.

"I would ask for your forgiveness," Mata-ru said with supplication as they entered a side street "but Kel-so has requested your presence immediately." He gestured with one hand back towards the main street, "if you needed to attend to other business somewhere beforehand, would it be alright if you did so after your meeting?"

Straight to business. Sereeah liked that. Karinar might be an all-right place to come back to visit at some point she thought. Mata-ru stopped suddenly and stood at his full height, arms resting behind his back, his chin raised. Sereeah stopped in response to him. Alarmed at the abrupt gesture, she instinctually delved into her senses. Nothing pheromonic...but there... he's serious now, she sensed.

"Master Kiensei?" he questioned.

"Um. Y-yes. I'll meet with Kel-so first of course," she spoke, trying to cover up her hesitation.

"Very well." He motioned to his immediate left at an unassuming door. Its angular shape accented with curved panel inlays afforded it the guise of appearing unremarkable compared to others around it. A series of knocks and scratches in what seemed to be some sort of code was applied to the door. A few seconds passed and the mechanical clacking of metallic parts was heard. Soon after, it cracked open with an obscure person peeking out.

"Ka'kwha. Miran mi'soh (*Hello. The guest is here*)" he said quietly through the crack in the door. Mata-ru stepped to the side and bowed slightly. He bid a quiet and quick farewell to Sereeah and left her there by herself. The door creaked, opened, and she stepped inside.

Inside the room was dark with slivers of daylight streaming in from small round windows up high. The air was stagnant and still with a mustiness from its time spent in stasis. It was like this was formerly a place of business but was no longer operating. Layers of dust and debris on the stacked and covered furniture revealed that the space had remained largely unused for some time. In the corner, a single flickering light shone on a lone figure. Sereeah approached cautiously but unafraid, lowering the hood of her cloak.

"Welcome" the figure said in a voice she recognized.

"Kel-so I presume?" she said in a standup-ish tone, her brow rising to present a soft expression. Suddenly, a clicking noise was heard as the cold metal of a gun barrel was pressed into Sereeah's head from behind and the safety feature of the weapon was removed.

A tinge of fear coursed through her body, but she remained still and quickly began assessing the feelings of this unseen character behind her. Not hatred, no. Cockiness maybe.

"Is this how you greet all of your guests?" she calmly spoke trying to buy herself some time. Not arrogance, she felt. Malice? That's not it.

The dark grey figure rose from his chair, the flickering light lapping at his silhouette. She could instantly see that he was extraordinarily strong, with almost chiseled features. His face had white, or light gray stripes crisscrossing it from both left and right. His tall head growths were also crisscrossed with the same markings, but instead of arcing outward, they curved inward making him look like some kind of demon of an ancient world. His shirt was tight fitting at the top with the collar rising up and hugging his thick neck. He had green painted pauldrons and vambraces of a metal she didn't recognize. A utility belt around his waist held up a black waist cloak or something that flowed almost to his ankles and was tattered at the ends. Two plasma pistols, one on each side of the belt in holsters told her that this one needed to be watched carefully.

"You are not my guest, alien. This is business, pure and simple," Kel-so said with measured gruffness.

"I like that about you," she said cooly. The one behind her had no intention of pulling the trigger she figured. No sense of urgency, or fear. Completely calm. She bet that his finger wasn't even on the trigger. She wagered she was fast enough to disarm him before he knew what hit him, but those dark hands of Kel-so were close enough to his pistols that she probably wouldn't survive long after. Time to use an old trick.

She relaxed her body, allowing her taught muscles to release. A tingling sensation under her arms signaled her biological defense had kicked in. Her species weren't widespread across the planet like others, and many a tale had been spun about Rishkas and their ability to influence others. Some of them were actually true. Most weren't. This natural defense wasn't automatic, and it wasn't infinite. But the pheromones she released stood a good chance of easing the tension. Perhaps just enough for her to make a quick retreat if necessary. A brief moment passed as the invisible chemical surrounded her, the still air did not help its dispersion.

"I like that you want to get down to business, just like I do," she stalled. The man behind her cleared his throat, a signal that it was working. She turned slowly, her deep eyes meeting the brown ones of the Tesska behind her. His dark blue face was accented around his eyes and mouth by a lighter shade of blue. His white head growths had only a hint of markings, but they were also blue, she noticed. One growth was slung across his chest and across his opposite shoulder. She kept her gaze as she slowly and tenderly removed the growth off his shoulder and gently placed it back to its natural hanging state down his chest. "You didn't really want to shoot me? Did you?" she asked soothingly with a smile, placing both of her hands on his chest; her eyes soft and sultry.

The gunman dropped his weapon to his side and smiled back at her. He blinked as if in a daze. Heh... she was right. His finger wasn't even on the trigger, she saw with a quick glance. "Now," she wheeled back to face Kel-so and putting on an air of diplomacy, "where were we?"

Kel-so chuckled menacingly and crossed his striped, bulging arms across his chest. "You are no Kiensei," he snorted, "but your tricks are good enough to make them believe that you are." He took his seat at the table and motioned for her to join him oppositely. Sereeah slowly made her way towards the dusty table, her eyes locked onto Kel-so's. She tilted her head slightly and traced a finger over the top of the back of the chair she was meant to occupy. Kel-so was having none of it. He kicked his leg out underneath the table catching the leg of the chair opposite of him. It lurched out quickly and caught Sereeah in the hip, startling her.

"Sit." He grumbled. "Enough of your foolishness." A slight breeze began to blow from behind the dark Tesska as if an air circulator was suddenly activated. A look of confusion crossed Sereeah's face as she slowly sat down, keeping cautious. The flickering light on the table before her revealed a scowl curling the upper lip of Kel-so. "I know about you and those tricks of yours," he nodded to the gunman who was still smiling at her from behind. "I also know this," he said lowly as he dug into his belt and tossed a circular metal fob on the table at her. She blinked quickly as it rattled to a halt nearly in front of her. She had seen plenty of those before. She had handled quite a few of them. There's only one type of organization that used them.

"Trade?" she questioned, her face becoming sterner. He inclined his head slightly in acknowledgement. She picked up the smooth-edged fob and rolled it in her hands momentarily. She twisted the activator ring and her breath at once seized in her throat as a virtual image of herself flickered to life.

"Where did you get this?" she said nervously. She hadn't realized that a bounty had been placed on her head since leaving the dispatch office. It was strange though; the fob didn't have the same weight as the one's she was used to. There also wasn't a bounty amount on the image. She stared at it intently, something was amiss.

"You think you're the only one with tricks?" Kel-so said. "I can make it just like the real thing... if I have to," he grinned. "The Dark Fire has long arms and I'm here to make sure the job gets done. Now, if you're done playing around, let's get on with this."

Sereeah remained silent. The imposing Tesska had made his point clear that he was in no mood to play games anymore, nor was he one to be trifled with. He also made it poignantly clear that the

Dark Fire wanted this done and that they would do whatever was necessary to see that it was.

"Very well, I'm listening," she said quietly. She stayed poised in her seat, ready to spring into action just in case things deteriorated. Things had not gone as she had expected thus far.

"About eighty kilometers from here is a small village called Hadeneska'tsiya, or 'Village of Sacred Trees' in the Common tongue. It's fairly primitive by Planetary standards but still carries some modernistic elements according to Karinar's own standards. Meaning, limited technology and communications abilities but advanced enough to sustain a thriving tribe." He paused for a moment and produced a virtuamap showing the general location of the village. The pulsating red dot looked as though it was situated in a valley near a mountain range northeast of their current location.

"About two weeks ago, a messenger from the village came into town on his way to Kanónsoni'ta. He carried news of a child who was believed to be Ki capable. His mission was to report it to the census bureau on behalf of their Narkash so that the Kiensei could be notified. Let's just say..." he paused, "...he never made it." Kel-so's eyes glowed menacingly through the vertically projected holomap at the woman across the table.

"So, are we just going to ruck it into the bush to go and get this... child?" she asked, waving a hand inquisitively. Eighty kilometers of walking with packs would take them several days' worth of travel at the very least. Not to mention keeping up with a child on the way back. She wasn't prepared for that. Come to think of it, she didn't even know the age of the little brat in question, and she was not about to start changing diapers, or loincloths, or whatever these people used.

"We will take scootsters most of the way and make camp about a kilometer outside the village. From there, we'll walk to the village to make contact. I will do most of the negotiating with the tribe there.

Even with your costume and appearance of a Kiensei, they will be wary of you just like any outsider. You must be prepared to do as I say, when I say it. Am I clear?"

Sereeah nodded her head. It became painfully clear to her that she was a mere tool in this little endeavor, and a gnawing worry began to form in the pit of her stomach.

Kiensei Runan Kai Asato dropped out of portalspace just within the designated commerce zone of the continent of Karinar. Considered newly minted by many of his peers, Asato had received this assignment about eight months after being formally elevated in rank at the Grand Monastery on Korosento. Having spent the past few months 'passing the knowledge' as it was colloquially known, his sesni, the Yarishma male called Tokka, had expressed immense pleasure in Asato's accomplishments and had seen him off on the platform for his first solo assignment as a fully-fledged Kiensei Runan. Though it wasn't glorious, depending on one's point of view, this mission was one of peace and good faith. Something the Kiensei held dear, Asato thought. An outbreak of violent protests had begun in the capital over a Tesska man that had been found murdered, the suspect was a Jamiku trader from Deshu. Though it was initially billed as an internal issue, the Regalia, or queen, had petitioned the Planetary Assembly for Kiensei intervention to prevent bloodshed and escalation, since a delegation from the continent of Deshu had been sent.

The Tesska culture had a reputation for using 'eye-for-an-eye' resolution to such matters. The Regalia wanted to maintain peace without stirring up a conflict between Karinar and Deshu in an effort to show her constituents and her people that she was more than capable of leading. Peace, after all, was something the Tesska valued highly, though they would fight to the death if necessary. The

Kiensei, she heard, were specialists in these matters. His sesni had cautioned him that the people were fiercely loyal to their beliefs and that he should proceed warily, not to mention the vague status of Karinar within the realm.

According to Monastery records, the continent was still technically considered Neutral, but had gained representation within the Planetary Assembly at some point in the past via treaty. A delicate place to be in for a group of people considering that one of their own served as High Minister not that long ago. But the evidence was there that Karinar was working towards inclusion proper into the Realm, former Tesska High Minister Jakamis Haj had seen to it, so the request for a Kiensei dispatch was legal and valid.

Asato disliked politics and its seemingly endless wormholes. Though he knew it to be a necessary aggravation at times.

Asato stabilized his craft within the zone and hailed the continental security, formally announcing himself in Planetary Common. "This is Kai Asato, Runan of the Kiensei Establishment, here at the request of the Regalia. Requesting permission to approach the continent and land at the capital," he said in an open planetary-wide comm channel. A few moments of silence passed when the comm crackled to life as the landing master responded. "Ka'kwha. I greet you Runan Asato," the voice said. "Please continue to Kanónsoni'ta, sector 5-H and land at pad twenty. Be prepared for inspection and formal inquiry," the landing chief said.

"Acknowledged," the Rodlek Kiensei said and toggled a few switches on his left. Retaining clamps on his Syurist-12 portalspace booster ring opened smartly and loosed his triangular *Spearpoint-class* fighter to operate freely on its own. Pushing the throttle lever forward, the light craft instantly rocketed towards the continent, leaving the ring floating calmly behind.

R-3B10, "Rebi" as the mech was called, chirruped in response to the comm chatter. "Yes, Rebi, I hope to make this an expedient trip," Asato said to the mech. "Hopefully the negotiations will go quickly, and we can be on our way." Rebi spun its domed head around and squawked something. "Yes, I know you're long overdue for maintenance, I promise that we will get you taken care of just as soon as we return," Asato said. He had worked with Rebi before on a few missions. The mech was quite grumpy according to his opinion and other's collaborations with the mech. Perhaps it was a faulty personality module or maybe they hadn't had a complete memory wipe in a while, either way the mech was going to add a bit of, well... flavor, to the mission he thought.

The Spearpoint-class broke into the airspace and settled in at an altitude of just under a kilometer above the surface, heading directly for the capital. He took a moment to admire the beauty of the planet near sunset. The lush forests below, the rolling grasslands. The expansive mountains. What a jewel of the world he thought. Abruptly, Asato felt something odd. Like something, or someone, was pulsating within the Ki below him. It was gone almost as soon as it came but it was enough to intrigue the Rodlekian Runan. "Rebi, mark this location please," he said inquisitively. He rolled the *Spearpoint-class* fighter over quickly to get a decent look at what was below. "A village. Curious," he thought to himself as he passed over it. He rolled the craft over and continued on his heading towards Kanónsoni'ta.

He had barely completed his roll when his senses, imbued with Ki, fired suddenly and alerted him. He felt something heading towards his craft. Something hot, something fast. He yawed the craft with lightning reflexes to the right as a red blaster bolt shot past his canopy. Was someone shooting at him!? Had he done something wrong!? "Rebi, check for hostiles," he commanded the mech as his head began to swivel around, looking for the perpetrator. He saw nothing above him or around him in the sky as his fighter continued its course. "Rebi, what do you have," he bit out. The mech had extended its internal sensor in conjunction with the Spearpoint-class's array with the intent on finding anything and everything it could.

Much could be said about the mech. Grumpy as it was, it was particularly good at scraping data from just about any source available to it. A series of beeps, chirps and squawks and the display screen within the cockpit lit up with data. "A small skirmish in the forest below. Natives... and local fauna," Asato said. "Very well, nothing of our concern for the moment." Rebi squawked in disagreement. It then sent a string of data to the HUD in front of Asato showing targeting data. Asato was in no mood to argue with the mech. "It was an accident Rebi, nothing more. I will not go back and *accidentally* return fire. Let us keep our course and fulfill our mission," he said. Rebi closed down the sensor arrays with a grumpy chirrup and proceeded to guide the craft to the coordinates.

Sereeah and Kel-so sped along the forested surface of the planet on narrow paths, mostly used by native foot traffic but wide enough for scootsters to follow. They had packed heavy, not knowing exactly what they would be up against. She was behind him and slightly to the left in the small formation, following him along every curve, over every hill. She had checked to see if any weapons were available... nope. *Scatdung* she swore to herself. No tangible way to defend herself out here. Probably on purpose, she thought. This deal was getting worse by the minute.

Kel-so held his left arm upward with a balled fist to signify her to stop. The two small scootsters came to a halt in a small clearing surrounded by the native trees. Tall, strong, with needle-like leaves on them. The orange and yellow sky signified that sunset was upon them. Kel-so shut down his scootster with a squelch and stepped off. Sereeah did the same, mimicking him.

"We will make camp here for the night and set out at first light to the village," the Tesska said in a gravelly voice.

The two began unpacking their scootsters and setting up the makeshift camp.

Bedrolls were out, a small cookfire was crackling and the two were sitting opposite one another. The daylight of the planet was still present, but quickly waning. Neither Kel-so nor Sereeah made a single comment. The air was thick with tension as the two sat in silence, not looking at one another, not speaking to one another, not so much as a nod or wink. She tried to sense the emotions of the Tesska across from her but couldn't discern anything. There were, after all, limitations to her species' abilities. But she had to try. She did, however, sense something strange. It was barbaric. Almost primal in nature. It haunted her and wouldn't escape her.

"What's wrong with you," Kel-so finally asked, poking a stick at the crackling fire in front of them.

"N-nothing," she said plainly. She didn't want to show her hand of cards unless necessary.

"Yeah? You could have fooled me if I was an idiot," he said in response. Kel-so's demeanor changed at once. He raised his head up as if scanning the area around them. He quickly placed his hands on the handles of the pistols in his belt and stood up. The usual sounds of the forest had quietly disappeared, and all was a silent as snowfall on Mount Lulum.

"What?" Sereeah said, noticing the change. The Tesska didn't respond, his head turned slowly as he scanned the brush. "Look, if somethings about to go down, at least give me the chance to fight," she grimaced. Kel-so's became hardened. He tossed her one of his blaster pistols. "I expect you to return that, dead or alive," he said stoically. Not a sound could be heard at the camp, save the crackling of the fire. The two occupants held up their pistols in readied defense, waiting for an unknown assailant. A chirp of an insect. A crackle of flame.

A shriek sounded suddenly from the left flank and two Bespare launched themselves out of the brush at the two. Their furry tetrapod bodies about twice the size of a Shirpcat moved swiftly out of the cover of the brush towards the Tesska and Rishka. Quick shots from Kel-so and they were dispatched, falling dead before they could even reach the firelight circle.

"Bespare," Kel-so said caustically. "They hunt in packs and are quite intelligent."

"How do we fight them?" Sereeah said in mild panic.

"Just stay calm, they will launch at least one more wave before giving up," he said calmly. "As Tesska, we evolved to hear them coming a long way away and learned ways to defend against them."

"And what way is that?" she asked nervously.

Kel-so grunted lightly. "You kill them, before they kill you."

The Rishka held her pistol upright, her hand shaking slightly. Handling known assailants was one thing, she thought, but unknown ones... well...

A screech from the forward and right flank signaled the next assault. "Don't shoot at their heads, aim for their centers," Kel-so shouted as the creatures leapt from the underbrush. His blaster erupted as he squeezed the trigger, firing resolutely at the assailants. In nervous fashion, Sereeah waited. Two Bespare launched themselves out of the underbrush and began rushing towards her. Their muscular rear legs pounding the ground and kicking up dirt as they charged her. She squeezed off a few rounds, missing their intended mark. Behind her she could hear the equal bursts of Kel-so's firing at the assailants coming from his side.

The evil determination from their indigo, vertically slitted eyes was paralyzing. Their fur was long and darkly mottled to blend in with the surrounding brush, a natural evolution of sorts. Their faces were angular and had a pronounced snout that formed both their sharply toothed mouth and sensitive black nose. Their smaller but equally powerful front legs brandishing four claws, one in the middle being profoundly larger and more distinctive. It's likely function, to tear flesh and disembowel. She continued to fire and continued to miss her mark. The Bespare advanced closer and closer, intent on ravaging her. Suddenly a muscular, dark arm appeared beside her face and fired several shots. One creature down, the other stumbled and groaned in pain as it fell on top of her, dead. In reaction, she mistakenly fired a few shots as she fell. They sailed into the air wildly.

"What's the problem," Kel-so shouted at her. "You aim, you shoot. That's it!"

"I'm sorry, I'm sorry," she hurriedly excused herself, pushing the creature off with a huff. "I've never seen these things before."

Kel-so growled at her. "Well now you have. Shoot or die," he said.

The two waited anxiously. The Bespare were intelligent as Kel-so had said. The remaining creatures held back. Patiently waiting to see if a weakness could be found and exploited.

"I'll take first watch," Kel-so said. "They're still out there, and they're watching us."

"I thought you said they'd give up?" Sereeah piped.

The large Tesska glanced over his shoulder and with a biting glare said, "I also said they were intelligent. They may wait and attack again, but if we're lucky they'll give up the fight."

Chapter 9

The skyscape of angled architecture over the mountainous range of buildings began to glow with hues of blue gray, turning into streaks of oranges and yellows as the sun began to rise. On the eastern parapet of the common area, Ashira sat on an observation bench with the thrum of busy Korosento all around her. Her eyes closed momentarily as she took a deep breath with the morning rays kissing her face. She had spent the rest of the night wandering about the place. She had filled her time and boredom by visiting every single tourist spot, reading every single informational plaque, and wandering aimlessly through almost every shop. She had stayed out of the lounges and bars as most needed a cover charge of money that she didn't have. She did, however, figure out a way to temporarily relieve her hunger worries. In a moment of clarity, she had noticed that many food stalls offered a free sample of some of their items. She made sure to take advantage of every single one, even if it was something she didn't particularly enjoy eating. Food was food at this point, and survival meant getting what she could get. It definitely wasn't enough to fill her stomach, but it was enough to sustain her in the immediacy. The ruse lasted for only a fleeting time as many of the vendors figured out that she had no intentions to purchase and began pulling the sample trays away as she approached. Exhaustion was something else she was struggling against. She hadn't slept much at all in the past two days and the added strain was beginning to take its toll.

Ashira sat quietly when all of a sudden, she heard metallic footsteps clanking their way towards her from behind. A brief moment of instinct flashed through her mind believing it to be a set of Crimat battle mechs, likely due to her mind fog. She had fought against those clanking nuisances for years and the sounds they made were almost unmistakable. She snapped her head around to face them and prepared herself mentally to fight, her eyes narrowed with a curved corner of her upper lip, her muscles tense like coiled springs.

"Greetings citizen" the police mech said through its monotone vocabulator. "Please refrain from sudden movements for your safety and ours."

Ashira's nerves began to settle slightly, and tired confusion began to cover her face. Two blue-gray police mechs stopped six paces in front of her with their glowing, yellow photoreceptors and static features trained on her face: their lanky arms by their sides hovering just above a set of blasters.

"What's going on officers?" she asked.

"Please present your identification citizen" the mech on the left said.

Her mind began to churn. "What in the world do these gnarlies want this early in the morning?" she thought. "Have I done something wrong officers?" she asked aloud. Her voice a mix of mild annoyance and confusion.

"Repeat. Please present your identification citizen," the mech on the right said, mirroring the statement.

Ashira stood slowly, turning to face the two mechs. Crossing her arms across her chest, she snarked out a simple "no". The two humanoid mechs stood still while processing the response. She didn't want to give them any more of her time and pressed them to justify their presence.

"Unless I'm being officially detained under reasonable articulable suspicion of a crime that I have committed, am committing, or am about to commit I'm not required to show you anything," she said with cool confidence. Her knowledge of local laws gained from her Kiensei studies and the fact that she didn't have an identification card to begin with were well at-play. It was a strange situation for her to be in. All adult citizens of the Realm aged 18 standard years and older were required to possess an identification card issued by their membership government as part of recent security enhancement legislation. All except the Kiensei. They did not nor were required to issue any official identification due to their general status on the planet and mandates within the Establishment itself. Some viewed this as a usurpation of transparency and equal requirements under law and was one of the solid points argued by dissenters and others who opposed the Kiensei.

"You are under suspicion for involvement in a reported theft in the area" one of the mechs said.

"Suspicion alone is not reason enough to accuse or interrogate" she shot back. She learned that one from Damae.

The mech on the left took one step closer and extended its left arm, palm pointing skyward. A hologram appeared in front of her from the mech's hand. It showed a security video of her walking after the little Multorn girl and entering the refresher station.

"You were seen accompanying the suspect. You were also reported as lingering within the area for an unusual amount of time which could mean you were aiding her by marking targets for theft or engaging in vagrancy," one of the mechs said.

"Since when is it illegal for someone to peaceably enjoy a public space during its operating hours?" she inquired mockingly, as if a mech would notice the nuance. "If you want to talk about the little girl, I'll tell you what I know. Other than that, I have nothing else to say."

"Please proceed" one of the police mechs said.

"I wasn't accompanying her. I saw her take something that belonged to a pair of Scarbeck, so I followed her to see where she was going. I had hoped to reclaim the items and return them, but she disappeared."

"Why did you not report the incident to the proper authorities?" one of the mechs asked.

"It was food of some type. How can food that's been eaten be used as evidence?" Ashira countered. "Is your plan to wait a rotation or two and try to collect what's left? Did you even go inside the refresher to see if anything was remaining?"

"There was nothing left of the evidence by the time we arrived" one of the mechs said.

Ashira stood akimbo, posturing a defense against the prying mechs. "No evidence, no case. Are we done here?"

"Do you attest, under penalty of perjury, that you do not know the suspect?" the mech on the left replied.

Ashira huffed in annoyance. "I don't know her. All I can tell you is she's probably homeless and hungry. When I went into the refresher, I was able to get a decent look at her condition. She abandoned what was left of one of the stolen items which happened to be a sweetbread of some sort. I believe she was in the process of eating it when I came in and scared her. That's my official statement."

"Thank you for your time citizen. Should you remember anything else or have further information, please contact the local precinct. Have a nice day," the mech on the right said. With that, the two police mechs turned around simultaneously and walked stiffly back towards the plaza.

Ashira shook her head with disdain at the questioning that had just transpired. First it was sedition, now she was accused of aiding and abetting and, what was that other? Vagrancy? She felt relieved that she was coherent enough to stand her ground. Though the thought of a jail cell actually didn't sound so bad right now, what with a place to sleep and food to eat. She turned and sat back down on the bench and looked out at the sunrise while pondering her situation. She needed a plan, and she needed one soon. Unfortunately, her body forced her to stay put as her eyelids drooped, then shut as she fell asleep sitting upright in the warmth of the morning sun.

It had seemed like ages had passed when Ashira jerked awake in a startled state. Rubbing her tired eyes and trying to clear the fog in her head, she looked around, first through blurry vision, trying to assess the situation around her. Her eyes becoming clearer, she saw the projection of a laser clock at the corner of the quadrant superficially mocking her as the current time revealed she had only been out of it for about ten standard minutes. Ashira stood up and stretched to alleviate the rigor that had set in on her tired joints. Though short, the power nap had done some good in salving her troubled mind enough to formulate a plan. Credits were what she was lacking, so she looked at all the places of business around her and decided she needed to get a job. It was still early in the morning, so some establishments weren't open but there were plenty of others that never closed. By her reasoning, someone needed help somewhere and her time in the Establishment and Imperial Army should be of help in landing even the most basic of jobs.

Easier said than done.

Ashira spent the next painstaking hours visiting the various eateries, shops, and lounges in and around the Plaza. She had never asked nor applied for a job, so this was wild space for her. Mostly, she got the answer of 'we're not hiring.' But what really stunned her after about the twentieth attempt was the commonalities of rejection. Twenty attempts and nothing to show for it. Twenty attempts and what she realized was that she was either too young, because the places that served alcohol had a minimum age requirement, or she had no experience, which was ridiculous. Her time in the Imperial Army of the Realm placed her responsible for equipment and personnel worth millions of dollars. It made no sense that she could drive an ASH-TE tank or fly an *Spearpoint-class* fighter but probably couldn't get a job at a scootster wash... which she hadn't tried yet as she couldn't find one in the area. She did have one moment of promise though. It was a little repair shop tucked away near the east side. The Brosnian that ran the place was willing to allow her to prove her skills. She had repaired a customer's personal communicator in a few minutes time which impressed the owner. When asked how she acquired her skills, she made mention of her former-Kiensei status, which unfortunately led to her being asked to leave because the skittish Brosnian was afraid of the negative press and what it might do to his business. It seemed as though the world was against her.

In times past, when the path ahead was clouded, she had been trained to clear her mind and meditate on the Ki. With the bustle of the area, there wasn't much opportunity to do so without drawing undue attention to herself.

"I need to get out of this place" she said softly to herself in disappointment. "I thought I could get on my feet here, but that didn't happen. I need somewhere to focus and plan my next move." She sat down next to a burbling fountain on the nearest bench to ponder her options. She tried to remember what was around the area from some of her previous patrols and couldn't come up with anything that would fit the bill. She looked around at the multitudes of passersby and saw an elderly human woman opening up a botanical stand across the way and decided to ask her. Her wrinkled face was a new one this sea of diversity and also because it wasn't too far to walk on her tired feet.

As Ashira approached the woman, she did so gingerly so as to not startle her. She noticed that the woman was struggling a bit and surmised that it was either good fortune or the will of the Ki that caused this intersection. She was a petite, plump old woman with short, fluffy, white hair that looked like curly clouds on her head.

Her skin tone reflected the many punishing rays of the various suns she had encountered in her lifetime. She was visibly stooped over, likely due to her age or some bone condition, but it did not slow her down much. Her modest light green tunic and trousers appeared to be hand made as did the ruffled white apron with little yellow flowers she wore over top of the ensemble. She worked meticulously with her weathered hands unlatching security shutters, placing arrangements, and watering some of her wares.

"Excuse me? I have a question if you don't mind," Ashira asked as she approached the woman just outside of her vendor's stall on the perimeter of the large cone-shaped spire.

The woman turned her white-haired head to face the person who had interrupted her. Her blazing green eyes locked with Ashira's as she assessed the young Tesska. Her face was cheerful, with decades of wrinkles testifying to the amount of smiles she had worn.

"I'm not quite up'n runnin' sweetie. Come back in a quick spell," the woman said with a gentle, unbroken voice. She smiled slightly while turning her head back to its former position.

"I was really hoping you could help me with...." Ashira was abruptly cut off.

"Would you'uns be so kind as to bring us that thar bucket of soil over yonder?" the woman asked while gesturing with a withered hand. "It's a might bit heavy fer me."

"Uh... sure," Ashira obliged with marked confusion. She grabbed the handle of the plasticene bucket and found it to be lighter than she thought. But of course, it would be heavier to someone older. She quickly carried it over to the woman and set it down beside her.

"Thankee my dear," the woman said without looking. "Now, would you'uns be so kind as ta hang up my digi-sign? It's hard for me to reach up thar what with my back all crook'd up." The woman pointed with a faintly crooked finger to a corner within her stall. Ashira just nodded and without a word, went over to the corner inside the stall and picked up the sign. She dusted it off lightly with her hand and hung it up in its apportioned space. Ashira smiled. A memory of chasing down a Kasini Springer and her accomplice to get her sword back with the elder Sesni Busen came to mind. It had been a good lesson in patience and that was exactly what she needed to do at this moment.

Ashira approached the elderly woman again, this time without saying a word and clasping her hands in front of her. The woman slowly pivoted where she stood to address the Tesska, hobbling a bit on her aged legs.

"One last thang dearie," she said as she looked at Ashira with tender eyes and another warm smile. "Brang this here old woman a stool ta set on?" Ashira returned the smile with her own and went back into the stall momentarily. "And getcha one fer yerself," the woman called from outside. Ashira returned with two square, creaky wooden stools with well-worn cushions on top. She placed one stool next to the woman and stepped back to allow her the room to maneuver. The elderly woman plopped onto the stool with a grunt and a sigh. "Well, set down a spell and enjoy tha mornin' with me young'n," she said. Ashira sat down as asked, her tired legs grateful for the reprieve.

"You'uns has mah thanks for tha help this mornin'. It's getting' harder to get it all done by mah onesie, but this is whut I do. Day in and day out. Now, my dear, whut kinda flowers was you'a looking fer?" the woman said.

Ashira felt slightly embarrassed for not having any money to buy something, but she had already invested herself into this little encounter. "Your flowers are very lovely," Ashira said. "But unfortunately, I...I don't have any money to buy anything. I was merely wanting to ask you for some direction. If that's ok?"

"These here flowers and plants are some of tha finest from Charndry. Gazzair and me used'ta travel thar and back every week when we was younger. I miss him. I made him a promise to keep this here a goin' as long as I was able." Her face trailed off looking behind Ashira, as if to some distant memory, then snapped quickly back to reality. "Oh, but whar are muh manners. The name's Iraila Berttal. What's yers dearie?"

"My name's Ashira" she said with gentleness. "It's nice to meet you."

Iraila tilted her head slightly and raised her eyebrows while clasping her hands in her lap. "Such a purdy name fer a purdy young lady. But my, you's thin as a cane stalk. You needs to eat more." Ashira would have loved nothing more than to tell her that she was absolutely starving at this point, but that would be rude. Instead, she just smiled and nodded courteously to the elderly woman.

"You's look awful young to be out here all by your onesie. Whar's you'a from?"

Ashira assumed it was universal knowledge that her kind were from Karinar. The Tesska weren't so widespread like Humans, Multorns, and other species that it was too difficult to know, but still, she politely indulged the elderly woman.

"I'm from Karinar originally. I was born there. I came – *we* came—to Korosento when I was young," she said, correcting herself.

Kiensei muhashki were usually brought to the monastery from an incredibly early age as was the norm. The young ones were allowed to know their home continent and city and were encouraged to embrace much of their cultural heritage, as she had in her own dress and garb. She remembered during the time spent with her clan that the topic of 'parents' would naturally arise from time to time, particularly when the concepts of health and physiology were taught. It was during those times when a Guidance Mentor was temporarily assigned, either to a group or singularly, from the same species, if possible. This was instituted, she later learned, to help the monastery younglings when learning about their own physiology and individual cultures as part of their overall training. It was good for Kiensei to know, understand, and empathize with the many varied species, races, and cultures of the world that they were expected to serve. Especially their own.

Hers had been Sesni Taash. A fellow Tesska woman, also from Karinar.

She had been fortunate, by her own admission, to have had the calm, patient, wise and compassionate nature of the respected Kiensei Sesni to aid her in those early years. Sesni Taash guided her in understanding the various cultural aspects of the proud Tesska people and even aided her in modifying the sash that was gifted to her to fit her chosen garb. But the most significant thing was the gift of her headpiece.

Headpieces were both symbolic and ornamental, Taash taught her. The venerable sesni's headpiece was crafted using the teeth of the feared gultarv, which Taash had defeated in defense of herself and some delegates during a tribal dispute mission many years ago on their home continent. The small, curved teeth were arrayed in a manner that accented the beautifully curved and colorfully patterned growths on her head and was gifted to her by both tribes after settling the conflict.

Ashira's was different. Crafted from pure platinum by the skilled craftsmen of her tribe, her headpiece was specially forged to signify her triumph over a foe without killing it, without violence; one of the highest forms of honor to the Tesska. Ashira had peacefully bested a formidable Bespare after it snatched her on a hunting trip with her father with intent to devour her...without killing it. Even more amazing was that she returned to her village riding the beast when she was barely a standard year old. As the story was told, the Narkash, or leader, of her tribe had presented it to her founder, Sesni Asato, when he arrived to take her to the monastery so that she could wear it when she came of age. As Sesni Taash explained it, the three points of each triangle represented the Keesha, Vehrar, and Apta: the mental, physical, and spiritual aspect of all living things while the three triangles on each side represented the Watah, Tari'ha, and the Narak: the creator, the land, and the Ki, respectively. All of which connect to the central piece being the wearer and their common connection to all things. It was her most prized possession. Though possessions were forbidden by the Establishment, cultural items were allowed in small numbers.

Most of the younglings dismissed the thought to learn about their parentage due to the fact that the communal nature of the Establishment, in essence, became their parent. There were some, however, that did want to learn more and were always met with soft rebuke with the reasoning that it would lead to affection, which was forbidden. A brief thought flashed through her mind. The Kiensei were forbidden, but she's no longer a Kiensei. *Her* parents might still be there. Wonder if they had any other children after she was taken? Could it be possible that she has a sibling!? Or both! Could she go there? Should she go there? Would she be welcomed?

"What about you? If you don't mind me asking," Ashira said to Iraila.

"Not much to tell really," the aged woman said. Her eyes lifting skyward in repose. "Me an' Gazzair grew up on Myrna. A beautiful place, even when compared to tha likes of this fine city. We got wed when we's was about nineteen standard yars and moved ourselves here. Such a purdy place. We both luved'ta garden and thangs. We wanted kids, but thangs just didn't work out fer us, so we decided to put all our luv inta our gardenin'. That brought us here. Looong time ago. We'd grow our plants thar and sell 'em here on this jungle made up 'a stone an' steel. People here jus luv that sort of thang. But listen at me all blatherskitin' off at tha mouth. Did you'un say you was a headin' somewhars?" Iraila said kindly. Her calm demeanor beaming from her worn face.

"No, I didn't but I am... well... lost," she said sheepishly.

Iraila kept her smile and just blinked her emotions. "Yer lost? Mmkay. Whatcha lookin' fer?" she asked again in a sweet yet direct manner.

"I... don't really know," Ashira replied, mimicking her counterpart's tone.

"Well now, you'uns can't be lost if'n ya don't even know whar yer goin' or what'cha lookin' a fer now can ya?

Ashira realized quickly that it was going to be a losing battle to try and match wits and barbs with this lady. She reasoned that honesty would be the best route and tactic with her. She thought about her options. Information was easy and mostly free. She wondered if she would risk asking for some food. The shooting comet prize would be a cot or something to lay down on, but that was too farfetched.

"I was considering looking for a quiet place to meditate," Ashira said. "I thought I would find it here, but I was obviously wrong. Would you know of any place?"

Those bright green eyes stared at her as if they could see past the tired façade in front of them.

Iraila's features changed to a puzzled look as she crossed her arms. "Meditate? "Like one them mystic Kiensei people or sumthin'?" Her face morphed to a more frustrated look. "They ain't caused me nuthin but trouble since that war they done started." She began gesticulating wildly with her hands. "Taxes gone up and people don't buy my wares hardly no more and the cost to just... *live*... has gone up too. Used to be that peoples could count on 'em Kiensei to do the honorable thang, but I ain't got a clue what's a happnin' now."

Ashira felt a shiver up her back as she recoiled at hearing the words from the elderly lady. It occurred to her in that moment that not everyone she would meet would be amicable towards the Kiensei and even if she wasn't technically one of them any longer, she would still be tainted by association no matter what. She wanted to argue back that the Kiensei didn't start the war, they were trying to stop it, but that probably wouldn't get her anywhere. She thought it best from now on to keep that little fact about herself quiet until she could tell if it was safe.

Iraila's features returned to their normal, pleasant form. "Sweetie, I thinks better when I has a bit o' coffa. Run on over yonder to Durden's spot and get us a cup," she motioned to an adjacent vendor with a waving hand "and maybe a baked-round or sumthin."

Ashira was slightly confused. She was extremely tired, and her mind was not sparking on all ignition couplers at the moment. For a brief moment she got excited at the thought of some food. "You want me... to..." she said as she scrunched her face in confusion.

"Yeh. Don't worry 'bout it. Durden owes me any who."

Ashira looked at her blankly and blinked.

With a large nexu-like grin, Iraila saw the confusion. "Aww... my little embernectar drop. Bless yer heart." She reached over and patted Ashira's hand. "Go on over yonder to Durden's," she pointed. "Tell em' you want two cups o' coffa and a baked-round fer me n' you. He don't charge me none."

"Oh... okay." Ashira lit up in utter astonishment. "Thank you!"

"Hurry back now and we'll see if we can gitcha fixed up," Iraila said cheerfully.

Ashira did as asked. She resisted the urge to stuff the entirety of the amazing smelling round and fluffy piece of warm, freshly baked bread into her mouth. Sitting back down beside Iraila, she handed the requested items over to her benefactor. They both sat in silence as the steaming coffa and buttery bread-rounds disappeared. Ashira felt as though food and drink had never been so good and silently wished for more.

With a final upturn of her cup, Iraila spoke in satisfaction.

"Aah. Mmmm. That's better now ain't it?"

Ashira nodded in blissful agreement. "Thank you... so much."

"So. You're a lookin' fer a quiet spot to do some thinkin'. Best as I can figure, that would be the Sho Lin Memorial Park. She was some kinda fancy politickin' type what did some good fer the Realm backin' its heyday... or sumthin like that. But any who, I been thar a few times with Gazzair. It's a purdy place. Flowers smell so good when they'a bloomin'. Its mandatory to stay quiet out of respect and all," she waved a bony finger at Ashira "so doncha' go a hootin' and hollerin' or tha law'll git'cha."

"Sounds perfect," Ashira said with an unassuming chuckle. "How far away is it?"

"Oh... I'd say, 'bout two kilometers yonder way as tha whisper bird flies," Iraila said, waving a hand in the general direction.

Ashira wilted on her stool at the thought of more walking. Her face reflected her body's protest against being pushed harder and further. The coffa and bread had helped, and she was grateful, but she was running on fumes. She rose stiffly and sauntered over to a nearby bin to toss her cup. Leaning back with her arms raised over her head, she rolled her head around her shoulders and stretched while taking a deep breath. She turned around and was surprised to see Iraila right behind her, their opposing features greeting one another.

Startled at the appearance Ashira spoke in surprise. "Thank you Iraila. For the food, and the coffa. I needed that and I really do appreciate it," she said trying to compose herself.

Her words were met with that ever so cheerful and expansive smile.

"Why sweetie, you'un helped me jus' as much as I helped you. That's what folks is 'sposed to do. The way I was raised, when ya see someone in need, ya help em' no matter what. Them Kiensei folk use'ta be like that all tha time. Use'ta see 'em around quite a bit, but not no more. Maybe someday they be like it again," Iraila said.

"Maybe," Ashira smiled in return as they both headed to the stall to regain their seats.

The two had talked together for about a half hour when Iraila looked longingly off into the distant cityscape.

"Well. Let's get youns on yer way. I got thangs to do and all," said Iraila. She reached under her apron and into her right pocket, withdrawing it with a closed hand. "Come 'ere young lady," she said with some authority.

Ashira wasn't paying attention but stepped straight to her new friend out of respect, stopping in front of her. The elderly woman rose up off of her creaky stool with a huff and straightened herself as much as she was able. Iraila looked Ashira square in the face with a kind and gentle seriousness.

"Now listen. You best remember what I done said today 'bout helpin' folks, ya hear?" Iraila said as she clasped Ashira's hand softly.

Ashira smiled weakly and said "I will. I promise." She felt something being pressed into her palm and in looking down in surprise she saw some money chits flash in the morning sunlight. Raising her gaze in astonishment to that unforgettable smile, she opened her mouth to speak but was very quickly interrupted.

"Nope," said Iraila shaking her head slightly with her eyes locked on Ashira's. "Don't wanna hear it so don't say nothin'. You take that there and get you a hired scootster or something else ya be needin, ya hear me? I knows yer tired. I knows yer hungry. Despite all that, yous was willing to come help me and even sit a while to jest talk. Most people woulda jest paid me no mind. You done a good thang miss 'Shira and I knows thars more to ya than meets tha eyes."

Ashira was speechless. So much so that she couldn't find the words to express her gratitude. It was a rare thing for her to not have anything to say, and *that...* was saying something.

"Oh, and one more thang 'Shira" the elderly woman said with her signature smile. "May that Ki flow ever within."

Ashira leaned back in utter shock as she gave the old woman a look of sheer dismay. Iraila just kept smiling, leaned sideways and looked over Ashira's shoulder and nodded her head towards something. Ashira turned around to see a replay of the news report from much earlier. Her own image once again projected in large scale up in the air.

"Just 'cause I'm old and talks funny don't mean I don't know thangs or pay attention," Iraila said softly.

Ashira wasn't much for physical shows of affection, but she hugged Iraila tight and whispered a genuine "thank you" in her ear with the words struggling to navigate past the lump that had formed in her throat. After a brief moment of embrace, she said her goodbyes and headed for the nearest hired scootster hailing station.

Perched unassumingly above the plaza on the pinnacle of Matume, a lone figure sat. Its gaze watched from a distance as two people embraced one another in shared kindness, the result of mutual small acts of selflessness. Its glassy green eyes blinked approvingly at what had happened there. Its head slowly turned as it followed the lithe figure of a young Tesska walking towards the edge of the plaza. With a soft coo, Raiju spread her gold and white feathered wings and leapt into the morning sky.

MORI

Chapter 10

The orange, enclosed, ferry transport hovered to a slow and steady halt at the hailing station near the Sho Lin Memorial Park. Ashira paid the Lishqua driver his fee, which included almost all the chits she had been given and stepped out of the scootster onto the formed durastone platform bathed in the mid-morning sunlight. The park was about three-hundred meters long, one-hundred meters wide and was carefully nestled between parallel rows of taller building segments. The entirety of the space could be observed from the multitudes of windows opening from its borders. Besides rigid building structures, the park was bordered on three sides by angular, hand chiseled stone planters holding a mix of imported flora, from Dahnee, according to a bronzium informational plaque anchored in the ground. There was sweet smelling Marltree with its small white flowers that grew in clusters, making the tree appear to have white balls of fluff all over it.

There were Chryshmum shrubs, whose larger trumpeted blossoms displayed hues of pink and purple and were the favorite resting spot for rarely seen butterflies. There were also the shorter Maicess, whose low-lying foliage and bowl-shaped blooms changed colors from shades of blue to orange throughout the day, depending on the amount of sunlight to hit them. Iraila was right, it was much quieter than any other place she had visited in the expansive city. Ashira wished she had known about this place sooner as she looked up and around, noticing that there were few, if any, skyway thoroughfares above the park due to a restriction in airspace carefully signaled by hover beacons. The earth-toned walking surfaces had been specifically formed to appear like ancient hand-placed stone segments in order to convey a sense of timelessness to the reverent place. The park was bisected through its pivotal point with a wide main walkway with smaller, curving pathways that branched off the main walkway at various points to allow meandering through the individual gardened areas.

As far as she could tell, there was only one official in a pristine Korosento Tsugint Guard uniform slowly patrolling the area. She couldn't tell whether it was a mech or a Tsugint inside that armor as it moved in a mechanical fashion yet made almost no sound with its steps. Its armor was polished to a shine the likes of which she had never seen before with no knicks, scratches or imperfections whatsoever. Its D9-TA5 rifle looked as though it had literally come off the assembly line only moments ago. As it walked, it took a specific route and all its movements were snap-tight, at the point of being pre-programmed. It looked like what the Tsugints called a 'buffy', but she could tell by its movements that it was specially trained or programmed.

In the center was a tall, bronzium statue of former High Minister Sho Lin. The statue stood about ten meters high and portrayed the delicate build of a human woman but with a regal poise. Her face emanating strength and resolve, her flowing headdress and elegant robes reflecting her strong will and conviction. Her hands were at her midriff holding a circular crest in each. In her left, the symbol of the High Realm. Her right, the symbol of the Kiensei Establishment. At the base, two Rolthdogs sitting poised around her feet. The years of patina only added to the elegance of the cast statue.

Passing a large, rounded durastone seating area, Ashira walked up to the statue and read the carved bronzium plaque:

> *"Engraved upon each of us is the mark of greatness, a testament to the potential that lies within. I envision a*

world where our individual strengths are not hoarded but shared equally. A world where our differences are not shunned but embraced, recognized as the very threads that weave the tapestry of our collective strength. We are all of us, the people of this world, where every voice carries the weight of significance.

-High Minister Sho Lin

Dedicated to the memory and honor of the Realm citizens, members of the Realm Defense Cooperative, and members of the Hikarino-Kiensei Establishment who perished in service to one another during the Great Portalspace Euruption. – M.A.R 1745

She remembered some of her history lessons about that era, known as the Epic Peace, and how the Kiensei numbered in the hundreds of thousands then. A time when the monastery was too small to house them all. A time when remote monasteries were established to allow the Kiensei quicker response to civil unrest. "A better time I'm sure," Ashira said quietly, placing her hand on the plaque. After a quick review of the area, she decided to take a seat on the round durastone disc she had passed previously. It rested about 60 centimeters higher than the walkway and was about 3 meters in diameter. Walking back towards the disc she saw the looming white fortress of the Kiensei Monastery in the distance as it was framed by the structures on both sides and the landing platform on the bottom. The statue, it seemed, was facing the monastery in some philosophical atavism for the Realm to forever look towards the Kiensei.

Ashira seated herself in the center of the circle crossing her legs in front of her. Straightening her aching back, placing her hands on her knees and closing her eyes, she took a deep breath in through her nose and slowly released it out of her mouth. Ashira's fatigued form found a moment of respite as she immersed herself in meditation. The city's cacophony was hushed, replaced by the gentle cadence of her breath. She ventured inward, inviting an imbibe of herself to the Ki.

Visions appeared to her in various sweeping and fast forms. Sounds echoed in her mind's eye; sensations skittered across her skin. A hand reaching out to her... faceless figures surrounding her. Murmurs of anguish, cold floor, hunger, despair. A warm embrace, rest, soft... comfort. Sadness. Loneliness. A nisi training nisi? Armored battle. Heat and sweat. A dark figure with an undistinguishable raspy voice. Crimson? Now white? Friends. Sea of black glass? "Then die" an apparition says in a booming voice. Blackness and emptiness. Wolves? Red, penetrating eyes. Starfields? Portalspace? No, something different. The sound of a screeching owl and a blinding white light snapped her back into reality almost instantaneously.

Ashira blinked sleepily. Nothing in her meditation made sense, it was scattered and chaotic. But then again, sights through the river of Ki could be misinterpreted. She had improved her ability of discernment since Ruma Sniings' assassination attempt of Damae over a year ago, but right now she was too tired to concentrate and so the effort had been wasted. She looked around and it slowly became clear that some time had passed. The shadows had shifted significantly than when she had first sat down. Did she sleep sitting up again? No. The Ki didn't let her sleep. It was trying to tell her something, but what, she couldn't discern in her exhaustion. Unexpectedly, behind her, a familiar voice rang out in loud aggression.

"It is requested that all visitors maintain an atmosphere of quiet respect" the singular Korosento Guard shouted behind her.

She turned her head to view what appeared to be the guard brandishing his rifle and forcibly reprimanding some teenagers for some loud antics they were engaged in near the statue. She knew that voice, she'd heard it thousands of times. "So, it *is* a Tsugint" she said quietly to herself. She wondered who he had angered or what malfeasance he had done to garner that kind of assignment. After some small measure of condescension from the teenagers, they left and the entirety of the park was empty, except for the guard and Ashira.

Off in the distance, the low rumble of a *Dominator X-class* assault ship quaked as it slowly raised its hulk from the planet's surface from the mooring docks near the distant monastery. A familiar feeling washed over her, and she stood up in response from the hard, round seat. Taking a few steps towards the monastery, she stood still and closed her eyes briefly, reaching out with the Ki. She couldn't divine much in her state but... there it was. The familiar tendrils of her former sesni, like branches from an evergreen tree reaching outward and upward. Kina was on that ship. She quickly withdrew herself before he could reach back. Her mind wondered where he was going and what battles he would win. What mischief he'd wind up in... and all without her there to watch his back as she had done for years. The thought of her former sesni leaving the continent in continued service—without her—saddened her. There he was, Kina Wykera. The hero off on some mission to save the world and here she was, alone, with nothing. And no one. A discarded shell of a person set adrift.

The malady of regret began welling up inside her. What was she thinking? Is this really the path she wanted to take? How did it come to *this*? Did I make a mistake in walking away? Memories of the times she spent alongside her sesni flooded her wearied mind. The missions, the battles, the... comradery. The purpose. She always was his closest ally in battle, just like he was to her. They were a team. But now, no more because of her choice. But what choice did she have really? They wouldn't listen to her, didn't trust her, and were quick to discard her down a refuse chute at the least sign of malcontent from the Assembly. Ashira's heart sank lower. She looked longingly as the ship slowly pivoted in the sky, its bright orange engines flaring to half power signaling the beginning of its exit maneuvers from the city, the ensuing rumble a few seconds behind. She missed the feel of a ship under her feet. She missed the wondrous variety of continents, islands, and people themselves. Her heart yearned to fly again.

"Eh, that's a beautiful site" the guard said, standing right beside her and facing the same direction. Ashira jumped and blinked in wearied fright as she did not hear nor feel the Tsugint approach her.

"You scared me soldier, didn't see you there," she wearily quipped. "Must've been lost in thought." She shook herself lightly, an attempt at regaining her composure. She surmised that she must be more tired than she thought to let someone just sneak up on herself like that. She glanced down and caught sight of a well-worn pathway that she had been standing on. The guard had stopped just short of her at what appeared to be a specific spot for some other purpose.

The silvery lenses of the exquisitely polished Tsugint helmet turned to look at her briefly before returning its gaze at the distant ship.

"I bet the view from there is better than here" the guard said. "At least it was the last time I was on one of those. Wonder where they're headed?" She was right. This guy had to have done something wrong to get stuck here.

"No telling" she said, placing a hand on her hip and waving her other hand nonchalantly at the sky. "Likely to some forward staging area in preparation for some frontal assault," Ashira replied.

The Tsugint guardsman turned his head again and looked at Ashira momentarily before looking at the departing ship once more.

He let out a hint of a sigh that sounded more like a deep breath, his helmet masking it.

"You know" he said, "even if we no longer serve one purpose doesn't mean we don't have a purpose at all."

Ashira looked at him quizzically for a brief moment. A Tsugint speaking to a deeper purpose? Through all of her traversing of war theaters, her trials, and tribulations with the Tsugints, she knew that they were created specifically to obey orders. They were highly loyal and would fight to the death in defense of the Realm against all enemies, foreign and domestic. But there was more to them she had learned. They were good and honorable soldiers, and even a few of them she could name as a friend. Where some saw an expendable creation number, she saw a soldier who had his own thoughts and feelings. A distinct person, each one of them. Maxus especially. Maxus, one of her few friends. Ashira often wondered what he thought about this whole mess of a situation. Would he be disappointed in her for leaving? Would the respect she had so painstakingly earned become so frivolous given the situation? Maybe one day she'll get the opportunity to ask him. Maybe.

And what about herself? Ever since she learned that she was chosen as a nisi, all she knew was warfare. It was exciting at first and she couldn't wait to show everyone what she was capable of, including Kina. She had made a mockery of those new training gundams designed to simulate the battle mechs that the Divisionists used, and she had thought it enough to prove her battle-readiness. Kina didn't, however. She could remember a few times that her excited outbursts landed her in a bit of trouble with the Demios of the Council... and with Kina. But the war itself had been a complete diversion from the foundational teachings of the Kiensei Establishment. Respect for all life being central to the Establishment but *'here, use these throwaway soldiers to get the job done'* had been the marching orders of the Emperor. A stark contradiction as if the

Kiensei rushed headlong into battle wearing symbols of peace on their chests with *'Born to Kill'* painted on their foreheads.

"What I'm trying to say" the Tsugint continued quietly "is that I know what *my* purpose is. My life is not meant for happiness. My purpose is to be useful and to do so in an honorable way. Hopefully, I'll make some manner of difference in whatever I do so that I have lived and died well all for the benefit of others. *That* is my purpose, and in my opinion, the purpose of all of us Tsugints."

Ashira was intrigued by this Tsugint soldier. She had never thought to ask them about their feelings on the war or their lives in general. Some had offered up explanations in numerous ways on their own, but as far as soliciting a genuine response, she had not. It didn't mean she didn't care about them, she cared about all of them and many times she had wondered if she had been fit to lead knowing she was leading many of them to their deaths. Like Sesni Asato and Kina, she too, valued the lives of these men.

"It's an interesting place to be stationed here, how'd you get assigned to it?" Ashira asked while trying to keep the conversation light. The two stood still, continuing to watch the hovering ship maneuver in the distance.

"I chose this" the Tsugint said. "I wasn't assigned. I'm still part of the Diplomatic Service unit attached to the Guard, but this posting is special. My armor has to be pristine, day in and day out. My weapon, the same. My movements, perfect. It's an honor to guard this special place. They say it's the final resting spot of one of the greatest High Ministers during the Epic Peace as well as some other unknowns. By special decree from the Emperor, an environment of quiet respectfulness is to be maintained at all times. And so, that's my purpose here. I'm an honor guard and I'm proud to serve."

Ashira turned to look at him with confusion painting her already exotic face. Her hands neatly clasped behind her and resting at the small of her back. "I have always heard that most Tsugints were assigned to the front lines in a fighting capacity or some other support role. I never thought they got to choose much of anything. I don't mean it in a bad way, it's just not something I'm used to hearing. It's refreshing actually to hear it from someone who's experienced it."

The Tsugint guard turned his body slowly to look around the park as if looking for someone. His head turned quicker than his body as he actively scanned the area for other people, yet his rifle remained motionless in his robotic-like grip. The park was still empty other than himself and her.

"Look" he said, turning to face her "I've been out there slugging it with the rest. I wouldn't mind doing it again. As it turns out, I'm not fit for duty of that sort. For us Tsugints, if we can't perform, we either get shipped back to the Foundry, thrown in somewhere as cannon fodder, or assigned to some administrative duty. In the worst of things, our minds are blanked, and we become janitorial staff or... how should I say it... scrapped. But they don't socialize that last bit. It just so happens that I found out about this post from Commander Xima when I was shipped here. It's me and five others who share a similar..." he began to trail off "disinclination for crowded spaces."

Ashira raised her eyebrows, horrified as she shifted to a less formal stance, her arms by her sides. "*Scrapped...* how does one *scrap* a living, breathing person?" she questioned intensely trying her best not to vent her frustrations.

The Tsugint stood still and unwavering. "Well, it takes less time to transplant organs and limbs from one Tsugint to another than it does to culture a brand new one. Especially if a Tsugint already has cybernetic replacements." He turned his head towards her. "We're all the same genetic makeup, so there's no rejection. In some extreme views from people in the Realm, we're like organic versions of the mechs we fight against."

Ashira's face descended into disgust at the thought of using real people in that manner. How could she not have known this? Her face hardened; her lip arched upward. "That's... just horrible. To think of it like that." This line of thought irritated her, as such, she began to lose some of her practiced composure. "To me, the Tsugints are people, real people. Not some piece of property meant for wanton disposal. I've fought beside others..." she caught herself mid-thought, the Tsugint's head turned slightly "... *argued* with others who think Tsugints are just that. Disposable. From what I can tell, the Realm is lucky to have people like the Tsugints. There are many who sleep comfortably at night without a second thought of who is ensuring that comfort." She caught herself and took a breath to calm herself down. "I'm sorry, enough of my ranting. You said something about a fear of crowds?"

"No." he said plainly "I just don't like being around a lot of noise. People chattering mixed with other loud noises, it fills my head, drives me crazy and makes me nervous for some reason. I didn't start out that way for sure so go figure huh? Some of the regulars labeled me as a 'gutless non-hacker' when I left the front, even though I was willing to deploy. The scientists called it 'an undesirable but functional mutation' when I was assessed by them after I had a breakdown of sorts during the Third Battle of Gormoran."

Her breath seized in her chest at hearing that name. She had been there too. It had been a three-pronged continental invasion operation and a bloody one at that. A lot of good soldiers died during the first wave. Her and Kina's gunship was shot down, so was Demio Suramosa's and Demio Shiroi's. She ended up trapped with Reikuno in a Divisionist surface gunboat underground and would have died in that metal tomb with her had it not been for Kina and Reikuno's Sesni, Undiabolo coming to their aid. Her mind leaped to remember if she had had any significant interactions with any Tsugint soldiers outside of her usual, but none came to mind immediately.

"So, the stress of battle you think," she asked, "or you're saying it developed over time?"

"Doubtful" he said. "I was a radio comms soldier that was live-testing experimental gear on the battlefield. Something about different frequencies, signal amplitudes and newer gear installed in my helmet for consideration of inclusion to standard loadouts. It felt like a thousand conversations going on in my head at once when things got hot and heavy. I ended up wandering around like I was lost, my head buzzing, until a medic spotted me right before an enemy shell exploded nearby and threw me into a boulder. I spent the rest of the battle in triage for a broken nose and busted chin and even then, I couldn't remember my name for more than a day. But its ZX-0217, "Hammer" they call me. They say they couldn't prove whether or not the gear had anything to do with the episode when they shipped me back to the science bay, so I got shipped here as a last resort before getting mind wiped. Luckily, Xima realized I still had something left to give and mentioned this post... so here I am. Don't get me wrong, the selection process is brutal and only the most disciplined and committed actually get the job. But you see, in the end, I still found a purpose. I have a high attention to detail; I like to think and ponder on philosophical questions to keep the noise down in my head. This post requires an attention to detail and the setting is nice and quiet so I can think. It all worked out. What about you? What's your story? Haven't seen you around here before."

Ashira turned away from Hammer crossing her arms. She looked up at the swaying branches of one of the flower-covered trees. "There's nothing much to tell, and what I could tell isn't worth mentioning," she said but was secretly reminding herself of her arrest at the reluctant hands of Commander Xima. "I was just passing through and thought this would be a good place to stop for a bit."

Hammer spoke with a hint of inflection in his voice. "You mean a good, quiet place to stop and *meditate*... while facing the Kiensei Monastery?"

"No," Ashira said lightly, looking over her shoulder to send a half-hearted smile to the Tsugint. "Just a place to stop and think for a bit."

"Hmph. Yeah, just to think for a bit. Well," he sighed "it's been nice talking to you. My lieutenant should be on his way to relieve me, so I better get ready for the change of guard. If it weren't against regulations, I'd tell you to go over there by that tall planter and take a nap, you look like you could use one."

"Is it really that obvious?" Ashira thought with a hint of embarrassment. It did sound nice, genuinely nice... but she couldn't risk it or put him in a difficult circumstance. "I should get going too. It was nice meeting you Hammer," she beamed weakly. "Maybe I'll stop by again sometime."

Ashira, with her arms clasped together and holding her own shoulders, began trailing towards one of the far corners of the park where walkways penetrated like manufactured riverbeds back into the interior of the sector when Hammer called out once more.

"Oh... if you happen to find yourself several blocks west of here, you might find something of interest," Hammer said. She didn't have the energy to call back, so she mustered her arm to rise up and her hand to wave at him.

"West is where I'll go then," she thought.

The young Tesska was heading towards a passageway as Hammer watched her leave. He waited in silent introspect on the appointed spot for the procedure. Right on time, the figure of ZL0-309, "Freq" they called him, came steadily into view. The lieutenant approached with the same mechanical precision that Hammer had performed. Eventually, the two honor guards came face to face in their gleaming armor. A quick salute and they both spun their rifles sharply with them both stopping in a vertical position at exactly the same time and exactly the same position with a loud '*clack*' as their gauntleted hands clasped the weapons. A procedural inspection of the armor and weapon of the incoming guard by the outgoing one followed with laser-like precision movements. The two moved past each other then turned about face in mirror-like accuracy. Another salute and the procedure was complete. The park was empty and the quiet permeated every square inch of the area with only the light hum of distant scootsters and other transports. A slight breeze tickled the leaves on the ground, and they skittered in response.

"Anything good today, Hammer?" the lieutenant asked quietly.

"Eh, you might say so, sir. One incident with no casualties and one VIP."

As Hammer turned on his heel to face the path back to the barracks he spoke quietly, just enough for his superior to hear. "...but you'll never believe who it was."

Freq replied with sarcasm oozing from his voice. "Yeah? Who's that? Let me guess, another public official with their secret not-so-significant other?"

"Better than that. Much better. I just had the privilege of talking to—*the*— Commander Mori."

The lieutenant quietly scoffed. "Boonswaggle! You're so full of scatdung Hammer. Like that time you told me that the Emperor himself came and spoke to you or when you said that prefect from the Harrin District was in love with you?"

"Oh yeah? Look over at the western corner then."

A few seconds passed before Freq spoke, in an uncommonly louder fashion.

"Why you lucky son of a danksucker," he said in disbelief.

The sound of Hammer chuckling was all that could be heard as he made his way back to the barracks.

Ashira had walked about as far as she was physically capable of. She didn't know how much time had passed, but the glow of an approaching evening began to appear above the rising shadow lines against the surrounding buildings. Her body ached. Her joints groaned. Her stomach gnawed in hunger. Her head throbbed. She needed to rest. The expected evening thrum of the section she was currently in seemed to mock her. Everywhere around, people of the district were chatting, laughing, eating, and otherwise winding themselves down after another day's activities. She noticed the poorly hidden stares from some of the bystanders at her haggard appearance and it made her slightly uncomfortable.

"What was I thinking?" she questioned herself in despair. "I had everything I could need back at the Monastery. My fellow Kiensei, I guess? Not anyone I could call a faithful friend though, well... other than Kina. Food to eat. A bed... oh gosh my bed." Her mind swirled through all of the basic amenities she wished she had at the moment. Whispers began rising around her and more and more people began to look her way. Her disheveled appearance did not seem to meld well with the people in this sector. She knew that she needed to get out of there or risk causing an unwelcomed stir.

Suddenly, out of the corner of her eye she spotted an unassuming alleyway and decided to slip into the shadows before the crowds started to churn at her presence. She ambled back through the winding capillaries that served as support corridors for the various apartments, shops and restaurants of the section, whatever section it was; the echoes of the main thoroughfares becoming fainter. The light was much dimmer back there. The stagnant air felt thick and humid, with the various smells of garbage and other undesirables hanging in the air like mines, erupting on her senses as she walked by. She turned a corner and was faced with a dead end. There were three black and rusty refuse containers framing the end of the alley. Their apparent state of disrepair and overflow showed that the sanitation crews did not frequent this spot. Her survival skills were all she had right now. She was in a mostly forgotten spot in an area that no decent person would visit.

Ashira slowly made her way towards one of the corners. Her body could go no further. She was utterly spent and was on the verge of collapse. With the last bit of effort she could summon, she slowly climbed into a void left where two containers had been set corner to corner. "At least no one would see me *if* they came back here," she said to herself. She had barely planted one foot down when she surrendered to the planet's gravity and crumpled to the ground landing flat on her back. She slowly sat up, feeling the damp, cold stonecrete underneath. She took in a deep breath of the rank, humid air and exhaled slowly. Pulling her knees up to her chest and wrapping her arms around them, she laid her head against the rough, unforgiving, and cold metal of one of the containers.

"What am I doing" she whispered sadly. "Why did I do this? *So what...* if the Realm has a poor opinion of me? *So what...* if rumors fly through the Establishment? I should've accepted the offer to come back," she reasoned with herself. Her chest began to tighten as her hidden emotions began to break free. "This was all a mistake, just another mistake. I don't know what to do. I don't know where to go," she thought. She shifted her tired form slightly and pressed her forehead against her arms that crossed her bent knees. Her shoulders began to heave slightly as sadness spilled out like a wellspring. Ashira leaned slightly against the slimy wall of a dank, dark corner of an unremarkable back alleyway. Gentle whimpers gave way to mournful sobs as she sat there, hungry, exhausted, alone... and cried herself to sleep.

High above, Raiju was perched on a parapet. She looked down into the alleyway below at a lone figure curled up in a corner, her large eyes blinking knowingly at the state of affairs. She shook her head quickly, ruffled her feathers, and tucked her wings in tight as she settled in to keep watch through the night.

Chapter 11 – Then

The first round of discussions had not gone very well. The Tesska people were angry and cried out for blood in the streets outside of the capital palace. The Regalia's delegation had made little progress in their bid to quench the threat of violence. Asato had asked that he be kept unannounced at first in an effort to assess the situation, and in return he would be vigilant, and reactionary only should violence break out. He wanted to be sure to remain impartial to ease the forthcoming negotiations. After representatives from both sides came to a stalemate and agreed to pause deliberations until the next day, the Kiensei Runan was bidden to speak with the Regalia herself to apprise her of what had happened.

He arrived late in the evening to a palace that was immaculately lit from the outside. Multilayered lights shone upwards to accentuate the curved architecture of the palace complex and to supply additional security. The architecture stood as a testament to the Tesska peoples in that it presented curved features reaching towards the sky. Sweeping structure and layers of coloration and patterns were plain to see—similar to the ever-diverse display of the people themselves. Its harmonious blend of organic form and geometric shape, a reflection of the Tesska's deep connection to nature.

He was met at a secondary entrance by members of the Royal Guard. The main entrance harbored protestors and would have likely caused more harm than good should he have approached in that area. The guards were clad in furred cloaks and shiny, metallic armor about their heads, their shoulders, chest, and upper legs. The armor appeared to have been forged from several different metals given their intricate designs and differences in coloration. Energy staffs glowing and crackling with red electricity were their main form of armament, though at quick glance, Asato noticed the shape of a plasma pistol hanging by their sides under the cloaks.

"Master Kiensei," one of the guards said as she approached him, "no weapons are allowed while visiting the Supreme Hallowed." The moniker was simply another name for the Regalia but used as a more intimate description by a select few. "Please hand over your sword." She held out her hand while the second guard held his activated energy staff at a ready position.

"Of course," Asato said calmly, "I am at the Regalia's service." He slowly untied the sword with its black scabbard from his belt and handed it to the guard without incident. The sound of shouting and chanting filled the air not far from where they were. Asato turned his head slightly in recognition as his hand was extended. The guard took it and held it close as she bowed in measured acknowledgement. He returned the gesture and together, they entered the palace.

The small group passed through lush gardens and courtyards that provided tranquil oases amidst the vibrant city life. The serene spaces were adorned with exotic and native flora alike. It was rumored that the gardens were used by some of the Tesska elite for quiet contemplation and communing with the people's ancestors.

Looking upward, Asato noticed the palace's highest point, called the Zenith Observatory. A tower that was used by the Regalia and other high-ranking officials to imbibe the breathtaking panoramic views of Karinar 's mesmerizing landscape as well as to gather as a governing body, not unlike the High Council of the Kiensei Establishment. The observatory was also used by many of the indigenous leaders to study and discern guidance from the cosmos, particularly the Narkash, where leaders of all tribes across the continent would meet yearly to discuss issues, resolve differences, plan directives and report on the people under their purview.

The many smooth-walled corridors they walked along when they entered the building interconnected various chambers and specialized areas. Each one adorned with unique artwork and artifacts that stood to showcase the people's artistic talents as well as their many historical achievements. One such in particular was a very well woven tapestry that appeared to depict the Viala Atrocity. Asato's history was a little rusty, but he remembered that at one time, the Realm Fair had been held there, but after an attack that left hundreds of thousands of citizens dead, the fair had been summarily canceled. The tapestry depicted what appeared to be the bravery and inclusion of the Tesska peoples in repelling the attack on the city of Viala.

Before long, the group arrived at the heart of the palace. The Grand Meeting Chamber, a vast and awe-inspiring space, was where the Regalia would hold court and entertain guests. It was also where other important gatherings and ceremonies were held. Upon entering, Asato remarked to himself at the walls that were lined and embellished with shimmering mosaics depicting Tesska history and mythology. Its ceilings adorned with a mesmerizing constellation of stars that represented the culture's guiding spirits and beliefs. But most alluring was the massive roaring fire pit in the middle of the space. Fire was sacred to the Tesska people. It was a symbol of life and renewal, a messenger and carrier of prayers, a source of healing and purification. And at its core, symbolized the sacred connection between the people, the spirit world, and the natural world.

"Ka'kwha. Greetings Sesni Kiensei," the smooth and elegant voice of the Regalia echoed through the chamber as the party approached the regal platform. Asato stood at the base of a white marble staircase leading up to the elaborate throne. The throne itself, a white marble monument inlayed with curved strips of polished obsidian to mimic Tesska markings as well as various precious metal inlays that represented cultural values of the people. As if bursting forth from behind the throne, metallic rays of various metals radiated upward and outward to almost twice the height of the throne itself. The Regalia stood in front of the throne. A tall woman of fit stature stood as a poignant monolith at the top of the stairs. She was regally clothed in white, flowing robes, trimmed with gold ribbon along the length of the sleeves and with fur around the neckline. Her light green face was accentuated by light blue marks extending upwards and curving away from her piercing yellow eyes. An intricately chained gold head piece adorned her brow and helped accentuate her striking features. The rounded marks on her cheeks revealed the strong bone structure of her face. Her tall and elegantly curved growths had alternating curved stripes along their length and the pattern was repeated down her long head tails that reached to her knees. The head tails were adorned with gold bands near her cheeks and then again near their ends.

Asato opened his arms wide and bowed deeply at his waist. A suggestion from his sesni before he left, to signify his willingness to come before the sovereign in perfect peace and perfect trust.

"Greetings and peace unto you, great Regalia," Asato said loudly. "How may I be of service?"

A distinct look and slight wave of her hand was all that was needed to dismiss the guard accompanying the Kiensei Runan. She began a slow, yet deliberate descent towards the Kiensei, her long and flowing white robes floating like clouds on the marble stairs as she descended. A few intelligible whispers, the crackling of the fire, and light taps of her feet were all that could be heard as she approached the Rodlek Runan—her eyes fixed on him. Asato remembered to keep his hands open and outward per his sesni's suggestion, contrary to his own people's custom of putting their hands together and steepling their fingers.

"Sesni Kiensei. I trust that you understand the gravity of the situation presented?" the Regalia said softly. Her voice was deeper than expected and yet smooth as spinnersilk.

"Indeed, I do, highness," he responded in kind. "I understand that your people have a cultural responsibility to maintain balance amongst themselves by trading like for like, in almost all situations, this one being of the highest profile currently."

"Certainly, that is one way of presenting it," the Regalia said. "My intention in calling you here was to help me reinforce to our people that peace, not violence, is a more suitable way to achieve that balance. Even though our traditions may dictate blood for blood, I believe we can allow diplomacy to reign supremely in both our minds and our hearts."

"A most noble cause, highness," Asato said, bowing his head slightly.

"Please, Master Kiensei, tell me what you saw today," the Regalia said.

Asato took a moment to reflect on the day. He touched his ornately engraved face mask in silent remembrance before he spoke. "I noticed that the Deshu delegation wanted to make a case for extradition to their home world so that the suspect could be tried there, but the people and your delegation rebelled against it, their point being that a fair hearing would only take place here on Karinar."

"And what of your thoughts on the matter?" the Regalia asked straightforwardly.

"I believe that a tribunal hearing on either continent would invoke a feeling of bias on both sides. I suggest a neutral space to hold a hearing," Asato said gently. "I understand that Karinar is in the process of applying for full membership to the Planetary Realm. Perhaps your majesty would be willing to allow a non-biased group to hear the case and adjudicate accordingly in Korosento?"

"No," the Regalia said sharply. "A trial will be held here," she pointed to the ground at her feet. "No exception. The offense occurred here; the tribunal will be here. The ancestors demand such."

Well, that didn't work, Asato thought to himself. If he couldn't lure the resolution off-continent so that it could be better controlled, then he would have to take a more proactive role. "If your majesty would allow me to independently learn the facts surrounding the incident, perhaps I could better serve you and your people," Asato said. "I fear that I would do you and your proud people a disservice otherwise."

A pause resonated throughout the expansive chamber. The popping and crackling of dry wood burning on the massive fire was all that was heard. The Regalia slowly blinked twice; her face unreadable as a durastone wall as she stared at the Kiensei Runan. She was in deep thought. Considering all her options.

"Very well," she said loudly. Her voice echoing powerfully within the chamber. She turned and raised her visage to address all that would hear her. "I decree that this Kiensei be allowed unfettered access to any and all information surrounding the incident. I also decree that he be allowed to come and go as he pleases amongst our people to carry out this task." She turned her penetrating gaze to the Rodlek Kiensei once more. "I further decree that he have no more than three days to do so, counting today, before I pass judgement on the matter myself." Her face was solid as stone as she announced her final decree. "Anyone who hampers or otherwise delays the Kiensei will be immediately punished according to... *my*... desire." The chamber was completely silent.

Three days' worth was not a lot of time, Asato thought. Not to mention it was actually less than three now. He would have to act swiftly if he was to bring an amicable resolution to this incident. "My thanks to you, majesty," he said as he bowed low once again with his arms outstretched.

The Regalia turned to ascend the staircase back to her throne. "One of my valets will attend to your needs for the evening. All available information will be waiting for you. I bid you goodnight and I trust that tomorrow will be productive in the resolution," she said with her back to the Kiensei as she ascended the staircase.

With that, the guards escorted him to his room for the night.

Sleep did not come willingly to Asato. He was slightly uncomfortable with the lavishness of the accommodations provided by the Regalia, as if being entreated into something beyond his will. His room was large, about five times the size of his humble space within the Grand Monastery on Korosento. The same finishes he had seen on his way to the Grand Chamber were present here as well. Smooth, cream-colored walls with ornate patterns and embellishments that mimicked the wonderfully diverse markings of the Tesska people. A fireplace crackled and popped at the opposite end of the room from the exceptionally soft and opulent bed, again, much more luxury than he was accustomed to. Light from the fire danced about the room and supplied just enough light to see all that was within the space. A few tall, rectangular windows were set on either side of the fireplace with long, white, sheer dressings. The data was accurate, he thought. The Tesska certainly treat their guests well, as dictated by their cultural beliefs.

He stood by the fire, deep in thought. One hand gently rubbing his face mask, the other across his midriff. A gentle knock came from the very thick, wooden door. He turned and approached the door to open it, as a call of 'come in' would be insulting. He unlatched the black and rustic-looking closure and opened the door to reveal a palace page.

"Greetings sir," the page said with a slight bow.

"My greetings to you as well," Asato answered.

"The Supreme Hallowed has decreed that you receive all information regarding the issue at hand. I present you with this," the page said, raising a small wooden box with handwritten documents and data tablets contained within.

The Kiensei Runan took the box with a respectful nod of his head. "My thanks to you and the Regalia," he said lowly.

The page clasped his hands together. "Is there anything else you need this evening Master Kiensei?"

"No. Thank you. I am fine, good night," Asato said respectfully.

The page took a step back and clasped a single fist at his chest, making a bow at the waist. "Rava'shi tash'ki (may the spirits give you rest), the page said and made his retreat as the door was closed.

Asato rested the box on the bed, and it sank slightly in the plush mattress. He rifled his fingers through its contents. Handwritten eyewitness accounts. Diagrams of the crime scene. Photographs. Those he would have to pore over individually. Two tablets were included. Rebi wasn't with him in his room but was still nestled within the mech socket of his ship. He keyed the comm on his wrist. A fleeting moment later it beeped in response and Rebi chirped an inquisitive response.

"Rebi, I'm going to connect my communicator into a few tablets. I want you to process them and sort the data within. I want you to cross reference everything, and I mean everything. I want you to look for commonalities and connections. Understood?"

Rebi grumbled a response that Asato understood as the mech being unhappy about having to stay with the ship while he got to lounge in luxury.

"I understand, Rebi. But you're built for extreme environments. A night in the cool evening of this continent won't deactivate you, I promise."

Rebi chirruped and squawked a response that expressed its discontent of having to work in such conditions and that added concessions would have to be made when they returned.

"Very well," Asato huffed in resignation. "I'll ensure you receive a proper buff and polish as well. Does that satisfy you?" Rebi chirped an acknowledgement. "Good," Asato said, "transmitting now." He pulled a data link cable from his belt and connected the first tablet to his comm unit. The steady fading pulse of green on the comm device signified the data transfer. A solid green told him it was finished. The process repeated for the second tablet. Once again, the Rodlek Runan hailed the mech.

"Transfer complete Rebi. I have physical documents to pore over for now. We will reconnect in the morning and go over what you discover."

A crackling grumble through the comm told Asato that the mech was not at all wanting to wait that long. He shook his head slightly in mild frustration and closed down the channel. Asato sighed heavily through his mask and grabbed a group of documents out of the box. He made his way over to the bed, sat down, and began poring over them. Crackling and dancing flames were his only company that evening.

Morning came early and the Kiensei Runan rose and prepared himself for the day's events. The sun had not risen yet and it was still pitch-black outside.

Two more rotations to go.

His thought was to make his way back to his ship since unrestricted movement had been granted. He wanted to confer with Rebi to collaborate on what he had found and cross reference it with what the mech had found. He readied himself and opened the door to his quarters. A different palace page greeting him sharply.

"Good morning, sir. Do you need anything that I might be of assistance with?" the page said quickly. The young Tesska man stood sharply at attention, his splotched face held high, his hands behind his back as he addressed the Kiensei Runan. Asato was surprised. He was not expecting the palace staff to be up and ready at this early hour. Had they been watching him?

"No, thank you. I wish to go to my ship and confer with my mech at this moment. Is that permissible?" he said. The page bowed slightly and motioned with an open hand for him to continue down the hallway to the main lift. "The Regalia has permitted your unaffected movement, sir," the page said in response. "She also has allowed you your weapon as well." The page brought his other hand around from behind his back and made a courtesy bow as he held the sword hilt openly as if it were presented on a platform. Asato took his weapon with gentleness, securing it with a natural motion to his belt as he had done so many times. The page followed him to the lift and escorted him outside of the palace.

"Sir, before you go," the page said, "here is my comm link key. Should you need assistance or have information for the Regalia, use this." Asato nodded in acknowledgement.

Rebi squawked and blipped as Asato approached the ship. The sun began to creep just over the mountainous horizon signifying the early hour. The light flowing like hot liquid iron across the expanse of the beautiful planet.

"Yes, Rebi. I know you finished the task a mere few minutes after receiving the data," Asato said, fully expecting the mech to complain about having to wait such a long time. It was easier to placate the grumbling mech rather than argue with it. "We organics require a few things that you do not. Thank you for being patient." Rebi spun its head side-to-side in mock defiance but bleeped a conciliatory series in acknowledgement. "Now, what can you tell me?" Asato said poignantly.

The mech blipped, squeaked, squawked his grumpy response. Producing a virtuagraphic image, it made its findings clear. Asato grabbed at his face mask and studied the diagrams in earnest.

"It appears on the surface that the victim was poisoned" he said initially. "The toxicology report showed an elevated level of asrinack." The mech beeped an agreeing response, but also made a point in return. "You do not believe this to be caused by the Jamiku suspect?" Asato questioned. Another blip and series of bleeps summarized it all. Asrinack was a chemical used in organic construction material preservation. Perfectly harmless in lesser amounts, as those found in general exposure during construction. However, in extreme amounts, it was deadly within a day of exposure.

"So, based on the evidence you studied, the Jamiku defendant was present on video with the victim." Asato paused, watching the interaction from various angles. "It could be surmised that the victim was poisoned by the defendant based on a high-level view," he said. The video showed the Tesska male in direct contact with the Jamiku defendant at a local social establishment. The hand of the Jamiku grasping and covering the entire top of the glass that the victim had requested before it was handed to the victim and subsequently being drank in its entirety. The timestamp of the video and the time of death corresponded with the use of a poison, particularly asrinack.

"Rebi, enhance the view surrounding the hand on the glass," Asato said quietly. The mech did as asked. The expanded view showed splayed fingers and no sleeves. Which led Asato to believe that no device or other subterfuge could have been used. The Jamikuan's hand was empty, there were no accompanying devices due to the bareness of the arm. Asato postulated that he was only being friendly under the influence of whatever was being consumed.

"Rebi, show me the video of the outside of the establishment please," Asato said curiously. The mech chirruped that all but one camera had been available. One, in particular, had went out of service about an hour before the incident in question. Rebi's continued bleeps and blips further conferred that the remaining video did not show anything of significance. "Convenient, isn't it? That one camera that could show us what we need wasn't working. Where was this taken?" Asato asked. The mech squawked a simple response. "Then Tsit'awih is where we shall go. Ready the ship, we leave at once."

Chapter 12 – Then

The *Spearpoint-class* fighter lightly touched down in a cloud of dust near an already moored freighter. The engines made their signature whine as Rebi completed the landing cycle and shut them down. Through the dust, the outline of a Tesska man approached. He held up his hand as a show of greeting to the new visitor. The bubble canopy of the craft pivoted open and Asato nimbly extricated himself from the cockpit. Adjusting his outer garment and closing it in the front, he walked towards the approaching man.

"Ka'kwha. Hello." The man yelled out.

"Hello." Asato offered in return.

The two came close enough that the dust no longer obscured their view. The look on the man's face was one of both confusion and perhaps bewilderment as he realized what, or who, was in front of him.

"I am Kai Asato. Runan of the Kiensei Establishment," Asato said politely, proffering a small, but respectful bow.

The man balled a fist at his chest and spoke a phrase in Tesska that Asato did not understand but took as a sign of greeting or respect.

"M-master Kiensei," the man stuttered, "how... unexpected it is to greet you. I am Mata-ru. May I ask what business you have in our humble town?"

Rebi lowered itself from the mech bay on the ship and trundled up beside its current master. "I am here at the request and authorization of the Regalia of Karinar," Asato said calmly. "Rebi," he motioned at the mech. A virtuagraphic representation of the decree from the Regalia was promptly displayed. "I am here to investigate an incident at her request. I do not intend on disturbing the people of the town, I only intend to ask a few questions."

"Y-yes sir," Mata-ru said.

"Have many ships landed here recently?" he motioned to the freighter on his left.

"No sir. That ship came here only a couple of days ago," Mata-ru said.

"Have you seen any of these two men?" Asato motioned again to Rebi. The mech bleeped and again produced a projection of the two men. The Tesska looked quickly and blinked.

"No sir."

"What about the establishment in this pictogram," he motioned again to Rebi, "do you know of it?" Rebi squawked in frustration at having to project all those images. It also bleeped concern at having to repeat this process over and over again to every person they met. "Please excuse my mech," Asato said to Mata-ru. He knelt down and explained quietly to Rebi that it could assist the effort or be shut down for the remainder of the mission, which would delay its buff and polish session. Rebi rumbled and made its dome shake in displeasure. Asato stood up again as Rebi displayed the establishment.

"I know of it, yes sir," Mata-ru said.

Asato produced a hologram projector from his tool belt and displayed a crude map of the town to save himself from the frustrations of Rebi. "Would you be so kind as to help me locate it?" The Tesska pointed to a small building. "My thanks to you," he said and made a bow to show respect. Mata-ru returned the gesture. "Rebi, let's be on our way," he said raising his hood over his head.

Mata-ru watched as the two figures became smaller and smaller as they traveled into town. Looking around to ensure he was alone; he produced a small communicator and keyed it.

"What is it?" came a low, gravelly voice.

"It's me. We have a problem," he said.

Sereeah didn't sleep one wink that night. Neither did Kel-so. He stood guard, watching, waiting for an attack. He could hear the Bespare circling outside of his sight in the underbrush, and he waited for that unmistakable cry. Sereeah found herself jumping at the slightest crack of a twig or chirp of an insect. She was resolved that this bivouac business was not for her.

Kel-so sniffed sharply and holstered his weapon. He approached the Rishka and held out his hand, motioning for her to give up the weapon he had loaned.

She recoiled at the notion of having to give up her only way of protecting herself.

"They're gone," he said. "Moved on. They lost six of their pack, so the pack was likely small to begin with," he said. "Now give me back my pistol."

She reluctantly handed it over.

"Now, let's get this packed up and get us ready to head to the village. You handle the camp, I'll handle the Bespare," he said, holstering the second blaster and unsheathing a curved knife.

"They're already dead," she said quizzically.

Kel-so shot an annoyed glance at her.

"Okay, Okay. Do your... whatever. I get it," she held her hands up in mock surrender. She remembered that the Tesska don't wantonly waste pretty much, well, everything. She rolled up the mats and stored them on the scootsters. She went to douse the fire and Kel-so stopped her. She watched as he removed the front feet in a measured and calculated fashion, raising each one up to the sky and saying something she didn't understand. She watched as he swiftly and expertly removed the pelts, folding each one neatly. He requested her to bring him an empty pack from his scootster which she obliged without question.

"Now, pack these items in that," he pointed to the pelts and pack in succession, "they will be a gift to the tribe and will help ease tensions."

She set to work and again watched as the Tesska dragged the skinned and field dressed animals, two at a time over to the fire and placed them crossways. The stench of burning flesh soon hovered low. He went to his scootster and came back with a small vial of some liquid of sorts that Sereeah was unsure of. He stood in front of the small mound of smoldering carcasses and held the vial above his head and in a loud voice cried out "Var likan osha'tira (Thanks for their sacrifice)" then smashed the vial on the mound. He quickly retreated just before a loud *whoosh* sounded. Flames erupted, engulfing the mound, and disturbing the air nearby in such a way that Sereeah's cloak was moved slightly, the sudden blast of heat startling her.

She finished packing and stood as he approached. He reached down and grabbed the pack with one hand, shouldering it with ease. "Let's go. We should be there in about an hour or so," he said. "In the meantime, we should go over your story, and I shall prepare you to meet the tribe."

Asato stepped out of the bright sun into a decently lit establishment, a local eatery with social games. It had a rustic look to it with rough finished wood forming the majority of the base construction and finishes. Supporting columns were made of solid tree trunks that had been preserved with a waxy substance to maintain their natural appeal. Trusses were tree branches of the same finish with what appeared to be imitation leaves, but he couldn't tell. In all, it gave the ambiance of being in a forest. A cultural farce, he thought. It was earlier in the business day, so the patronage was noticeably light. Perfect for keeping a lower profile, he thought. He saw who appeared to be the proprietor behind the bar. A weightier Tesska male who showed no lack of resources in his appearance. Evidently this was a successful business. The purple-skinned man had white, wavy markings on his head growths and white markings on his face. Even some of the markings on his arms were more rounded with softer edges as opposed to the sharp lines of others. *Truly this species was beautifully diverse,* Asato remarked. In true Kiensei fashion, he sidled up to the bar with no fanfare and awaited the man to come to him to engage the conversation.

"Welcome, friend," the man said, finally noticing one of his first customers of the day. A traveler by the looks of him... or it... or something. That cowl-hidden face was definitely one of a non-resident. He'd seen plenty of them in the past few standard weeks. It didn't matter though, money was money. "Is there something I can get for you?" he said approaching amicably.

Asato had noticed three large containers sitting on the credenza behind the man, each with their own concoctions slowly being churned and chilled at the same time. He chose one that appeared to be a mixture of fruits with a water base. "And a drinking tube with it, if you please." His mask had a port to accept drinking tubes so that it could maintain the proper air mixture necessary for his survival. With a jangle of intricately designed bracelets that appeared to be of gold in several shades of color, the green-hued drink was put before him. He opened the port on the bottom of his mask and to his enjoyment, the drink was quite delicious. He had finished half of it when the moment he had subtly waited for happened.

"Can I offer you anything else, friend?" the Tesska man said.

"As a matter of fact, you can," Asato said, producing his personal virtuaprojector from his utility belt. "I'm looking for information regarding these two men." He activated the projector and the image of the two men rose into view. "They were present in this establishment not long ago. It seems one of them, the Tesska man shown here," he pointed, "ended up missing."

The man crinkled his face at the picture, then at the hooded... person thing... in front of him. What was going on here? A strange customer asking questions about someone he didn't know? This was ridiculous. He wasn't an information service; he was a business owner. He couldn't possibly remember every single person that visited his establishment. "I have no idea what you mean," he said dismissively. "You're here to drink, eat, or play. If you're not spending, I got nothing to say pal."

"Rebi?" Asato said quietly. The mech had been patiently awaiting just behind him, understanding full well what was about to happen. The Regalia's decree promptly came into view just beside Asato. In a discreet fashion, Asato unsheathed his sword and gently laid in on the bar in front of him as he rose his own face to the bartender's.

"Uh oh," was the first thought through his head as he read the royal decree in front of him. That symbol, that image. It was the Regalia herself. He had heard a rumor that a Kiensei had come into town. And this was certainly a Kiensei that also had a decree from the Regalia for unrestricted assistance. His face devolved into one of servitude and compliance. "M-my apologies, Master Kiensei," he said quietly with a slight bow. "How may I be of service to you and the Supreme Hallowed?"

"My question still stands," Asato said lowly, "Do you know any of these two individuals? They were seen at this establishment recently. It appears that one of your cameras was inoperable at that time as well. What can you tell me about that?"

The man thought for a moment. He knew better than to lie to a Kiensei. Legend had it that those mystical magicians could read minds. It was even worse to go against the Regalia. He couldn't lose his business; it wasn't worth it. "The man there," he pointed to the

Tesska, "he came into town a few days ago. He was a runner from one of the rural tribes on his way to Kanónsoni'ta. He stopped here in town to rest before continuing on. Heard he had some census information or something. It's pretty usual for the rural tribes to use runners to report on things like births, deaths... you know, stuff like that."

"Do you know which village?"

"I do not."

"And the other person in the video?" Asato asked.

"I don't know who he was," the man said truthfully. "He drank a lot and we had to cut him off. I think he was just some trader who was out to have a good time in an exotic place. We get that a lot here." The man rubbed the back of his neck. This wasn't easy, but he knew the consequences were worse. "We get suppliers from other civilizations from time to time. How else do you think you were able to enjoy such a lovely beverage?" he said with a sheepish grin and a poor attempt at salesmanship.

"And the camera?" Asato asked cooly.

The man sighed and looked towards the ground. "A-another Tesska man approached me. Said he had s-some personal business to attend to. He paid me a sizable amount of money to disconnect one camera. I-I didn't ask any questions." He knew he shouldn't have done it, but hey, money was money.

A pause passed as Asato digested the added information.

"And this man. Did you get a name?"

"No, I didn't. No names."

Asato thought for a moment. He could ask for a description, and it might help in his investigation, but the amazing diversity in the Tesska people would make a description very challenging to decipher especially in their own land. Still, it was worth it since Rebi was excellent at digesting information.

"I want you to describe the Tesska man to my mech here, and in the meantime, I need to call someone," Asato said, excusing himself briefly. He stepped away from the bar, just out of earshot from the proprietor. He keyed his communicator.

"Yes, Master Kiensei?" came the voice of the palace page.

"I have a question regarding the government's census process. How often is census data collected?" Asato asked.

"Data is collected once per year. There is a two-month collection period that spans the ending and beginning of our traditional calendar," the page replied.

"And where in that calendar are we currently?"

"About midway through the second quarter, sir."

Asato thought for a moment. It became obvious that for census data to be reported outside of the normal period, something special or tragic must have to occur. "What about the remote tribes?" he continued. "Would it be normal for a runner to be reporting census data outside of the normal collection timeframe?" he asked the page.

"It would certainly be strange. An extenuating circumstance would have to happen for that to occur," the page said.

"Have you ever known of such an event?"

"Mmmm. No sir. Then again, I'm still quite young," the page said.

"Very well. I am currently in the town of Tsit'awih. Would you be so kind as to send me locations of known remote tribes near this town?"

"Certainly sir," the page complied.

"Thank you. When I have something of substance to report I shall let you know," Asato said closing down the comm channel. He approached the counter and placed some money chits gently on the bar top, more than enough to cover the beverage. "I thank you for your time," he said. "Rebi, it's time to go."

Outside, Asato transferred the data to the mech. In an abbreviated time, it chirruped that it had processed it, but that it had received some interesting data from the *Spearpoint-class* fighter. Rebi chirped in a gloating manner that it had been smart enough to keep the sensor arrays active and that the person they had met at the landing pad had sent a communication right after they left.

"I wouldn't think it would be remarkable for a landing pad coordinator to communicate in the discharge of their duties," Asato said.

Rebi bleeped a retort.

"The communication went outside the borders?" he said surprised. "That is certainly interesting. Any chance you would know where exactly?"

Rebi beeped a frustrated negative. Then rattled its dome and chirruped that another transmission had occurred that stayed relatively local and that it could provide a general area of where the transmission went.

"Very well, let me see," Asato said. Rebi's virtuaprojector hummed to life. A yellow pulsating circle indicated an area where the transmission could have been sent. Asato stared at it intently. "Now, show me the villages that the page sent us." Rebi made small red dots appear. Another moment passed as the Kiensei Runan looked intently. The yellow circle was close to two villages in a mountainous area. It wasn't exact by many standards, but it was interesting enough to give pause. "What about that village I asked you to mark on our way in?" Asato said curiously. Rebi blinked one of the two red dots near the yellow circle.

A small knot formed in his stomach. Pieces of this puzzle were starting to fit together in his mind, and it began to worry him.

"Rebi, we need to get back to the ship."

"Yes?" Kel-so said quietly into his comm.

"We have a problem," the voice replied. "A Kiensei, a *real* Kiensei has landed in Tsit'awih and is asking questions about the runner from the village. He is under decree of the Regalia."

A sharp pang of alarm hit Kel-so's mind. The coverup was in question and now the Supreme Hallowed was involved. This would greatly complicate things. Maybe he should have just destroyed the camera instead of bribing the owner. "Stall him if you can. We haven't picked up the package yet, but we are almost to the village." A quiet beep sounded as he closed the comm.

"Everything alright over there?" Sereeah asked. She couldn't hear the conversation but thought it prudent to see if she could learn anything that might be useful to her. She didn't trust the man in front of her any further than she could throw him, and he looked rather weighty.

"We need to hurry," Kel-so said. "You know what you need to do, right?"

"Yes."

"Good. Here we go."

The two had walked through dense, hazy forests, across swishing grassy openings, and along creeks of babbling water. They were in the middle of a tall, evergreen forest when a narrow path began to appear, as if it had been travelled many times. Up ahead was an opening, the light of day becoming brighter the closer to the edge of the forest they came. Stepping out of the wood, the two found themselves on top of a hill. Looking into the shallow valley between them and the next hill was a village nestled contently and surrounded by tall trees of various kinds... *the* village. Approximately thirty dwellings were visible.

Their rounded and circular shake-shingled roofs looked like large brown mushroom caps from a distance. The exteriors were made of rough log and adobe construction with rounded, oval, or square windows that had the look of more modern compartmentalization for individual spaces on the interior. Well-worn dirt streets passed between the main rows of dwellings. In the middle of the village, however, was a singular rectangular building. It was long and had an angular roof of the same shake-shingle type. It appeared to Sereeah that this could be a community meeting house or a place for tribe council.

"The Ravaraki tribe," Kel-so said. "Our destination."

"We have a problem," the voice said through the secured private comm channel. "A Kiensei has arrived and is under decree of the Regalia to investigate another matter, but it overlaps with ours."

Baron Vohlm snarled at this news. This carefully planned extraction was now in danger of failure. The benefactor would be most displeased with news of this sort. But most importantly, the secrecy of it all was paramount. "If this operation goes awry, you know what to do."

"Yes," the voice said. "Preparations are already in place."

"Good," Vohlm said dryly. "As soon as the target is acquired or you have confirmation of failure, execute your preparations," he grumbled and closed down the comm. He looked up from the long, expansive table where the other members of the Dark Fire leadership sat in convocation. Lord Grunnery glared at him in displeasure.

"This... will not please our benefactor," Grunnery growled. "To appease him, we shall absorb the costs of this attempt should it be unsuccessful, though that likely would not satisfy him." He clasped his hands together atop the large table. His long, thin Manchurian mustache twitching along with his lip.

Duke Chimaz Balereon spoke up. "My lord, our asset in the Martellian Commonwealth reports that they have acquired a package. Perhaps that would be enough appease the benefactor?"

Grunnery growled lowly. "Perhaps. I shall inform him as soon as we have resolution of the Karinar operation."

Chapter 13

The sun had already risen, and the day's norms of a trillion people had already begun. The noise of routine steadily rose in the district. Raiju sat unmoved on the parapet still watching over the still figure below. Ashira had barely moved, if at all, through the night. The Ki moved within her suddenly. She sprang from her perch, opening her wings to glide. She was needed and it was time to act. Her green and white feathered wings carried her towards the alleyway below. Spiraling downward effortlessly with silent avian gracefulness, she came alight on the front edge of a black dumpster. Something was coming. Her two vigilant eyes scanned the alleyway for signs of movement.

The din of the main thoroughfare added no aid in discerning between sounds of an intruder or the rustling of a bit of garbage in the light breeze. Suddenly, there it was. A shadow appeared in the distance. It moved quickly and quietly, dodging in and out of the darkened corners of the alleyway... and it was headed her way. Raiju waited in silence and watched the figure as it came closer. Soon enough it was time to act. She shrilled and hooted loudly. The figure stopped dead in its tracks and looked at her. Seeing this, Raiju continued the performance by hopping slightly, stretching her wings, and making short, cooing sounds. Good. She had gotten its attention and now it was headed straight for her.

The figure crept closer and closer while she stayed still. Watching the figure as it watched her in return. Soon, it was close enough. Raiju leapt into the air and fluttered just above the still sleeping Ashira. She hooted softly as she spiraled her way back up to the parapet perch she had kept for the past many hours. Through her green eyes, Raiju watched as the figure slowly raised itself over the abutted corners of two dumpsters and peered below. The next pathway was opened, but would she take it? The bird cocked her head in wonderment.

Ashira was dreaming. She was walking down a wide, dirt path bordered by the black of space and twinkling of star fields, shrouded to the front and rear in a thick, wispy, grayish fog. All around her, whispers in tongues she couldn't decipher cadenced in syncopation with the sounds of her footsteps. As she walked, the ground behind her continuously collapsed with a low rumble and fell into nothingness, leaving her with the only possibility of continuing forward. When she stopped, so did the collapse. When she continued, so did it. Behind her, she heard an unfamiliar, modulated voice call out wistfully *"left me."* She stopped, turned, and gazed into the gray mist in confusion. There was nothing there. She whirled around looking into the fog in all directions for the voice's owner but found none. She continued forward along the path, her footsteps crunching in the gravel underfoot. A faint apparition that she could not identify began floating through the mist, above her, beside her, passing through the path only to reemerge elsewhere. The fog swirled as it moved around the apparition. Ashira should have been alarmed and wary, but the apparition felt warm, comforting. Familiar. More voices began to echo all around her, out of sync with one another. *"Recklessness in you"* one said. *"Influences of the dark,"* said another. Ashira's head swiveled in vain, trying to find the source when she stopped suddenly at the sight of the apparition in front of her, the fog billowing around it.

"Who are you?" Ashira cried out in confusion.

A voice sounded and echoed as if it were composed of many beings. High- and low-pitched voices emanated uncoordinated.

"*Your potential... see your future*" it said with strange familiarity. Ashira blinked in measured reflection. Hadn't she heard that before?

A faint light began to pulse slowly in the distance, cutting through the thick fog. The apparition disappeared as the ground began to rumble and shake. She began to run towards the pulsating light with speed unnatural. The fog began to roll back, quickly revealing infinite space and stars. The dirt pathway fell away, dissolving into dust and fading out of sight, but to her surprise she did not fall with it. The rumble became a pounding roar. The pulsing light became brighter and brighter when suddenly she felt the urge to leap toward it, like an instinctual response. She leapt, her arms and hands outstretched into nothing. The barely audible screech of a owl was the last thing she remembered.

Ashira began to open her eyes as she felt something or someone tapping on her head. Her vision was blurry as her senses slowly began to return. She could make out what appeared to be a person in front of her. In a jolt of adrenaline at the belief she was being attacked, she threw her hands up towards the person in defense and scooted as far back into the corner as she could.

"Get away... from... me" she croaked in a half-coherent manner. Her throat scratched as her eyes struggled to focus.

"Oh! You're alive!" said a young girl's voice in surprise. "Thought maybe you were dead or still passed out from drinking too much booze or something."

"I...... don't drink" she said wearily, her voice sounding like she had swallowed a bucket of sand. Though at this moment she'd drink just about anything. Her head was no longer pounding, but her body was stiff and very sore from the durastone accommodations from the night before. She blinked her eyes a few more times until the blue face of a young Multorn girl stared back at her with large, cheerful green eyes. The very fibers of her body protested as she struggled to get moving.

"Well now that I know you're not dead, what are you doing back here?" the little girl asked.

"I... fell asleep. I thought... it would... be... a safe place for the night," Ashira said shakily.

"Safe for the night!?" she said surprised. "Good thing the garbage loaders didn't come, or you'd be a squashed bug! Are you sure you didn't drink too much? You don't look like you belong here."

Ashira gradually made herself rise to one knee, then two. She stretched her arms up high and rolled her head around to loosen her neck. On sore and shaky legs, she finally stood up as stiffness reminded her that she had slept in an awkward position.

"I *don't* belong here" she concurred raising her brows and looking down at the ground. "I don't even know where *here* is." She coughed to clear her voice.

"You're in the Balma district. It's one of those... what did mama call it?... socio-species neighborhood-thingy? I dunno what she said. It's basically a fancy neighborhood made to look like regular people live here even though its fancy," the little Multorn said with a big smile.

Ashira didn't recall the district's name, nor could she remember if she'd ever been there. But she did recognize the type of place she was in. It was one of many newer interspecies communities designed to bring citizens from all backgrounds together instead of individual siloed communities of a single species. The silos, of course, being a result of the multitudes of refugees and evacuees being relocated due to the war.

Cocking her head sideways, her head growths wobbling slightly the little one asked "well, if you don't belong here, where is your home?"

She coughed to clear her throat. "I... left my home."

The little one nodded, placing both hands on her hips. "Yeah. Me and mama had to leave our home too. It was scary at first, but mama found us a place to go until we can get a new home."

Ashira, with her senses finally working again, recognized her from the Pliaza. Little blue face, dirty outfit, bare feet. "Hey, aren't you the little one... that stole some sweetbread and disappeared into a refresher... at the Pliaza?"

"Well yeah, duh, how else am I supposed to eat?" the little one snarked.

Ashira was taken aback. She half expected the little girl to run, which would not have worked in Ashira's favor since she was in no condition to give chase... and the fact that chasing a child might be frowned upon if she was spotted.

Ashira looked with a wearied but playful smirk at the Multorn. "How indeed. Speaking of which, you happen to know where I can get something to eat and maybe some water without stealing it?" she said while raising an eyebrow and curling her mouth in one corner.

The little girl rummaged in her hidden pockets on each side of her dirty romper. She produced what appeared to be a military ration bar and thrust it up towards Ashira.

"Here, take this. I get these from those men that walk around in those white and red mech suit-looking things from time to time. They don't taste too good, but they're food when I don't have none. There's a jug of rainwater over there," she pointed to a corner where a downspout protruded "it's safe enough."

Ashira glanced at the dirty little hand holding a bent and mashed ration bar and wondered if she should risk eating it... yep... she realized quickly that she was hungry and she needed food now.

It was gone in an instant and Ashira couldn't remember if she had even tasted it as it slid down her throat. She closed her eyes briefly and sighed.

"Thank you little one. Thank you very much."

"My name's Eilidh!"

"Eilidh. I like that name. Mine's Ashira. How old are you anyway?" she said, climbing out of the corner and walking over to the translucent jug to take a drink. The lukewarm water quenched the fire in her throat and instantly she felt relief. She stretched her arms and legs. Her back protested. Her neck was stiff. Hard surfaces were unforgiving.

"I'm seven!" she said standing akimbo.

Ashira scrunched her face in a quizzical manner. "And you live…. where exactly Eilidh?"

The Multorn crossed her arms and turned her back towards Ashira. "I'm not 'spossed to tell. Mama told me not to tell. It's a secret."

Sensing Eilidh's natural curiosity in her, Ashira decided to feign disinterest. "Well, ok then. I don't want to get you in trouble with your mama, even though she isn't here. I heard about a place a few blocks from here that may be of interest. I think I'll head that way. It was nice to meet you. Thanks again for the ration bar."

Eilidh watched with novelty as Ashira stiffly ambled past her and down the alleyway. Usually, she was shooed away or scolded or sometimes the scary police robot thingies came to try and get her. But this person with faint stripes on her face was different. She could tell. *Some people just gotta stick together* she thought.

Ashira made several turns in the labyrinthian back alleyways heading westward. She wasn't lost by any means, but Eilidh didn't know that. She could sense the curious little, blue-skinned girl peeking out around the corners, following behind her in her best sneaky fashion. After the fifth corner she turned, Ashira spun around and waited with her arms resting behind her in a quasi-militant fashion. In a moment, a little blue face with green eyes peeked furtively around the corner and saw her standing there with a smile.

"Heeeyyy... how'd you know I was here?" Eilidh asked in self-disappointment.

Ashira just kept smiling at the little girl. "You are really *really* good at sneaking; I'll give you that," she said with a wink and a gentle finger at the young girl. She then touched one of her ears. "But I'm really *really* good at hearing."

Eilidh came out from the corner and stood in front of her with her hands behind her back, mimicking Ashira. She began rocking back and forth on the balls and heels of her feet.

"Welllll.... You're going the wrong way."

"The wrong way to what?" Ashira asked inquisitively.

"Um. I dunno. But it's not that way," the little one mumbled.

"What's not that way?"

"Nuthin'. I-I was speaking a-a-another language" the little Multorn said trying to backpedal the conversation.

Ashira was amused at the young one's attempt to think on her feet and repressed the urge to laugh aloud at the innocent antics. She instead raised her chin and her brows as she looked down emphatically at the suspicious-acting child in front of her.

"But what would happen if I went that way? Would I get in trouble? Or would *you* get in trouble?"

Eilidh kept rocking on her feet with her eyes roaming everywhere but in Ashira's direction. "Um. Maybe I might get in trouble."

"Well, what do you think would happen if I went that way by myself? Would you still get in trouble?" she asked.

"No. But the big men might try to hurt you. They keep a watch out for bad people." Eilidh said.

"So you think I'm a bad person?"

"Nuh uh. You didn't chase me away or throw stuff at me or nothing."

Ashira thought for a moment, then squatted down to look the child in the face. "Eilidh, what do you think can we do so that you don't get in trouble and the big men don't try to hurt me?"

"I dunno." She spoke noncommittedly.

"What if... *you* took me there, and I tell them you were a hero and rescued me? Would that keep us both out of trouble?"

"What's a hero?" Eilidh asked. She stopped rocking and raised her eyes to meet Ashira's.

She smiled softly. "A hero is someone who does really good and brave things to help people, no matter what."

"Yeah! That's me! I wanna be a hero," Eilidh nodded with an excited smile; her little head growths bouncing with joy.

"Well then, my little hero. Lead the way." And the two continued on through the alleyway walking side by side.

Ashira and Eilidh emerged from the alleyway system into a rarely seen area of topside Korosento. Nestled within the intricate latticework of elevated walkways, forgotten service tunnels and maintenance catwalks was "a camp!?" Ashira said in wide-eyed surprise.

At quick glance, she could see the outlines of ramshackle dwellings and other structures that appeared to be made of scavenged materials from the city's underbelly and progressive works. From patched up tents, to repurposed cargo containers and even shanties constructed onto the sides of ventilation shafts, the outward appearance showed an innate resourcefulness to its inhabitants, all dappled in diffused sunlight. Ashira looked upward as there wasn't much direct sunlight, but light, nonetheless. This was due, she noticed, to the camp's proximity to some colossal skyscrapers that shielded it from view from both ground and sky.

"Yup." Said Eilidh, extending a hand towards the camp. "That's where I live. It's called Skyshade Haven."

"Skyshade?" Ashira asked inquisitively while looking down at her.

"Yeah. That's what I named it. It sounds fancy. Like those big buildings." She said while pointing skyward.

"Hey! You there! What are you doing here?" came a shout from the right. Ashira turned to see a husky, three-eyed Braundt approaching her. Ashira was not in the best condition to fight anyone, but she would do what she could to if forced.

"Hey Tumps, you leave her alone! I rescued her. I'm a hero and I say leave her alone." Eilidh shouted back at the approaching Braundt.

"Ve don't know her" came the deeply accented voice of an equally burly Humboldt with a broken horn approaching from the left. Ashira raised her hands and began to back away. "I don't want any trouble. This little girl found me. I wandered this way by myself, and she tried to stop me," she said. It wasn't the whole truth, but she was trying to protect Eilidh from getting into trouble.

"Eilidh, you go on back to your mother. We will take care of this one." Tumps said, motioning with his head. At that, Eilidh took off at a run towards the makeshift entrance to the camp.

"Vat are you dooink here?" the Humboldt questioned curtly. He sidled up to the Braundt as they both stood as a united front against her.

"I've been on the streets for a few days now. I was wandering around and got sidetracked. I'll leave if it's too much trouble. I don't want to cause any problems," Ashira said sternly.

"How do we know you aren't some spy and that you'll rat us out to the authorities?" Tumps grumbled.

"Hey Tumps, Markhiz! Leave her alone and get back to your own business." Came a shout from the camp entrance. The three of them looked towards the sound and saw a slender blue Multorn woman standing there with her arms crossed. Eilidh was with her, peeking out from behind her legs. She was dressed in brown cargo pants with dark brown boots. Her yellow shirt was fitted to her slender form with the sleeves rolled up near her shoulders. She appeared to be mid-thirties in age, but the weathering of street life had taken a slight toll.

"She ah-could be spy!" Markhiz shouted back, waving his arms above his horned, red head.

"Aw go stuff your ears you big oaf," the Multorn said while swatting a hand towards the Humboldt. "And Tumps, man... with three eyes you can't see that she's too young to be a snoop? She's a teenager! You really think the Imperial government is recruiting children to risk their lives in the back alleyways to come find the likes of us?" The Multorn approached the three. "Now. You two" she said sternly, pointing a scolding finger at the two offending males "go on about your business. And as for you," she wheeled around, her long blue head growths swinging elegantly, her voice afire, "why are *you* with my daughter?"

Ashira began to feel like a glitching virtua-vid repeating the same message over and over. Her mind wandered towards the possibility of this situation being a terrible idea, yet again.

"I left home." She began with a sigh. "I've been wandering the streets. She found me," motioning to Eilidh "even gave me something to eat out of pure kindness. I'm sorry if I caused a commotion. I mean no harm and will leave in peace," she said with a respectful bow, resting her clasped hands in front of her. At least the peacekeeper part of her Kiensei training was still of use, she thought.

The Multorn woman proffered a reserved look towards Ashira. She shifted her stance to favor one leg and tapped her toes slightly on the opposite foot. She looked the newcomer up and down as if trying to gauge the worthiness of the story presented. Her mind was sharp, her countenance reserved but she was willing to see the worth of a person. She made a slight sucking noise on her lip as she began to speak.

"If you left home, then that means you have a home to return to. If you're in a crisis, then why not just go back?" she said.

"It's complicated." Ashira said plainly.

"So is being on the streets," the Multorn retorted.

"So, I'm quickly learning."

A moment of silence passed between the two. They stood opposite each other. Each waiting in stalemate for the other to move or speak. Ashira took the opportunity to contemplate what had been presented to her. She had always had something or someone with her, wherever or whatever she was doing. In battle, she had Kina or another sesni or another nisi or the Tsugints. In the monastery, it was always other Kiensei. When she was on patrol in the city, it was never a thought or concern that she was by herself because she always had a home to return to and an entire establishment to support her. She had never really been alone and on her own. Not even the Wahaskah incident made her feel completely abandoned—there were other muhashki there. But now, all of her safety nets and crutches were gone. Yes, she could go back, and the Kiensei would take her in. Things could try to revert to the way they were, but would they really? She knew it would never be the same. And then there was the war. All the killing and death. Pain and destruction. All a complete contradiction to who she was and what she stood for. The concept of being a peacekeeper, she could handle gracefully. Being a cog in a war machine, not so much. And then there was Kina. Her single biggest regret of the whole ordeal was leaving him behind. She would bring him with her if she could, but that was nearly impossible. He had his own struggles to handle, let alone what she wished she could lean on him for.

"I don't know how else to explain it" she said. "I just can't go back. Does that make any sense?" She knew very well how to explain it, though it likely wouldn't serve any good purpose in this moment.

"It does, to a degree. Everyone has their own reasoning and for now, your business is your own. Let me make one thing clear though" the Multorn said seriously. "There are many people here who depend on this place for their very lives. To lose it could mean certain death in one form or fashion. The people here have been able to make an existence from practically nothing and to upset that would destroy them. Is that a burden you think you can carry?"

Life and death were things Ashira knew very, very well. The dichotomy of a peaceful existence in a time of planetary civil war was certainly a dream that anyone could wish for, even at the most menial level. It was clear that trust would have to be earned here. Luckily, she was somewhat of an expert in gaining the trust of wary people. She decided that leading with a bit of truth should help start the relationship off on a good footing.

"I understand your point, and I don't take it lightly. Yes, I have a home to go back to, but everything inside of me rejects that possibility for many reasons. I had no idea what I was getting into when I left, I see that. I'm not asking for a handout. I can pull my own weight if that's what you're worried about" Ashira said.

"Sweetie, handouts are generally all we've got to look forward to" the Multorn said. "You got a name?"

"It's Ashira, mama!" Eilidh piped up excitedly from behind her mother, her face beaming with delight.

The elder Multorn walked up to her and extended a hand. Ashira clasped her forearm as the other reciprocated.

"Don't make me regret this, Ashira" she said seriously while pulling her closer and locking eyes with her. The two exchanged a knowing expression "The name's Taria. C'mon," she nodded behind herself, "I'll take you inside."

Chapter 14

Ashira was genuinely impressed at the resourcefulness of the little hidden community. A perimeter wall of sorts had been fashioned out of pieces of scrap metal and scavenged construction fencing to supply a means of protection. The individual hovels were crude but very functional given the lack of raw materials. There were many distinct species present, which was not surprising. This was still Korosento after all, the capitol of the entire planet. She had been to many levels of its underworld either on assignment or, well, on the run, and had seen what poverty, disparity, and dereliction looked like in many forms, but this was different. There was no squalor despite the rough external appearance. There were no outward shows of drunkenness or addiction, brawling or other debauchery that tended to emanate the lower one descended into the bowels of the city. This was simply a group of people who were desperately trying to make the best of a tough situation.

"Not what you expected is it?" Taria asked as they walked in between the individual sites.

"It's pretty amazing actually," Ashira said. "How long has this place been here?"

"It was here before we came, and that was about two standard years ago," Taria said. "It's grown quite a bit in that time. When we got here, there were about twenty people. Now, we have over fifty."

"But why so many do you think?" Ashira questioned genuinely.

"In case you haven't heard or been living outside of the world, there's a war going on. The cost of living has increased, taxes are rising, there's a massive influx of people moving to escape the conflict. Korosento just can't handle it all," Taria said. "What about you? What's your story?" Ashira touched her chin, pondering how much information she should allow herself to divulge as they continued to wind their way through the camp. She decided to keep her immediate past quiet for the time being while she continued to think of a way to explain her situation. She knew that the questions were coming sooner rather than later. What surprised her more was how educated and experienced this lady sounded.

"I'm afraid there's not much to tell. I left home. Things just didn't work out for me there. So, I left" she said sheepishly. She quickly decided to redirect the conversation. "I understand the need to survive, but aren't there shelters or communal housing available for those in this type of situation? I thought about trying to find one myself," she said.

Taria's mouth curled as she huffed. "Hmmpf. Have you ever been in one of those places before? Based on your question I'm going to say you haven't." Taria was candid about most things. Direct and forthright. "You're welcomed to go and try it out," she said sarcastically "but I'm sure we'll see you back here after a day or two."

"You're right. I haven't tried one of those places."

"Well. Between the stale air, communicable diseases, moaning and wailing, and the bed vermin, I'd say it's a regular luxury experience. Oh, and there's that added risk of getting snatched in the middle of the night too," Taria said insincerely. "Don't forget that Korosento is a big place and it's easy to get disappeared pretty quickly."

The three arrived at a small, rustic dwelling that was constructed next to a mechanical chase for one of the adjacent mega high-rises. The simple structure sat flat on the stonecrete ground. Its walls were a patchwork of rusty, flat metal sheets, sun-beaten duraplast panels that looked to be salvaged from some old crates. The low and narrow door appeared to be a repurposed battleship hatch, but instead of actuators, it had to be manually opened. Simple and effective.

"We're here Ashira! Home!" said Eilidh.

Taria reached out and put a hand on her shoulder. "You can stay with us temporarily until you decide what you want to do. You know the way out, so if you decide to leave, you just leave. We have rules here, ok? Rule one: you treat everyone with respect. Rule two: there's no fighting whatsoever unless you have to defend yourself or another person. Rule three: no stealing. Nobody here has much of anything to begin with, but if you take something that doesn't belong to you, you better believe we will *all* come to reclaim it. Rule four: share. We all do our best to gather what we can to help one another. Share with others and they will share with you. Rule five, the most important. Don't tell anyone about this place. We know it's not legal to be here and the last thing we want is to be dismantled and scattered. If someone wanders in, we'll deal with it as you've already experienced."

"I understand," Ashira nodded with a straight face. Living under the weight of rules was nothing new to her. These, on the other hand, were different as compared to what she was accustomed to. These rules were meant to protect life not just an ideal.

Eilidh trundled up to the door, grasped the crude latch and opened it. It made a slight screech as the aged metal slid on its worn tracks. From inside, another accented female voice sounded. "Aye, you back home love?"

"Hey! Siobhan!" Eilidh happily cried out and ran inside to greet the person. Sounds of a cheerful reunion poured out of the doorway.

"That's Siobhan" Taria said. "She stays here too. It might get a little cramped, but you'll at least have a dry and safe place to lay down. Rains are forecasted in the next day or two I think, so it's good you came when you did. Good for you at least, maybe me too."

"I'm grateful for your generosity. But why are you helping me?" Ashira asked curiously.

"Let's just say we can benefit from each other for a time. It's not what you think, I promise. So don't run off scared or anything," Taria said with a genuine, chuckling smile. "Other than that, it just feels like the right thing to do."

A Kiamnik woman came into view in the doorway, carrying Eilidh on her left hip. "I'm sorry it took me a fair bit, but I did manage to gather some grand stuff from the usual spots.... this... time." Her red face quickly devolved at the sight of Ashira from one of happiness to one of shock, her words trailed off as her mind whirled with the new arrival. "Ah, spirits alive! What's *she* doin' here!?" The Kiamnik said in a surly voice. Her flowing red head tendrils becoming stiff and still.

Ashira at once sensed through the Ki that this person did not like her. For what reason, she couldn't tell. Maybe she was being territorial? Or maybe she thought Ashira presented a threat? She wasn't sure at the moment.

"We collectin' rubbish off the street now, are we?" the irritated woman said wobbling her face at Taria; her head tendrils undulating in corroboration with her mood. Ashira squinted slightly and clenched her teeth in shock at the sound of being called trash.

"Relax, relax." Taria said soothingly, motioning with her hands to calm down. "She wandered into camp with Eilidh in tow. She's clear. She's going to stay for a bit to allow her to get acclimated. Then she can decide what she wants to do. Besides, one extra set of hands around this little slice of paradise might be helpful for all of us. Ok?"

Siobhan lowered Eilidh to the ground and whispered to her to go inside. The little Multorn did as asked. Siobhan closed the door behind her and took two steps towards the pair: standing at her full height, crossing her arms. "I don't be likin' it. Not a bit, not at all." Siobhan said scornfully.

Taria scowled back at the Kiamnik, rolled her eyes then turned to face Ashira. "Would you please excuse us? Go on inside and Eilidh will give you the grand tour, OK?"

The dark blue and bilious eyes of Siobhan bore into Ashira as she walked past the obviously upset Kiamnik and through the door to the shack. Once inside, the hushed sounds of an intense discussion could be heard occurring between the two women outside.

"Don't worry," Eilidh said reassuringly, "they'll be fine. Now, come see my spot!"

Ashira found herself in a dimly lit and cramped space that looked to serve as both living quarters and storage. It wasn't dour by any means, though it wasn't cheerful either. The interior walls were lined with shelves made from diverse types of salvaged duraplast and housed a haphazard assortment—from rusty tools to scavenged electronics and maybe a battered virtuabook or two. A single, small viewport was set into one wall as a makeshift window, allowing a sliver of the limited lighting from outside to filter in. Furniture was minimalistic, cobbled together, but functional. A lumpy mattress covered with a patchwork quilt made from old, discarded clothing was seen in one corner. A few, handmade sheets of patchwork fabric hung from lengths of rope and scrap wire to serve as dividing curtains within the space. A small, rickety table stood in another corner, supported by a stack of old circuit boards. A few makeshift stools, constructed from repurposed metal piping and scavenged padding, supplied some type of seating. A small, salvaged heating unit stood in the corner nearest the doorway and appeared to be the only heat source on chilly nights. Next to it was, she assumed, an interesting cook stove made from an old repulsorlift engine component. Above it, some battered and handmade cookware hanging on the wall.

As the little Multorn took her hand and began to lead her towards the rear of the space, she regarded at how well things were organized. Shelves, hooks, and even the rafters held a variety of items and supplies. She also noticed that, despite the rough exterior, there were some touches of personalization and comfort. A small group of bioluminescent plants in discarded cups and bowls sat on the windowsill casting a soft, calming glow. A threadbare tapestry hung on one wall supplying a glimpse of a world far removed from the chaos of the one outside.

Pulling a well-worn, patchwork sheet back, Eilidh revealed a small pallet that served as her bed. It was an assortment of discarded cushions, recycled stuffing and other soft items that had been scrounged, bundled together, and covered with fabric to create a cohesive and functional bed. On the walls within her little space were hand drawn images she had created using color sticks that varied between planets, stars, animals, and what Ashira assumed were people of differing species. In the middle of the pallet laid the rugged semblance of a stuffed toy Shirpcat. The little Multorn let out a squeal of delight as she leapt face-first into the amalgamation of fluffiness. She grabbed the stuffed plaything, hugged it tight and rolled to her side. Ashira remarked at how the drabness of the camp and the dilapidated place Eilidh called home did not seem to dampen the brightness of the little girl's spirit. She, herself, couldn't remember a time where she could say she felt the same. The life of a Kiensei was one of structure, order, and routine. Yes, the younglings did get to... well... *be* younglings, but it was different. It became even more different when the Civil War broke out.

Especially for her.

She and her fellow nisis, equally, were children that had been pressed into military service instead of learning how to be keepers of the peace. Untrained, inexperienced children forced to lead heavily trained soldiers to their deaths. Children forced to make incomprehensible decisions that adults typically shouldered, that held demonstrable consequences. Children that were forced to grow up much sooner than was natural.

Innocence lost.

No… *stolen*… by the Kiensei. By the Divisionists. By the inability of people to solve their differences without killing one another. The *many* being made to suffer because of the *few*. She hated to admit it to herself, but there was some truth to Reikuno' words.

There were multitudes of thoughts flowing through her mind, so many that she momentarily lost touch with the present—her eyes seeing but staring blankly into the beyond. It wasn't until Eilidh noticed that she was delving into the depths of herself that she snapped back to the current reality.

"Ashira? Are you alright?" Eilidh asked.

Her eyes blinked wildly for a brief moment as she briskly and minimally shook her head. A small smile turned the corners of her mouth as her acknowledgement of reality returned. What happened? She had to deflect quickly.

"H-how long have you been here?" Ashira asked, trying not to let on that she had been daydreaming.

"Um, I don't really know. A long time. Since I was really little."

"What about school? Aren't you supposed to be enrolled in one of the Primary Academies?" she asked.

"Mama and Siobhan teach me. They're real smart. Like really really smart. They teach me to read, write, and do lots and lots of calculations. I'm also learning how to speak Kiamnik! I'm probably smarter than all those other kids in real school," Eilidh said with a hint of innocent confidence as she rose to a sitting position and placed her hands on her knees.

Ashira chuckled amusingly at the little Multorn. "I bet you are. A little more practice and I think you'll be a master at it." Suddenly, her senses alerted her to presences approaching. She raised her head in sharp focus, turning to look over her shoulder.

In that moment, Taria and Siobhan came through the portal door. The former hosting a look of mild annoyance mixed with resoluteness and the latter carrying a countenance of defeat.

"Sorry for the... *discussion*... Ashka." Taria said coyly.

Siobhan quickly corrected the Multorn. "It's *Ashira*," the Kiamnik said critically as she cut an irate look towards the Tesska.

"I'm sorry, I'm sorry. Really bad with names," she said while pointing to herself; a grimace painting her face. "We'll work on getting you a spot set up," she said while motioning to Eilidh and Siobhan. "Right ladies?" she said. "In the meantime, let me show you around the camp and introduce you to some of the more agreeable folks around here."

"Thank you. I would appreciate that," Ashira said. She and Siobhan exchanged an uncomfortable look as they passed one another, shoulder to shoulder, as she exited the domicile.

Outside and away from earshot, Taria looked with curiosity and pointedly asked, "do you know Siobhan?" Her eyes narrowing slightly with suspicion.

"No. I can't remember if I have ever met her before or where it was if I ever did." She was being completely honest in her response but felt the sense that something had happened in their discussion that made Taria feel otherwise.

"Mmkay. I just get the feeling that there is some sort of unresolved tension between you two" Taria said with concern.

Ashira honestly had no other answer to give. "Well, whatever it is, I don't know about it. I promise," she said, holding a hand up to reinforce her statement.

The two walked along and among the various makeshift dwellings. Taria properly introduced Ashira to many of the residents including Tumps and Markhiz, whom she had already met. Though gruff at first glance, Markhiz was a tradesperson and was very skilled with many systems including electrical and plumbing. He had worked many years with a building company on several high-profile residential buildings but lost his job due to the influx of people seeking refuge from the war. The labor market became flush with other tradespersons willing to work for lesser wages and so, he became yet another casualty of the conflict. Now, the Humboldt was working to tap into the utility feeds of the mega-high rises towering above the camp to help provide the residents with some of the most basic of necessities. Tumps, as it were, was helping Markhiz and learning the trades he had mastered. Tumps was also a victim of market saturation, but instead of trade work, he worked as an educator in one of the many primary schools in the lower levels of the metropolis. Lack of adequate pay, overbearing hours, and an ever-increasing cost of living Forced Tumps out of his home on level eighty-one. He ended up on the surface by happenstance one day while mentally preparing himself to sequester to the lowest depths of the planet. His only desire at that time was to breathe the freshest air just one time before heading below and yet, he found his way here.

She also met Krishom, a Lurgic male who had worked in a product distribution warehouse that had made adjustments in workforce using mech automation and, as such, retired his role of moving and sorting stock. Ashira learned that he had tried to re-educate himself on the new automation with the intent of becoming a repair technician and maybe workflow administration but was again trumped by automation. Mechs were repairing mechs and managing other mechs in his industry now, which left little room for him. She met Amankaba, a human female who, like others, was displaced due to an overwhelming workload in the Korosento Importation & Customs Inspection office. The substantial number of refugees and increased centralization of trade within Korosento caused occupational overload in the woman, forcing her to resign in order to maintain some semblance of sanity. She had been threatened with termination due to an incident where she buckled under the increasing pressure of her role. For the sake of her own mental health, she left willingly.

There were many others, each with their own story ranging from Mech Programmer to Cargo Loader, Jewelry Dealer to Scootster Mechanic. All had a story to tell of their once peaceful lives, usurped by economic, political or some other upheaval such as the civil war. These were good people who were just trying to live.

And then it came to Taria herself. Ashira waited until the opportune moment to ask the Multorn the ubiquitous question. As they continued to walk along the passageway created by the scattering of dwellings, Taria opened up.

"I was a supervisor in the financial division of a small mining firm." Taria said. "I had a good life. Graduated with top honors from the Royal Imperial Academy. Married to a successful legal consultant. Had it all," she said. "I had lost my job due to restructuring after an acquisition by a larger firm, which I think was because of the war. The government tried to subsidize in order to keep small businesses like ours in business, but it wasn't enough. We were fine though; we could still make ends meet. I looked for other work, but my skillset just wasn't in demand. I was homeschooling Eilidh when one day, my husband Graven calls me unexpectedly via virtuameet and tells me he doesn't want to be married anymore. Says he wasn't happy with his life. It gutted me. We had built a good life together, had our daughter, everything seemed fine. He just up and disappeared and left us with all the burdens. Without his salary, I couldn't afford to live anymore, and it pushed us to the streets. I tried my best to find work, but the financial sector had collapsed by that time into centralized government roles for the war effort. It didn't matter that I had an education or tenure, I just couldn't find a job. I didn't really care about myself, but Eilidh? How could a father do that?" she asked, but not expecting an answer. "How could a father abandon their child? Those were the questions I asked myself.

Anyways, I went to shelters but found that most either didn't have room or were just detestable. I didn't want to put my child in that situation. I also didn't want to run the risk of her getting kidnapped or worse, taken from me by the Imperial government."

Ashira had no answer. She was amazed, and even a little inspired by the resiliency of this woman and feeling humbled by the fact that her own situation wasn't nearly as bad as Taria's. She was, however, taking the opportunity to learn about the people around her, something Kina had encouraged her to do many times. Taria had asked her at least twice on their tour, in various polite ways, what her story was, but she had only offered bits and pieces. In hearing the fullness of Taria's, however, Ashira spoke up as a show of trust. After all, this woman had shown her kindness and offered her help where others had not.

"I was abandoned too," she spoke. "I spent years thinking I was part of something that valued me and my contributions. I gave my full loyalty and life, but at the first sign of trouble, backs were turned towards me, and people set against me. So, I made a choice. I had to leave." Taria nodded in curiosity about the cryptic nature of the statement but decided not to press for more. Instead, she opted to share more of her own life in hopes of coaxing Ashira to open up just a little more. She too liked to get to know the people around her.

"It's good to talk about things like this," Taria said affably, placing a friendly hand on Ashira's shoulder. "It certainly doesn't make it go away, but just getting things off your chest tends to help. It helps me at least. I like to get to know people I'm around, and I'm simply fine with people getting to know me. Being out here, we have to work together to survive and knowing who you're around helps us work better together. But you still haven't asked me yet."

"Asked you what?" Ashira questioned; her face scrunched. She had no clue what she was supposed to ask.

The two stopped and faced each other.

"Why haven't I relocated to the lower levels?"

"Well, the thought had crossed my mind, but I try not to delve into people's personal business," Ashira said abashed.

"It's okay. Really. It's the reason why most people here in this camp haven't done it too." The two turned and began walking again. Taria gesticulating with her hands like a teacher in front of a classroom. "You see, Korosento isn't as all glamorous and starshine like the Realm would want you to believe. There's a certain level in society that one crosses into that makes it virtually impossible to recover from."

"You're talking about a level of poverty," Ashira said plainly.

"That's right. The way our society is built has a black hole in it. As long as you stay away from the event horizon, you're good. But once you're in it, you're in it."

"Okaaay..." Ashira said, searching for relevance.

"Think. What's one of the key things one has to have in order to live in our society. One thing that is constantly asked for when you get a loan to buy a scootster or sign the contract on a personal communicator service. The one thing that is attached to your Realm ID, even if you travel the world."

Ashira had never had to deal with any of those things. She was completely lost on what Taria was after.

"No? Nothing?" Taria probed. *Strange* she thought. It wasn't that hard of a question.

"Okay. You got me." Ashira surrendered, playfully shrugging her shoulders.

Taria lolled her head over on its side and cut a roguish look towards Ashira. "An address," she said.

"An address?"

"Yup. Can't get a job without an address, unless you get paid straight cash, but then the government will find out eventually because of reporting laws, or you have to find a spot to keep them, so they don't get stolen. Can't get a bank account without one. Can't sign legal contracts without one. Can't get your Realm ID now without one since the new security measures went into place after the attack on the power grid." Taria said.

"I see where this is going now." Ashira said with enlightenment. "Without an address, no job. No job, no money. No money, no home. No home, no address. I get it now. That's enough to make your head spin like an out-of-control gunship."

A confused stare came from Taria that lasted a brief moment. "You got it kiddo." She clicked her tongue and winked. "And it's the same in the lower levels only down there, it can get dangerous. People disappear down there, either willingly or not, and my fear is that Eilidh would be one of them. Also, the police force gets more aggressive the further down you go as well, which matches the crime level I hear. They would just as soon as arrest me for something so minor as Eilidh's truancy, then they'd find out she didn't have a home, then they'd take her from me, and I probably wouldn't see her again. I just can't take the risk of losing my daughter in any case. It's still a risk here topside, but just fewer ones. I know there's decent places in the lower levels, like in the 30's, but you still have to have money. And if I'm going to be broke, I'd rather be broke as a joke up here where at least there's fresher air and natural light."

"I can't blame you for wanting to protect someone that close to you," Ashira said downcast, her eyes falling downward. Her thoughts flowed to the many times she had protected Kina and to the times he had protected her. She wondered what he was up to in that moment. It was distant, but she could still feel that telltale breeze from her sesni through the Ki.

"Can I ask you a question?" Ashira enquired.

"Sure. Shoot." Taria said with some excitement. She had finally gotten the young lady to start engaging.

"What's Siobhan's story?" she asked.

Taria chuckled and smiled. "Siobhan is a bit of a hothead sometimes and can definitely be a handful. But she cares. Genuinely cares. About me, about Eilidh. Give her some time and you'll see what I see... her heart of gold. She means well and is just protective, but I agree sometimes it comes out in a less than positive way. But as far as her story goes, its hers to tell."

The two had made their way through the camp, meeting new people along the way. Ashira seeing them all through new eyes. On the way back, they ran into Markhiz again as he was finishing the pipework on a rainwater reclamation system he had devised. The intent was to capture the water from the rainstorms and use it to support some of the needs of the camp. It wouldn't be potable by any means, but non-potable water supplies still had their uses. Ashira smiled at the Humboldt and the two had a cursory discussion about water pressure relative to the pipe size used and height of the storage tanks. It was amazing to some of the residents at how intelligent the Tesska was to be so young. Taria took notice as well. When they arrived back to Taria's place, Eilidh met them at the door.

"Ashira, on behalf of the citizens of Skyshade Haven" the little blue Multorn said aloud, "I present you with... a ..."she paused as she searched for the proper words to speak. "... a bed" Siobhan said sardonically. The young Multorn motioned regally with her arms and hands through the small doorway into the abode. "I *WAS* gonna say something fancy, Siobhan." Eilidh said with a feisty head bob.

The Kiamnik's head tendrils waggled in surprise at the remark. "What's with you wantin' to be all posh all the bleedin' time, eh?"

Ashira entered the dwelling with warmth swelling within her heart. "Thank you," she said while making a genuine nod to each person. Siobhan turned away and gave no notice to the gesture.

"It's yours," Taria said. "It's made to be portable in case you need to take it with you. Beats sleeping on the cold and scraggly stonecrete."

"Mine?" Ashira asked in mild disbelief. Possession was forbidden within the Establishment, just like affections. But then again, she was no longer a Kiensei. Right? In retrospect, her current situation was almost just like her dorm in the Monastery. She had a bed. She blinked in disbelief. But this was *her* bed. A possession. As long as Taria would allow it at least. This was a start.

"Yeah, yours. Like I said before, we share."

In the midst of the much-needed cheerful moment, a chill needled Ashira through the Ki. In the corner sat Siobhan with a petulant, piercing stare aimed right at her.

Chapter 15

Time had passed and Ashira had found a way to integrate herself with a loosely knitted work team whose efforts to bring the most basic of necessities to the camp had been floundering. The rushing of disparate thoughts and reservations had subsided. Her spirit was calming more as each day passed. She had made friends with Markhiz, Tumps, a human male named Belors Hirudin, a Tallin woman named Shi'ma and a few others who shared the same goal and formed the work team leads. With her help and aptitude for tinkering, thanks to Kina's teaching, they had successfully completed Markhiz's reclaimed water supply project. They had also successfully tapped into the potable water supply pipe prior to the monitored meter, which provided a small but steady supply of fresh water without alarming the systems from the Korosento Public Works. Water drainage was already supplied via the storm drains present near the perimeter of the camp. A small boon, but a welcomed one.

When questioned by Ashira how Markhiz came by the various fittings, valves and other pieces, the Humboldt explained how some of the other residents formed scavenging teams. It was a way for everyone, even the least skilled to contribute to the success of the camp. Some would scavenge topside for food and other things that the wealthier residents would discard. Or they would go to community food pantries when they became available, but those were harder to come by. Others went to the shallower levels, market service corridors, and religious groups of all species could be found there. But a very few were brave enough to trek deeper into the lower levels to level two. The regional junkyard, as he put it.

Markhiz was squatted and stooped over with a wrench, tightening a connection on a leaky pipe. "A dangerous plaze to go to. Ze rats and vermin might make meal of you," he pointed a long finger at Ashira. "Some peoples come back sayink they are ghosts down zere. They hearink whisperings and spooky-like things," he wiggled his fingers. "But... all ze good stuffs iz down there."

"Who goes down there?" she asked.

He stopped his work and lifted his horned head slightly. Raising an eyebrow, "Siobhan" he said quietly then went back to his work. "She lead ze team."

All things being equal, she had quickly made friends... except with Siobhan. That one would not seem to capitulate to kindness or any attempt she had made. Ashira sensed she was intelligent, highly intelligent, and also very guarded against her attempts of friendly connection at every turn. Something was missing and she could not figure it out. Siobhan had an amazing aptitude for electricity and power systems Ashira had learned. More so than any other resident. Taria had been right though, the Kiamnik was kind-hearted, especially towards Eilidh, Taria and some of the other younger residents. Even though things were improving in the camp, food was still limited. There were times when they had little to nothing to eat, but Siobhan always made sure Eilidh had something, even if it meant she would go without. It was easy to tell that she did care, deep down. Siobhan would work with Eilidh on studies, play games with her, tell her stories, and draw together with discarded bits of color sticks. She treated the little Multorn as if she were her own daughter. There were times when Eilidh would have night terrors and Taria's attempts at calming her back to sleep would fail, but not Siobhan's. No matter how tired she was, she would coax her own sore and stiff frame out of bed to go curl up beside Eilidh on her little makeshift palette and sing to her what sounded like traditional Kiamnik folk songs. And wow, she could sing alright. She had a voice like spinnersilk.

It was those tender, fleeting moments that brought tiny amounts of justification to the horrors of war for Ashira, something she still struggled with.

As Markhiz continued working, she looked around the camp at the many faces and wondered what they may be toiling with internally. Everyone she had met here so far had a story, a struggle, a fire that led them like a beacon, just to keep them going.

What was her fire? Ashira's mind began wandering back to the war and to the many missions she had endured with Kina. Visions of war-torn civilians flashed in her mind and overlayed themselves with the reality of the present. The people in the camp looked eerily like her memories. The dirty faces, the appearances of dejection. But they were safe for the moment from the wider evils within the world. She had sacrificed pieces of herself for them, and they didn't even know it.

The Tsugints were different. She had hypothesized that this was on purpose. The faceless helmets and congruent armor hid the dirt, physical and emotional, from outside view. The Kiensei, not so much. On really dry continents, like Sharharah and parts of Mikoth, it was really hard to stay clean. The Tsugints had a special under suit that allowed flexibility, breathability, yet maintained water and dust resistance. How good it always felt to get clean after a mission she thought. Like washing away the stains of battle, a shower was a small comfort. If only they could do that to one's memories, she thought. A moment of ideation leapt forward in her mind. She thought about Markhiz's system for a moment and corralled her wandering mind. "Hey Markhiz. When was the last time you had a shower?" He raised his face at her with a look of embarrassment and surprise. He said not a word, but turned his head slowly left and right, taking a sniff at each direction.

"Uh." He thought for a moment. "L-last rainstorm. Wh-why? I smelly?" he said sheepishly.

"No. Not yet anyways" she said jokingly. "I was thinking about using your system to make some showers. Just because we're out here doesn't mean we can't get clean. Right?" Ashira said.

She had used outdoor showers before, on the battlefield when things got really messy. They were crude and weren't a luxury by any means; the water was usually cold or barely warmed by the sun, but they worked efficiently to knock the dust and dirt off.

"Um. Y-yeah, I see." He said in his deep voice, nodding his head in agreement. He finished his task and stood up. "Ve talks to Shi'ma. She goink with team tomorrow to get empty carbon crates and plasticene they find. Ve use dat. But," he chuckled, "your idea, your projekt" he said, waving one of his large hands with dismissal.

It took two days of tinkering and managing the obstinate nature of plasticene, but Ashira, along with Shi'ma, had fashioned some basic but functional stalls using the recovered crates. Plasticene panels were fashioned to serve as doors. Markhiz had stored away a few broken fire suppression nozzles and some spring-loaded valves. Turns out they made surprisingly good shower heads. Taria had some bits of rope and Ashira fashioned some handles from leftover pipe. She attached them to the valves and gave them a tug to test it. Success! Many of the residents passing through the area began noticing what she was up to. The smiles she spotted from the community members reassured her that this was definitely a good thing.

"Wow!" came Taria's voice from behind her. "Nice idea there, where'd you learn that from?"

"Aye, where'd ye be learnin' that from, then?" came the probing voice of Siobhan from her stance beside Taria. "Go on, spill it. We're dyin' ta know." She said in a goading manner.

Ashira decided not to answer the belligerent Kiamnik. Instead, she decided to skirt it altogether by redirecting. "Now all we need is a little soap," she said to no one in particular while marveling at her work. She was feeling accomplished and pleased with her creation. She continued to feel a sense of aggression towards herself, but she also felt something more overarching from Siobhan whenever she was around. It was almost as if Siobhan emanated a feeling of hurt more than anger. She still couldn't put a finger on it but her instincts as a trained peacemaker motivated her to continue to look for ways to quiet the Kiamnik's tumultuous spirit. But would she welcome it?

Ashira's contributions continued to improve the camps quality of life as time continued on. Her strong and gentle influence led the camp to gaining better basic amenities such as access to clean water, sanitation, and even protective measures against raiders from the lower levels that some of the residents had spoken about and openly feared. Whether she knew it, approved of it, or not... she was living out the holistic creed of what a Kiensei should be—a servant of the people and a keeper of the peace. Even Siobhan had begrudgingly agreed to allowing her to help in tying into one of the electrical feeds to the high rises... a dangerous task, make no mistake. At the end of the day, the camp had what it needed to sustain its humble ragtag group of citizens. Except food. That continued to be a troublesome aspect. One that wasn't easily solved.

The camp knew that growing its own food was a probable solution, but one that would take time to nurture to fruition. Seeds were easy to come by in the dumpsters and discarded foods of restaurants and the high rises themselves. Ganjan fruit, Rummen melons, ungerminated Chand, and even Hoba rice. Those were easy to find... fertile soil was not. The limited sunlight of the location was also an issue. It was detestable by many standards, but the vermin of the area made for easy and accessible sources of protein. But this was about survival, not opulence. Ashira had passingly mentioned this survival tactic that some of the Tsugints used, when necessary, albeit without the inflection of her former alliance. The looks in return varied amongst the camp citizens from contemplation to outright disgust.

She remembered the first time she smelled the enticing scent of grilled Pancha meat wafting from a makeshift grill, the sizzle of dripping fat on hot surfaces, the wafting of smoky scents it produced, the juiciness of that first bite regardless of where it came from. Food was one of the universal meeting grounds for any civilization. This she already knew. But the act of a community coming together to feast on the least of acceptable means that society had ordained became the bedrock foundation of her understandings of what people generally needed—they needed connections. They needed each other. She saw her contributions just as that, the enabler of interconnecting the people there and in that, she found peace. She found herself. She found purpose.

She realized that, in its hubris, the Kiensei Establishment had disconnected itself from the very people that brought meaning to their existence. Instead of peace, harmony, and on reliance of one another, the people of the world had embraced indifference, bigotry, and a focus on the narrow-minded self over the beauty of diversity.

But there was still Kina.

His humble beginnings that sparked a genuine love for those whom he served was something she had come to miss. She understood that beneath that rough exterior existed a furnace of love for those who were considered lesser, the downtrodden, the outcasts. In their time together, they had formed a special familial bond that all the Kiensei had sworn to disavow. Though the members of the Establishment regarded themselves as 'brothers' and 'sisters' in what had become a superficial moniker, Kina had genuinely felt what it was like to have a family and also what it felt like to lose it. Something many in the Establishment were not fortunate to have experienced. His need to belong, to love and be loved, to serve, and to support was only partially filled by his duties as a Kiensei. If he left the Establishment too, she would be there for him, as he had been there for her. She vowed this to herself. She knew that his loyalty wouldn't allow him, though. His deep well of love, unfathomable as it was, for those he cared for and protected stood in the way of what she knew was in his heart. So, it was up to her to carry that legacy forward... outside of the Establishment. She didn't need the Establishment to tell her *who* she was. She didn't need the Establishment to tell her *what* she was. But she still missed those connections. The Kiensei were still just... people too. But they were on a path she could not follow.

Ashira was deep asleep one evening on her makeshift bed. Of the various lumps, bumps, and nuances, she had worked out a way to sleep as comfortable as she could. She was dreaming again. Premonitions permeated her dormant, but churning mind. Rest did not come easily to her anymore, not since leaving. Many times, when she closed her eyes, her mind was filled with dreams and visions of things beyond her understanding. Sometimes she dreamed of warzones, of death, of explosions, of screams. She couldn't help it. Usually, she would seek the guidance of a Sesni or Demio, like Harichi, to help her understand her dreams.

Many times, she had experienced this phenomenon. More so after the enigmatic encounter on Rigort. Tonight, it was a dark temple. Quiet dripping water echoing in a massive cavern. Lightning suddenly flashing all around. A dark figure attacking her. She fights back, but strangely, the figure does not tire like a machine filled with rage. It relentlessly pursues her. Brazen and crashing blows assault her relentlessly. *"Surrender"* a familiar voice reverberated quietly. *"Save him. Your destiny. Rise against the darkness. Help balance."* A flashing blade bulleted toward her. Suddenly, she snapped awake. Something was on her chest!

A shadow crept through the darkness of an alleyway. Silently moving between corners, dumpsters, and detritus within. It moved with calculation, with purpose, with malice through the dark. The figure came to an opening and peered out of the shadows around the corner. There was the camp that the informant had mentioned. It was protected though, with walls and a sentried entrance. Not something that had been mentioned. A Braundt, and a Tallin kept watch in the dimly lit opening of some sort of perimeter around the camp. The job had to get done, no matter how, no matter what. Seeing an opening, the figure darted swiftly for a darkened area just outside the perimeter wall. There it was. A chink in the armor. Enough hand holds to scale this pitiful defense. Looking around to scan the possibility of discovery, the figure began to climb, slowly, so as not to cause a sound of clinking metal in the makeshift fence. Landing without sound on the other side, the figure turned its head, looking at every corner, every walkway, every door. There it was. The hovel of the child that they were after. All was quiet for now, and they intended to keep it that way.

The shadow crept slowly, intently towards the target area. The lack of lights and other forms of defense and deterrence certainly helped them along. It was late in the evening, or early in the morning, depending on one's view. Because of the dilapidation of the camp and lack of resources, it was easy to infiltrate and burglarize. The two guards could be heard in the distance, casually chatting about the previous day and other things. The whisper of pipes, the hum of the city's industry, all normal for this area.

Making its way towards the abode, the shadow prepared itself to infiltrate and complete its task. The rudimentary locking mechanism on the makeshift door was no challenge. Producing a lockpick kit from its utility belt, the shadow began its silent assault. The child within would be theirs as instructed. A quick spray of silicon lubricant on the guiding tracks and the locking mechanism... to quelch any alarming squeaks or noisy clacks... and the burglar set to work. Only a few moments passed when the subtle click of cotter pins falling into place and the stator giving way all signaled a successful attempt. Slowly and steadily the closure turned, and the door slid open slowly to expose the dimly bioluminescent interior. It was warmer inside than out as the unseen flow of warm air rolled out the doorway and touched its face.

One to the left, asleep on a palette. Two in the right rear, on a makeshift mattress. A flutter of... a bird? No, couldn't be. It looked up into the rafters, to the corners, and around the space and saw nothing. The shadow crept forward on all fours, silently making its way towards the rear left corner of the shack to where it assumed the child slept. A ragged curtain wall and a short escape route was all that separated them from a payday the likes they had not seen in a while. The snorts, huffs and sounds of deep sleep filled the dimly lit shack. Peeling back the curtain revealed the innocent little Multorn, asleep in her puffy bed, unawares of the danger a mere few feet away. The shadow produced a tranquilizer module, a necessary implement to keep the little one quiet for exfil. Inching closer and closer, the shadow brought the module mere centimeters from the little one's neck... one last check on the sleeping... good. In one swift motion, a hand was placed over the sleeping child's mouth. The button was pressed, and with a miniscule hiss, the prey was subdued and plunged into a sleep so deep that it would take many hours to awake from. Quietly, she was bundled tight and slung about the back of the stealthy intruder. The sounds no more than as if the child had tossed in her bed. Her arms and legs tucked carefully so as not to create an accidental disturbance. Without a sound, the shadow began creeping slowly back towards the door.

Unexpectedly and without warning, one of the inhabitants stirred. The creature froze in place, their attention laser focused. It was the one by the door. A short blade was produced from a hidden sheath, and it gleamed a cold blue hue in the minimal bioluminescent lighting. The shadow quickly surmised that a simple jump, a deliberate thrust, and the stirred would be quickly silenced. The bundle on its back would make no interference to its agility. The door was nearby, so the escape would be quick.

Ashira swatted at the thing on her chest with wild abandon and hit nothing. She felt it jump as she swung and then again as it promptly returned to its unwelcomed perch on her chest after her arms had stopped flailing. It was a bird. An owl? Her eyes focused quickly. She'd seen these creatures before in more than one location. Its eyes, a green so pure, gazed back at her. Ashira blinked in shock. This... creature... was speaking to her? Through the Ki? She had connected with animals before, this was different. The creature was... connecting with *her*.

"Rise swiftly," she heard its words in her mind. *"Life in danger. Innocent in danger. Need you. Act!"* she felt its thoughts resounding in her mind like a strong wind roaring through trees. In one swift moment, the owl leapt into the air. Her senses sparked to life as the Ki called to her. Something was there! Something was coming at her!

As the owl moved from her view, a shadow leapt from the floor straight at her, the sheen of a blade visible in its hand. The being was upon her. Its weight immobilizing her legs. Her hands caught its wrists... its hands, one reaching for her throat to strangle it, the other lunging a blade for the same to sever it. Ashira could feel the warm stench of its breath on her face as it tried to push its hands forward. It was strong. Snapping her head forward, she headbutted the creature in the face, sharply forcing it to recoil in a pained grunt. Her left leg freed suddenly, she pulled her knee to her chest and kicked with all her might into the abdomen of her attacker. The shadow went flying and crashed to the floor in a loud racket as cobbled together chairs and bric-a-brac clattered about the space, waking the other inhabitants. Both springing to their feet expertly, the Tesska beside the palette and the shadow on the floor stood at the ready, facing each other. Eilidh's head bobbing unconsciously on its back quickly revealed the intruder's intention.

"Who are you!?" Ashira barked loudly. "What are you doing here? Let her go!" Ashira prepared herself for battle, glaring with white-hot heat at the foe before her.

The shadow chuckled ominously as it coughed to regain its breath. Its darkened form poised for attack with the blade gleaming at the ready.

Taria and Siobhan sat straight up, hurriedly shedding sleep from their bodies and faces. Taria gasped at what she saw, her daughter on the back of... something... and Ashira standing, battle ready, facing the intruder.

Siobhan cried out. "Oi! What in the blazes are ye doin' here!? Get the radgy scatdung outta here before I kill ye!" She leapt from the bed and rushed towards the intruder. In quick reaction, the shadow thrust the blade contained in its hand over its shoulder to within millimeters of the throat of the unconscious Eilidh. It stared Siobhan in the face with piercing silvery eyes.

"Stay back." It called in a wet, slurred voice. "Or the whelp will die."

"No!" Taria shouted in alarm. "You monster! Why would you do such a thing! Take me if it's of any consolation, just don't hurt my daughter! Please!" She scrambled forward, fighting through restrictive bed dressings in an effort to reach her child, but was grabbed by Siobhan.

"No, love! There's no reason in it." She spoke with authority, grabbing Taria's frantically flying arms and hands.

The dark figure stood still, unrattled by the commotion from the two on the bed. Its head swiveled steadily back and forth between the three occupants. It took one step towards the door. Ashira mirrored it, taking a step as well. Her muscles tense, her mind sharp, like a spring compressed and ready to release.

It took another step, she took another.

"Let her go" Ashira said sharply. Her skin becoming warm with the blood flowing intensely through her body as her heart pounded in her chest. She was ready to fight and there was no way this thing was getting away.

"You don't understand Tesska. I'm in charge here. She's coming with me, or we both die," the slithery voice said. "You don't seem to understand that either way, you lose," it said with a rotting, toothed grin.

"No. *You* don't understand. I said let her go or you're the only one who's gonna lose something," Ashira snarled as her eyes narrowed in razor focus. She opened herself up fully to the Ki and her body surged with the power it afforded her. She felt the rushing tide flow through her like a flood barreling down a mountain side. Not in anger, but in controlled defense of an innocent. She rocketed her left hand out and, using the Ki, grabbed the blade. She pulled on it earnestly as if it were chained to a boulder being dropped from the sky and the creature's grip didn't stand a chance. The blade flew across the room to Ashira's hand, but as soon as she caught it, the room erupted in smoke. The creature had employed a smoke bomb to try and mask its escape, but Ashira was ready for it. She closed her eyes and held her breath to prevent the chemicals from affecting her. In an instant, she lunged at the doorway, feeling the creature's movement through the Ki, but grasped only air. It had barely made it past her and was out the door. Ashira rolled elegantly, dropping the blade, and launched herself through the doorway into the cool night air. She opened her eyes and exhaled... there it was, heading for the wall on the south side.

Menial lighting had already started to glow within abodes and doorways began to open as the commotion had roused many of the other residents. The creature expertly ran through the thoroughfares and between the narrowly spaces hovels, jumping obstacles and dodging stabilizing lines. Ashira gave chase. The Ki imbuing her with supernatural speed and agility as her body drank it with natural ease. She couldn't see the creature clearly, but she could feel it, and she was hot on its trail. She had to get to Eilidh. The creature was agile and possessed great strength, even with a child strapped to its back. It made every effort to knock over boxes, toss obstacles, and otherwise hamper Ashira's chase. But she was ready for it. She ducked and dodged, leapt and slid around everything the creature tried to put in her way. That little girl didn't deserve this, and she was sure she wouldn't let it happen.

Siobhan and Taria fell out of the smoky doorway, coughing and gasping for breath. Siobhan fell to her knees and in catching herself, her hand fell upon something... metallic. A knife. She closed her fingers around it and fought through stinging tears, her eyes burning from the smoke. Gritting her teeth in anger while trying to clear her lungs, she set off at a staggered, coughing run to try and catch up to Ashira and the intruder. Taria stood up, bracing herself against the doorway, coughing as well. Taking a ragged, deep breath of clean air, she cried out hoarsely "Help! Help us! An intruder has taken my daughter!"

Residents looked about in startled confusion, not knowing where to look or what exactly to do. Many of them caught a glimpse of a blur passing by as Ashira chased the shadowy creature through the camp. In an effort to garner support, Ashira cried aloud "he's heading for the south wall!" Tumps, one of the main guards that night, was within earshot and began running in that direction on the outside of the wall. Siobhan also within earshot, also headed that way just behind the Braundt.

The creature was agile and lithe. Even so, Ashira was able to match its moves equally. It made it to the south wall and in a feat of amazement, it leapt onto the side of a shelter, grasped an unseen handhold, then launched itself towards the top of the wall. "No." Ashira said to herself. Her emotions rose as she felt the swell of the Ki within her. She stopped and reached outward with both arms lasering in on the creature. She caught it mid-air as it reached the pinnacle of the wall. She squeezed it, held it tight, keeping its arms, and legs immobile. She squeezed so hard that the creature yelped in pain. She didn't care at this moment. Taking a child, let alone threatening to harm it was grievous to her.

"*No.*" a familiar voice sang to her from within. "*Not in anger.*" It wasn't darkness of intent she reconciled to herself. It was justice. She had watched Kina do it before, pushing that boundary, skirting that line between revenge and justice. She knew what she was doing. This evil thing needed to feel the sting of justice and she was the only one able to mete it out. "*Peace.*" the voice continued. "*Let go... anger. Let go,*" it said. Ashira blinked, stupefied by what she heard as it clashed with what she felt.

Across the wall, she heard Tumps call out in confusion. His gravelly voice rang out. "Is it stuck or something? I don't see any wires or a levapack."

Siobhan also called out over the wall as if she knew what was happening. "Let it go! We're here, we've got 'im!"

Ashira released her grip through the Ki and the creature fell into the waiting, burly arms of Tumps. But the fight was still within it. A wailing groan split the air. The creature had produced a second, previously hidden blade and stabbed the Braundt in one of his three eyes as he continued to hold the writhing intruder. Siobhan, quick to assist, grabbed the hand that held the blade. She smashed its arm hard across her knee and with a crunch of splintering bone, the arm broke, and the blade was captured. The creature screamed in pain and flailed like a wild animal, still in the strong grasp of the Braundt. A swift jerk of its knobby head backwards smashed into Tumps' face forcing him to release his grip. A swift kick to Siobhan's midriff knocked the wind out of her briefly as she dropped to one knee. Eilidh's head, bobbed limply as the three jostled about.

Just then, Ashira launched herself across the wall in a graceful leap to join the fight. In one quick motion, she landed in front of it, a look of burning determination splayed upon her face. Its eyes went wide in surprise just before a fist landed on one of them, then a right cross to its jaw, followed by a left-hand body shot and finally with a swift right roundhouse kick to its head... all with careful accuracy to not harm the bundled child on its back. Ashira felt a familiar *thunk* as her foot connected. Tumps, his third eye bleeding profusely, lunged at the creature as it slumped to the ground, almost as dead weight, and swallowed it in his large arms. Siobhan set to work quickly as she fought to regain her breath. She used the captured blade to begin cutting away the wrappings that held Eilidh on the creature's back. The little Multorn was out cold, battered and bruised from the ordeal, but she was alive.

Multitudes of residents came pouring out of the camp towards the conflict to help. Especially Taria. Like a charging bull, she bounded over to Siobhan and grabbed the limp form of her child and held her tight, sobbing uncontrollably. Markhiz came to aid Tumps in securing the creature and taking control of it while Tumps retreated, his eye drooping pitifully with blood. Other citizens lent a hand as well, supplying light, a bit of rope, extra hands. Lanterns and crudely constructed lights revealed the creature to be a Ghasto male with dark, almost black skin. He was still alive and sucked air forcefully in pain and exhaustion. Ghasto were known to be hired assassins in the Realm given their physiology. Most of the species were quite peaceful and ambivalent, but some took to lives of crime. Siobhan took control immediately.

"Bind 'im tight!" she shouted. "Let's get a medkit here for Tumps, and someone tend to his eye! Taria, take her back to the house," she pointed to Eilidh, a small calmness to her voice. "Someone, go with them and help look after Eilidh's wounds." The Kiamnik rattled off orders expeditiously, her tendrils flicking angrily in time with the lantern light. As the Ghasto was bound, she stood upward and over him. She was furious and it was clear her anger was roiling. She trembled almost uncontrollably as her emotions took over control of her body.

"Yer foul deed won't go unpunished, ye bastard!" she shouted at the intruder as she punched him hard in the face. "Ye'll pay for the pain ye've caused!" She punched him again; her fist making a wet, meaty smack as she connected. Her complexion deepened to a darker shade of red, her tendrils twitched like striking serpents. Ashira stepped in between her and the prisoner, raising her hands to stop her. "No Siobhan. No!" she said, trying to calm the agitated woman. "He's done," she said, trying to placate the irate woman.

People from within the camp had seen some of what had transpired. The unnatural speed, the floating intruder, the amazing feats of agility. They were nervously gathering around the collection of combatants, whispering amongst themselves. Siobhan stared at Ashira, breathing heavily with a look that would burn a hole through a steel plate. Ashira sensed something was wrong. The anger emanating from the Kiamnik felt through the Ki like she was standing under the blazing sun. "I've got a bad feeling about this," she thought to herself.

In the flickering light of lanterns and headlamps, Siobhan was livid, and she didn't care who was on the receiving end of it right now. Her hatred blinded her. Hate for this Ghasto. Hate for this living situation. Hate for Eilidh's sake. And hate for... *her*. Her breathing was hard and heaving, like a bellow encouraging a forge. Like hot molten steel pouring from a crucible, Siobhan let her feelings flow out and envelop the Tesska in front of her.

"And just who are *ye* to be orderin' *me* 'round here, Huh!? *Commander Mori*!?" she yelled at the top of her voice with spittle flying.

Chapter 16

The whispers and murmurs of the crowd increased. The crimson Kiamnik stood face to face with Ashira, her breathing heavy as her emotions pulsated throughout her body.

Ashira had to think quick. "What's your deal Siobhan? I get the frustration at this guy" she said cooly, pointing at the new captive. Ashira tried to remain calm, but steadfast concern painted her face. Siobhan evidently knew who she was. She called her 'commander.' Many of the Tsugints knew that, but she obviously wasn't one of them. Did she work at the Monastery? She wasn't a Kiensei; she wasn't even Ki adept. She bent down to check the jury-rigged restraints on the captive.

"This piece of scatdung near snatched me child!" she barked loudly, pointing at the bludgeoned and bound Ghasto sitting on the ground. "He earned his demise. Period." Taria stopped in her tracks as she heard Siobhan's voice ring out. With Eilidh in her arms, she turned sideways to listen to the ruckus. Her face forlorn as Siobhan's weakness spilled out.

"Are you saying we *kill* him?" Ashira retorted sternly yet calmly. "We are *NOT* the judge, jury, and executioner here. We need to let the authorities handle it," Ashira postulated. She rose to her feet and stood offset from Siobhan and the Ghasto.

"Oh ya. That'd be just juicy as a fruit now, wouldn't it? Bring the coppers here so they can get us booted?" she snickered at the idea. "Then what? Sure as they come an' take 'em they'll come back an' clear us out now. Right? You dinna think of that one did ye?" she nodded mockingly at Ashira.

"Killing him is not the answer Siobhan," she said resolute, ignoring the attempts to verbally attack her.

"What'd ye know about it? Huh? Ye surely knows what killin' be all about." She darted her face towards the Tesska. "What would ye do to defend what's yers? What would it take to tarnish that gleamin' Kiensei halo ye're sportin' huh?" the Kiamnik said heatedly, waving a hand at her mockingly.

Ashira was stricken. The word 'Kiensei' hadn't even been toyed with in any conversation, implied or otherwise, with the brusque Kiamnik or any other resident. It was obvious now that she had withheld that tidbit of knowledge about Ashira when she first arrived at the camp, but now the secret was out. It wasn't too farfetched to think that maybe she had seen a Holonews broadcast or read some plain diginews rag at a news stand. Maybe she *did* work at the Monastery? Or maybe she was part of the military?

People within the camp began to gather closer at the sound of the verbal conflict brewing. It was a rule, after all, that the people do not fight with one another and many of the residents became uncomfortable at the sudden turn of events. Some came closer to eavesdrop, some appeared ready to jump in at any moment to diffuse the brewing situation.

"Siobhan, I don't know what I've done to you or what you think you know, but I don't see where it has anything to do with the current situation," Ashira said calmly, trying to deescalate.

The Kiamnik bristled against her. "Oh... of course not." She said with hatred oozing from her voice. "Why would a *KIENSEI* give a bleedin' thought to *ME and what I need*," she shouted "even if I cared more 'bout them and the cause they so... *HONORABLY*... support? Huh!?"

Whispers began arising amongst the gathering crowds. Whispers of 'Kiensei,' of 'Spy,' and 'Warmonger' amongst other terms rose up into the night sky like smoke from the emotional bonfire in front of them. Ashira at once felt uncomfortable in this situation as it continued to escalate. She looked around at the crowds. The looks. The stares. Some faces were rife with anger, others with apprehension, some with cold fear. She could sense all of the above. There were myriads of intentions flowing from the crowd. On running, intentions on... ousting her. The captive Ghasto began to chuckle through a blood-stained grin. Ashira needed a moment to think. Arguing with Siobhan was like beating one's head against a wall. What would Kina do? Nope, more like *'What would Teka do'* because she knew in that instance what Kina would have already done, and it wouldn't have been pretty.

A voice from the crowd sounded aloud. "You're a Kiensei? If you're so high and mighty, then *you* think of something."

Ashira knew there was no way around it. She had exposed herself defending Eilidh, and that was worth it to her. She had saved an innocent life, the calling of a Kiensei, even if she was no longer one. The calling she missed dearly. She closed her eyes briefly as she inhaled a deep breath to calm herself, the cool night air flowing into her nostrils.

"This isn't about me right now, this is about him," she said, pointing a finger at the captive. She turned her sight to the captive on the ground. "Who are you? And what did you want with the child?" she asked the Ghasto. It disturbed her that a young child was targeted. No response. She squatted down to come face to face with him. His silvery eyes flashed in the glow of the lanterns.

"Tell us," she said tenderly, trying to sound emphatic. Again, no response. Those silvery eyes just stared back at her. In aggravation she raised her voice and leaned on his mind through the Ki. "Tell us now!" Nothing but a bloody, toothed grin in response. It became clear that this one wasn't about to talk, and his mind was too strong to force him. Well, the Suramosa and Wykera method didn't work, she thought to herself. "Okay Markhiz..." she sighed "what do we do with this one?" Ashira asked, raising her face to the Humboldt.

"Iz tough call. Ve kill him, ve are guilty. Ve turn him in, ve get exposed. I no know vat to do right now." He said shaking his head in disbelief.

"Do what you will," the captive grumbled wetly. "Like I said, either way, you lose. They know where I was; they know what I was seeking, and they'll come again." His silvery eyes cut a look across the gathered crowd.

The word *'they'* sent a chill up Ashira's spine as she stood back up and stepped a short distance away from the scene. *'They'* could mean anything. A gang. A cartel. A slaver's troop. It was easy for criminal elements to find success in the massive metropolis capital, she knew that. This was the first time, however, that she had been exposed to it so blatantly on the surface as opposed to the lower levels.

Siobhan grinned slyly. "*That* Kiensei" she seethed, pointed an accusing finger at Ashira while addressing the crowd "cannot do what needs to be done here." She slowly began circling Markhiz and the captive. "So let *me* finish it for the good of all of us."

"I *was* a Kiensei. But not anymore," Ashira said plainly, staring into Siobhan's face. She made sure to speak loud enough for the others to hear her defense. "I took issue with some of the things the Kiensei do and with how they operate in certain manners... and I left, willingly."

Whispers in the crowd sang like tree frogs in the night. "They can do that?" was one comment that could be distinctly heard.

Ashira's senses felt the heat of anger, the intention of malice and the darkness flow around Siobhan. She watched as the Kiamnik faced the bound captive then quickly produced both blades that formerly belonged to him, spun them smartly in her fingers and before Ashira could react, plunged them into each side of the captive's neck. She uttered some unfamiliar curse in the Kiamnik language to his face, touching nose to nose as she did. The Ghasto gurgled as his last exhale bubbled as a bloody springhead from his contorted mouth—and was forever silenced. Markhiz looked in shock as he let the captive go and it slumped forward. Gasps erupted from the crowd.

"Siobhan!" came the sapient call from Taria from behind the gathered crowd. "That's enough! Let these people handle that filth. You come with me; we need to talk."

The Kiamnik stood, then spat on the ground at the dead intruder. She cut a burning stare at Ashira as she slowly acquiesced to Taria's request. This was not over by any means. The gathered crowd parted as she left the scene like a ship gliding through water, then folded in again once she had passed by.

"*Now what?*" was the burning question in many of the resident's minds. Some of them left the scene, wishing to recuse themselves, some to get away from the now exposed Kiensei. It was clear that the intruder was guilty of kidnapping and assaulting a child. It was also clear that one of their own was now guilty of murder. In the realm of street justice, the debt was settled. In the realm of political justice, they were in trouble. Ashira explained to those that remained, Markhiz being one, that had they left him alive they would have had options at the very least.

Now they had nothing but problems.

A pair of blue-scaled Carpens came forth. Brothers. They were part of the team that traveled far below with Siobhan. They had done time in prison many years ago for fraud but had paid their debt to society. Unfortunately, they fell victim to bigotry, which is how they ended up at the camp. Their red and stalky eyes panned over the dead body. They turned and whispered something to themselves, which Ashira could barely make out. It sounded like they had an idea. Markhiz stepped up beside her.

"You really Kiensei?" he asked quietly in surprise as they watched the two brothers continue to whisper and gesture to themselves.

"I was. But not anymore. I don't like having to repeat myself so much," She spoke while crossing her arms.

"You scarink some peoples here methinks," he said quietly.

"Yeah, well I was scared for Eilidh," she protested. "That's why I did what I did. I certainly didn't mean to scare anyone, but I had to do what I had to do... for Eilidh."

"Siobhan, she vaz scared too, you know," said Markhiz. "She have anger problems. That's vy she here. Seeink you all magicky beatings up zis guy," he gestured to the body, "maybe she scared of you too?" Ashira wanted to argue the point of Siobhan's fit of rage being scarier than her own less lethal tactics but decided against it for now.

"Are you scared of me?" she questioned pensively.

The Humboldt waited a moment before he responded, which didn't help Ashira's self-esteem at that moment.

"Mmm. No. You havink a good heart. You vant to help. Most peoples here, know zis. Zis unfortunate event though," he waved his upturned palms towards the fallen foe, "not your fault. You go. Make peace. I takink care of zis. I thinkink I know vat ze brothers vant to do."

Ashira turned her head and looked up at Markhiz. She was used to being a leader, especially during the hardest of decisions, like when she almost lost her entire squadron above Jadonz, or when she was almost overrun by the enemy on Filkia... all due to her own stubborn will to win. She was used to taking charge and leading by example. It dawned on her that it might no longer be necessary in every situation. Markhiz stepped forward and began speaking to the people. He began by openly defending her actions, then explaining that Siobhan had made a mistake, but ultimately that the real problem was what to do about the dead Ghasto. She turned and walked back to the camp, listening to the conversations behind her. As the last words became intelligible to her expanded sense of hearing, she barely heard the words 'deep below.' This situation wasn't right, and it pained her to realize that she had to accept it. Whether she liked it or not, she was committed to helping these people. But that didn't mean she had to be involved in every little thing that went on.

Ashira saw both Taria and Siobhan sitting outside in conversation when she walked up to what she considered 'home' for the present. It might not be for much longer, she wagered. Taria noticed her approach first and made a small head gesture to Siobhan that appeared to alert her to Ashira's presence. Siobhan made no effort to acknowledge her... not even so much as her usual pointed glare. Her face was hidden mostly in a shadow.

"Well. Sporty evening, isn't it?" Taria said sarcastically as Ashira walked up. Her face awash with sadness and frustration.

"Is Eilidh all right? Can I do anything to help her, or you?" Ashira said.

"Not right now I'm afraid," Taria said, exhaling loudly and tossing an empty injection module up to her. "She got banged up a little bit, but nothing's broken. She's still out cold thanks to that. But... she's alive and she's here."

"A sedative," Ashira said, turning and inspecting the empty module in her hands. It was odd to see one of those here as they were usually found in the Realm's Military Medical Centers, either here or abroad. In short, the general public pharmaceutical dispensaries didn't use them.

"Yeah, and not one I've ever seen before," Taria said. "But understanding *now* that *you've* been about a bit..." she trailed off while shrugging her shoulders.

Ashira didn't like where this was headed. She could sense that she was about to be asked for something that she probably didn't want to do. "What you're saying is that you'd like to know more about it, and you believe I'm the one to get that information for you?" Ashira said bluntly.

Taria looked up at her. "Sit down for a minute will ya? You're making me nervous," she motioned with her hand.

Ashira did as she was asked, taking Markhiz's comment to heart, and sat down a few paces away from Taria, and a few more from Siobhan who still hadn't made a sound or looked at her. Taria took a deep breath and wet her lips.

"Ashira...," she exhaled "I don't care that you're a Kiensei or was a Kiensei or whatever you are. I didn't ask, and you didn't tell. There are a lot of people here with bags of bones in their clothing storage. The fact is this, you put yourself in danger to save my daughter. You did something where others wouldn't have or even couldn't have. I'm grateful. Thank you." Ashira was relieved to hear the kind words.

"You're... welcome," was all she could muster, her expression softening; her apprehension fading.

"Siobhan here," she nodded her head in the Kiamnik's direction "also did something that others wouldn't have, though a bit more extreme we all can agree. Had we gone to the authorities, our little slice of heaven here would be in danger. But still, we're safe right now because of what was done."

"Aye, we are" Siobhan croaked. She raised her face up into the pale light. It revealed the fact that she had been weeping profusely, her crimson cheeks glistening. Her eyes were puffy, her voice, struggling. "Speakin' o' which, what's becomin' of our departed guest?"

Ashira leaned forward slightly as if to gain Siobhan's gaze with empathy. "I don't know... and to be honest, I don't *want* to know," she said with an eased exhale. "But what I do know is that Markhiz and two Carpen brothers are evidently handling it."

"Hurropin and Rennopin," Siobhan rasped. "The brothers. They'll likely be takin' the slug down to level two. It's a barmy mess down there, it is."

"Aaannnyway...." Taria cut in, shooting a glance towards Siobhan "what I'm concerned about is whether or not that dirtwad was telling the truth about that *they know where I was* foolishness. If there's more coming, I don't know if we can handle it, but I'd rather see the tube train coming before it hits me so I can at least brace for it."

"I'm not a security guard Taria. And I have no desire to be one especially if it ends up like this," Ashira said. "I did what I did to protect Eilidh in that moment, nothing more."

"That's nother what she's a'meanin'," Siobhan spoke, her voice cracking and squeaking. All things being equal, that was the first time the Kiamnik hadn't said a cross word, a loaded phrase or even an aggressive statement. Ashira was slightly surprised.

"Look, let me be straight with you," Taria held up a hand and interjected. "Your connections to the Kiensei and the Realm, that means you know people. Surely there's a way to find out whether what that guy said was true or not. Who knows, he could have been bluffing to try and save his own skin. All I'm asking is that you look into that for us. Would you be willing to do that?"

Ashira thought deep and hard on this for moment. She knew plenty of people, of course. But did she really want to go back and ask for help now? "I need some time to think about it," she said. A sound of movement came from within the shack and all three perked their heads up, looking towards the doorway.

"I'll go check on her," said Taria. "Think on it, but don't take too long if you can." Taria grunted as she rose and went inside leaving the remaining two in an awkward silence.

Siobhan traced a finger in the dust, her knees bent to her chest with her chin resting on them. Ashira rolled her head on her shoulders to stretch her neck. She ventured a glance over at the Kiamnik and was surprised to see her doing the same. She quickly averted her eyes and settled them on a nondescript corner of the dwelling. Siobhan made a grunting noise, as if to clear her throat. Ashira sniffed loudly, as if clearing her sinuses. The thrum of nighttime civilization on Korosento continued in the distance.

Neither of them, stubborn as they both were, wanted to make the first move.

Chapter 17 – Then

"Ka'kwha, miran tal'varin neya" (Hello, welcome traveler and friend), came the call from one of the village sentries. The Tesska man glanced briefly at the hooded woman behind the approaching tribesman. His face contorting into one of suspicion and into one of curiosity. His hands tightening their grip on the simple rifle he held.

Kel-so held his hand up as a show of peace. "Ka'kwha na'tal, miran. Neyo kwenarshi" (Hello friend, I come in peace), he said then switching to the Common speak. "We are here to see the tribe Narkash. Your runner brought word of a child. The Kiensei," he motioned to Sereeah, "have sent one of their own to see it."

The sentry balled his fist and bowed slightly. The word 'Kiensei' could barely be heard in his simple show of respect. "This way, please," he motioned as he welcomed them to the village.

The looks from the villagers evoked that of wonder, of curiosity, and of anxiety from some. It was not often that visitors of this kind came to the village. The hooded figure was not someone many, if any, had ever seen. She was mysterious, she was exotic and beautiful, and many were anxious at her appearance. But the fact that she was escorted by one of their own, seemed to help staunch the flow of suspicion at her arrival. Some watched from their covered porches as she walked by. Some stopped whatever task they were performing to follow her with their eyes as she traversed the dirt roads.

Sereeah could feel the gazes upon her. She could feel the emotions pouring out into the road as she passed. They were in awe of her... and she loved it. Her own nervousness was held at bay by the feeling of theirs. She could do this; she *would* do this. She ran over the plan in her head as she followed behind the two men on their way to... wherever.

Soon, they arrived at the village center. The sentry escorted them into the rectangular building they had seen from afar. It had a rough-cut wooden exterior that was covered with smooth, white adobe and to her surprise, large triangular openings, like windows without glass, along the side. Entering the building, she could see the opulence within that was hidden from an external view. Obviously, this is where business was handled in this tribe. Elaborate carvings were placed on the perimeter. The walls were smooth and appeared to be of clay that had been hand-smoothed and painted with local sources. A large fire pit was inset into the ground at the center of the smooth wooden plank floor. A fire crackled within it. Smoke rose upward and dispersed itself through a gable of sorts set within the roof peak. The ceiling was of an open architecture, rough trusses spanned the entirety of the space with various earthen trinkets of unknown meaning hanging sporadically throughout.

"Wait here," the sentry said quietly and left expeditiously.

She waited until it was just the two of them. "What's happening," she said quietly.

"The sentry is likely summoning the Narkash, the leader and matriarch of this tribe. You must understand, for a child to be selected by the Kiensei Establishment, it is a great honor to the people," Kel-so said quietly. "You need to make sure to act like it."

One by one, the people of the tribe began appearing at the door. Some looking around in wonder, some just making their way in without incident. All knew the gravity of the situation. Some amount of time passed, and the great meeting house filled with all from the village. A low murmur of conversation surrounding the strange new visitor filled the space as many waited on the matriarch to arrive. Impatria was her name.

The sentry approached Impatria's home. He stood in the road just outside and looked up. On the covered porch sat the Narkash herself. An elder female Tesska who had watched over and led the tribe for many, many years. She sat on a simple, carved wooden bench with her hands on her knees. Her wide set features were creviced with wrinkles but still of a striking blue stripe pattern over white. A carved wooden headpiece graced her forehead like a crown. Her wrinkled orange skinned face was still elegantly graced with white patterns upon her forehead that coalesced along the ridge of her nose then diverged like wings across her cheeks, under her eyes. Her natural skin clothing, a true testament to her tribe, bore the traditional markings, dyes, and embellishments of her people's heritage. Around her neck hung a smooth jade-like stone of spiritual importance. About her waist was a leather belt with various beadwork pouches and pockets to hold the various implements of her station. Behind her, hanging on the wall of her home was a large, round wooden totem with long strings of yellow, blue, and gray stones and beads.

The sentry balled a fist at his chest and bowed low towards her. "They are here, Impatria. A Kiensei has come for the child," he said proudly.

She nodded in acknowledgement. Her hands were resting on her knees as she enjoyed the day's pleasant weather. She raised one of them to dismiss the sentry. He, in turn, knew that it meant that the tribe was to assemble in the longhouse, and he would spread the word. Using the same hand, she grasped at the stone hanging around her neck and tilted her head back slightly. She closed her eyes and took a deep breath. The time she had both hoped and feared for had come at last. Never in her life did she believe a Kiensei would be born in her tribe. Her own heart both leapt and sank when she saw the fearsome Bespare entering the village that night, the child riding on its back, smiling in amusement. It was such an honor to be chosen by the ancestors and spirits to receive such a child. But she knew the pain that must be borne by the parents. To wish for, hope for, and be blessed with a child was a wonderful thing. Now, the pain of letting the young one go was theirs to bear.

"I will go to the family and bring them to the gathering," she said. She reached beside her and grasped at her walking stick, a tried-and-true friend in her old age. The tardiness of age hampered her ability to move swiftly, but she could still move freely at least.

Impatria made her way steadily towards the house. The weight of the moment was heavy on the aged woman's shoulders as she ambled along the dirt road. She rapped gently with the head of her walking stick on the wooden door. A light, wooden clacking sound signaled the closure was opened and the door began to swing inward. The purple-skinned face of Bo-ram peeked out from behind the door. He blinked quickly in surprise at seeing the tribe leader at his door. He swiftly opened the door fully.

"Impatria," he said with surprise as he bowed low. "Welcome, please enter." He gestured with one open hand for her to come inside. She smiled and without a word, entered the dwelling.

"Is Asi-ri and Ashira home?" she asked quietly as she made her way inside.

"Asi-ri!" the man called out to his wife. "Impatria is here to speak with us." Impatria winced slightly at the outburst. Why this man always became anxious when she came around, she would never understand.

She made her way slowly into the cozy yet comfortable home. The adobe fireplace was glowing with a warm fire, supplying light and heat to the common room. Her foot kicked an unsuspecting straw toy ball laying in the footpath. She looked down as it skidded across the floor and saw other items that otherwise belied a well-kept home that a young child lived and played here. It didn't bother her; she knew that children needed space to play and that it was challenging for parents to keep a clean home sometimes. She loved children. And she loved the wonderful joys they brought. Children were a gift, and they were a responsibility. They were awe-inspiring and frustrating all in the same breath, but mostly inspiring.

"Forgive us Impatria!" Bo-ram said as he hurriedly gathered the ball and other items from the floor and furniture. She watched as he gathered toys, blankets, clothes and just about every item within reach as quickly as he could in a rushed attempt to present a home worthy of her visit. His arms became so full that items began falling out just a soon as he stooped to add another. She shook her head slightly, her wizened chin swaying gently. She hadn't the least care of how the home looked. She cared more that the two parents had faithfully served the tribe, had given their time and talents to its continued success. She cared more for their well-being knowing what she was about to tell them.

The space was quaint but welcoming. A large armchair made from tree branches and vines sat beside the fire. It had cushions fashioned from animal skins and stuffed with feathers from various game birds. The walls were smooth adobe, much like the rest of the house. Few wall hangings were present; a large woven night-catcher with multicolored beads, a hand-carved wooden animal, and even a scraggly picture or two that the child must have drawn using charcoal from the fireplace, not to mention an obscure handprint or two from the same. Other seating was available of the same type, but it appeared that the little family enjoyed time just sitting on the floor most evenings. A small wooden table was the centerpiece of the room. It looked as though the family shared a meal or two recently just there, along with some of the charcoal artwork.

"Please, sit Impatria," Bo-ram said ushering her to the chair by the fire, the best seat in the house. Asi-ri appeared from what appeared to be the bedroom with a rag in her hand; she had evidently been washing her face in an impromptu manner.

She bowed much like her husband had. "Impatria," she said with an air of respect.

Impatria took a seat and nodded her head in response to the welcome. "Please, sit down Bo-ram and Asi-ri," she said calmly, her hands resting on top of her walking stick. She was doing her best to not alarm or upset them. It would be soon enough that their entire existence would be upset. A few more moments of peace were more than deserved, she thought. "Where is Ashira?" she asked lightly.

The two parents looked at one another in confusion then back at her. "She is at Zamita's learning about healing," Asi-ri said. Zamita was the tribe's elder healer. He possessed the knowledge of natural herbs, poultices and rituals surrounding the traditional medicine for the Tesska people. He, like Impatria, loved children and enjoyed spending his remaining days wowing them with the natural wonders of their world.

Impatria took a deep breath and pursed her lower lip, urging her voice to come out. "A Kiensei has come," she said, looking squarely at the two across from her. "You and Ashira honor us greatly. It is time," she concluded. Sadness filled their faces. It *was* time. But they barely got to know her. Only yesterday she was born, it seemed. Had it been three years already? They knew it would happen eventually, but the inevitability of the fact had never fully sunk in until now. Bo-ram grabbed his wife. She in turn rested her head on his shoulder holding back tears just as much as he was. This was their baby girl, and now, she was to be taken from them, never to be seen again. How they had longed for and begged the spirits and ancestors for a child for so long. How joyful they were when Asi-ri learned of the conception. How anxious they were as her belly continually grew as the baby came ever closer to arriving. The indescribable joy of feeling her move for the first time. Asi-ri used to sing to her unborn child at night when the baby was restless. Then, that night came. The stars were smiling down on them, bearing witness to the miracle about to happen. The air was cool and comfortable as if the world was ready to welcome her. The insects sang songs as an offering to the night. The joy Bo-ram felt when she came into the world. His outburst in the night, waking and stirring the tribe in his excitement.

Now, their daughter would be gone... forever.

But the little girl was a Kiensei. She had a gift that was beyond understanding but well respected by her people. A destiny awaited her that was greater than theirs. Honor and gratitude would be his and Asi-ri's until the end of their days, but that wouldn't fill the hole left behind. He would give it all up, leave it all behind... for her. She was and would always be his 'Little 'Shira.'

Bo-ram summoned what courage and composure he could and hugged his wife a little tighter. "What do we do, Impatria?" he asked quietly. The markings on his face belying the dark sadness he felt.

Impatria realized the pain in their faces was but a shred of what was really going on inside their hearts. The child was like her own. All the tribe's children were like her own and she cared deeply for every single one of them. "We shall go to Zamita's and gather her. From there, the Kiensei waits for us in the longhouse. We will go together, and I will be with you."

Asato and R-3B10 had made their way hastily back to the landing pad. The male Tesska that had greeted them was nowhere to be found. Pity, Asato thought. There were a few follow-up questions he'd hoped to ask but time, it seemed, was of the essence. A connection had formed around a village. And that village was where he was headed towards next. The Ki, he understood, acted on its own will. As a Kiensei, it was his responsibility to listen to the Ki and follow what it willed. He did not believe it mere coincidence that something, or someone, had caused a disturbance when he first arrived. He believed it was the will of the Ki that brought him here.

And he believed that it was the Ki that was calling him to this remote village.

"Rebi, make ready to liftoff as soon as possible," he said, gracefully leaping into the cockpit. The mech squawked an awkward response after signaling the ship to raise it up into the bay. "What do you mean something's wrong?" Asato asked. Rebi cheeped and chirped something that sounded like an attempt at sabotage had been made on the ship. "Can you isolate the problem and repair it?" Asato said with aggravation as he began flipping switches and rotating rocker levers to start the ignition sequence. If anyone had toyed with his ship it had to have been that Tesska man they met on arrival. The man would need to be questioned further since it was likely he had tampered with a Kiensei vessel, but it would have to wait. Rebi's dome spun back and forth wildly as it interrogated the ships sensor arrays and diagnostic computer. "An attempt to hack the autopilot?" Asato said in confusion as Rebi displayed the issue on the HUD. Rebi beeped and chirped, squawked and borped as if complaining, until the issue was cleared. "Yes, Rebi, I am glad you are on this mission," Asato said, placating the grumpy mech. It was true though. Had it not been, then the Kiensei Runan could be on his way right now to somewhere unknown, likely never to be found again. A cloud of dust rose as the *Spearpoint-class* fighter lifted off from the ground. After a short ascension, its main engines fired their orange ion bursts and the craft rocketed towards the village.

Nearing the red, pulsating dot on his navicomputer, a thin, gray column of smoke appeared in the distance. Curious, he thought. "Rebi, let's investigate," he instructed. "Let's circle around that spot and see if we can find a landing." Rebi updated the Heads-Up-Display to show that this location was near where it triangulated one of the radio transmissions. They were close and it seemed as though they weren't too far behind whoever this was.

The ship rolled left in a slow circular turn. Asato could see a clearing in the trees below and what appeared to be the remnants of a fire pit. "Set the ship down Rebi," he said cooly to the mech. The mech was a step ahead of the Kiensei Runan and had already scanned the area for biologics and tech. It chirruped that there were two scootsters below, but they were inactive. No signs of life were detected.

The fighter touched down and the whine of the engines ceased. Asato stood upright in the cockpit, cautiously scanning the area before disembarking. Two scootsters with packs. The remnants of a fire still smoldering. He approached it and saw charred remains of bones as if a feast or sacrifice or something he couldn't understand had occurred. The ground was upheaved and disturbed all around. Footprints from both people and animals were found everywhere. A singed pock mark on a tree was plainly visible. Definitely from blaster fire.

"A battle of some sort," he mused to himself. That could explain the errant bolt that zipped past his ship on his arrival. He investigated the site further, walking its perimeter. He stooped down, his robes enveloping his form. Footprints, two sets of footprints. "Rebi, chart a course for the nearest village," he said. The grumbling from the mech was all he heard. Something about battery life and reserves. "R-3B10," he said sharply. "You have days of battery capacity and another of reserves. We need to move, now." A small rotation of Rebi's dome and a slight rattle was the only reply.

Zamita sat cross-legged on a colorful woven mat in his simple hut. Small clay jars, ampoules, dried herbs, and talismans hung from twine strings above his head. Clay jars of assorted sizes were placed around and contained all manner of perfumes, poultices, salves, and other items of his calling as the tribe's healer. In front of him, wide-eyed at what the aged man was saying, was a little hybrid Tesska girl dressed in a green dress with light green vertically zig-zag patterns. Her leather wrapped legs were set wide and she was leaning forward on her small hands in complete amazement. Zamita reached up and loosened the string on a small jar and brought it down. "And this," his breathy and aged voice said, "is Blepheron Root." He placed it under his nose and sniffed, then did the same under the child's. She sniffed lightly and let out a satisfied "mmm" at the sweet scent. "We use this for our eyes," he explained, blinking his at her. She smiled and blinked her large, round blue eyes in return.

A knock came at his open doorway and a shadow was cast inside. The two looked up and saw Impatria there, her hands atop her walking cane. Zamita gave a bow of his head in respect. "Narkash, what can I do for you? Is your knee bothering you again?"

"No, Zamita," she said with a serious look on her face. Zamita took immediate notice of such and could tell her visit was not a social call. "A Kiensei has come, it is time," she said, looking at the child seated on the floor. He nodded in acknowledgement and sat up to his full height as best as his aged body would allow.

"I will prepare the ritual. Please come inside," Zamita said. Impatria did as asked and behind her came Bo-ram and Asi-ri. Ashira's little round face lit up and the budding white markings morphed slightly at seeing her parents.

"Mama, papa!" she exclaimed, standing up and running to her mother. Asi-ri stooped down and wrapped her arms around her daughter, as she had done so many times before.

But this would be one of the last times.

Zamita walked about his hut, opening various jars, and gathering different bundles of herbs and other plants. A rattling sound echoed as he chose a large, gilded gourd that was used as a shaker. Impatria and the others sat down around the small fire pit that smoldered with a little heat emanating. Ashira sat in her mother's lap, curious as to what was about to happen.

"Look mama!" the little one piped up, not recognizing the seriousness of the situation. "Hims has toy!" she pointed to the gourd in Zamita's hand. "I want play" she entreated.

Asi-ri smiled down at her daughter and Bo-ram placed a loving hand on her head. The hybrid mother Tesska placed a finger over the young one's lips and whispered 'shhh.' "Be quiet Ashira. This is important, ok?" Not to be denied her fun, the little Tesska stretched out her hand and quickly the gourd flew across the small space into her eagerly awaiting grip. She shrilled with excitement as she shook the ceremonial gourd with great fun. Impatria smiled at the antics as did Zamita. Bo-ram scolded her quietly and took the gourd from her hands, handing it back to the aged healer in front of him. Ashira began to fuss at the apparent travesty unfolding before her.

Impatria rolled stiffly to her knees and reached for the child's hands as she began to flail about in protest. The elder Tesska smiled at the little one as their eyes met. "Zamita has something special for you. A gift," she said to the child. Ashira settled down at hearing this. The funny old woman had always found ways to make her happy. "But you need to sit still, Ok?" Impatria said. "OK," Ashira said, and settled into her mother's lap, a finger finding its way into her mouth.

Zamita went to his creaky knees and blew on the smoldering fire, encouraging a small flame back to life. He stuck the ends to two bundles of herbs into the fire, alighting them and allowing them to burn for a moment before he blew them out. Smoke wafted from the ends like ghosts rising from the past. A pungent smell filled the hut as he began chanting an ancient Tesska prayer. He rose slowly. Waving the smoking and smoldering bundles about the others present, walking around the outside of the small circle gathered there. He grabbed the gourd and began shaking it loudly, chanting and singing the blessings of his people, asking for the spirit's blessings upon them.

He shook the gourd forcibly about the heads of all present, even little Ashira, who was unamused at him getting to play with the gourd and she couldn't. Zamita finished the small ceremony without fanfare, but to the graciousness of Impatria, Bo-ram and Asi-ri. Impatria reached a finger into one of the pouches on her belt. The blue powder inside was made from pulverized dried berries and mixed with ash. It symbolized the coexistence of life and death in one. She motioned for the parents to stand as she herself did so. One by one, she placed a vertical mark on the chins of the parents, a symbol of their sacrifice, and uttered the words "tuay'mai, tuay'mai" as a remark of thanks to the parents, the spirits, and ancestors.

It was time to go and meet the Kiensei.

Chapter 18 – Then

The gathered tribe began to part as Zamita entered the longhouse, a bundle of smoldering herbs held in front of him with both hands. His face, calm and stone solid. Behind him, Impatria. Her face cemented with the seriousness of what was about to take place. Behind her, Bo-ram with one arm around the shoulder of his wife Asi-ri, who was carrying the child Ashira. Bows from all tribesmen, tribeswomen, and other children were proffered in respect as the Narkash passed by.

The gathered crowd parted until two figures were seen waiting by the central fire pit. One, a dark-skinned Tesska man, and the other... a robed female Kiensei whose beauty was unknown to their people.

Zamita stopped in front of the large fire and held the smoldering herbs up in both hands towards the sky. He shouted an ancient blessing before tossing the bundle into the flames. Silence permeated the expansive longhouse, save for the crackling of the fire. Impatria stood, her hands on her walking stick, facing the two strangers. An eerie silence passed before she finally spoke.

"A great day is upon us," she began, raising her hands. "Our people have been blessed with a Kiensei. We have been given a great honor by the ancestors to nurture her and support her until such time that she takes her place amongst the honorable ones of the world." She turned to face the two parents; their faces rife with anxiety painted over with mock courage.

"Bo-ram, Asi-ri, do you accept the honor given to you by the spirits and ancestors of the Tesska people?" she asked aloud.

Bo-ram, stepped forward and balled his fist to his chest tightly. He bowed low and in equal volume said, "We do."

The crowd of over seventy-five was silent in respect.

"Zamita," Impatria said quietly, both addressing him and commanding him to perform the sacred ritual.

The aged Tesska man pulled the gilded gourd from his belt and began singing out in his people's native tongue. He danced in his aged form around the large fire pit, the gathered crowd in silence. His wizened voice undulated between high and low pitches as he faithfully recited the ancient and time-honored verses. He shook the implement with fervor as he passed around the blessed family, singing the ancient blessings he was once taught ages ago in honor of them. The spirits and the ancestors all danced with him and within him.

Sereeah was unamused. This archaic show of... whatever... was a waste of time to her. She wanted to get this over with as soon as possible and get the hell off this continent and back to real civilization. She was ready to be done with this job and put everything about it behind her. She risked a measured glance to Kel-so beside her. His face was just like theirs, in solemn awe of the traditions playing out before them. She had to keep her little ploy intact, just for a while longer.

The song and dance ended and Impatria nodded to Asi-ri. Reluctantly, she knelt down and placed the child's feet on the wooden plank floor. Ashira earnestly grasped at her mother's neck, wanting to be picked up again. Asi-ri whispered something to the child, and she turned to face the hooded woman across the way from her.

Impatria spoke up authoritatively, "Master Kiensei, we present you with Ashira Mori, daughter of Asi-ri and Bo-ram. We place upon you the honor of the Tesska people and the hopes of the Ravaraki tribe."

Sereeah glanced at Kel-so from under her hood. He nodded slightly to her in acknowledgement. She lowered her large and enveloping hood, revealing her crimson skin and dark purple hair. Some within the crowd gasped. Many had not seen such a being so beautiful before. Surely this was one of the honored Kiensei, they thought. She took a moment to assess the feelings about her. Wonderment, awe, and a slight tinge of fear. Good. All was working well in the moment. She looked across the space at the child before her. Her large, piercing blue eyes staring back at her in reservation, as if the child was trying to decide who and what she was.

Sereeah smiled, acting as genuine as she could. She knelt down, allowing her falsely crafted robes to flow outward from her form and extended her hand towards the child. Immediately she turned and buried her head into her mother's chest with a defiant grunt. Asi-ri whispered to her and forcibly turned her around to face the Rishka woman. Ashira shouted out a defiant "No!" in protest. Many in the crowd began to stir at the act. It was an honor to be chosen by the Kiensei, to defy it was disrespectful. Bo-ram tried his voice. He spoke quietly to his daughter, trying to reason with her sudden surge of rebellion. "Not nice, not nice papa," she said aloud in protest. Unbeknownst to all, the child could sense through the Ki that this woman was disingenuous. She was no Kiensei, and Ashira knew it. A high-pitched whine sounded in the distance as many of the people looked up and outward. Someone else was coming. Kel-so gingerly walked up to Sereeah and feigned fealty. "We should be going soon, Master Kiensei," he said heavily. His eyes told her that they were about to be in trouble if they didn't move soon.

Kai Asato throttled his ship faster towards the waypoint he had Rebi set when they had first arrived. Something was happening, a rippling within the Ki. He could feel it. It urged him forward. He felt as though he was needed, though he could not deduce exactly what it was about.

A clearing came into view. The village he saw not long ago. No signs of people in the streets however, though a wide, gray tail of smoke was rising from the central building. "Set us down outside of the village Rebi," he called to the mech, "and stay with the ship to keep it secure once we land." An acknowledgment sounded from the usually defiant mech. The *Spearpoint-class* fighter landed and Asato expertly launched himself from the cockpit and landed smartly on his feet. Raising his hood over his head, he began walking swiftly into the village.

He could hear commotion filtering out of the large meeting house as he approached. Through the large triangular openings, he could see a large crowd of the local people gathered inside. There it was again, a familiar surge in the Ki. He had felt it before. A show of power was not warranted right now, he would keep his intentions quiet and be peaceful. The feeling he had was one of distrust, of defiance. Like a stubborn log jamming up a river, refusing to let go. He made his way quickly to the main entrance. He peered inside and could see a large fire crackling hotly in the middle. Many of the people looked on in disappointment, confusion, and in frustration as a small child wrestled and fought with, he assumed were, her parents. But over what? A crouched figure abruptly caught his attention. Another Kiensei Runan?

The Rishka woman was dressed in what appeared to be traditional robes, but with some distinct discrepancies. She didn't look familiar at all to him. He had met many of his fellow Establishment members in his time but the identity of this one escaped him. A thought passed through his mind as he stepped away from the doorway. He keyed his comm. "R-3B10, tell me the description of the person that the owner of the cantina gave you." The mech knew that when it was addressed by its formal designation, it was serious and not to respond negatively. The mech did as instructed as quickly and succinctly as possible. "Thank you," Kai Asato said when the description was finished. "Now, contact the Monastery on Korosento and see if a female Rishka Runan was dispatched here recently." A moment passed while the mech did as asked. The comm unit cheeped back to life with a simple 'no' from the mech.

Asato instantly found himself in a challenging situation. The final pieces of the puzzle he had been working on began falling into place. A Ki-receptive child was here, right here, in front of him. That was the source of the disturbance. Someone, an imposter, was trying to steal the child. The runner that was murdered came from this village and was attempting to report the emergence of such. He could not, must not, let this happen. "Rebi, tell the Monastery that I have discovered a Kiensei imposter trying to kidnap a Ki-receptive child. I am engaging at once." He closed down his comm and stepped through the doorway, his senses on full alert.

"Come child," Sereeah said calmly with her hand extended. She did her best to paint her face with gentleness in an effort to lure the child to her. "No, No! I no want to!" Ashira rebelled, thrusting herself deeper into her mother's arms. Looks of disappointment began displaying on many of the people gathered. It wasn't them she had to fool; they already believed her ruse. But this stubborn child refused to come with her.

Kel-so whispered something in her ear. Perhaps she could try her natural ability? He stepped away from her slowly, so as not to be affected by it. Sereeah came close to the family and knelt down. The child glared at her from her mother's grasp as she pushed herself as far into Asi-ri's chest as possible. Sereeah smiled and opened her arms. That familiar sensation signaled that her limited reserves of pheromones were released and were now temporarily depleted. She fluffed her cloak to spread the invisible chemical as best she could under the guise of comfort.

Even at such a youthful age, Ashira sensed the intention of this… person. She stretched her short little arm out, fingers splayed, and pushed. It was a reaction, the only reaction she could muster. She pushed the bad stuff away. The invisible cloud. She could see it where others could not. This person was mean despite her friendly face. Ashira pushed and pushed hard. She pushed the bad stuff towards the fire. The fire that burned everything.

Sereeah fell backwards as if someone, or something had run into her. The crowd gasped. The disrespect of this child was dishonoring to the tribe. "Ashira!" Bo-ram chided her. The little one looked her father in the face, pleading for mercy. "I can't like it papa, I can't like it," she said in her own innocent defense.

Murmurs began rising from the gathered peoples. To refuse the Kiensei was to bring shame upon the people. Bo-ram and Asi-ri were deeply conflicted. They knew that it was Ashira's destiny to be with the Kiensei, but the very fabric of their beings yearned for her to stay with them. Asi-ri was just about to stop the entire ordeal, shame, or no shame when suddenly, a booming voice came from the door.

"Perhaps I can be of assistance," Kai Asato said loudly. Heads turned and swayed as all eyes turned upon the Kiensei Runan in the doorway. The many gasps of the people could have sucked all of the air from the large space. It was an honor to have a Kiensei visit, but two Kiensei, now that was unheard of. The blood in Sereeah's veins ran icy cold with fear. Her eyes almost clouded over knowing that the worst possible scenario had happened. This new arrival was certainly authentic, and she was certainly not. Her impersonation would surely land her in an inescapable prison. Deal or no deal, threats or no threats, she was not about to tussle with this man. She glanced around the space quickly, looking for an escape. Those large openings would do nicely.

"What is the meaning of this," Kel-so said sharply.

"I was about to ask you the same thing," Asato replied as he shed his outer robe in preparation and made his way towards the fiasco. His gaze focused on the Rishka woman. "Who are you?" he asked intentionally. The crowd parted and pulled back from the new visitor as he slowly advanced. The look of this... Kiensei... was fearsome. His features were sharp, his skin was unnatural looking and those... things on his face were alien to the people. Many retreated out of fear. They had never seen a being such as this. Bo-ram and Asi-ri clasped their daughter tightly in an effort to protect her.

"I-I... was sent here to claim this child," Sereeah said nervously as she regained her footing.

"By whom?" Asato retorted calmly. "Certainly not the Kiensei Establishment." More murmurs arose from the crowd. A flick of the Rodlek's wrist and the mock sword hanging on the Rishka's belt flew to his hand. Unbeknownst to all who were present, his eyes looked down at it behind his glasses. He swiftly knew what it wasn't. Dropping it to the floor, he raised a heavy foot and smashed the plasticene prop with the heel of his boot.

"And you," he raised a hand, pointing to Kel-so. "You fit the description of a man suspected of murdering a runner from this village. What do you say to that?" Impatria's face became stern. She had sent her most trustworthy runner many days ago. She had begun to wonder why he had not yet returned.

Kel-so grinned menacingly. Kiensei or no, he was not about to be captured. He could run. He could get away. He might even be able to take this alien to its grave. "You have no proof," he said.

Asato's expression could not be ascertained simply by looking at him. But in this moment, he curled a corner of his mouth opening in what would pass as a grin. "Care to come with me and plead your case to the Regalia?" he said, goadingly. The crowd stirred at the sound of their monarch's title.

A grunt came from the dark-skinned Tesska. It was time to fight. Live or die, he didn't care. His gambit had failed and if he was going down, he might take this fool with him. He quickly grabbed Sereeah and pulled her in front of him as he unholstered one of his blasters. He pulled her close holding her about the neck and put the blaster to her head. Perhaps he could barter a way out of this for both of them. "Move, and she dies."

Sereeah was in shock, she was so focused on the Kiensei that she didn't feel the emotion of Kel-so beside her. She didn't want to die. Her mind raced. If she could lie her way out of this mess and pin it on him, well, at least she might get out alive. "It's his fault," she called out in panic. His forearm was choking her. She grasped at it in an attempt to free herself. "He made me do it! He threatened me and my family! I had no choice!"

"Stand down!" Asato barked. The crowd moved back towards the walls and openings, some retreated entirely in fear, escaping the longhouse completely. "No one needs to get hurt. Let us work through this peacefully. I'm sure the Regalia will give you fair quarter if you come quietly." Kel-so knew better than that. His death warrant was already signed if he was captured. The fire crackled as the two parties stared at one other.

Sereeah was in full panic, she was able to dip her chin just enough to loosen the strong Tesska's hold around her neck. She bit down hard like a wild animal. Kel-so screamed in pain. He pushed the Rishka imposter hard towards the Kiensei and immediately brought one of his pistols to bear, waiting for a clear shot. His free hand grasped at his second weapon. Sereeah was surprised by the shove and stumbled, falling on her knees at Impatria's feet, gasping for air. He squeezed the trigger and fired a shot at the Kiensei.

Kai Asato's senses sparked like a lightning bolt as he anticipated the desperate move. His hand had already grasped the hilt of the sword on his belt and imbued it with the Ki. In a flash, he swiftly brought it to bear. His green-hued sword blade snapped forward instantly in just the right spot to deflect the blaster bolt headed for his face. His visage was bathed in a glowing green color as he stared past his weapon at the offender. The crowd shuddered at the sound and sight of the legendary weapon of the Kiensei. "Last chance," he growled to the insulting man as he began walking towards him. Several more shots came as the Tesska man fired both blasters in a desperate attempt to kill the Kiensei. Asato harmlessly deflected every shot without stopping his advance, the Ki surrounding him. He reached out with his off hand and used the Ki to pull the pistols away from the assailant, instantly disarming him. They made a metallic clink as they hit the wooden floor and skittered to a halt.

Sereeah saw her chance. Everyone was focused on the Kiensei and Kel-so. She quickly rose to her feet and bulldozed her way through the crowd, knocking an older person down and leaping through a triangular opening. She was a fast runner. If she could make it to the scootsters and then her ship, she was out of here. She threw off her cloak to give herself freedom of movement and to lessen her weight. Adrenaline flooded her body. Firey energy burned beneath her skin. She barely felt her feet touch the ground as she ran for her life.

"Go!" Impatria cried out, pointing in the escapee's direction. Several Tesska adults gathered their wits and gave chase.

Three tribesmen nodded at one another. Asato saw it. They rushed Kel-so from behind and tackled him to the ground. He kicked, struggled, and yelled but was subdued in a matter of moments. Seeing the danger had passed, Asato sheathed his sword and returned to his usually calm spirit.

Her legs ached, her chest was on fire, but the adrenaline was like someone had injected jet fuel straight into her veins. Sereeah's heart pounded as if trying to escape her chest. She ran harder than she ever had in her entire life. The shouts of pursuing villagers grew steadily fainter as she outpaced them out of sheer fear. Luckily, she had remembered the path they took into the village and in retracing their steps, she eventually found the scootsters hovering exactly where they had left them.

She grabbed a handlebar with one hand, and with the other she supported herself on a knee. Her chest heaved as she struggled to fuel her body with air. She couldn't allow them to follow her. These primitives lacked the ability to use comms easily and effectively, so she quickly decided to destroy one of the scootsters to increase her chances of escape.

She tore a piece of cloth from the bedroll stowed on the back of one of the scootsters and tied it to the throttle handle. Flipping toggle switches and pressing the ignition button, the scootster bellowed to life. It whined as the fixed throttle allowed it to soar to maximum power almost instantly. The sounds of pursuing tribals came closer and closer. Sereeah ran over to the smoldering firepit and grabbed a rock, one heavy enough to hold the foot pedal down. She stood back as she readied herself to drop the stone just so, and instantly... woosh... off the scootster went at max throttle. It didn't go far until it smashed loudly into a large tree and sputtered in a mechanical death throe.

Hearing her pursuers coming closer, she ran over to the remaining scootster and hopped aboard. A comfort settled her nerves a bit as it rumbled to life. She was almost there. Squeezing the throttle and pushing the foot pedal, she tore out of the clearing, heading back to her ship, and freedom once again. She was done with this planet. Done with this job. Done with the Dark Fire. She had other skills, skills she didn't want to rely on, but they had helped her survive before and they could do it again. She could do this. She could disappear.

Sereeah never let up on the throttle as she rocketed towards the landing pad. In a bit of controlled chaos, she slid the scootster sideways to a halt only a few meters from her ship. The man called Mata-ru was nearby. He looked at her with a confused expression. She had no time for him. She just wanted to get out of here.

"Master Kiensei?" called the man. "Are you alright? Did you accomplish what you came here for?"

She made no effort to acknowledge him. She hurried herself up the ramp to her ship and quickly seated herself in the familiar leather chair that was like an inanimate friend to her. She clicked buttons and rocked toggle switches. The cockpit lighted to life as systems came online, lights flashed, panels beeped, and the engines spun up to full rotation. The ramp retracted and with a thud, sealing the ship airtight. She reached over and pushed the throttle forward and the *Pyrixis* lifted off in a cloud of dust. *Almost there*, she thought. Her breathing had slowed a bit, but her heart still pounded like a smith's hammer on an anvil.

The blue tinge of the atmosphere above Karinar gave way to the star-speckled blackness of space as she entered orbit around the planet. She checked her sensors, no pursuers. She might get out of this thing. She reached over and entered the coordinates for a portalspace jump just to get her to another continent so that she could gather her thoughts. The computer blipped and began its calculation cycle. Pushing a few more buttons on the console in front of her activated the autopilot to take over. She rose from the chair, her body shaking from the withdrawals from the adrenaline. She needed a drink.

The ship turned slowly as the calculations were continuing and the ship came into alignment. She could see the stars moving across the cockpit viewport as she shakily grabbed a bottle of liquor in the cabin wet bar. She poured herself a generous portion and immediately downed it. A grimace and a cough followed as the harsh liquid burned her throat. She poured another and downed it too. She chuckled as the burning liquid flowed down her throat. The dots of stars stretched into lines as the ship made the jump into portalspace. She took a deep breath of release. Almost at once, warnings and alarms began blaring from the cockpit. Her eyes went wide with fear as the swirl of portalspace suddenly became one giant bright white ball of light. It filled her dark pupils as her eyelids peeled further and further backwards. Her mouth began gaping open.

She was headed into the sun!

She leapt and stumbled into the cockpit, but it was too late. Without fanfare or warning, the *Pyrixis* plunged itself into the core of the sun at unprecedented speed... and was never seen again.

Mata-ru watched as the freighter left atmosphere. He had made sure to hack the autopilot as soon as the fake Kiensei arrived. If she had come back with the child, he would have reversed it promptly, but she hadn't, so that liability had to be dealt with. He had also tried to hack the real Kiensei's ship in an attempt to salvage the operation, but it came with complications. He had never tried one of theirs before, so it had been a bit hasty and sloppy. He assumed that her arrival alone also meant that Kel-so was compromised. He looked around and found two large rocks. He placed his comm unit with Kel-so on one and smashed it to bits with the other. He gathered the pieces and decided to throw them into the scrub surrounding the landing pad. The Dark Fire would not be pleased with this failure, but he was sure he could keep their anonymity intact. It was time for him to disappear as well. That real Kiensei would likely be looking for him. He could dissolve into the brush or one of the other remote tribes for a while, just until the heat wore off.

He keyed his other comm.

"What do you have to report?" came the deep, gravelly voice.

"The operation failed. The Kiensei arrived and caused too many complications. But no worry, your anonymity is still intact," the Tesska man said.

"Our benefactor will be most displeased with this news. Pray that it is not you that will be silenced next," the man said and the comm went silent.

Chapter 19

Siobhan eventually caved, knowing within herself that it was the right thing to do. Having committed the most grievous of offenses amongst the two, by her reckoning, she spoke up first. Quietly though as her voice was still recovering.

"I suppose I owe ye an apology for what I done," she began. "I'm sorry, truly I am. Ye helped us, ye helped Eilidh. I'm grateful too. Hadn'a been for ye, she'd likely be gone now."

Ashira blinked for a moment in disbelief. The Kiamnik was actually being nice to her now? It felt strange. "Water under the bridge," Ashira replied in an effort to soothe the situation. "Though I gotta ask... why didn't you tell me you knew I was once a Kiensei when I got here?"

"I be believin' it's fair to say I don't have a lot of trust for the Kiensei," she croaked pointedly. "And it be fair to say you dinna know me and I was all about protectin' meself and the others. But first, ye need to know something true. I have a problem with me emotions sometimes." Ashira nodded in acknowledgement since she had just recently experienced it. "I don't be knowin' why, but it's sumthin' that's hounded me from when I was a wee one. Once the flame is stoked, I canna control it. It's why I'm here."

Markhiz had been right, Ashira thought. "You don't owe me an explanation, Siobhan," Ashira said. "You made your apology, and that's good enough for me. I probably should have said something when I arrived, but I was afraid that the camp wouldn't allow me to stay if they knew who I was."

"That's fair, but please, Ashira," Siobhan entreated with an open hand. "I already be knowin' about ye, trust me. Allow me to explain meself to be fair unto ye." Ashira raised her eyebrows and nodded in surprised agreement, choosing to remain silent. This was certainly a different side of Siobhan she never thought she'd get to see.

Siobhan cleared her throat. "I served under Admiral Brocurn. A stiff blighter if ever there was one, but a good'n. Ensign Siobhan Mallory, officer of the Engineering Division, specialist in Power Systems and Propulsion," she said with mock dignity. She sniffed quickly, clearing her sinuses, and laid her head sideways across her forearms facing Ashira; her head tendrils barely undulating. "I was there at the first battle of Humaran afore me promotion, and again at Usan Lota aboard his flagship, the *Beneficiary*." Ashira knew both of those battles very, very well. They were both extremely involved and carried high casualties. And she knew Brocurn too. He had been instrumental in rescuing her people on Cronus. "There was an issue with yon' ship at Usan Lota whilst waitin' fer ye to come back from that busted up continent. In the rush to get to Usan Lota, Brocurn ordered the reactor core to be overcharged, more than allowable tolerances. It blew a couple o' stasis field generator stators which caused an electrical system imbalance..." Ashira was getting lost in the tech-talk. She could follow along pretty well having apprenticed to Kina in more ways than just the Ki, but this was getting too deep.

"Um," she interrupted. "You're losing me here. Sorry," Ashira said.

Siobhan stopped and actually grinned at her. A first for the two.

"Basically, its meanin' that the ship didn't have full power. And a recalibration o' the energy load balancers needed doin' to equally distribute remaining power through the ship, but it would'a cause certain systems to go offline briefly. We were long inta' the battle, so it needed to wait or else risk losing weapons, or shields, or portalspace capabilities, or all of it. Me superior, Lieutenant Roland

Caine, arsehat of a human, ordered me to do it. I objected to save the ship. He persisted under threat of court martial. I objected again, so he started to do it himself. I got angry, so I decked him hard. Knocked him clean out I did. I avoided the brig on account of the security recordins'. But still landed me smartly inna Dishonorable Discharge it did. Ruined me life. There's none too many opportunities for a soldier what's been kicked out."

That sounded familiar to Ashira. Remarkably familiar.

"What about an appeal?" Ashira asked.

"Tried it. Went to Brocurn himself before me court martial. Dinna do any good. Even appealed to the Kiensei General above him, Kai Asato methinks it was. I got nuthin' in return. Not even so much as a *thanks fer playin' but no chance cubes fer ye*," Siobhan said.

"Did you actually speak to him? Asato?" Ashira asked. She knew Demio Asato very well, and it was not in his character to ignore something of that caliber. Demio Asato cared for the soldiers in his charge and looked after them carefully.

"I dinna," she said, shaking her head. "But after I heard nothin' back, I figured he wouldna' cared enough to look inta' someone like me. Probably saw me appeal and tossed it" Siobhan said, placing her forehead on her arms. "Any who, it landed me here when they kicked me out," she sighed "and that's where I met Taria and Eilidh. I haven't been happy in a while and they both make me feel that way," she said, raising her gaze skyward.

"Aw. How sweet," came the sarcastic voice of Taria from the doorway. The Multorn mother stood there with her arms crossed and leaning on one shoulder. A smile beamed from her face. They looked up at her simultaneously, not knowing she had been standing there listening. "Don't mind me," she chuckled as she approached them, regaining her seated position. "You two seem to be getting along now, so I don't want to mess it up or anything."

"How is she?" Siobhan asked.

"Still out cold. She had rolled herself off her bed, so I put her back. Thinking about turning in myself, but I don't want Eilidh to wake up without me there."

"Depending on the dosage," Ashira piped up "she may be out for an entire rotation."

"Aye, she might," Siobhan concurred.

"Wow! Look at that. You two actually agreed on something," Taria joked. She reached out and picked up a random piece of trash, tossed it up into the air and let it fall back down to the ground. "Yep. Gravity is still working. So, I guess it's authentic then." The two chuckled in amusement. "I think I can hang in there until she comes around."

"I'll stay up with ye" Siobhan said.

Taria looked square into the Kiamnik's face, a look of seriousness glowing forth. "Siobhan, you said 'me child' when you were wrangling that Ghasto. What exactly did you mean by that?" The Kiamnik's head tendrils stiffened slightly as she stared blankly into the distance. She took a deep breath.

"I always dreamed of havin' a family. But I canna. Seems me anger problem isn't me only one," Siobhan said wistfully. "Bein' round Eilidh gives me a joy I've always wanted. Bein' round you gives me a peace I've always be needin'. I love Eilidh like she was me own and I'd give me life for her."

Ashira admired the sentiment but took this as her cue to leave for a bit. This was a private moment between them, and she didn't need to be a part of it. Instead, she thought a walk to check up on Tumps was more appropriate, and it was time to stretch her legs a bit. "I'm going to go check on Tumps. Be back in a bit," she huffed, rising to her feet.

"Don't forget what I asked you to consider," Taria called out.

"I haven't. I'm thinking about it and a walk might just be the thing to help me clear my head," Ashira said over her shoulder. And she set out to find Tumps.

Along the way, she processed the events of the evening. She reminisced about her time on Wahaskah, when she was alone, with no one to support her. All she had was her training, her training as a soldier. She remembered a conversation she and Kina had about that very thing. An injured Tsugint lay before her on a stretcher with her holding his hand in support. Kina explained that times were different, and as such, he was forced to train her as a soldier, not as a peacekeeper like Teka had trained him. It was confusing because her time as a muhashka was spent learning about peace concepts, conflict resolution, accepting differences and other things a peacekeeper would and should do. Then, from Phisis and forward, it seemed all of that particular training flew out the porthole in the middle of portalspace in lieu of battlefield tactics, weapons training, and subterfuge. It seemed as if the Establishment itself had no idea what it was about anymore. She wondered if things would be different if she was still a Kiensei, but not a soldier. Kind of hard to do really as most able-bodied Kiensei had been pressed into service in some form or fashion. Even Reikuno. She was adept at and enjoyed the peacefulness of healing and internally disliked warfare combat. She had mostly stayed at the monastery and helped out in the Medical Bay. But she was still there on the front lines from time to time when her sesni called. Thinking about her made Ashira think about alternative roles. Maybe a monastery guard? Or a diplomat? Lore keeper? No, too boring. An explorer maybe? There had to be some kind of balance in this, she was sure of it. A sudden trickle of reality flowed through her mind, and she shut the idea down completely.

"Nope," she whispered to herself. "No way but forward."

As Ashira approached Tump's humble abode, she saw Shi'ma exiting the doorway. The Tallin woman never seemed to portray any sense of emotion and it was generally hard to tell what was going on in her mind based on her demeanor. So, it was a bit of a shock when she visibly became nervous at Ashira's approach from the darkness.

"I'm sorry," Ashira said, holding her empty hands up. Shi'ma recoiled at the sight of Ashira's hands rising. "I didn't mean to startle you. I just came to check on Tumps. Is he OK?" Shi'ma stopped in her tracks and gave a slight nod. She began side stepping slowly as if to move herself out of Ashira's path. This made her feel uneasy as it appeared that Shi'ma was afraid of her. She started to try and placate the nervous woman when a grunt came abruptly from the doorway as Tumps appeared along with a Lapin male she had never seen before.

"Tumps!" Ashira cried out in relief. "You OK pal?"

The Braundt looked up at her and a half-hearted grin curled his snout. His eye was completely bandaged up and was splinted to one of his other eye stalks for support. He grumbled in his usual manner.

"Mmmm. Yeah. I'll be fine. That thing got one of my eyes good, so I'll have some adjusting to do with using two now. Other than that, just some bumps and bruises."

The astute Lapin stepped forward towards her in a militant fashion with hand on his chest. He wore a light-colored cloak that appeared to have some stains on it from his work on Tumps. The hood was down, and his long ears were laid back and secured near the ends, probably to keep his hearing ability intact while also keeping them out of his way. His voice was moderately light, fast paced, and carried a hint of sophistication with it.

"So, you must be the Kiensei what saved the day and all, eh wot?" Ashira sighed in exasperation. It was wearing on her that she continually had to explain herself, so much that she felt like a broken virtuadisk.

"I'm not a Kiensei," she said flatly. Should she consider making a sign and attaching it to her forehead or something?

The Lapin casually strolled up to her and stood fully upright on his powerful legs, his hands clasped behind his back in parade rest.

"Well then Ms. I'm-not-a-Kiensei, you certainly act like one but never you mind then, milady. I still believe congratulations are in order and a bang-on job well done in handling that blighter, wot wot?" He extended his yellowish furred hand to shake hers. She looked at it, then looked up at him as he was about two standard feet taller than her. His regal, whiskered smile and his true intentions were welcomed. She clasped his hand, and he gave a sharp shake.

"Silba, milady. Silba H. Gagst at your service. Formally of His Lordship's 2nd Medical Brigade on Cochella," the tall Lapin postured.

Ashira had to force herself *not* to crack a smile and laugh at the sight of a tall, rabbit-like creature that spoke in a manner she'd never heard before yet one that seemed comical in nature. She failed at *not* smiling.

"Pleased to meet you, Silba. I'm Ashira..."

"Mori, eh wot?" he said in his quick-witted manner, cutting her off. "Nasty business with all that Monastery burning wot? Saw you all over the Holos I did," he sniffed and adjusted his whiskers. "Can't blame you misself for not wanting to hang around that mischieva any longer. A right foul git, the lot of it. Top hole of a soldier you were from my understanding. Why in my day a good soldier was worth standing up for, not to mire down in political mumbo jumbo." He snorted indignantly as he turned on his heels to face the other two, hands clasped behind his back. "Well," he sighed "it's been an eventful evening, and I should be heading back home to the missus and all. Righto."

"Thanks, Silba, for coming out this late," Tumps called out. "We greatly appreciate your support."

"Ta ta for now," he waved a paw as he walked away into the night. "Shi'ma, you change that dressing twice daily now, yeah?" he called over his shoulder.

"Who was *that*?" Ashira asked, gesturing with her thumb in confusion.

"Eh, that's Silba. He lives just down the way. He's a bit chatty, but a good medic. We try not to call on him unless it's an emergency," Tumps said.

"I'm sorry you lost an eye. Had I known that Ghasto was still armed, I would have done differently," Ashira said.

"Never you mind," Tumps said, mimicking Silba's tone and demeanor. This made Ashira laugh, which she hadn't done in a while, and it felt good. "How's the little one?" he asked.

"She got banged up and was still out cold when I left to come find you, but she's alive."

"And our... *visitor*?" he grunted, regarding the Ghasto.

"Dead. Markhiz and two brothers are handling the rest," she said.

"Hope that's the last of it. I'm not giving up another eye, just saying," he chortled.

Shi'ma stayed back and didn't say a word. Ashira could sense the fear within her but couldn't understand why it was there. Instead of pressing the issue, she still wished her a good night and decided to return to Taria's.

The three of them stayed up, taking turns with short naps, and watching over the little Multorn. The sun rose in the Korosento sky as they all three sat at the makeshift table. They took turns playing a game called Sands of Time to ease the waiting; a creation from Eilidh that actually ended up being quite fun, Ashira thought.

It was about mid-day, each of them taking turns stretching, going for a short walk, taking a short nap, or playing a game, when the little girl stirred in her bed. Taria was just outside, Ashira was taking a short nap, and Siobhan was keeping watch. Siobhan blinked in disbelief as the little girl moaned weakly and moved her slightly bruised arms. She jumped up and ran to the doorway, a surge of energy filling her.

"Oi! Love! She's a wakin' up!" the Kiamnik woman called out. Taria was inside and at the bedside within seconds. She knelt down and stroked her daughter's cheek, urging her to come to. Gently calling her name and patiently waiting. A few moments passed when one little eye cracked open and looked around. Then the other, which was darkened with bruising.

"Ma...Ma?" came the weak little voice, cracked from a parched throat.

Taria placed both of her hands on her daughter's face and came closer, tears meandering down her smiling cheeks. "I'm here baby, I'm here," she said, her throat seizing up. "And Siobhan's here too." She kissed her daughter's forehead, desperately holding herself together.

"Aye, ye little nugget o' fun. Ye gave us quite a stir, d'you know that?" A tear formed in Siobhan's eye, pooled, then escaped down her face.

Ashira woke, hearing some commotion. She sat up groggily and stretched her arms above her head with a yawn. Wiping her sleepy eyes, she saw something... a paragon of beauty. She saw two people who cared for one another, tears flowing happily, and an innocent child who was fortunate enough to have people who cared so deeply.

She saw a family. Something she never really possessed herself.

The warmth, the harmony, the peace she felt radiating through the Ki in that moment was pure joy to her. She realized that it didn't matter whether she was a Kiensei or not, it didn't matter whether people *knew* she was a Kiensei or not. It didn't matter if it was a Prefect, or the leastmost of society that needed her. What mattered was that she had done the right thing. She had selflessly helped those in need simply because they needed it, and she was fortunate to be here to do it. She was where she believed the Ki wanted her to be, and the essence of the Ki had responded in kind.

Chapter 20

Astandard day had passed and Eilidh was up and about, nearly her usual, springy self again. Aside from some soreness and the ever-changing colors of some of her bruising, she was on the mend. It had taken some carefully worded explaining to Eilidh about what had happened, but the little one's demeanor hadn't missed a step. Tumps was recovering nicely and some of the camp's residents stopped shying away when Ashira wandered by or spoke, even Shi'ma. Others though, still held some reservations.

Ashira had been thinking about Taria's request. It was early afternoon. She had just returned, carrying a repurposed plasticene jug from the fresh water supply, when she heard murmuring inside the dwelling. She couldn't make out what the conversation was about from outside, so she decided to head in to see if she would be included, or if it was private. She entered the dwelling to two seated women looking at her with concern splayed across their faces.

"Sorry, didn't mean to interrupt," she said as she put the jug of water in the corner near the stove. She was trying to appear nonchalant and let them dictate the situation.

"Nother a problem," Siobhan said. "We were just discussin' how we might could better protect ourselves in the future."

"About that," Ashira began. She grabbed her chin, a slight habit she had picked up from Kina, who got it from Teka. "I've been thinking about it."

"And?" Taria asked hopefully.

"I do know people," she gestured with a pointed finger. "I don't necessarily *want* to talk to them, but if it's for the good of the people here... I'll do it," Ashira said.

Siobhan came up to her and offered her a hand in friendship. Her face a solid rock of genuineness. "Thank ye. It means a heap, no lie."

"Don't thank me yet," Ashira said, shaking her hand. "I haven't yet figured out *how* to do it, but I know where to start at least."

"Every journey begins with a single step," Taria quipped. "What do you need from us?"

"Nothing," Ashira said, pursing her lips. "I might be gone for a while, but I'll be back. But first, I should probably clean up a bit." A confused look came her way from the two women. "I'll have to pass through some public spaces to get where I'm going. The last thing I need is to..." she trailed off, knowing what she wanted to say might hurt a bit.

"... look homeless?" Taria finished her sentence with a smirk. Siobhan cut a glance over at Taria.

"I... was going to say *without attracting attention*."

"I get it, I get it," Taria said, waving a hand coolly. "Tell you what..." she began as she stood up and scooted a chair across the floor with a screech. She stepped up on the chair and reached up into the rafters and pulled down a large round metal tub. "You go rinse off real quick in those amazing combobulations you and Markhiz came up with and I'll wash your clothes. I can see they could use a little tending to," she said as she heaved the tub down to the floor.

Ashira took a step backwards, crossing her arms across her midriff. For the first time in a long time, she actually felt... embarrassed or anxious... she didn't know what it was, but it felt strange to her. Her face began to feel warm.

Siobhan watched the color in the Tesska's face darken a bit. A smile crept up in amusement. "Aye love! You done went and scared yerself a Kiensei ya did!" she said as she began to giggle.

Scared? She wasn't *scared,* Ashira assured herself. "Wh-what... am I... s-supposed to wear?" The words had difficulty emerging from the usually calm Tesska. Siobhan's giggle escalated into a full-on belly laugh. She began laughing so hard that it sent her to her knees. Taria smiled in amusement at what she believed was going through Ashira's mind at the moment. The sound of laughter made its way outside to Eilidh, who was playing with a toy that one of the scavengers found. Curiously, the little girl walked over and poked her head through the doorway.

"What's so funny?" she asked mutedly as she looked around. Spotting the tub on the floor in front of her mother—bath time! She threw off her clothes quickly and ran into the room to the complete and utter surprise of the three standing there.

Taria blinked in bewilderment as her bare-skinned child came running in; the child's face painted with a bright smile, amongst the multicolored bruises. She placed her child's head in the palm of her hand and took a breath. "Really young lady? Seriously?" she questioned, raising an eyebrow in amusement, and trying her best not to encourage her daughter.

"What?" Eilidh asked in confusion. "It's not bath time?" Siobhan began coughing between laughs on the floor amidst the bedlam. Ashira was bewildered at the events unfolding in front of her, her face becoming warmer by the second, her face also a mirror of confusion. She had never seen anything like it before.

"No baby," Taria said with mock exasperation "it's for Ashira." Eilidh wheeled around at once to Ashira and with a scrunch-faced grin said "tub-baths are sooo fun, you're gonna *love* it!" Siobhan rolled over on her back, sputtering and coughing between laughs, trying hard to catch a breath. Ashira's eyes were wide. There was no way she was getting in that thing. A passing thought reminded her that Monastery life certainly did not train her for this.

Taria couldn't help but laugh a little too. "Ok, Ok, Ok," she chuckled "the tub is for *clothes* this time. Eilidh, go pick up yours and bring them here, please. They could use a good wash... and go get dressed in your other outfit. You can't be running about naked as a doodlefly." The little Multorn bounded over to where her clothes had landed and picked them up, still as bare as the day she was born, and brought them to her mother. She then bounded playfully over the mounds of her bedding to a box in the corner where she slept to retrieve her other outfit.

Taria noticed the shocked and confused look on Ashira's face. She pushed the tub aside and walked over to a shelf, opened a paperboard box, and produced a large, gray piece of soft cloth. She tossed it over to Ashira. "Here. You can dry off and wrap up with that until your clothes dry. I'll walk with you to the showers and gather your things while you clean up. Ok?" Ashira was silent for a moment, not something that happened very often. The gravity of what had transpired began to sink in and her mind began to ease.

The Tesska and Multorn exited the dwelling and headed towards the showers. On their way out the sound of Siobhan and Eilidh laughing and playing together could be heard. Taria remembered the uncomfortable expressions that Ashira portrayed in her expressions as they walked. Not to mention her blushing, at least she thought it was blushing. She had never seen a Tesska blush before. She didn't even know they could. Go figure. "You've never experienced a real family before, have you?" Taria said.

"No. I haven't," Ashira said truthfully. She had seen families in war zones, families in settlements, orphans, adopted and many other variations. The Kiensei colloquially called each other '*brother*' and '*sister*,' just not in a true familial way. But she had never been witnessed to what truly went on in the home, which is why she acted the way she did. It was unfamiliar to her.

"I appreciate the honesty. Kids are both amazing, and frustrating at the same time," she sighed wistfully while gazing upwards. "They make you smile; they frustrate you, but you still love them no matter what. Speaking of which, do you remember your parents?" Taria asked.

"No. I don't," she said plainly. "When children are brought to the monastery, they're no longer allowed to see or speak to their biological parents. It helps prevent affection, which is forbidden. At least that's what the rules say," Ashira replied. "Affection can lead to fear and envy, which can then lead to anger and jealousy, then to hate, then to suffering. The Kiensei are taught not to attach themselves to prevent seduction by the Kage." Taria proffered a look of mild confusion. She had never heard one so young speak like this. "The darkness," Ashira clarified.

"Sounds like isolation to me," Taria replied. "Isolation is what makes us less like real people and more like mechs and gundams. It disconnects us from reality and polarizes our views. Case in point, you were extremely uncomfortable back there, right? Because you had never experienced what it was genuinely like to be in a family? How can you know love if you don't subject yourself to it? How can you have true compassion if you don't know what it feels like to experience it, or rejection for that matter?"

"I see your point," Ashira said, though rejection was something she knew all too well. Her early childhood memories of the daycare were vague, but she remembered how everything was very structured: meals, showers, bedtime, training etc. All mostly governed by nanny mechs. "Right now, I'm just glad I don't have to sit in a tub in the middle of the room," she conceded, trying to inject a bit of humor into the conversation.

Taria smiled. "Yeah, we may be poor, but we're not indecent. Well, most of us at least. I'm just glad I don't have to chase Eilidh through the camp anymore after a bath. Lemme tell ya," she said rolling her eyes with a chuckle.

"Eilidh is lucky to have you and Siobhan," Ashira said.

"Well, we wouldn't have her right now if it weren't for you," Taria said. "You'd make any parent proud; I know I am. I'd adopt you in a flash if I could... wait... how old are you anyways?" Taria threw an arm across Ashira's shoulder as they continued on to the showers and proffered a one-armed hug.

"Seventeen," Ashira said. She allowed Taria's arm to remain. She could sense the feeling of acceptance, the feeling of genuine... something... she couldn't describe it, coming from the Multorn woman, but it felt good. It was uncharted territory for her, but at that moment, she was willing to let it in and enjoy the unknown for once.

Ashira sat refreshed in a chair across from Eilidh, wrapped up in the soft, gray cloth. It felt good, warm, and comfortable like that gesture from Taria. Her clothes were hanging in the corner near the stove where Taria was cooking, drip drying in the radiant heat. The two were playing Sands of Time, and Eilidh was winning, though not on purpose.

"Oi. Ye shoulda' seen yer face Ashira," Siobhan poked verbally. "Looked the shade of a simian's arse it did!" she chuckled.

"Siobhan! Language!" Taria called out from the makeshift stove. Some decent produce had come in from a recent scavenge and there was enough for a fragrant and hearty stew. The scent wafted throughout the humble home much to the pleasure of all within. Ashira tried to remember the last time she had a hot meal like this and couldn't. Her growling stomach, however, reminded her that it didn't matter. After bouncing from battle to battle for years, eating rations and meal bars, this was a treat.

"What's an 'arse' Siobhan?" Eilidh piped up.

The clank of a ladle and the hunched shoulders of Taria spoke volumes to her frustration. "Yes, *dear...*" she said with deep sarcasm, "explain to her what that is." Ashira and Siobhan traded glances at one another across the room. A playful nod of the head and mischievous smile from Ashira returned the poke back to the Kiamnik woman well enough. Siobhan rolled her eyes in silent protest.

"Eh... its nother a word I shoulda' used nugget," Siobhan conceded, her fingers combing through her head tendrils. "Don't be usin' it now, ye hear?"

"Then why'd you say it?" the little girl asked. Taria glanced over her shoulder with a jabbing grin. Ashira scrunched her lips and glared at Siobhan with a crinkled brow and raised eyes as if to say "yeah, why *did* you say that?" The Kiamnik tilted her head back and looked up at the ceiling, muttering something under her breath.

Taria approached each member and handed them a bowl of steaming stew. "She made a mistake baby, let it go. She's sorry. Right Siobhan?" Taria glared at Siobhan's guilty face. "Now eat your food because its bedtime soon."

The little family ate their meal in the soft glow of a single lantern, though one could say it came from the hearts of those who lived within it. They talked, they played games, they genuinely enjoyed the time well spent. Ashira wondered to herself if this was what it was like to have a real family? It was strange, but... so good. She found herself enjoying the fact that she was being taken care, for once, of out of the kindness of others' hearts whereas she was used to taking care of herself and others. After things were tidied up, Eilidh was put to bed and Ashira got dressed while the other two women went outside to enjoy the cool, evening air. Ashira joined them shortly. They all sat down, each reflecting on the day amongst themselves.

"What's your plan Ashira?" Taria asked. Siobhan hummed a note of agreement.

"Well, I have no desire to go back to the Monastery and I won't entertain the thought. But there is someone I think could help and I'll need to see if they're still stationed here first." A look of mild confusion was sent her way. "Then I'll see if I can get a message to them, and we'll go from there."

After a while of general conversation, story-telling and mild banter, the three women headed inside to get some sleep. Ashira closed her eyes knowing full well what the next day would bring.

Chapter 21

Ashira woke up early—very early—before the sun had even begun to rise. The day before, she had found a piece of paper and a writing utensil. She had written something down but showed no one. The note was carefully stored in a pouch on her belt. She quietly slipped out of the home so as not to disturb anyone else. She nodded silently and with a shared sense of respect at the sentries as she left the camp behind in the darkness. She walked back through the alleyways that had brought her there initially, the sounds of Korosento civilization becoming increasingly prominent as she neared the district. Standing in the shadows at the entrance to the service corridors, she looked out on the society she had left behind for a time. Nothing had changed. The people that were awake at this hour were all doing exactly the same thing as before. Going to work, coming home from work. Eating a meal. Sitting down with friends and laughing. All of the same things the little hidden society she had stumbled upon had with one significant difference. These people didn't fully understand what it was to do without the amenities they so cherished, and not long ago, neither had she.

She stepped out not knowing or caring if people were staring at her again. And it didn't matter either way. She had found something new, something better. She couldn't help the entire world; she couldn't help the entirety of Korosento. All she could do was help the people of the camp. A place where she had found something pure and good. Something worth trying for; a purpose. And it gave her hope.

Ashira walked along the surface streets lost only in her own thoughts. She thought about Kina. She thought about Maxus. She thought about the civil war at-large. She looked to the stars and remembered how much she missed flying in the upper atmosphere, gazing at those distant balls of fire. A small, nondescript sign caught her eye on a wall at a junction. Faded and worn, it was exactly what she had been looking for. She stopped for a moment and saw the first rays of daylight in the distance. She was unsure if this was the right thing to do, but she had to do something regardless. "Taria said a single step. Let's see where it goes," she said to no one in particular and she turned toward the direction the sign indicated. Back to the Sho Lin Memorial.

Entering the memorial was surreal. When she came through initially, she was lost in many ways, even though she didn't want to admit it to herself. She looked around and spotted a familiar form in the distance, a soldier in that unmistakable gleaming armor. She wondered if it was Hammer for a second but decided it best not to disturb him and let the situation play out on its own. Walking up to that prominent durastone circle felt more natural this time. Her mind was more at ease. Her body was not exhausted and utterly spent as before. She could focus more now instead of blindly delving into the Ki like a muhashki. This time she had a specific agenda. Off in the distance, the sun painted the Kiensei Monastery in light orange hues as it started its journey through the sky. The cool morning breeze tickled her skin and rustled the leaves of the trees. She felt it, the Ki through the trees in her mind. She was ready.

She took a cross-legged seated position in the middle of the circle and closed her eyes. She let her consciousness sink into the river of the Ki. She floated along as it ebbed and flowed. It carried her, sang its peaceful song to her like water gently lapping at the shore. In her mind's eye she saw stars, innumerous stars overhead, representing the light within the people of the world. The wind whispered past her, she whispered something back, speaking her desire and letting the wind carry it. The trees swayed in response. Kina was still there in the Ki, that familiar rustling was unmistakable, but it was distant. He wasn't in Korosento, but where exactly he was, she couldn't say because the Ki didn't work that way to her. She touched the celestial river, allowing it to soothingly lap at her hand, she whispered again, it reverberated, and the trees rustled in response. The wind touched her face like a gentle echo... there, that's who she was looking for. Thunder rumbled lowly in the distance, a warning maybe. But against what was not known. Her consciousness slowly rose back to where she was seated, her mind settled, and her eyes slowly opened. Time had passed and the sun was a little higher in the sky. She found it was the norm for her when meditating that deeply. Which is why she had to be careful where she did it. She knew she would be safe there in the memorial. Last time, her vision was chaotic and disorganized. Likely due to her exhaustion, her chaotic spirit and not knowing exactly what she was seeking. This time, it was extremely specific.

She watched the lone soldier make his rounds, knowing he had passed by her many, many times. She put her hands down on the durastone to help herself stand up. A walk would do her some good to stretch out the stiffness. Her hand touched something. Something unexpected, but not unwelcomed. Its familiar cylindrical shape had graced her hands many times before. "A ration bar," she said aloud as her fingers curled around it. She turned her head and saw the black lenses staring back at her from the eastern corner, where the guard changing ceremony was held. A barely distinguishable nod from the soldier and one in return from her solidified the exchange. Not one to turn down free food, not anymore at least, she ate it quickly and was reminded how bland they really were. "That has to be him," she thought as one corner of her mouth curled upward.

She approached him slowly, his gleaming armor not making any movement. In the distance she heard footsteps, glancing briefly she saw another guard coming down the path. It was time to change guards she thought, so she had better make this quick. "Hammer?" she questioned quietly. The soldier ever so slightly shook his head. "I'm sorry, my mistake," she said looking away.

"It's... Freq," said the guard as quietly as the helmet would allow. "Lieutenant Freq....... *Commander*." Her eyes went wide in surprise. She had never heard of him before, but evidently, he had heard of her. Probably from Hammer, she surmised.

"I'm not a commander anymore," she said quietly.

"Hmpf," he chortled, "as far as I'm concerned, you still are," he said.

Ashira fiddled with her fingers for a second, unsure of the soldier's response, then looked again at the distant solider still approaching. She summoned her courage and stood at her full height. "I need some help Freq, if you're willing?" she asked. The Tsugint stayed silent. A few moments passed. "I can understand if it's against regs, but it's not much," she said. Still no response. There was a time when she could have simply ordered him to help her, but that time had passed. She thought nervously for a moment, though she didn't show it. "Please?" she entreated.

Since she was technically a civilian citizen now, maybe a little politeness would help her cause. The footsteps got closer and closer. Suddenly Freq snapped to attention and turned sharply to face the incoming soldier. The change of guard procedure unfolded in front of her, and she remarked at how precise the movements were. Spinning rifles, function, and cleanliness checks. All very impressive. As the two guards passed one another at the end, Ashira thought at the very least she could compliment them. A little embernectar could go a long way, she had learned.

"Nicely done," she said genuinely.

"All clear sir," the incoming soldier said quietly.

"Come with me commander," Freq said.

The other soldier broke protocol. He dropped his arms down and turned around. "What!? You mean I have to stay out here?" he protested quietly.

"Listen Hammer, you got to hang out with her last time. This time, she hangs out with the rest of us. You can't always brag about the fun stuff that you *mostly* make up," Freq scolded playfully.

There he was. Ashira smiled at the soldier. "Sorry Hammer," she chuckled "maybe next time, ok?"

Hammer slumped slightly and exhaled a breath of dejection. "Ma'am, yes ma'am," he sulked as he reluctantly resumed his duties.

"Officer on deck!" one of the soldiers in the barracks called out as the lieutenant stepped inside. Immediately, four soldiers stopped what they were doing and snapped to attention.

"At ease, men," Freq said. The men casually went back to their business of polishing armor, cleaning a weapon, or watching a holovid. The barracks weren't what Ashira had thought they were from what she could see from behind the lieutenant. These guys had it made in the shade compared to most. There was a communal area with what appeared to be wonderfully comfortable seating. A full kitchen off to the side with..."is that a Percolux coffa machine?" Ashira saw in astonishment. There was a hallway in the rear that was lined with six doors, one for each soldier she guessed. Three individual restrooms, widescreen virtuaprojector with resolution scaling... man these guys were in paradise.

"Anything good today, sir?" VX0903 said, as he sat at the table polishing one of his pauldrons and not paying particular attention.

"You might say that Bounce" he replied, keeping quiet about the guest behind him.

"As long as it's better than whatever Hammer will probably conjure up when he gets back," VC0402 said, sitting with his back to the lieutenant as he blew non-existent dust off of a piece of his disassembled rifle.

"Eh, it might be Squelch," Freq said coyly.

The other two soldiers were seated on a couch, busy watching a virtuavid rerun of a speedster race and paid no attention to who was at the doorway. Freq removed his helmet revealing his barely visible blonde hair with very precise lines cut down the sides. Standing in a very official manner, he cleared his throat.

"Men! We have a guest. Let's show her some courtesy," Freq said loudly, stepping aside. Four heads turned towards them. Four sets of eyes stared in disbelief. The two soldiers on the couch glanced at each other briefly, then glanced around the room quickly at the others. In a split second all four jumped to their feet and simultaneously stood at attention, snapping a salute, and shouted 'Ma'am!' Ashira was humbled.

"Please, you don't need to salute me," she said.

"Just showing a bit of respect, commander" Freq said.

"Well... at ease, I suppose," she said humbly.

The two soldiers by the couch came around the end and were smiling as they walked up to her. One had silvery hair and a tattoo on his forehead, the other had the usual blonde hair, but his was longer and parted neatly on one side. She looked at them and a memory flashed through her mind. She couldn't remember every single Tsugint's name she had come in contact with, but she had seen them before, but where?

"Good to see you again, commander," the one with the silver hair said. "Sure is," said the other.

Ashira squinted, her mind a flurry of memories as she tried desperately to pinpoint where she had seen these two. A symbol she saw on the wall down a corridor flashed through her mind. Ra'andal? Firehawk Division!

"The ship *Crematoria*!? Above Ra'andal!? That was you two we knocked out in the galley! Right?" Ashira quipped. She and Reikeno had endured yet another ordeal from the siege of Ra'andal on the *Crematoria* where she and Reikeno were forced to defend themselves against a virus that infected the Tsugint soldiers aboard. Freq chuckled to himself at hearing that. The soldiers had told that story a few times since taking the assignment. It was just funnier coming from the one who actually did it he thought.

"You're... Stablos, right? And Sharpe?" Ashira guessed, pointing a finger at each of them.

"Yup, that's us all right. Surprised you remembered us actually," Sharpe said, rubbing the back of his silvery head sheepishly.

"Now, *Lady Mori*," Freq said with mock regality "you mentioned you needed some help. Not sure what we can do but lay it out there and we'll see what's possible."

Ashira nodded her head. She reached into a small pouch on her belt and produced the piece of paper she had written on and handed it to Freq. He looked at it curiously but with a hint of confusion. He unfolded the paper and read its contents. His brow furrowed a bit as he finished and folded the paper back up.

"You sure this is all you need?" he asked.

"It is," she replied with confidence and nodding her head.

"Well, all right then. Make yourself at home for a bit while I handle this. I'm sure the men here won't mind swapping a few war stories, right fellas?" he said looking around the room at the smiling faces. The nods in agreement said it all. "We don't get visitors here, so this is a welcomed treat. Xima isn't supposed to be here until tomorrow for his regular check-in so no worries on us getting in trouble. If he does show up unexpectedly, well, we'll just call it a *morale boosting exercise*," he winked. With that, Freq headed to his quarters and reemerged about fifteen minutes later to join the revelry.

Ashira stayed for a while, chatting with the men and swapping stories of the missions, battles, and skirmishes they had all been a part of. It felt good to be with them again, if only for a brief time. She appreciated their support just as much as they appreciated hers. The mood was light, the camaraderie deep, and the respect they all had for one another was high. They laughed; they remembered. And the coffa was awesome. Why in the world couldn't she have requested one of those machines on some of the ships she was stationed on? Oh yeah, that whole possessions thing.

It was nearly evening when a metallic knock came from the door. Immediately the conversations stopped, and all heads swiveled to face the door. Ashira looked at Freq, he looked back at her and inclined his head in assurance. He had made contact and the contact had arrived.

"I think that's for you," he said with subtlety.

She leaned forward on the couch putting her elbows on her knees, her face looking at the floor. She took a deep breath, stood up, and headed towards the door.

"Well boys, it was nice talking to you," she said with a smile. The metallic knock came again. "I'll see you around, I guess, but thanks again for your help." All five men nodded at her with steely loyalty. She pressed the door actuator, and it slid open with a hiss. She stepped out into the cool, evening air to a cloaked figure with its back turned to her. The door closed. A familiar voice soothingly spoke to her.

"I received a request at this location of the utmost urgency and that I was the only one to provide it?" the figure said.

"Here goes nothing," she thought.

"Hayto-kah, Sesni Asato," she said softly in the native Rodlekian speech. It was a phrase they had shared often during her time as a muhashki and becoming rarer with her time as a nisi. It had always invoked a sense of camaraderie and understanding when used between them.

The hooded figure of Kiensei Demio Kai Asato turned swiftly to face her. His masked and goggled face beamed with what she had come to know over the years as pleasant surprise. "Hayto-kah! Little 'Shira!"

Chapter 22 - Then

The Ki swirled about the longhouse with purpose. Ashira felt it. Her mother had grasped ahold of her in an attempt to both shield her and hold on to her for just a little while longer. She felt something pure, something comfortable, with this new stranger. Many of her people shied away from him because of his appearance and his power, but she could sense something... comforting about him.

She pushed and wrestled with the arms of her mother. She wanted to be free now, the mean people were gone, and she wanted to meet this person. "Mamaaaa..." she complained in frustration as Asi-ri grappled with her suddenly inconsolable child. "Want down! Want... down!" she began to cry out. Pushing at the imprisoning arms of her mother. "I want Ka'kwah, mama, I want Ka'kwah!" she grunted as she continually tried her best to force her mother's grip to subside. Something within Asi-ri stirred. Her grasp loosened as she let her daughter free.

Kiensei Runan Kai Asato found himself in the middle of a group of people who had never seen a real Kiensei before in their life. Most of them pulled away cautiously. Some looked on in awe at his display of the Ki he wielded. He turned slowly gauging the feelings of those still present and earnestly searching for one that was in charge. He found her not too far from himself.

"Master Kiensei," Impatria uttered as she agedly made her way towards him. "You honor us with your presence."

"The honor is mine," he said quietly with a bow of respect for the tribe's leader. "I apologize and beg your forgiveness at what has transpired here," he motioned openly with one of his long-fingered hands.

Kel-so huffed and grumbled on the ground nearby as several members of the tribe pushed their full weight on him, pinning him down.

"Please, tell us what has happened," Impatria asked softly. Her experienced eyes gleaming in the light of the fire.

Asato stood upright at his full height and steepled his hands as a show of respect. "The Kiensei Establishment received a request from the Regalia to investigate a source of unrest for your people. I am the Runan that was assigned to the task. Who that other person was, I cannot say. All I can say is that I discovered many discrepancies during my investigation, and they led me here. It appears that the source of the unrest was centered on..." he searched earnestly for the child. "Her," he pointed, finding the curious little face staring back at him.

All heads turned towards the child. Her beautiful blue eyes were fixated on the strange man standing before her. A small grin of acknowledgment crossed her chin as if she could feel the intent of what was to come.

Ashira had been set free from her mother's grasp. She had made her way forward, unbeknownst to the many standing around in amazement at the strange Kiensei before them. She could... feel... his gentle spirit. He was different than the other one.

She made her way towards him, slowly putting one small innocent foot in front of the other as she approached his tall and otherwise fearsome presence. She was not afraid, however. She was... curious. She made her way towards the man, her fellow Tesska parting and making way as she gingerly passed through and by them. She stopped just short of him, one arm tucked behind her back, the other at her chest in a seemingly royal fashion; something she had observed before.

The eyes of the gathered people were trained upon this moment.

Asato knelt down on one knee and extended his hand towards the little one. She wasn't afraid of him. Her essence within the Ki was one of strength and courage he felt. She smiled at him, her large round eyes never wavering. Her curious face beaming at him without prejudice. She extended her hand and took his.

Immediately the Ki surged in his body. A sense of peace, a sense of power, a sense of... fearlessness inundated his spirit. He watched as she nodded to him as if to acknowledge the unity they shared in the flow of Ki. He returned the gesture in kind. Surely the Ki had sent him there for more than just the mission. Surely it had sent him to bring this little one home to the monastery where she belonged.

"Hayto-kah little one," he said, smiling his species' best smile behind his mask. He knew it wasn't visible from the outside, but he tried his best to project it from the inside.

"Hayka," she said in her innocent little voice, trying her best to emulate the phrase. She liked this person, she thought. He was nice. He was kindhearted. She could tell.

The low comments amongst the crowd relayed their approval. Impatria smiled in agreement. Bo-ram and Asi-ri wept silently together, holding one another without any other recourse.

Their little girl... was truly a Kiensei.

Their pride was all but eclipsed by their pain. She would leave them soon; they realized this fact all too well. And they would likely never hear from her again.

A day's celebration ensued. Dancing, feasting, singing, and traditions that were many centuries old were invoked. Asato humbly accepted the generosity of the tribe as they bestowed the best they could offer towards him and the child. It was more than clear that these people valued the gifts she possessed and what it meant for her place in the wider world. Her parents were given places of honor, their home decorated on the outside with gifts and embellishments to signify their honorable sacrifice. One rotation remained in the decree, however. Kai Asato knew he must report back to the Regalia herself and settle the matter at hand once and for all. He sidled himself up to Impatria and keyed his comm.

"Master Kiensei," the page called back.

"Tell the Regalia I have captured the one responsible for the crime. I'll send you coordinates for the village. I do not have the ability to transport him. Can you send aid?" Asato said.

"Certainly," he said.

Impatria raised her hand. "I wish to speak," she said. Asato graciously handed her the comm and showed her how to use it. "This is the Narkash of the Ravaraki."

"Ka'kwha. I greet you Narkash of the Ravaraki," the man said respectfully.

"The man who was killed was my most trusted runner. He was to bring news of a child, born in my village. The child is a Kiensei," Impatria said.

"Are you certain?" he asked in disbelief.

"The Ki is strong with the child," Asato said. "I wish to take her with me to the Kiensei Monastery on Korosento."

"This is... wonderful news Master Kiensei. I shall inform the Regalia immediately. Narkash of the Ravaraki, you honor your tribe and the Tesska people," he said. A subtle click signaled the close of the channel.

An hour or so passed and a distinct rumble was heard from inside the longhouse. Many of the people stopped what they were doing and looked skyward in confusion. Music ceased; dancing paused.

"I suspect that would be your transportation," Asato said aloud to the bound and seated Kel-so. The sound of many footsteps approached. Odd he thought. That many to come and gather one criminal? Without warning, armed guards in formal armor entered the longhouse with long, gilded staffs ushering the people to make way. The Regalia herself appeared in the doorway like an angel. Gasps from the people were heard and all bowed low as her tall and elegant form glided into the room.

"I thank you Master Kiensei, on behalf of the Tesska peoples, for your service," the Regalia said.

He bowed low in response. "It is an honor to serve the people, your highness."

Two guards picked Kel-so up and began dragging his bound form out to a waiting ship. "Narkash of the Ravaraki," she said loudly. Impatria's cane tapped on the wooden floor as she came near. The elder woman dipped her head in acknowledgement as she stood in front of the Supreme Hallowed. "I am sorry for your tribe's loss. I entrust you to come and pass judgement on the man who took the life of one of your own in accordance with our long traditions." Impatria nodded in agreement. "I also hear there is something good to come of all of this," she said, her elegant head slowly rotated, her eyes scanning the room. "Where are the parents and the child?" she asked. A shuffling noise was heard as Bo-ram and Asi-ri, carrying little Ashira, made their way forward. They made low bows as they approached. "You bring honor and pride to our people," she said loudly. "May I have your names?"

"I am Bo-ram, Supreme Hallowed," he said with wonderment in his eyes. "This is Asi-ri and our little 'Shira," he shook his head slightly, "I-I mean, Ashira."

Ashira looked at the tall woman in front of her. She looked nice. She thrust herself away from her mother's grasp and held out two short little arms and hands towards the Regalia and said "Up!" with no reservations.

"No, no Ashira," Asi-ri said, "we do not do this to the Supreme Hallowed." The Regalia's eyes went wide, and a smile morphed the markings on her face at the little one's gesture. She took a step closer and reached for the child in return with a small chuckle.

"Hello little one," she said taking Ashira into her arms. The astonished looks from the gathered people and the parents showed that this was not normal but certainly welcomed. Gasps, whispers, and smiles permeated the large space. "You are special amongst our people. You make us very proud; did you know that?" she soothed. Ashira nodded. "Hims says Hayka," the little girl said proudly, pointing to Kai Asato. "Want down now," she wriggled and grunted. The Regalia chuckled and set her down and watched her run back to her mother. She motioned with two fingers over her left shoulder. An attendant who had waited in the doorway stepped forward carrying a tied bundle made from intricately woven cloth of the finest quality.

The Regalia nodded to the attendant who promptly opened the bundle. The corners fell revealing two, shining and ornate headpieces. They were made of gold and platinum and bore multicolored gold inlaid stripes and raised embellishments of vines, leaves and flowers. A central diamond shape of shining platinum was engraved with the royal seal. "A gift for you," she said to Bo-ram and Asi-ri, "in honor of your sacrifice for our people. Wear them with pride and all that see will know of your honor."

"Tuay'mai, Regalia," Asi-ri and Bo-ram both said with fealty.

"Master Kiensei," she called for and motioned to Asato, "I assume you are familiar with the name Taash?"

"Yes, your highness, she is one of our Establishment and also of your people," he said.

"Then I also assume you know of her sash?"

"I am not overly familiar, but I understand she wears one," he said quizzically.

She raised another two fingers over her shoulder and again and attendant brought another tied bundle similar to the other. Again, the Regalia nodded, and the bundle was opened. A plum-colored sash was revealed. It was made of a velveteen material with intricate dark patterns embroidered into it. "When she is old enough, give her this as a sign of honor and gratitude from her people," she said. The humble Kiensei took the item respectfully and promised he would.

"I too have a gift for when the child is older," Impatria spoke up. The Regalia motioned for her to continue. The aged woman trundled up to the Kiensei and reached into one of her beaded pouches. A tinkling was heard as she produced a metallic headpiece. Three silvery triangles on each side, hinged together and connected to a central, four-sided piece. Beads strung together formed the parts that would eventually hold it on her little head. Again, the Kiensei took the item humbly.

The Regalia stayed for a short while longer and even went with the tribe as they collectively escorted the Kiensei and the child to his awaiting ship. R-3B10 was there waiting. Little Ashira ran up to the mech and cocked her head inquisitively at the strange thing that made funny sounds. She extended a little finger and poked at one of its optical sensors. Rebi squawked in disapproval much to the shrill of excitement Ashira made at the sound. She did it again and tried her best to mimic the sound. Rebi was not amused. It extended a grasper and poked her in the nose. The little girl laughed and poked the mech again. Rebi poked back a little harder. She blinked momentarily and poked harder herself. "Rebi," Asato said with warning, knowing this would not end well. Rebi rattled its dome and chirruped that it wasn't the one who started the whole mess. "There will be plenty of time for that later," Asato said.

The little girl sat in the Kiensei's lap as they lifted off and headed into the starlit sky. Her blue eyes went wide at the view of her world from so far up and of the seemingly infinite sky ahead. She sat perfectly still taking in everything her little mind would allow. Her head swiveled back and forth as the *Spearpoint-class* fighter docked with the waiting portalspace ring, the clicks, bumps and hisses all new to her.

"Are you ready for a ride?" Kai Asato asked little Ashira, looking down at her. She looked up and over her shoulder from her perch in his lap and nodded vigorously. "Take us home, Rebi," he said.

Her eyes were never wider, and her smile never larger as distant stars stretched into lines and the churn of portalspace exploded in front of them.

The flickering yellow virtuagram of Lord Grunnery rose in front of a hooded man. "You have news?" he asked. His deep voice inflected with hopefulness.

"My lord, the effort on Karinar failed. We shall bear the costs of it as recompense," the holo said dryly.

"Money is of no consequence," he snarled. A brief moment of pause passed. "This is most... *displeasing* Grunnery," he said with anger hanging on each syllable. Five long and spindly fingers appeared from a fluted sleeve and contracted as if grasping at some invisible object. The yellow virtuagram writhed; the hands of Lord Grunnery clamored at his throat. Gurgling sounds came as the Hallen nobleman struggled to breathe.

"But... we... have... another..." Grunnery squeaked, the words struggling to form.

The spindly fingers opened, and the virtuagram appeared to collapse. The Hallen's chest heaved as he struggled to catch his breath.

"Explain," the hooded man said sternly.

Grunnery coughed in an effort to clear his throat. "Let me assure you, my lord, the Karinar incident is clean. Our sources have reported that they were able to acquire a package in the remote Morevallian archipelago. We will deliver it to you as soon as possible."

"Good," the man said sharply. "Success is the only recompense. Failure is death." The yellow visual flickered as the connection was severed. The cloaked man turned his tall and thin form to face his laboratory. His glowing yellow eyes pulsing with red blood vessels piercing the darkness of his hood. The blue-green lighting revealed a line of white medical capsules with clear covers had been placed in a row with myriads of sensors, probes and other scientific apparatus strung about. Some were already occupied; some were waiting for occupants. A long, thin finger pressed a button on his cloaked wrist. In a few seconds, the large metal door to the laboratory slid open with a hiss.

"You called, my master?" came the noble voice of a human male who was equally cloaked in reverent mimicry to his superior.

The yellow eyes gazed upon his apprentice. "Prepare the Ki transfer experiment Nobleman Stagnum. Our last necessary subject for this trial will arrive soon."

The other hooded figure of the Kageatsu known as Stagnum bowed in supplication to the command. "Yes, Nobleman Pestilent," he replied with fealty.

Stagnum hid his feelings deep. This was the last lesson for him to learn. Soon, his master would be dead, and the world would slowly work its way into his grasp.

Chapter 23

"This is a most unexpected surprise little 'Shira," Asato said in his most amicable voice. "It seems your ability to be more subtle has improved."

Ashira did not respond at once. She just stared solemnly into the patterned holes in the Rodlekian sesni's glasses, imagining what his eyes looked like behind them. In all their years together, she had never seen him without his necessary implements. This was difficult for her, asking for help from the very people she had walked away from. Deep down, she was glad he was here; she was glad that he had responded, and she was glad that he had come alone.

"Are you alright?" he asked softly, clasping his hands together.

During her time reminiscing with the soldiers, she had forgotten to rehearse what she was going to say in her mind. She didn't want to rely on the Kiensei anymore, for anything. But this was something she knew she could not accomplish by herself. Instead of trying to go it alone, she swallowed her own pride and asked for one of only two people she believed she could trust to help her.

"I'm fine, sesni," she said quietly. "I'm trying to get my feet back on solid ground and working towards making a life for myself." The first part was absolutely true, she was indeed trying to get settled so that she could figure out what to do next. The latter, not so much. She hadn't been successful at figuring that out just yet. "Can we take a walk, please?" she said, motioning back towards the park. He inclined his head and displayed his own open hand towards the path leading to the park.

The two figures walked side by side down the passageway away from the barracks. Ashira explained the situation with the homeless encampment and the incident with the Ghasto and handed over the injection module for him to study. Kai Asato listening intently and reserving his own comment until he had fully heard the young woman complete her story, pausing her only for clarifying questions. Demio Asato was confused about the plight of Siobhan. It wasn't a memory he was familiar with. He postulated that a clerical error of some sort could have prevented his review of the appeal and vowed to look into it.

The two walked along as they had done before, many years ago. The founder and the muhashki. The seeker and the adept. Behind them, the five Tsugint soldiers watched, admiring from the barracks' doorway, wondering what they were talking about, wondering if she would ever come back, and wondering how she could ever bolster her integrity so much more than she already had. All of them, had a deeper respect for the commander they had all come to know and admire. They certainly missed her.

The two passed through the park, through the elongated shadow of the statue of Sho Lin and onward towards the western passage back to the Balma district. As they walked, Ashira turned her head to tender a look at Hammer, still holding singular vigil in the park. She raised an arm in acknowledgement, he nodded ever so slightly to return the gesture, careful not to break protocol again, especially in the presence of an acting General of the Army.

"Ashira," Asato began as they passed into the streets of the district. "I am relieved that you felt comfortable enough to contact me. Though I am not sure how much I will be able to aid you. It seems I am to be assigned to the campaign at Harte Minosa in a few weeks and lead the Imperial efforts there where you and Wykera left off."

This was unwelcomed news. Her face became sullen, knowing it was a long shot to begin with, so it was not outside the realm of her expectation.

"However," Asato continued, "I believe Sesni Vikara has returned from Marishka's Dock. He is to be given a new assignment, but he may be able to look into your request concurrently," he said, touching his intricately engraved mask.

"Anything helps, sesni," she said with skeptical relief. She had quickly learned from those around her in Skyshade that help is help, regardless of its source. "Thank you. I was hoping maybe Sesni Busen could look into it as well. He is, after all, the resident specialist in the criminal underworld of Korosento." Demio Asato inclined his head.

The two friends walked into and along the service passageways leading to the camp. As they did, there were moments of awkward silence followed by brief moments of idle chit chat. Neither of them willing to address the elephant in the room. They talked about past missions; they mused about life in the monastery. They verbally danced around the fire of truth that burned between them as if playing a mental game of strategy. That is, until Demio Asato spoke up. He had waited long enough and had deduced it was the best and most forthright thing to do.

"Ashira, I need to apologize for my involvement in your decision to leave the Establishment," he said in a deep voice. Shame had crept into his mind since she left. Remorse was flowing freely; regret was welling up inside the honorable Kiensei Demio. "I cannot express how deeply I regret what happened." He had been deeply troubled by Ashira's departure. It stung watching such a talented and bright young individual completely renounce her only known way of life and knowing he had played a part. But he had to let her go. *They* had to let *her* go.

She stopped immediately in her footsteps, her expression unreadable. She had felt this conversation approaching, but the wound was still fresh in her mind. She sighed, exhaling repressed frustration, inhaling patience, and understanding. Her gaze softened, curiosity mingling with the pain etched on her heart.

"Sesni Asato," she said, her voice soft, "you were one of the few who I felt actually believed in me. Maybe not at the time, but you were the only one other than Kina that actually apologized for what had happened." She opened her arms, palms facing upward in nonverbal prostration. "Not even Demio Suramosa said a single word."

"Teka was one of your strongest supporters little 'Shira," he said quietly. "He spoke up to the Council in your defense and even wanted to chase after you and Kina when you left, but I halted him."

"But why?" she questioned intently. Teka Suromasa was a political savant, she believed, and she had also believed that the Assembly was the main driving force behind the council's actions. Her eyes widened; her focus intently fixed on her former mentor.

He paused for a moment. Touching his mask in deep reflection, knowing what he said next would carry an immense weight. His palms were steady, but his remorse was more than palpable. He moved his hands and clasped them in front of his chest. "Out of respect for you and your decision," he said softly. "Ashira, you are courageous, fearless, forthright and your moral compass reads truer than so many others I have ever met. You are wise beyond your years and the Establishment is a lesser institution without you. But you made a decision. A decision all your own. A decision that came from your innermost convictions with regard to who the Kiensei are, and who you are. But one influenced by our own failings, and my own I will admit." The tall Rodlek bowed low. "I cannot speak for the council, only for myself. I am sorry, Ashira. Please forgive me," he said.

Ashira was stunned. His actions were completely unexpected, but she welcomed them openly. Her heart leapt in her chest at the genuine gesture the honorable Demio offered. Her eyes softened and her chin quivered slightly as she turned away in an attempt at hiding her feelings. He stood up once again, but leaned towards her and offered an open hand. She glanced back, turned, and took it without question. Immediately the goodness she first sensed in this man when he came to take her from Karinar came pouring out once again. Oh yes, she remembered that day as it was one of her few remaining memories from her early childhood... before everything changed.

"I never wanted to leave," she whispered. Her voice laden with grating truth. "But after all I had accomplished, all I had sacrificed, I just couldn't stay," she said with sorrow saturating her voice.

"I'm very proud of who you've become," he said. His mask and glasses doing their best to hide the features they covered. "You should be too." She grinned in return.

A familiar chirrup sound pierced the air as the comm unit on his wrist lit up.

"You should probably get that," she said, knowing that it was likely the council summoning him back for some new event happening somewhere across the world. He nodded in agreement.

Unexpectedly, a strange scent wafted its way to the pair. It was pungent and ashen like something had burned. It smelled like "...biofuel transporters?" Ashira thought, her face twisting in confusion. Those loaders were usually used to haul things off in great quantities and were usually found at construction sites. Fear gripped her at once as her mind wandered towards a scenario she had hoped would never come and Asato sensed it.

"What is it, Ashira?" he rumbled with concern.

"Nothing good," she said aloud. Worry cemented her face, and she began running down the passageways towards the camp with Asato following closely.

In the distance was destruction. It was all too familiar for Ashira. From where she stood at the opening from the alleyway, it was a scene of desolation, of ruin. She had seen this too many times to count in too many cities. But this time it was different, this time, it was *her* home instead of someone else's. The camp was gone. Every square inch of it.

Nearby she saw the pincers of several WEB37 loader mechs grabbing at piles of debris like scavenger birds picking at a dead animal. She watched with a knot in her gut as each mouthful was bitten off of a pile of debris then spat into a waiting biofuel transporter. The imposing transporters spouted their foul stench as they bumbled along on their morphotracks to the recycler stations awaiting to devour their cargo of scavenged debris. She saw spindly-armed NAK-1.5's picking apart some of the various amalgamations of pipes and wires that had ferried their drinking water and other hard-earned infrastructure upgrades. Sparks flew as, one by one, wires were severed and repaired, or pipes were cut and welded. Her heart sank deeply as her eyes found the very spot where she had slept for quite some time. It was now barren. Her home was gone and so were the people that lived there. The memories all just wisps of dust in the demolition where something pure and good once stood.

"Greetings citizen," the FOR.3 Foreman mech said through its vocabulator as it approached. "Please refrain from approaching the site during salvage operations," it said in its monotone voice. The FOR.3 was a more robust version of the FOR-series of mechs. It was designed as humanoid, much like the FOR.5. This model had thicker body plates for better protection on construction sites along with improved scanning and ambulatory functions to navigate pits, holes, and uneven terrain.

Ashira was upset. "What are you doing!?" she shouted at the mech. "There were people... living, breathing people who lived here! There were *children* here!" She stepped menacingly towards the mech, her arms flinging wildly in frustration.

The mech held up a jointed, three-fingered hand in an effort to stop her. "Citizen. It is illegal to threaten a government sanctioned operation and its duly appointed representatives," it said in monotone warning.

"Since when does the government deal with destroying lives of those it's supposed to protect?" she bit out, still approaching the mech.

"Ashira, stop," Asato said astutely; placing a hand on her shoulder in an effort to prevent her from doing something he knew she would regret. "Let us keep calm," he said with reassurance. The Kiensei Demio positioned himself in front of Ashira, placing himself between the two. "Perhaps the foreman would be so kind as to explain this... sanctioned operation," he said cooly. He removed his ornately patterned cowl slowly, revealing his striking features. He placed his hands on his hips, conveniently exposing the sword hanging on his belt.

The mech elevated its head across the entirety of the Rodlek's imposing figure, using its opto-scanners to accurately assess his station. "Yes, Master Kiensei," it rasped digitally. "Pursuant to Korosento Code 893, Section 12B, Article 7.1, Subsection W.4.93, Paragraph 9..." the mech began. Asato was not amused, neither was Ashira.

"Get to the point foreman," his voice boomed.

"Yes, sir," it said. "In congruence with the law, all unauthorized residences within public spaces shall be immediately dismantled, its occupants relocated, and the site sanitized and reconditioned back to its original state," the mech said.

"Where are the people," Ashira asked aggressively from behind Kai Asato.

Asato motioned for her to remain calm. "Foreman, I demand to know where the people of this encampment have been relocated to," he said authoritatively.

The mech paused momentarily while parsing the data network. It produced a data tablet from its back and tapped at it with what appeared to be reluctance, and in a few moments, it spoke up. "The citizens have been reassigned to level seven."

"Level seven!?" Ashira piped up. "Is the air even breathable down there? Where exactly did they get moved to?" She remembered distinctly how stuffy and bitterly recycled the air was on Level Thirteen. She shuddered to think how much worse it would get the further down one went. She had never been that far down, and rumor had it that Level Two was as low as one could go. If the people were forced down there, then they were as good as lost forever. Poor Eilidh, she thought, she didn't deserve this. None of them did.

Turning its optical sensors towards her, the mech responded with a canned response. "I'm sorry citizen, the details of the reassignment are currently restricted per Korosento Code 243, Section 40J, Article 3.27, Subsection R.9.204, Paragraph U.21. You may solicit the Korosento Public Information Portal for further information."

Demio Asato bore down on the unassuming mech, bending at the hip and bringing his face closer. "Anything you can say to me, you can say to her," he said imposingly.

"Processing," the mech responded dryly. A moment of stillness passed amongst them as the mech filtered and sorted the command through its response tree. "Acknowledged. Level Seven has been designated as a reassignment level for all non-permanent residence status citizens of Korosento. The Korosento Transient Benefactory Act, also known as CSB 8213, established that all citizens without a permanent residence shall be moved to level seven as they are discovered. Certain areas of the level are still restricted, but many sections have been or are currently being rehabilitated to house the multitudes of displaced organics due to the massive influx of refugees from other parts of the planet in response to the needs arising from the civil war."

"So, it's out of sight out of mind then?" Ashira shouted angrily, stepping from behind Asato. He caught her with a singular hand, gazing down at her with an air of remaining calm.

"This will not solve the problem Ashira," he said calmly. "The mech is merely stating the law. And the law applies to all of us, whether we agree with it or not." He motioned to the foreman and dismissed him.

Ashira closed her eyes and huffed in frustration, but knew he was right. "This is ridiculous," she said with bated breath, shaking her head and throwing her hands up in frustration. "Those people were innocent. They were only trying to live, to survive!" She was one of them too. She knew that relegating them to such a deep level was essentially erasing them from the world. There was no telling what might happen to them down there, and there was no one to care for them, to protect them.

"I understand," Asato said quietly. "But the law is the law Ashira, and none of us are above it. You know this. Sometimes, we must let go the things we cannot control."

She glowered at the scene as he stared at her through his veiled implements. The distinct chirrup of his wrist comm sounded again. He looked at the comm, then at her as she looked at him.

"I'm sorry, but I must return to the monastery," he said with remorse. "I have done what I can. I promise that I will speak to Sesni Vikara on your behalf. What becomes of it, I cannot guarantee unfortunately."

As usual, politics stood in the way of the innocent people of the world, she thought. If Kina were here, they would be halfway down the lift shaft by now. But he wasn't. It was only her. "Thank you, sesni," she said abrasively. "I understand. Good luck on Harte Minosa."

Sesni Asato walked up to her and knelt down on one knee. "Here, take this," he said gently while opening his hand to offer her a few chits. "You can always come back to the Monastery if you decide to. But do so only if it's truly what you want to do, not if you believe what is expected of you. To do one, you must let go of the other."

For a split second, she was ready to refuse them, but she remembered Taria's words about handouts. She also knew that he wouldn't have offered them unless he genuinely meant well. He was, of course, her friend and a Kiensei after all. It was this kind of selflessness from the Establishment that she missed. She understood that his hands were politically cuffed just as much as hers had been... but no longer.

"Thank you, master," she said, taking the chits and stashing them in one of her belt pouches. She reminded herself yet again that she wasn't a Kiensei as she continually had to do, and as such, she was no longer intrinsically bound to the same codes of conduct that they were. Let go indeed. She could let go, but *what* to let go of was her decision, and hers alone.

"The Ki shall flow within you, always... little 'Shira," he said gingerly.

She watched her friend rise, turn, and walk back towards the alleyways in which they had arrived. He pulled his cowl back over his head, stopped and turned with a shallow bow and steepled fingers. He reminded her not to give in to her anger or fear and to use that beautiful mind and fearless spirit she owned to do what was right and just.

She didn't know it then, but this was the last time she would ever see him.

Ashira stood at a distance and watched as the last of the debris, which had been painstakingly scavenged by the former residents, was loaded. The last biofuel loader puffed its disgusting gray plume as it rumbled away. The silence left behind was eerie to her. Once, there was a small community of people with a singular goal to just survive. The voices, the people, the laughter, the sense of community. She thought longingly at how much they had accomplished, how hard they had worked. All destroyed and tossed away like garbage. Now, there was emptiness. Both in front of her and within her. She stared at the void where the shack belonging to Taria, Siobhan and Eilidh had once stood, where she had rested her head at night. She remarked to herself at how that little place had kept her sheltered for a time and reminisced on the good that remained. The smiles and laughter of Eilidh played back over and over in her mind. She was sad, however. She thought about Taria. She even thought about Siobhan. She thought about little Eilidh and how she was sure her parents fought valiantly to protect her... as she, herself, would have done—*did* do. The wheels and cogs of the Imperial government had turned. This time, not to her favor as they had done so before. Level seven was a long way down, and level seven encompassed the entire metropolis.

Ashira walked along the streets of the Balma district in a numbed daze. She had nowhere to go, no reasonable way to get there if she did, and no one to turn to if it happened. The citizens flowing around her went about their usual routines. The laughter and normalcy of a day's release echoed in her mind as she struggled to find peace. She had found a place to belong, much like the Kiensei, and again, it was ripped from her. "Alone again," she said to herself.

"Maybe that's the way it's supposed to be for me," she thought. She felt like a ship without a rudder, tempest tossed upon the waves of destiny. She was afloat for now but had no clue as to what she was supposed to do. No clue as to where she was supposed to go. She had come to realize something that had nagged at her soul for some time now. The realization that life as a Kiensei had failed her in some way. It had failed to teach her how to simply... live. Live as a regular person in the wilds of civilian life. Instead, she had only learned how to fight, how to be a warrior. How to be a soldier. It wasn't enough that by many Planetary standards she was still a child, and that the Establishment had no problems sending children into battle to kill, to watch others die, or to die themselves.

There were many thoughts waging a war in her mind. But instead of fighting with herself, she fell back once again on her training. She needed somewhere to go for shelter. She thought about the Pliaza, going back to Iraila. No. She didn't want to be burdensome to the elderly woman. She thought about seeing if the boys at the park would let her camp there for a bit. No. Xima would eventually find out and that would cause more trouble for her brothers than it was worth. She thought about returning to the Monastery again. She snickered at her own hubris. No, that would be ridiculous. There was no way she was going back there. She was stuck in a rut and had no idea what it would take to get herself out of it. But she was confident that there was a way, and she would find it.

"Think, Ashira, you can do this," she said encouragingly to herself.

Unexpectedly she heard something. Wings? Wings propelling something through the air. She looked up and saw the silhouette of something... a bat? No. Some other winged creature gliding on the artificial currents above. Something like a cold chill crawled lightly across her skin causing her to instinctually adjust her shoulders. It was the Ki. She couldn't explain it, but she knew this creature. She didn't connect with it. *It* connected with her. It... *called* to her.

A gasp marked her own realization that this could be the same creature that saved her from the Ghasto. She looked up in wonderment and studied the creature as it circled back, its silhouette distinguishable against the evening sky, and flew over her once again. It was... leading her. It drew her in like a magnet pulling on ferrous material. It wanted her to follow it.

She walked along the crowded thoroughfares, ignoring the nightlife and the peoples of the great, ceaseless city. Her gaze, skyward as she followed the creature along an unknown path, oblivious to life all around her. All at once, it accelerated forward. Outpacing her as it flew on ahead. Her connection to it had ceased and she didn't know what it wanted, or what she was supposed to do, other than... just follow it. She watched as its figure became less of a silhouette and more a darkened dot against the creamy orange lit sky. She didn't run after it; she didn't feel the need to.

Ashira came to an intersection. She had lost sight of the bird and wondered if she done something wrong, or it... just left? Closing her eyes and centering herself in the Ki, she could feel it. It was there, perched in a swaying bough in her sensation. It was calling to her. She could almost make out what seemed like... words? Was it trying to talk to her? The warmth on her face helped her discerned the direction she needed to go like feeling the sun as it shone down. She turned and walked down a nondescript passageway. There were parts of her that resisted the urge nervously, but they were overwhelmed by the parts that felt as though this direction was right. It felt *right*. It felt... peaceful. As she walked along, making turns, and following new paths, her sense of peace became stronger. The final left-hand turn brought her to an overlook. A spot where the service corridor met a place where the skyline opened up. A hidden gem of a view she thought initially. A view into the distant skyline imbued with light and darkness alike. In the distance, the descending sun shone its golden orange glow against the sky like a fine work of art. On a ledge, the outline of an owl... *the* owl... tempted her gaze. She stared at the figure; it stared back. It... *connected* with her once more and she allowed it to permeate her thoughts. She could not discern the ancient language that reverberated in her mind, but she could understand the intention it projected. It wanted her there, in that place, in that moment. She began to approach it slowly with short, measured steps.

She called out to it, her voice cautious but steadfast. "What do you want with me?" No answer. It just sat still, gazing back at her with its gilded feathers tucked in neatly.

She tried entreating it with subtlety through the Ki, asking what it wanted and why it wanted her. Again, no answer. It continued to stare at her as she cautiously approached, its bright eyes continually drawing her in and drowning her in their power. She tried to connect with it. She stopped in her approach and closed her eyes, reaching an open hand towards it. Almost immediately her eyes snapped open as her attempt was pushed back.

"No," she thought she heard.

Suddenly, her vision began to blur slightly, and her senses dulled minorly. She blinked and shook her head at the sensation that tried to cripple her. It wasn't painful, it was... strangely calming, but strange, nonetheless. This was unlike anything she had experienced before.

Her vision began to reciprocate backwards and forwards, centered on the owl, along with a low oscillating sound. "Why?" she called out, her own voice sounding ethereal. "What do you want with me?" she entreated. Again, no answer.

Those blazing green eyes continued to stare as she stared back, those eyes the only focus in her pulsating vision. Ashira stood as if in a meditative position, not knowing what to do next when the owl spread its wings, stretching them regally. Its deep green eyes still locked on hers. It leapt and began speeding straight towards her almost as if... it was going to attack? Ashira felt strength return to her and she raised her forearms in defense. Only... the bird landed on her arm as light as a feather. Her vision normalized; the low oscillating sound ceased. She slowly lowered her arm, leveling it with the ground.

The owl looked at her then cocked its head to each side as if studying her for a moment. Those green eyes blinking from time to time in curious introspection.

"Hi," was all Ashira could say in bewilderment. This was one of the most bizarre things to ever happen to her, and she had seen some pretty bizarre things. The owl responded with blinking eyes and a chirping sound. She instinctively brought a finger towards it, gently stroking its feathered neck. The bird responded as if it accepted the gesture. It was all very strange. In that moment, Ashira felt as though she had known this creature her whole life... but she hadn't. She couldn't have. What *was* this feeling... this... *connection*?

"You got a name?" she asked humorously, her voice laden with wonderment and perplexity. She chuckled slightly to herself. Yeah, right. As if this thing is gonna...

"Raiju," an angelic yet whispery voice echoed in her mind like windchimes in a breeze. Ashira blinked. Did this thing just *talk* to me? She thought. "Raiju?" she said aloud. The bird hooted happily.

"Ok then, Raiju...," she chortled slightly, "what are we doing here?" Ashira was completely confused. Those green eyes bore into her. She seized only for the briefest of moments, every muscle in her body firing as if a bolt of lightning had run through her... but without pain. Blackness and silence enveloped them. Abruptly, from a singularity of light... stars began to churn, celestial bodies came into form. Ashira found herself standing in a field of tall grass, near a lake, of sorts. A border of tall trees behind her, gently swaying. "This..."

she said breathily. Her face mirroring the recognition she felt deep inside.

"I know this place. I've seen it before, like from a dream." Raiju cooed softly; strange voices whispered in ancient tongues as a breeze tickled the tops of the tall grass. The cool air was comforting, peaceful. Ashira was thoroughly amazed and confused all at the same time.

"Who... or what... *are* you?" she said to the owl still resting on her forearm.

"*Guide,*" an angelic voice twinkled in her mind.

"A guide?" she questioned aloud. "Guide to what, exactly? I don't understand."

"*Destiny,*" the twinkling voice responded. The owl blinking steadily.

"Where did you... come from?" she asked, her face full of wonder. A distinct and different female voice flowed like a rolling mist out from the swaying trees behind her. "I am Amamikoto." She knew that voice. She knew that... person.

Ashira turned swiftly on her heels to face the familiarity behind her, only to find nothing. She looked frantically, searching for something, anything that would help her understand. The memories of Rigort began replaying in her mind. Some inexplicable, some downright frightening. And yet, the days they spent there, were like a few seconds in real time. She realized then that this was all beyond her understanding. She felt the Ki moving strongly about her and decided it was futile to fight against it. The Ki was calling to her.

She knelt down with Raiju still perched on her arm, the ground underneath her undulated as if they were ripples on a body of water. Raiju leapt, and resettled on her shoulder as Ashira tucked her legs beneath her. She closed her eyes, placed her hands on her thighs and gave herself to whatever the Ki had in store for her.

She let go.

"The Ki flows within me and the Ki flows for me," she whispered, but her own voice rolled like a storm in that place. It echoed over, and over, and over. It echoed as if she had voiced it over and over and over again, but she had not.

All became silent. The last resonances subsided. Her senses returned to her. She smelled the lifestyle of Korosento again. She heard the hum and thrum of scootsters and of people. She felt the cold, hard ground beneath her. She opened her eyes and saw Raiju perched out in front of her on the parapet.

Raiju locked her gaze to Ashira's. She briefly ruffled her feathers then extended her wings and took to the sky. Ashira saw something in the distance that had been hidden by the bird's silhouette. She looked up, but Raiju was nowhere to be found. In the glowing distance, once hidden... was the outline of a building. She knew that building. A moment of clarity washed over her. A peace. A tranquility. The boughs of the sentinel evergreens swayed and danced with the quiescent breeze of the Ki to her. She literally had no idea where she had just been, but it was clear to her where she needed to go.

"Thank you, Raiju," she uttered softly.

Chapter 24

Ashira stood in the imposing shadow of one of the many high rises of the illustrious Imperial District. She looked at the large building in front of her, the Burja Mantoori building. Named for its architect, its greenish hue against the skyline was indicative of some of the metallurgy in its construction was a clear sign of what the building was, and more importantly, who lived there. There were many people of high status, some of whom she had directly or indirectly met on assignments in her former life. But she was only interested in one in particular. The rounded peaks of the building represented the shoulders, according to the dedication placard; the weight-bearing attributes of those housed within. Prefects of the Realm called this building, amongst others, home.

Security here was tight. It had to be. But with all of the preparations, attempts had been made and a few even succeeded on the lives of those who lived here. Korosento's criminal element at times was like trying to wrangle a hydra that already had a thousand heads by lopping off a few hundred at a time. Ashira knew the intricacies of the patrols and the systems used by the building. After all, she had once patrolled here and provided security escort for one of the more prominent residents. But that was a different time... when she had credentials to grant her access. She didn't want to commit a crime by breaking and entering... but thought a carefully, albeit unannounced, visit may be more acceptable. Who was she kidding anyways? To get in, she'd have to break-in. Not something she was overly excited about, but it was the only path she had in front of her, so she had to take it.

She continued to sit in the shadows in the near distance, watching as the regularly scheduled Korosento Guard patrols came by... just as she remembered them. Exactly eight and a half minutes between each patrol. Not long enough to bypass the access control system at the lobby door... not to mention dealing with the TA-TL Doorkeeper mech too. She puzzled on this for a moment longer.

There was the skycraft landing and parking bay. No. Too high up. She huffed to herself in annoyance. "Think, Ashira, think," she grumbled to herself. At this point, she was kicking herself for making all of those security improvement suggestions after that incident with the assassin and the Amatricia Delegation dinner. No access through the ventilation system... it was now basic ion shielded because plasma shielding was just way over the top. No access from the roof... the sky lanes were restricted above, and she didn't have access to a scootster.

She looked up and had a moment of clarity. On the exterior of the building were observation rooms and elevator shafts that were encased in transparmor and bronzium alloy framing. The golden checkered patterns reminded her of some vertical chess board, or something like that. Between the structural sections of the building jutted small ledges of durastone that gave the structure both rigidity and aesthetic appeal, well, at least from the architect's view over a hundred standard years ago. Those ledges were navigable. She remembered something vague... a maintenance loading bay somewhere about a third of the way up that was used for servicing and maintaining some of the larger building systems. It would be a stretch, but she might be able to reach it. She just hoped the service portal doorway wasn't locked. She would have to wait until dark or else risk being spotted from the ground.

Nighttime came once again in its usual circadian rhythm. The continuous flow of airborne traffic around the various buildings of the sector was unrelenting as the time passed. Positioning herself unassumingly at a public refresher station about a hundred meters from the base of the building, Ashira waited for the opportune moment to move. She had taken the time, whilst waiting on sunset, to mentally map out her route. She had gone over each and every projected movement at least a dozen times. She was about as prepared as one could be for one who had designed the security detail for this building.

The patrol came into view. Two soldiers in their red accented Kintsugi Guard armor. A lull in the general foot traffic. The upward facing lights hadn't switched on yet. The time was now. She emerged from her roost behind the refresher and quickly, but steadily, made her way towards the building, careful not to expose herself. She turned and rested her back against the cool wall at the base of the building and watched as the patrol continued on and out of sight. She quickly looked around... no one was paying attention. Good. She turned around and looked straight up at the first platform. Checking her surroundings again, she summoned the strength of the Ki and leapt upward. She grasped the edge and quickly pulled herself up onto the ledge, lying flat to lessen her silhouette. A quick glance around and she moved to a crouch and prepared for her next jump. The lifts were stationary for the moment, the meeting rooms were dark. It was quite possible that the Assembly was still in session debating some intricate bill. No one noticed her and all was well... she made the second jump, the third jump, the fourth, the fifth, and so on. She jumped, climbed, and paused to observe, repeating the pattern at each landing until the portal was in sight. Suddenly, the Ki alerted her to something unexpected. She instinctively dropped flat on her stomach as a red laser light shot out from the side of the building, scanning the immediate area of the ledge. It slowly scanned across the horizontal plane of the entire ledge, then switched quickly to the vertical. Ashira had to move fast. In between the sensor switching planes she rolled herself off the ledge, hanging on to a fortunate hollow left behind from a bit of durastone cracking and falling off some time ago. She had barely fit three fingers on one hand into it and was holding on as tight as possible. "Hmm... upgrades," she mused. A multidimensional environment sensor, she thought. Had it detected her, she was sure she'd be spending the night in a holding cell... again.

The scan was progressing slowly, her fingers beginning to ache with the strain of the planet's gravity pulling on her. It finished its vertical sweep then switched again to horizontal. "This thing needs to hurry up," she thought. Her grip strength was waning, and she wasn't sure how much longer she could hold out. She knew it was a bad idea, but she looked down. A flashback to a previous military mission interrupted her concentration momentarily. Her fingers slipped slightly. The wall, she remembered. The ground was close enough for her to cushion a fall using the Ki, but it would cause a scene and crack open all kinds of fresh hell upon her. Her fingers began slipping more. She strained with all she could muster to keep her grip. Just a little bit more, she kept telling herself. The scan finished just as her fingers lost their hold. She hung in the air for a split second. Quickly thrusting up with her opposite hand, she was able to barely grasp the ledge, saving herself from a fall. Swinging her body weight sideways, she was able to regain a hold with her opposite hand. Pulling herself upward, she rolled onto the ledge on her back in satisfaction. She placed her hands on her midriff, closed her eyes briefly and exhaled a breath of gratitude for her fortune. "That was close," she said to no one in particular.

She rolled over to her knees and looked around. Only one more platform to reach the maintenance bay. A quick sensory exploration through the Ki and she leapt up and over to the platform. As she looked back, she realized she had made her move without a second to spare as the shapes of several people appeared in the windows where she just left, presumably to enjoy the view. A moment of calculated caution as she scanned the area. No patrols. No cameras. There was a keypad securing access to the building, but she had no credentials anymore. If she forced the door, an alarm would sound. Fortunately, she had been Kina Wykera's nisi and good thing he had taught her otherwise.

Some maintenance work had apparently been going on, so there were bits of discarded tech, bits of metal and other materials scattered on the platform. She found a bit of wire and a broken metal ring. The makings of an electromagnet. That would do for one part of the door, she thought. Rummaging around she found a small piece of thermoflect insulation. Its mirror-like finish was perfect for windows, but for her needs, it was perfect for bypassing an optical door sensor. The hard part was finding the sensor itself and making sure not to break its beam and again, setting off an alarm.

She fiddled with the keypad and eventually removed it enough to access the wiring behind it. Tapping into the power leads with the wires from the cobbled together magnet, she instantly realized her mistake. It leapt from her hand and attached to the door with a loud clang. It was stronger than expected, Ashira realized, as she winced at the sound. She hastily disconnected it and haphazardly reattached the keypad. She quickly retreated and ducked behind the nearest condenser unit and waited. Surely someone would have heard that. After what seemed ages with no one coming to check, she crept cautiously back to the door. Perhaps she should find the sensor first since that would be the make-or-break moment of this whole operation... "not operation," she reminded herself out loud.

Part of learning to wield the Ki lied in learning that "size does not matter" as Ungosh Harichi would put it. There were plenty of exercises that taught all underlings not to judge an object's size against the capabilities of the Ki. Commonly, the budding young Kiensei would fail at these tests designed to show them that even against seemingly large and ridiculously heavy objects, the Ki could be used to control them. Ashira smirked at the memory of her own failings and subsequent revelations. But there was a much bigger challenge that followed. Not in how large an object seemed, but in how small. Early lessons in the Kiensei Establishment were woven together like intricate tapestries. Misdirection was always the norm for the young ones as lessons were often meant to create failure, so that the real lesson could then begin. Once the learners understood the concept of *'large size doesn't matter,'* it was then that the larger lesson in *'small size doesn't'* would begin followed by *'many objects doesn't matter.'* It was one thing to control a single object, of any size, but an entirely different thing to control many objects, especially very small ones.

Ashira stood before the door, closed her eyes, and let herself feel the river of Ki flow through her body and across her skin. It tingled slightly as the sensation began at her shoulders and flowed down her arms to her hands. She let her other senses float along the platform mere millimeters above its surface, finding the smallest speck of dust amongst a sea of debris. Sensing the facets, the surfaces, the composition of every single particle. Strange, she thought, as she hadn't been able to do that in times past. Her abilities had grown in ways she couldn't explain. She raised her hand with an upturned and empty palm. All around her, a thin, wispy, and barely visible cloud of dust rose. Turning her palm over, it coalesced into a thin sheet about as large as a standard tablet. She had to be careful, she reminded herself. She had to space the particles apart just so... so as not to trigger the optical sensor while still revealing its location within the door frame. She placed her consciousness within the dust cloud and piloted it through the narrow crevices along the door; her eyes opening yet still sensing the position of the cloud. Turning a corner, panning around, until finally... a glint of laser light, barely in the visible spectrum. There it was just above the middle hinge. Pulling the miniscule dust cloud free, she released it to disperse like vapor in a breeze with her fingers splayed.

Ashira found the latching mechanism and, this time, carefully positioned the electromagnet, connecting the power leads. She made sure to hold the apparatus against the door before making the final connection to prevent another loud clang. With the magnet securely in place, she pulled on it sideways, thus pulling the latch free, effectively releasing the door. But now, the difficult part.

Ashira used the Ki to carefully release every crinkle, every divot in the surface of the small piece of thermoflect. It had to be perfect. She carefully raised the small piece towards the sensor path, guiding it flat against the door jamb to keep the distance intact. She slowly, very slowly, slid it inward until the beam was intercepted.

No alarm. Good. She curled a corner of her mouth in a sly yet confident grin.

She gradually opened the door. Initially just a small crack, then slowly and steadily more and more, continuing to hold that precious little piece of film perfectly still as she did so. After a few breathless moments, the opening was large enough for her to squeeze in. She slid inside swiftly and quietly before pulling the door shut. She pushed the sliver of film out without incident, and in taking a breath, used the Ki to push the electromagnet back to its location and closing the latch. She knew someone would eventually find the apparatus, but she would likely be gone by then.

This was a one-way trip. It would either end badly, or good. Nothing ventured, nothing gained.

Ashira made her way inside carefully. Using all of her talents and abilities, she found her way to the main elevators without detection. It was quiet in the building with hardly anyone traversing the halls at this time. No cameras on this floor yet; another win. There on the wall was the Kiensei Override mechanism. A simple use of the Ki... pulling, rotating, pushing, and the call light flashed a victorious green. Precious seconds passed as she patiently waited for the lift to arrive, hoping beyond hope that no one was waiting for her. She had a decent story prepped just in case, but hoped she wouldn't have to use it simply because her disheveled state would be her own downfall. The lift arrived with a smoothly toned chime. The doors parted to reveal that no one else would be joining her on the way up... she hoped. She stepped aboard and faced the keypad that stood in her way towards her destination.

Kina's override code came to the forefront of her mind. She wasn't proud of it, but since he was like a big brother to her, she wasn't ashamed of eavesdropping on one or two... call it twenty or more conversations he had had. Even the personal ones. It was her job anyways to look after him, she rationalized to herself, so the best way she knew to do it was by knowing everything about him that she possibly could.

She input his user ID code, 052577 and his passcode of 8810. The screen lit up a reassuring blue color to indicate a successful attempt. She pressed the appropriate button, the doors closed, and a gravitational pull towards the floor indicated that she was on her way up. The music was as terrible as ever, she thought. As fancy as this place was, they could at least put on something decent... like the Wavers or something more engaging than the music filtering into the lift.

She was nervous. It wasn't easy for her to just show up unannounced to Damae's apartment. After all, this was... *the*... Prefect Damae Miada, one of the most well-known names in the Realm, and she was breaking into her home. What would Damae say? What would *she* say? Kina wasn't there, she was sure of it. What if Damae made her leave? What if Kina showed up all of a sudden?

Her mind flooded with questions without answers as the lift steadily chimed the passing of each floor.

The familiar 'ding' of the lift and the sensation of her stomach rising announced the arrival to the destination. She had nowhere else to go, and no one else to turn to... except Damae. The doors opened and she took a step towards an unknown destination in a familiar land.

The comfortable blue tinge to the modernistic apartment was calming, in a way, as she stepped into the formal dining and reception area that was commonly used to host guests and delegates. Ashira had spent quite a bit of time here by Damae's side. It wasn't a feeling of 'home' more so than a feeling of comfort. She had always felt safe, at peace, while she was here. The illustrious prefect from Hachani had taken great care to not flaunt her opulence openly while still keeping ties to her homeland. Something Ashira had come to admire and respect about her. The decorations were subtle and minimalistic. A few pieces of native pottery here, an impressionistic painting there, an antique piece of handmade furniture over there. All bathed in the ever-changing light flowing in through the curved penthouse skylights overhead. Ashira made her way across the space, passing by the formal dining table. She perked up as the sound of footsteps came up from the stairs across the way. They were metallic. That had to be....

"Greetings Lady Mori," came the tinny voice of M-AR40 appearing at the top of the staircase. "Your arrival is most unexpected, but how might I be of service?" he chimed.

"How did you know it was me?" she questioned.

"Well, Master Kina is out on assignment at the moment, and I logically deduced that you would be the only other person with his private override code," the silvery protocol mech said. "Prefect Miada has ensured that even her maidens have separate codes so that she can track who comes in and out of her home."

"Good to know," Ashira said with feigned interest. "Is the lady prefect home?"

"Yes, Lady Mori, she is. She's currently on a virtuacall, but I will escort you to the waiting area."

Ashira's anxiety grew with each spiraling step down towards the open seating area. She largely ignored Ar-forty's clumsy attempt at small-talk conversation. Mostly about her ordeal. Even so, she loved this place. It had such a wonderful view of the Korosento skyline. The seating was placed in an open-air, vaulted space with a large open balcony bordered by large, white tapered columns. It was like a personal suite at the world's biggest opera. The semi-circular couches in the middle of the space overlooked the Imperial District and the Assembly Building proper. The golden water fountain burbling gently was always a welcomed treat. From what she had learned through listening, Damae had modeled most of the apartment from her homeland, including the elaborate floors of smooth durastone stained with red and black accents. The statues, Ashira could do without, they were kind of creepy, but who was she to judge. She viewed the space and at once wondered how many times Kina had been here because... well... he *had* been there, and she knew it.

"Please, be seated," the mech motioned. "The prefect will be with you shortly," M-AR40 said dryly. "Can I offer you anything? A beverage perhaps?"

"Just some water, please," she said.

Ashira immediately felt bad for sitting on the pristinely kept furniture in her state, so she sat on the edge in a less than comfortable manner, her arms and legs tucked as tightly as she could make them. Ar-forty disappeared shortly and arrived once again at her side with a monogramed glass of water. The lanky mech made a courteous bow and skittered off towards the chamber of the lady of the house.

In the distance she could hear the voice of her friend speaking to someone she didn't know. *Ciara* or something like that. She could hear Ar-forty announce himself cordially but with fealty. There were benefits to her Tesska physiology, of course, even though she was technically a hybrid. Apparently, he had not announced her arrival before now as the sound of a hurried excuse came along with... hurried footsteps?

Ashira braced herself for...well... *something*. She didn't know what to expect really. If she expected the worst and hoped for the best, she told herself that she would side skirt disappointment altogether. The sound of rushing feet came closer and closer, the echoes reverberating increasingly through the archway nearby. Ashira quickly downed the glass of water then rose from her timid perch on the couch, still trying to keep herself as tucked in as possible, her hands clasped in front of her.

This was her one chance. A last chance.

Chapter 25

The graceful and elegant form of Damae Miada quickly appeared in the archway in the rear of the seating area. She was clothed in a fine gown of gray silka that flowed around her like a delicate fog rolling slowly down a mountain. Jeweled and beaded strings flowed outward and across her arms from a central jeweled broach in the center of her chest. The straps framed her delicate decolletage. Her reddish-brown hair was down with seemingly infinite curls and pinned back from her face with a silver and pearl studded headband. She stopped suddenly at the sight of Ashira, her face melting into one of surprise and joy. Ashira's was one of humble obsecration.

"Ashira!?" Damae cried out in surprise as she spotted her. She at once broke into a hurried walk towards the young Tesska. Her flowing gown appeared to restrict her ability to actually run, but she gathered the bottom of the dress as best she could to allow her more freedom of movement.

Ashira sensed a feeling of relief from the lauded prefect, but respectfully, she closed her eyes with a gentle bow, almost refusing to look her in the face out of shame from showing up unannounced. She hadn't seen Damae since her trial ended and certainly didn't contact her when she left the monastery. But she was sure Kina gave her the usual emotion-filled news. She was overtaken by surprise when the prefect came upon her unceremoniously and wrapped her up in her arms, embracing her tightly... with a love she couldn't describe... even in Ashira's tousled state.

"Oh, my *goodness*," Damae exclaimed "it's so good to see you! Where have you been? Are you all right?" The flood of questions overtook Ashira. She was temporarily at a loss for words. She wasn't prepared to respond to whatever the prefect volleyed her way. She wasn't prepared for this... kindness. She wasn't prepared to deal with how she felt in this moment. Her tired knees began to shake.

"I... didn't know... where else to go," Ashira said brokenly with labored effort. Her chin began to quiver as she began to lose control of her carefully guarded emotions. She turned her head sideways on Damae's shoulder as if to keep the woman from seeing her facade beginning to crack. She felt the comfort as Damae's hold upon her tightened slightly and her hand gently cradled the back of her head.

"Are you alright?" Damae said once more but quietly. "Are you hurt?"

"No," Ashira gasped. It was all she could muster.

Her usually strong shoulders began to heave slightly. Her forthright chest tightened like a large animal was sitting on it. Her snippy-voiced throat seized like a great ape was choking it. Tears flooded her eyes as the deep well of emotions rose within her. The Kiensei were not supposed to give in to their emotions. The Kiensei were supposed to be in control of themselves at all times. The Kiensei were supposed to remain strong and professional even in the face of tragedy and disaster.

But she was no Kiensei, not anymore.

She could no longer hold it all back; the forces of emotion were too strong for her. She let herself go in this moment with someone she truly trusted. She allowed herself to be truly vulnerable for the first time in her life. She wasn't a Kiensei; she wasn't a peacemaker. She wasn't a commander in the army, she wasn't a protector. She wasn't the snippy little sister to one of the greatest Kiensei of the Establishment, she wasn't anything in this moment other than her true self. Just a person existing in this wide world steeped in turmoil, trying to survive and just live, day to day.

"It's okay," Damae whispered in her ear. "It's okay. I'm here." She hugged the young Tesska just a little tighter as her weight began to pull them downward. Ashira's legs gave way as they both slowly sank to the floor. This was something new, something different, something... pure, for Ashira. Instinctually, she raised her arms and clasped them around Damae in a show of equal affection. Something she hadn't done willingly in a while, not since almost freezing to death with Reikuno on that crazy mission. But that was an instinct to protect, this was one of surrender. In this moment she didn't have to be brave, she didn't have to be the strong one. In this moment, someone else was being strong for her. Her heart opened and poured out all that had been repressed for so long. And it was good.

The two sat there in the open floor. Just holding, just comforting, just being there in the moment. Ashira sank herself deeper into the loving and supportive embrace of her friend and allowed herself to be cared for, to be supported. As her façade continued to crumble like a glacier falling into the sea, the Ki also embraced her too. It swirled about her like a hot water spring, imbuing her with warmth and ease. Something was happening, an evolution was occurring within her. She felt... peace. She felt... serenity and a balance of sorts. And as she sat there with her friend... she felt something strange. She felt the life, the Ki itself within her friend, growing. The Ki existed in and amongst all things, organic and inorganic. Life, she knew, created the Ki, made *it* grow. Both of those, it seemed, steadily increased only ever so gradually surrounding her friend. Ashira was more than aware of her own adeptness to the Ki, but for some reason, a sensitivity had begun to evolve around her friend, but it wasn't *of* her friend... it was within her like a small light beginning to glow.

After a time, all emotions had subsided. Ashira inhaled deeply and exhaled slowly as if to cleanse her lungs from the remnants of sorrow.

"I'm sorry," she said remorsefully, releasing her hold on Damae. "I didn't mean to come here and turn myself into a puddle on the floor of your home, or to be a burden."

Damae leaned back and crinkled her face into one of pleasant annoyance. "What are you talking about? You know you are welcome here anytime, right? I'm just glad to see you're ok. Kina told me about what happened and that you just left. Something about needing to do this on your own. Does that sound right?"

Ashira looked into the beautifully concerned face of her friend. "Yes. I left. I just couldn't do it anymore. Not after the Demio turned their backs on me. Not after Reikuno betrayed me." She looked out towards the skyline. "Not even after Kina asked me back."

The two friends helped one another to stand up. Damae ushered her to one of the couches and the two sat together, side by side.

"It takes courage and strength to do things like that," Damae said. "You have your own personal convictions, and you stood by them. That's real strength, Ashira," she said encouragingly. "It's scary at times, for sure. But if we don't stand for something, we will fall for anything."

Ashira always enjoyed listening to Damae speak. She had a natural talent for connecting with reality and with the people. She had this innate ability to listen, to observe and equally understand what the plights of the people were and adjust accordingly. If ever there was someone she would want to be like, it was Damae.

"Now, you didn't come here to just turn yourself into a puddle, did you?" Damae asked directly. She wasn't one of the best prefects in the Realm for nothing. She could see that Ashira looked tired, road worn, and on the verge of exhaustion.

"No, I didn't," Ashira said truthfully. "I'm... at a loss Damae. I just need some guidance, a direction... something. I thought I could figure out life without the Establishment on my own. I guess I was wrong," she shrugged. A yawn crept up from within and showed itself on her face.

"Tell you what," Damae said. "Why don't you sleep on it, and we'll talk in the morning, okay? You look tired." Ashira offered no protest.

She was shown to one of several guest rooms in the expansive apartment. A rounded room with ornate columns bordering large windows giving the appearance of what Damae called the 'old country' of Hachani. There were sheer curtains as long as the room was tall. A large, light blue, circular rug with evenly spaced tassels that felt amazingly soft under her feet. Damae turned the bed down for her friend as she climbed in, with hesitation. Ashira had never felt something so comfortable in her life. The mattress was soft yet supportive and as she lay down, her body sank ever so slightly as the bed responded in return. The sheets were smooth and made of the finest linen and had such a clean scent to them. The multitudes of pillows available were such a luxury, but she didn't care which one she had at that moment. She lay her head down in complete comfort, in complete safety. Damae wished her goodnight with a friendly hand on her shoulder, and she was asleep before Damae even turned out the light.

The sun shone brightly overhead. An endless sea of sand was before her. The heat was oppressively assaulting her skin. Time wheeled overhead as she was instantly transported across vast wastes, covering great distances in an impossible timeframe. Light and shadow streamed past her like portalspace. She stopped suddenly at a rocky outcrop. From there she could see a white dome in the distance. An animal of some sort let out a low bray. A lone rider was approaching, hooded and robed, riding on some reptile-like quadruped. A child was running in the distance. The wind began to howl. There was a voice that rustled like leaves "there is one more..." though she couldn't make out who it was or its meaning. The windstorm whipped sand into a frenzy around her, turning into a cyclone. The pressure built up around her and shot her into the atmosphere like a cannon. She watched as the tan and desolate continent shrank to a dot and disappeared amongst the untold expanse of sea as she floated through the lowest orbit of space. Almost as soon as the continent disappeared, she turned forward and another land, a blue and green one, appeared in reverse fashion. Beginning as a dot, then quickly expanding in front of her. This land was beautiful, lush, serene. She blinked and was instantly transported to a cloud, where her vision was occluded. The vapor slowly drifted by and unexpectedly a vision of a fortress or palace appeared in the distance. The voice of a young woman echoed around her. "*Help me... I have no other hope*," it said with a strangely familiar tone. Unexpectedly there was a bright, blinding flash that shimmered green, then... fire and destruction. Thousands of voices resonated in a split second, then were silenced.

Ashira gasped as she sat up with a start, still in bed. She had been dreaming again. She placed a hand to her head and blinked to clear the fogginess. Her dreams were strange and carried a mix of emotion, destination and things that were mysterious. The Ki was showing her things, but what? Was it the past? The future? Or just something different entirely? She couldn't tell.

"Ashira? Are you alright?" Damae called from the doorway. "I heard a noise and just wanted to check on you."

"I'm... I'm okay," Ashira said, shaking sleep from her head. "Just a dream."

Damae was no fool. Kiensei and dreams usually meant something was about to happen, be it good or bad. She and Kina had had several discussions about them before when he had willingly opened up to her about his own. Many times, they were cryptic, sometimes frightening the things he described. She wondered about Ashira's dreams. They had saved Damae's life at one point, so she held concern that something was coming again.

"Well, when you're ready, come on over to the kitchen to get something to eat. I'm sure you're hungry," Damae said, smiling from the doorway.

Come to think of it, she was hungry. Very hungry. In fact, it had been at least a day. Maybe? "How long was I out?" Ashira asked, stretching her arms high above her head.

Damae raised her eyebrows and sent a smirk her way. "Oh, about fourteen hours I think."

Ashira's eyes went wide. "Fourteen HOURS!?" she exclaimed; her face full of bewilderment. That's the longest she'd ever slept before in her entire life. She groaned aloud while throwing her head back down into the pillow; her hands covering her eyes. Sleeping in wasn't something she was fond of; she was conditioned that way. The early morning schedule of a muhashki meshed well with that of a soldier, so what had begun in her childhood had continued on until recent times.

Damae turned and threw her head back, tossing her curly hair playfully. "Hurry up dozybird," she called out. Dozybird was a term of endearment her mother had used on her and her sister when they were little, and it was something she and Ciara used against one another as they got older in remembrance of their childhood.

Ashira made her way slowly to the kitchen where she saw Damae sitting quietly at a small square table sequestered into a quaint little nook. The nook was cozily recessed into the exterior wall like its own little bay and held an intimate appearance. It had three, small, round windows set at angles to offer a view of the skyline from a different side of the apartment. The light that came in was muted slightly. The prefect appeared to be contemplating something as she sat on one of the benches, resting on her elbows with her hands around a steaming mug of coffa. She looked out of one of the portals in reflective thought, sitting in her olive-green dress that was form fitting on the top, even the sleeves, but flowed out from her chest, hiding her figure below. The raised embroidered gold designs that resembled jubai eyes adorned the lower half and were large at the waist but gradually tapered smaller as they were repeated down to the bottom. Her shining reddish-brown hair was smooth on top, parted neatly down the middle and held in place by a golden headband with small points. From the headband down, her curls billowed across her shoulders.

Ashira approached quietly. It took a moment for Damae to realize she was there as she was lost in thought. But when she did, she glanced at Ashira and curled her mouth as if a sad thought had crossed her mind before changing her demeanor to something more cheerful. Ashira sensed that something had happened, and the prefect was trying to suppress her feelings. Aside from that, an absolutely delicious smell wafted through the kitchen and instantly her mouth watered as the scent pleasurably enticed her nose. Her stomach responded in kind with an embarrassing burble.

"Hi," Ashira said quietly with a slight wave of her hand as she approached. It was quiet in the kitchen. Something she never thought she'd hear... the sound of silence like this in a home.

"Come. Sit and have some food," Damae motioned, patting the seat beside her.

Ashira did as she was invited. She approached and slid in beside the prefect. Silence passed between them as Ashira watched Damae prepare an informal presentation of food for her. Out of a thick, black metal pan she scooped a large slice of a golden yellow bread that smelled of sweet grain, fruit of some kind, and embernectar. Over top of it she ladled a thick, creamy sauce that appeared to have mushrooms, roots, nuts and other ingredients simmered within. She placed the steamy and fragrant plate in front of Ashira with a smile and handed her a utensil.

"Something from Hachani that my grandmother used to make," she said with fond remembrance. "It always made me feel better, no matter what." The smell was intoxicating. Damae could have served her a pile of old vegetable peelings, and she would have eaten it. Her stomach grumbled audibly as if to usher her to indulge in the amazingness before her.

Ashira tried her best to be polite, but after the first bite, she just couldn't help herself. It was absolutely amazing. She had no idea Damae could make something so delicious... given the fact that she was also awesome enough to hold her own in a fight as well. Ashira finished the plate in no time, much to Damae's surprise. The prefect's eyes went a little wider as she asked her if she wanted seconds... to which Ashira nodded her head vigorously. Her mouth was full of the last bite as she mumbled something that sounded like a "yes, please." A pleasant smile graced Damae's face as she served her a second helping.

The two sat in the quaint part of the kitchen, enjoying the food, the coffa and the company. In between mouthfuls, Ashira and Damae reminisced on times past, making small talk. The Plageus incident. The trip to visit Mariss Butark, who Damae expressed she missed dearly. Ashira briefly mentioned her son Lusec Butark and the incident on Shimsae.

"Wait, what!?," Damae exclaimed, shooting her a surprised glance. "He *kissed* you?" she said with an incredibly surprised smile that spanned the entire width of her face.

"It wasn't like that," Ashira said trying to explain away the situation. It wasn't at all like that, honestly. It was a ruse to keep their cover intact. After all, she did start the whole thing with that 'engaged' foolishness.

"Nuh uh," Damae said with mock defiance and waving a finger. "You're not getting off that easy. C'mon. Out with it. I want details," she said ribbing the young Tesska playfully.

They talked about many things, and they talked about Kina. Damae expressed her feelings about him, about how her feelings had changed since they first met years ago. About how she loved the fact that he allowed her to be more of her inner self; less serious with the ability to just... laugh a little. Damae spoke about her gratitude to Ashira for understanding their relationship and keeping it secret. "But I have to know," she asked, "when did *you* know about us?" Ashira thought for a moment and took another bite. "I had my suspicions for a while. I could always sense a bit of yours and his intentions when I was around, but it was that one trip to Ra'andal that really confirmed it for me."

"Yeah, we had Teka to thank for your showing up unexpectedly," Damae said, rolling her eyes at the utterance of Teka's name. Ashira mimicked her reaction. "We were going to Ra'andal for what was to be a honeymoon of sorts since we never really got to take one," Damae said. "It's so hard living like this, but we make it work the best we can. I always worry about him when he leaves on a mission, but when you were with him, I knew you'd take care of him with everything you had."

"And what about now?" Ashira said. The fact that she wasn't there to look after him took on a more serious connotation.

"Now," Damae took a deep breath, rolling her fair features to face Ashira. "Now I just hope. There's always hope, right?"

After the third helping, Ashira found herself pleasantly full. Something she hadn't been in quite some time. The two had sat there for an uncounted amount of time in relative silence as she savored the food to her heart's content with Damae continuing to stare off into the distance at times while Ashira ate. Ashira sensed something in her, feelings of excitement mixed with feelings of fear. She finished her last plate and pushed it away from her gently to signify she was through. Damae looked at her through soft eyes, "did you get enough?"

Ashira leaned back on the bench; her stomach pleasantly satisfied. She took a moment to think but turned her head to look at Damae. "You make me wish I was born on Hachani, you know that right?" she said jokingly.

The two shared a giggle as suddenly the mood became more serious.

"Ashira," Damae said sitting up straight, "how do you deal with the loss?" Ashira's face scrunched in confusion at the unexpected question.

"Loss?" she replied.

"In your time on the battlefield, how did you deal with the loss of some of your closest companions?" Damae said.

Ashira pondered this for a moment before responding. "Well, as Kiensei, we were taught that loss was inevitable. Something that should be celebrated, not mourned. And that we should not dwell on the things that were or that could be, only the things that are. That changed with the Civil War. We were taught to expect casualties of all kinds and types, but we had to shift our focus to Tsugint soldiers mostly. For me, it always hurt losing the men that I was responsible for. Every time. I still have to remind myself that they served a purpose of their own and did so of their own accord regardless of any conditioning. In the end, all I could ever do is learn from the situation, learn from them, and move forward." Several moments of silence passed between them.

"I lost Ackla," Damae eventually said. Her face decaying into one of sadness. "She died on Opsis while we were there investigating an issue with the planetary financial system on behalf of the Imperial

Government. I feel guilty because I involved her in something that cost her life, and it cost her family their mother and wife."

"I'm sorry for your loss Damae," Ashira offered. "But I'm sure Ackla knew the risks when she signed up to serve. You can honor her memory by continuing the work she supported up until the end. It's not easy at first, but it gets easier as time goes on."

"Well now, you've certainly grown up beyond your years," Damae said with surprise.

"I've had some great mentors along the way," Ashira said, inclining her head towards the prefect.

Ashira thought of something. Something that might seem a little selfish given her unannounced status in someone else's home. She thought hard about it but decided that it was worth a shot.

"Damae," she began sheepishly. "Can I ask a favor?" The prefect looked over at her in mock surprise, nodding her head.

"Can I take... a bath?" She thought back to her time with Eilidh and how the look on the little Multorn's face was actually convincing that a bath was an enjoyable experience. She also remembered passing that spa and wondering what it would be like. Now was just as good a time as any to try.

The confusion that painted Damae's face was shocking to Ashira. Shocking to a point where she thought she might have offended her hostess.

"I've... never had one, plenty of showers, just... well... I heard they're enjoyable," Ashira awkwardly offered as an explanation, her eyes flitting back and forth.

"Girl," Damae said with an attitude of disbelief. "You've never had a bath? Seriously?" Ashira shook her head. "What in the world are they doing over there at that Kiensei Monastery anyway," Damae said sarcastically as she motioned with her hands for Ashira to get up. "Ok. Scoot. Let's go, right now," she said, her face full of determination at the young Tesska. Ashira knew that look, and it was never to be denied.

Chapter 26

Ashira was in pure bliss. She had never known something so wonderful, so immersive, so… amazing as a tub full of hot water laced with sweet smelling perfumes and suds billowing up like clouds. Eilidh definitely knew what she was talking about. Poor Eilidh. She couldn't forget about that sweet faced little girl. Her thoughts constantly returning to the little family that took her in and sheltered her. She couldn't forget about them; she would *never* forget about them.

Damae spent some time with her in the elaborate refresher, discussing various things, including Ashira's walkabout in the wilds of Korosento after leaving the monastery. They talked about the Tsugint soldiers at the memorial, they talked about Iralia. They lamented on Taria, Shiobhan and Eilidh and the hardships the little family had endured. Ashira had inquired about the bill that the foreman mech had referenced, to which Damae had no recollection of. Apparently, it had been placed on the Assembly floor for a vote while she was away. Purposefully so, according to Damae's deduction to help ensure it would pass without too much obstruction. They laughed at earlier adventures the two of them had, including the Y9 Landfighter incident where Damae showed Ashira just how accomplished she was at piloting one of the fabled and highly sought after crafts her homeland created. That adventure, it seemed, held a mutual impression on them both.

They talked about life. They talked about death. Both women concurred having experienced too much of it. They talked about the war. They talked more about Kina and how influential he had been on them both.

Damae offered a rare openness to her private self when she talked about her recent dispatch to Mickio and how her former love interest in former prefect Anritsu Rushama had caused a rift in her and Kina's relationship. Ashira reminded her that Kina wouldn't see it that way, to which Damae agreed, on experience of such. But Damae assured her that she had made it up to him in the best way she knew how, which garnered an embarrassed look from the young Tesska. Taking a cue from her expression, Damae changed the subject.

"So, what will you do now?" Damae asked.

"I'm trying to figure that out," Ashira said with a wistful look. She had already tried asking for a job to little success. She also realized that her arena had been limited and that expansion of her efforts would probably be beneficial. "I need to get a job, I know. I also need to find a place to stay. Neither of which are easy to do in this current economy. And..." she trailed off, "...I don't really know where to start."

"What do you mean exactly?" Damae asked. A look of inquisitiveness painted her features at hearing what Ashira had to say. Damae was well aware of many of the issues plaguing the Realm and Korosento proper, but this was different. This was someone who had experienced it firsthand.

"Well, my time in the camp showed me that there is definitely a fine line separating those who have and those who have not," Ashira said. "I met people who had meaningful lives and occupations that fell victim to, well, bad luck, I guess. Some were veterans like me. Some were well educated. Some had made mistakes but still paid their debts to society. But for it all, they ended up homeless and just scraping by."

Damae looked at the floor in disappointment. "I agree. The Imperial government *has* failed many people," she nodded in agreement. "The hard part is trying to figure out what to do about it. There's so much bureaucracy, so much red tape to cut through to get anything done now," she said. "The government is so large that I often find myself frustrated that committee after committee must be commissioned and consulted before we can take definitive action. Its only when a major disaster happens or something to do with the war rears its ugly head do we get the ability to act more quickly. Sometimes it's like fighting an uphill battle. Like we're pushing this large boulder up a hill only to stumble and watch it roll back down to the bottom again."

Ashira reflected for a moment on many things she had experienced during her years as part of the Imperial Army. She reached up, out of sight, and touched the miniscule scar on her left shoulder. A reminder from a previous battle. She reflected on the Kiensei. Something she had held in deep reserve finally came out. "Damae," she began, staring as if she was looking straight through the wall into the distance, "do you ever wonder if we're fighting on the right side of this war?" She listed her head to the side and rolled her eyes pensively to look at Damae. She figured this might not go over well. The prefect furrowed her brow in serious introspection at the question.

"The Kiensei Establishment isn't what it should be," Ashira said, "and the Kiensei Establishment's role in the war feels skewed. Every day that this war drags on, the Kiensei renege on their vow to be peacekeepers instead of soldiers. All I ever wanted to do was to help people, but all I've ever been, is a soldier, an agent of war. At first it was exciting, all the travelling to the innumerable places of this world, the combat, the feeling of making a difference. But as the war has dragged on, I'm not so sure about it. Kiensei are supposed to respect and defend life, all life, yet we lead living men to their deaths as they themselves destroy along the way." Ashira paused and took a deep breath. "We... *they* preach balance, but their actions fuel the conflict." Damae listened intently. "I'm no politician," she rolled her head back to center, "but it seems like the government is becoming the very thing we've been fighting against."

Damae's face degraded into one of reserved defense. "Ashira, that's not true. The Realm stands for diplomacy and reason. Listening before action. Yes, there's fighting and destruction, but imagine if the Kiensei weren't leading the effort, how much worse it would be. Imagine if undisciplined, unsympathetic officers commanded the Tsugints to do things that could be considered inhumane."

What Damae said was true, she thought. If the reserved nature of the Kiensei wasn't in command, what atrocities would be committed, Ashira thought. "I'm not trying to upset you, I promise," Ashira said apologetically. "It just seems like more and more power is taken from the representatives of the people and given to the High Minister. I experienced the fact that every time more urgent abilities were granted to him, new and sometimes harsher rules and laws were pushed down for us to enforce. That just doesn't sound like democracy to me. You remember our trip right?" Ashira asked.

"Of course," Damae responded kindly.

"So do I. Mariss and Lusec, both of them were Divisionists, but they looked like any other citizen. The only difference was that they believed the Realm had bogged itself down in policy and opened itself to corruption. I hate to say it, but I do see their position and it just makes me wonder. I mean, Olorzin, yeah that guy needs to go, but for all its worth, I also see part of what the Diffies are saying as well. It just makes me wonder how much truth is out there and how much has been left out."

Damae took a moment to sift through what her friend was saying. She was listening before acting, one of the tenets she stood for. Hearing Ashira reminded her a bit of herself, the spitfire young monarch that became the steadfast prefect. She calmed herself and allowed the fact that the young Tesska had become quite mature in her time away from the Establishment. Her disposition lifted. "So, you really think the Kiensei are becoming a worse version of themselves? Surely all of them can't be disappointing, I mean, look at you. You've certainly become something more. I know that I'm proud of you and who you've become."

Ashira leaned back and sank a little deeper into the tub. "I don't know," she said with a weak smile. She wasn't used to getting compliments. "All I can say is what Kina once told me, that there will be Kiensei who disappoint, but they will be far outnumbered by those who do the right thing. I have to believe to some degree that it's the same with the Realm. And as long as the Realm has prefects like *you* to embody that statement, I think we'll be all right."

Damae smiled at her in response, but her mind quickly moved towards him... "Speaking of Kina," Damae sighed reluctantly, "he'll be home in two days from what I understand." Ashira looked away as if staring into an infinite distance. With him coming home to Korosento, it meant her time here had ended. Though she was certain neither Kina nor Damae would mind if she stayed, she knew it likely wouldn't end well. Plus, married couples, especially secret ones, needed private time to themselves. She knew she would only get in the way.

"I understand," she said.

A chime sounded at the door.

"Who is it?" Damae called out.

"It is I," came the tinny voice of M-AR40.

"What's going on?"

"My lady, your guest has arrived."

Damae's demeanor instantly lifted at hearing the news. She turned to Ashira and crinkled her face in genuine happiness. "When you're done, come to my room. I have a surprise for you," she winked.

Ashira hated to leave that wonderful, indulging experience but knew that all good things must end eventually. She stepped out, dried, and dressed herself in a gown and robe Damae had left for her. She had never worn something so light, airy, and comfortable. How lucky her friend was, she thought, and made her way to Damae's private chambers.

Ashira approached the vaulted and arched door. She could hear joyful conversations, none of which Kina was a part of, which made her feel more at ease. She pressed the chime button to politely announce her presence. The door slid open, and she saw Damae... and someone else she hadn't met before.

"Feel better?" came the initial question from Damae. Ashira nodded her head blissfully in agreement. "Ashira, this is Linrah Grachine, one of my former handmaidens and a friend. Linrah, this is Ashira Mori also a friend of mine."

There it was. She actually said it. Damae... the great Damae Miada called her... *friend*. The joy in her heart swelled to expanses not previously felt. She was sure that Damae had many friends, but Ashira... well... she didn't. To hear someone so prominent address her as 'friend' was both gratifying and therapeutic at the same time.

The young woman that turned to address her had an uncanny resemblance to the prefect. Not surprising actually, since the legendary Hachani handmaidens were meant to dynamically act as decoys, bodyguards, and tactical servants to the Monarch of Hachani. She was wearing a dark blue pantsuit, the bottom of the legs opening up like a bell to give the appearance of a dress. Her hair was short and fluffed like feathers in the back.

Linrah extended a friendly hand of greeting to her, to which Ashira kindly returned. "Hi Ashira. Nice to meet you," she said with a polite smile.

"Nice to meet you as well," Ashira returned the gesture.

"I hear you might need something more robust to wear?" Linrah said.

Ashira looked confusingly over at Damae and didn't offer a response. She thought quickly. She hadn't changed her outfit since she left the Monastery just after the trial. She had worn the same bits of clothing for quite some time. She subtlety remembered at how certain parts had weathered and frayed with constant use but were still in decent shape. She looked intently at Damae, who was returning her look with one of sympathy. She reminded herself that Damae was no fool, and an observant and empathetic person to a tee.

"Do you still have those coveralls that Brustae used to wear?" Linrah turned and asked of Damae.

"I do," she nodded knowingly and quickly disappeared to fetch them.

Linrah looked over Ashira as if visually measuring her. She approached her and placed her hands on Ashira's midriff and slid them towards her hips, which made the Tesska uncomfortable in the moment. Ashira brought her hands up in a defensive pose, ready to strike at a moment's notice.

"Relax," Linrah said, assuring the Tesska of her intentions. "I outfitted Damae for years, so I know every inch of her figure. I also knew how to fit clothing to the various handmaidens on the fly without a proper kit. Brustae was the closest to Damae in every measure," she said, inclining her head towards the prefect. "You're pretty close too. After Brustae died, Damae kept some of her outfits just in case. I'm thinking I can tailor something to fit you pretty easily."

Ashira relaxed slightly. She wasn't used to being taken care of in this manner and she wondered how secretly uncomfortable Damae must have been to be subjected to constant prodding. Then again, she might have become accustomed to it early on.

Damae reappeared with a set of woven coveralls made mostly of deng'aroo material, which was known to be both comfortable and wear resistant. She handed them to Linrah who laid them aside on Damae's bed.

"I remember these," Linrah said to Damae, with a pleasant look of remembrance. "Give me about a day and I'll have something that'll serve you well Ashira," she said astutely to the Tesska.

The two friends sat on one of the couches in the open common room overlooking the sunset. It had been a peaceful day, a good day. One of the best Ashira had had in a long time. She knew, though, that the time to leave was drawing closer so she imbibed as much peace as was possible.

"Ashira," Damae said with a longing stare, "have you thought about your future yet? Like, what are you going to do next?"

This was a bit unusual to her. Yes, she had thought about what to do next, but Kiensei weren't taught to contemplate the future, only to live in the present. But she thought it was worth it to start changing a few things here and there. After all, she was no longer a Kiensei.

"Yes and No," she said honestly.

"Let's go through your options, ok?" Damae said. "What are you good at? What do you like to do?"

Ashira thought long and hard for a moment. Was Damae going to help her get a job? That would be great. A lot of her learned skills came from Kina. He taught her how to fix things. He taught her how to fly. He taught her mostly how to fight. "Well... I can fix most things. I can fly," she said, "but you already know that."

"Well, repairing and flying are two things that are still valuable," Damae said. "Why don't we start there? If you want my advice," Damae proffered, "you need to play to your strengths. You need to leverage your skills and aptitudes. If you want to start a new life outside of the Establishment, get a job, a home, and all the things a regular person wants, then you need to start applying yourself based on what you do best. Maybe you could join a trade? I think you'd do well."

Ashira blinked in genuine contemplation. She did have skills other than just brandishing a sword, that much she knew. How to apply them, however, escaped her at the moment. "I did try to get a job when I first left," Ashira said. "Most places either weren't hiring, or I was too young. There was one place though that was going to hire me, but they backed out once they knew I used to be a Kiensei."

Damae touched her chin in contemplation. "It's more about where you apply than to what you apply. You said you applied at the Pliaza?" Ashira nodded. "Yeah, that place is too volatile. Too many people pass through there, so the vendors get meticulous about who they hire. The best place to start is in the lower levels I'm afraid." Ashira was afraid of that fact.

"Oh!" Damae had a moment of inspiration. "There's this market, Travestamee it's called. I hear that it's becoming a popular place for topsiders to hide away for a while. You could get a job in there somewhere I bet." She said this, of course, having already been there herself... with Kina... many times.

This was a lot for Ashira to process. A lot to consider, and a lot to figure out. Too much at one time, she pondered. One step at a time.

"Damae, when you're at a loss or when you just can't see a path forward... what do you do?" Ashira asked emphatically. She knew within her bones that even the great Damae Miada had times where she was at a loss.

"Well, mostly I just make my own. When I find myself at a loss," she chuckled sheepishly, "it might seem a little silly, but I ask the universe." When she was little, there were times when life seemed so confusing to young Miss Miada. She and her sister used to spend some of their evenings out on the veranda at their lake home back on Hachani. As young sisters, they would take turns shouting out to the stars above all the things they thought they wanted in life. Not that it always worked, but as children, wonderment was the stuff of bliss.

"The universe?" she questioned in confusion. The returning looks on Damae's face said it all. "You're serious, aren't you." Ashira said warily. Blindly asking 'the universe' was something that she didn't believe would help her. She could certainly understand Ki meditation, but if shouting at the universe worked for her, maybe it was worth a try. "Well, alright then, tell me what to do."

Damae watched from across the expansive room as the young Tesska stood near the edge of the balcony. Her figure creating an outline against the creamy orange sky. Her shadow elongating itself across the floor. She watched her friend raise her arms above her head, her fingers splayed out like sun rays. She heard her whisper things, though what they were, she knew were between Ashira and the universe... and of course, the Ki.

Ashira woke the next morning much earlier than before. More closely to her usual time. Of course, she wasn't as exhausted as before either. She sat up and ran her hand across the amazing sheets she had slept in, trying to mentally imprint the whole experience in her mind as best she could. She knew, deep down, that it was near time to leave.

Outside she could hear Damae talking to.... "Kina," she muttered under her breath. A moment of surprise gripped her. Her pulse quickened. Was he here? The staticky audio from a glitching virtuacall quickly brought her back to ease. She could hear the conversation, especially if she concentrated. Something about an investigation? Ovarnum Dias? "What in blazes is Kina doing heading to Ovarnum Dias," she thought. A planned campaign to Exanas... "if only Ashira hadn't left," she heard him say. Her heart sank for her sesni. If she had stayed, she knew she'd be able to help him and help Damae. This wasn't an effective way to start the day.

The call concluded and she could hear Damae talking to Linrah and M-AR40. She was preparing to leave. Ashira quickly got up and left the bedroom to see what she might be able to do to help.

Ashira appeared with a willingness to help her friend. But instead, received immediate attention towards herself.

"Hey girl, sleep well?" Linrah said amicably, turning towards her.

"I did. And honestly, one of the best night's sleeps that I've ever had," Ashira said, rubbing her neck.

Damae was sitting on the couch, obviously engaged with a thought in her mind that everyone else wasn't privy to. Ashira glanced at her; she didn't avert her own gaze.

"Everything alright here?" Ashira asked in a leading manner. Her intent was to gauge the events and conversations she wasn't aware of.

"Eh, the usual," Linrah said, shrugging her shoulders and looking over at a concerned Damae.

"Yeah, the usual," Damae said, staring at the floor. She shook her head slightly, rubbed her face gently in her hands and stood up, approaching the two. "There's a special session of the Assembly that's been called and I have to go. But before I do, let's get you taken care of," she said, inclining her head towards Ashira.

Linrah brought out a plain white paperboard box and opened it. She pulled out the deng'aroo jumpsuit that she had tailored the night before. She had modified it to fit Ashira's figure, but she had also made some improvements. She had added some uniflex material to the sides of the legs, to add both strength and flexibility. She had heard from the prefect that Ashira was quite acrobatic when necessary. She had added chest pockets for added storage and had crafted leather vambraces and fingerless gloves for added protection and functionality for her arms and hands. Secondly, she pulled out a synthetic weave undershirt to add breathability and wicking should she get hot. Next, she presented a pair of Nubian leather boots, some of the finest in the world. Soft, supple, and very durable. Lastly, Linrah pulled out her old belt, or a modified version of it. Ashira was at a loss for words. Never had she been given anything of the sort.

"Thank you," she said to both of them. "I don't have anything to offer you in return," she said sorrowfully. Damae approached her and put a hand on her shoulder.

"You don't owe us anything. I promise," Damae said emphatically.

"Yeah, it was my pleasure to just be able to come visit my old friend," Linrah interjected. "I kind of miss the old days, the excitement of it all."

"Old? Who are you calling old," Damae snorted.

Ashira thought long and hard for a moment. She didn't have anything much of value. She had the few chits that Demio Asato had given her, that was about it. But there were two things...

"Where are my old clothes?" she asked.

"They're in the room you've been staying in, over by the window," Damae said, pointing a finger in the general direction.

With a resolved look and a nod of her head, Ashira took the box of vestments and disappeared briefly to change. She emerged in the new outfit, which fit her ever so amazingly she thought. In her hands, she held her Tesska sash. A mark of her people. One of the few individualistic items she was allowed to have as a Kiensei. She approached Linrah and held the item out in front of her.

"It's not much, but I want you to have this," Ashira said. "It's a traditional sash of my people. It's presented as a mark of a warrior, a mark of bravery" she said.

Linrah made a small bow and accepted the item with grace and humility. "Thank you," she said. Damae smiled at the gesture.

Ashira then turned and approached the prefect, her friend Damae, with a longing look of humbleness. Damae cocked her head with a pensive look, not knowing what to expect. Ashira held out her hands for her friend to take them. Damae looked on with mild confusion at Ashira, accepting without reservation what was about to happen. The two stood face-to-face for a moment. Silence passed between them as they stared at one another in friendship.

"Thank you, Damae, for everything," Ashira said. "I don't know how I could ever repay you, but I want you to know how much I appreciate you and what you've done for me. I'm grateful *to you* for taking care of Kina. I'm grateful for you taking care of me." Damae started to speak but Ashira released her grip and held up a hand to gently silence the woman in front of her. Ashira bowed her head slightly and in reaching up, slowly loosed the clasps holding the headpiece that framed her face.

Damae gasped quietly at the gesture. "Ashira! What are you doing?" she said.

Ashira pulled the painfully crafted item away from her head and turned it for a moment in her hands, remembering why she was given it so many years ago. She fumbled with the beads that once wrapped around her head. She looked her friend in the face and held her hands out with the headpiece laid across them.

"This is the most precious thing I have," Ashira said. "It's a mark of honor from my people. It was given to me by the matriarch of my tribe many years ago when Demio Asato found me. It represents many things, but mostly it stands for the value of balance and the strength of peace."

"Ashira... I..." Damae interjected.

"Yes, you will take this," Ashira said sternly... not using the Ki to influence her mind but nodding poignantly as she spoke. Damae blinked with surprise. Linrah tilted her head in surprise as well. "My arms are getting a little tired, so I'm going to need you to grab it," Ashira said, the corners of her mouth curling with a snicker.

Damae looked her friend squarely in the face. This was the person Kina had lauded so much, and she could see why. "You might have made an excellent politician, Ka'ze," Damae retorted as she humbly and respectfully took the item.

"Pppffft," Ashira playfully raspberried. "No way! Those people are just money-grubbing, power-hungry cheats and liars," she said and reached out to hug her friend as tight as she could.

The three shared many more moments through the remainder of the day. They laughed; they mourned, they remembered. They left the war and pain of life behind for just a little while longer. Just to be with one another. Hours passed and in time, Ashira looked out across the expansive balcony one last time at the sunset quickly arriving.

It was time for her to go.

Chapter 27

Ashira adjusted the new headpiece that Linrah had made for her from some leftover leather. It felt strange and not yet a part of her after wearing the other one for so many years, but this new one was wonderfully comfortable, just like the boots on her feet. It hugged her head exactly right, supporting her in a way that made things feel lighter. She tightened the strap on a satchel slung across her shoulder that Damae had given her as well, to help her carry some of the few items she had. The water bottle at her side was full and secured tightly... another improvement from Linrah over her old utility belt. One thing that bothered her though were the sleeves on the coveralls. She pulled and tugged a bit, then decided it was best to just roll them up. They were there if she needed them. She stood at the base of the apartment building she had illegally infiltrated just days before and looked skyward, quietly reflecting on the time well-spent with her friend.

She believed that Damae would be all right. She believed that Kina would be too. As for herself, well, she didn't know what lied before her, but she too, would be all right. She looked ahead, a cornucopia of people from all across the massive planet just... living. No real cares of the wide world beyond Korosento. Only what was in front of them and what their daily life would be like. No real thoughts of the future, she imagined, only what would get them through their day today. Not a bad way to live actually.

She began to make her way through the crowd when suddenly, a furry faced Lapin male bumped into her. "Watch it, will ya?" he chastised. Normally, her appearance would have belied her status as a Kiensei and thus garnered a regretful apology, but not any longer. Normally, it would be the citizen apologizing to her, but not any longer. Now, she was just a regular person too. The man stared at her in contempt.

"*You* watch it" she said unapologetically, staring him in the face. He just grumbled and shook his head, his whiskers waggling as he continued on his original path. And so did she... as a regular person, she reminded herself.

She walked along the familiar pathways she had once trod, either on patrol or on her way back to the monastery. Now, just flowing along with the tide of people with no clear destination. Her mind wandered to Eilidh, to Taria, to Siobhan. She wondered if they were okay. She wondered if they were even alive. She wondered what Kina was up to on his mission as well as Damae, and how she might have helped them if she were still a member of the Establishment. But no more. She wasn't. For once, she had her own problems to solve. For now, it was all about... her.

There were moments when everything within her being screamed to go back, to be what she was born to be, to be who she loved being. A Kiensei. But that wasn't her life anymore, not now, at least. Harichi once told her muhashki tribe that to be a Kiensei took the deepest commitment, the most serious mind. That just wasn't her anymore.

She heard someone cursing off to the side and she turned to see them flailing their hands about in frustration. She stopped to watch them for a moment, curious as to what had them so upset. They kicked at a scootster in frustration as it appeared that it had broken down. "Play to your strengths," Damae's voice echoed in her head.

She walked up to the Brosnian as he swore in his native language. She could see that it was a Bejon T-25 bike. Nothing too complicated but still easy enough to service. Parts were easy to come by as the T-25 was built to be highly customizable. She had heard that there were entire clubs dedicated to those like-minded individuals to gather, talk, ride, and trade... all around the Bejon.

"Hey buddy, what seems to be the problem?" she called to the Brosnian male as she approached.

He muttered something under his breath before turning to address the young Tesska. "I've been working on this blasted thing for months. Every time I fix something, something else breaks on it."

Ashira remarked at the bike for a moment. Seeing that it was more than just the standard Mauler Y-19 that powered the thing. There were several aftermarket modifications that, in her opinion, led to the continuous breakdown issues.

"I can look at it really quick to see if we can get you back on the road if that's alright?" Ashira said.

"What's it gonna cost me," he asked in reservation.

"Just wanna help you out, that's all," she said.

"To tell you the truth, I'd soon just be rid of the thing," the frustrated Brosnian spat out, copping a swift smack to the handlebars.

Ashira looked over the bike swiftly, but with a wary eye. This was a chance for her. With a bike, she could move around much easier and it would take her much less time to cover ground, but she didn't want to inherit someone else's problems either. The Y-19 was in decent shape, no cracks in the compressor. Aftermarket intake seemed to be for the Y-21 but was functional. Exhaust vents were clear. She could work with that. Sparkers were old, she didn't like that, but they worked. There was a frayed belt that needed changing but looked like it had some life left in it for now. Exhaust was in good shape. Repulsors... well... one of them needed a good purge and scrub.

She quickly opened the satchel and looked for the chits Demio Asato had given her, instead she found a small, green silken bag. Inside was... a grey paperboard card? A small, white flower was hand-drawn on the card with the letters 'D.M.' in it. She retrieved it and held it for a moment knowing her friend had also once held it. She turned it over and saw the elegant and flowing handwriting of her friend; her voice resounding in her mind as she read it.

Dear Ashira,

> *This is your life. <u>Your</u> life. Not a piece of hardware to be handled. Not a set of rules to follow. It takes great courage, and sometimes great sacrifice to decide what you will do with it and how you will live it. And it takes fearless determination to see it through. Ashira, find a passion and pursue it with all your heart. Dream big and never give up. Learn more, be creative, try new things and work hard at whatever you do. Embrace failure, learn from it, and live for the day. Love with all your heart and above all... make every moment count. Every step you take now, is a step you get to choose. I have watched you grow over the years. You have become a strong young woman with an indomitable spirit. You care for others more than yourself, which is the true nature of both the Kiensei, and the Realm, though you may not wish to acknowledge it. It gives me immense pleasure to tell you this: I admire your fearlessness. I love your willingness to do what is right for its own sake. The Establishment is lesser without you, but the Realm in its vastness, is more wholesome with you as a part of it. I am proud of you and honored to call myself your friend. Never forget that I will always be there for you and as always, the Ki will forever flow within you and for you.*

> *- Damae*

A distinct jangle revealed more chits. Ashira smiled genuinely at realizing her friend had given her one last gift and done so in a very sneaky manner. She returned the card and quickly counted what she had in total. Three hundred and some change.

"I got two fifty to take it off your hands," she said to the Brosnian.

He grabbed his chin and contemplated for a moment. "Erm. Two seventy-five and its yours," he offered while nonchalantly wagging a long finger, "fully fueled too."

"Deal," Ashira said, slapping his open hand to seal the deal, and she handed over the chits. He handed over the ignition codes and turned to walk upon his way.

"Good luck," the Brosnian exclaimed as he walked away counting his money, "you're gonna need it," he smirked under his breath. "There's a sucker born every day," Jubaial thought to himself as he pocketed the money. He might have had thirty chits in that piece of junk to get it running long enough to dump it off on some poor sap and get away before they noticed.

Ashira was so excited with her first major purchase as a 'normal' citizen that she failed to lean on her intrinsic senses to guide her. She fiddled with the intake to improve its function. She double checked the belt tension. That one repulsor might give her some trouble, but it looked like it would hold out for a bit. She tweaked and fiddled for a few moments then flipped the actuator switches on the fuel tank console and pressed the ignition button. The old bike rumbled to life. It wasn't the smooth purr she was accustomed to hearing from the T-85, but it was a sweet sound... a sound of freedom and possibility.

She hopped into the worn leather seat and positioned the satchel just off to her side. She looked around at the towering buildings to gain her bearings briefly and squeezed the throttle lever to ramp up the compressor. She pushed her foot forward on the pedal and the bike began sailing off towards the main portal.

The bike cruised above the lower streets of Korosento's topmost level. The lights below reminding her of the veiw as a ship jumped to portalspace. The sun was setting to her back, which told her she was heading in the right direction. Gantries whizzed by as she followed the main infrastructure conduits towards the great gaping maw of the central lift station of Korosento... the next horizon of her future. She pushed the handlebars forward, forcing the bike to dip sharply as she cruised below the gantries, immersing herself one last time in the surface of the great, sprawling metropolis.

Emerging into the central lift shaft, she floated the bike sideways and focused on joining the main traffic flow, a long spiraling train of craft on their slow descent into the belly of the great city. Silent whispers of the Ki trailed behind her; a delicate symphony interwoven with her every breath. It was a language she had come to understand—a cosmic dialogue between destiny and freewill, where the echoes of the past and the possibilities of the future converged.

Raiju sat hidden on the edge of the great precipice. She watched as the young Tesska rode towards something, a destiny that was her responsibility in guiding her towards. She took flight to follow her. That was her duty.

Ashira had spoken her desires to the universe, as Damae had suggested. She would find a way to get to them. She would find them. She would help them. She might fail, but she had to try. At least that's what she told herself not knowing what awaited her. She had spoken her desires to the universe on that balcony, and the universe had answered her. Maybe not in the way she had imagined, but through someone she admired and respected.

If you see no path before you, just create your own.

She pushed the foot pedal forward on the bike urging it faster towards the lower levels. Then unexpectedly....

sparks lit up the console as one of the repulsors blew in a puff of black smoke.

And unbeknownst to her in that moment, her true destiny was about to begin.

Epilogue

Ashira sat hunched over a data console aboard the sleek and modern gunship *Markina-III*. The smoldering ruins of the rice farming village destroyed by that thing called an *'Examiner'* left behind in the wake of portalspace. The few survivors were settling into their temporary quarters. She had been out of the loop on a great many things that had happened ever since she left Damae's funeral with Maxus. She had left many things about her old life behind.

She had to know. She had to know what had happened since The Raze had come to pass. Where did she now fit into this... subjugating Eminence? Her new benefactor, Chase Miarta had warned her that things had only gotten worse. Well, it had been pretty bad already. Having to run constantly and look over her shoulder for Examiners and Inspectors was another. "How much worse could it be?" she questioned to herself. Chase had given her access to every shred of information he had. Some of which had been hacked or stolen from the Eminence Network itself. He admitted that the information was haphazard, scattered, and in disarray, but that she was welcomed to whatever she could find and could do with it whatever she felt pertinent.

She keyed a button on the console and a diminutive yellow tinged hologram of Demio Teka Suromasa rose before her face. Even though they had disagreed in the past, she knew the wise sesni had something to offer.

"This is Demio Teka Suromasa. I regret to report that both our Kiensei Establishment and the Realm have fallen to those called the

Eminence. This message is a warning and a reminder for any survivors: allow the Ki to guide you. The Monastery is destroyed as is our once peaceful way of life. Avoid Korosento. Run. Hide. Do not sacrifice yourselves wantonly. But please, persevere. There will come a time where peace may yet come again. The Ki be with you, flow within you, and flow for you, always."

She closed down the virtuaprojection. Even in defeat, the honorable Demio still believed in what the Kiensei stood for. That much, she could respect. Ashira wondered what had happened to those in the Establishment she had interacted the most with. She keyed in Sesni Lamilla Dullani... missing, presumed dead. Sesni Aruca Valt... missing, presumed dead. Demio Mako Rinji... killed on Korosento during a failed coup. "Coup?" she snorted. "Since when do Kiensei stage coups?" Lady Aidial, killed by... a Nobleman Otosan? That name was unfamiliar. Otsi Tika... killed on Korosento during a failed coup. Kai Asato... shot down on Harte Minosa. Her chest was filled with sorrow at seeing the loss of her founder and long-time friend.

All of them were labeled as enemies to the Realm. If anything, they were enemies to themselves, but not the Realm.

Ashira continued searching through the data, looking for anything and anyone... refusing to look for those few names she held most dear. Mostly what she saw was... "dead." Were they really all gone? She took a deep breath in rebuttal to accept the truth, but she had run out of options. Was she the last one? She had to know. Her fingers regretfully tapped in 'Harichi.'

The database returned a cryptic response. *'Presumed dead, unconfirmed. Last known whereabouts: Korosento. Priority Target.'*

She reluctantly keyed in 'Teka Suromasa.' The database returned a similarly short and cryptic response. *"Presumed dead, unconfirmed. Last known whereabouts: Korosento. Priority Target.'*

She keyed in 'Damae Miada' even though she had borne witness at her funeral. *Cardiac Arrest due to exsanguination.* Her own heart hurt in that moment. It was hard to bear the finality of her friend's death, but there were just some things in the universe that were inevitable, she reasoned. She fumbled in one of her pouches and pulled out a small, folded and worn piece of gray paper. She opened it carefully to prevent any damage and reminded herself of a time well-spent. She folded it up just as carefully and returned it to its hidden home.

Ashira wiped a small tear from her eye and slowly keyed in 'Kina Wykera.' One letter at a time. *Killed on Phustama* the records showed. "Or more like murdered," she said aloud. She couldn't believe it. Kina was one of the most powerful Kiensei she had ever known. He rarely lost a battle. Whoever had killed him, had to have been more powerful than him, which was unconscionable to think. But more so... what was he doing on Phustama? The records didn't show any other details. If she hadn't had left, would he still be alive? Would *she* still be alive?

Out of curiosity, she keyed in her own name:

'Presumed dead, evidence indicated. Last known whereabouts: Crashed Destroyer 'Magnanimous.' Grid: S-8. Island: Mureport III. Uninhabitable," she read.

Maybe her little ruse on that island hadn't worked as well as she'd hoped. Still, she had injected a sense of reasonable doubt, which was much more beneficial than the Eminence outright knowing she was alive. After all, that dark, hooded figure she was forced to kill did say that she was supposed to be dead. She hadn't wanted to do it, but a fleeting memory in that moment of an incident on Korosento reminded her that she had to do... what *needed* to be done.

Since leaving the Establishment, one thing she had learned was how to disappear. She knew then that open operation in rebellion wasn't a possibility for her. It would bring too much unwanted attention and too much heat to her remaining allies. But there were other ways to help, other ways to fight. Information could be just as powerful as open conflict, and information could be used in the shadows.

A wave of memories ebbed in her mind. She keyed in three more names, one after the other. Something positive for a change, she thought, at seeing the information relating to those names.

A calm chime sounded as the door slid open and Chase Miarta came in to check on her. He approached her from behind, her head still lowered in focus on her studies.

"Have you found what you were looking for?" he questioned.

"Yes, and no," she said blankly. "The records appear to be incomplete regarding some of the Kiensei I searched for."

"Trust me," he said, placing a gentle hand on her shoulder. "An *incomplete* record is not necessarily a bad thing," he said with heavy inflection.

She looked up at him. His rock-solid face said it all. Some of them *were still alive*, just like her. He knew it but wouldn't say. It had to remain secret. It *must* remain secret.

"I'm ready to help," she said, her own face as stone solid as his. "But if I do this, I do it in my own way."

"We need all the help we can get my dear," Chase said solemnly. "Whatever you need, whatever you're willing to do, a Kiensei leading it gives us something more than we had before."

"I'm not a Kiensei, Chase," she said, turning to face the console again.

"Tell yourself whatever it is you need to," he said sarcastically, "but actions speak louder than words."

She spun around in the chair and stood up. Sometimes Chase could be just as confusing or bull-headed as old Harichi or even Teka. She didn't quite understand what he was talking about. What could she possibly give more of that others could not? She opened her mouth but was quickly interrupted as he held up a hand.

"Hope, my dear, you give us hope," he said inclining his head. "You give... *me*... hope. And uprisings are built on hope." The two stared at each other for a moment. Chase scrunched his mouth slightly and gave a small bow to excuse himself.

"Wait," Ashira said. He rose up, his face covered in curiosity. "If help is what we need, then there's a chance to get some in the bowels of Korosento," she said.

Chase crinkled his forehead. "Korosento? Are you saying we wander into the viper's nest then?"

She thought hard for a moment. The virtuavid of Teka would have assuredly been seen by the so-called *Eminence*. The closer they went to danger, the further away from harm they would be. The least expected choice. It was wild and maybe a bit reckless, but it made sense.

"Just like Kina would do it," she thought.

She curled one corner of her mouth and narrowed her eyes slightly: a wry and snippy expression. "I wouldn't have it any other way."